I0654492

The Streets Made Me

Larry D. Wright

Lock Down Publications and Ca$h
Presents
The Streets Made Me
A Novel by *Larry D. Wright*

Larry D. Wright

Lock Down Publications
P.O. Box 944
Stockbridge, Ga 30281

Copyright 2020 Larry D. Wright
The Streets Made Me

Lock Down Publications
Like our page on Facebook: Lock Down Publications @
www.facebook.com/lockdownpublications.ldp
Cover design and layout by: **Dynasty Cover Me**
Book interior design by: **Shawn Walker**
Edited by: **Lashonda Johnson**

Stay Connected with Us!

Text **LOCKDOWN** to 22828 to stay up-to-date with new releases, sneak peaks, contests and more…

Thank you!

Larry D. Wright

Submission Guideline.

Submit the first three chapters of your completed manuscript to ldpsubmissions@gmail.com, subject line: Your book's title. The manuscript must be in a .doc file and sent as an attachment. Document should be in Times New Roman, double spaced and in size 12 font. Also, provide your synopsis and full contact information. If sending multiple submissions, they must each be in a separate email.

Have a story but no way to send it electronically? You can still submit to LDP/Ca$h Presents. Send in the first three chapters, written or typed, of your completed manuscript to:

LDP: Submissions Dept
P.O. Box 944
Stockbridge, Ga 30281

DO NOT send original manuscript. Must be a duplicate.

Provide your synopsis and a cover letter containing your full contact information.

Thanks for considering LDP and Ca$h Presents.

Larry D. Wright #422542
Redgranite Corr. Inst.
P.O. Box 925
Redgranite, WI 54970

Larry D. Wright

Acknowledgments

The novels that I have penned were merely embryos incubating in my mind until I began reading the works by literary wordsmiths such as Donald Goings and Shakespeare. Their iconic prose stimulated my passion for writing and prompted me to give birth to my own cast of provocative characters. I could not have been successful without the people who supported me during the rudimentary stages of my career.

The Beginning of The End

"The streets ain't made for everybody; that's why they make sidewalks!"

Cookie – Empire

Larry D. Wright

The Streets Made Me

Prologue

My casket was beautifully handcrafted from fine mahogany wood, solid gold pallbearer handles complimented the master workmanship and the plush interior was stitched from Egyptian silk the color of a clear day in heaven. If a casket was a vehicle that transported you to the next life, I was being chauffeured in a Maybach.

Hundreds of fully bloomed rose petals were detached from their thorny stems and spread across the marble floor creating the illusion of a sea of crimson tears. Two white doves rested their angelic feathers in gold cages located at the head and foot of my casket. They chirped a happy harmony, oblivious of the sad occasion.

The top of the casket was closed, and there were whispers that I was not inside. Some openly hoped that I had somehow escaped death, miraculously surviving the lethal shotgun blast that tore away my flesh. Crime families silently wished that Lucifer had reached up from hell and snatched my doomed soul into eternal fire. I instantly became an urban legend. The rumors spread through the ghetto like Chlamydia.

"Najee, ain't dead!" a petite woman the hue of cappuccino blurted out while getting her nails done at an upscale salon in Atlanta. "I heard he was in the witness protection program because he double-crossed, Sosa," she continued as the Korean shop owner glued a three-inch acrylic nail to her finger.

"Girl, where did you hear some silly shit like that?" an irritated but sexy female voice inquired from the opposite booth while getting a pedicure.

"My baby daddy's cousin heard it from one of his boys at the car wash."

"Bitch, please! Men gossip worse than women do! Don't believe everything you hear," she warned, yet still downloaded the information into her memory bank. She couldn't wait to tell her hairstylist the juicy rumor.

Other theories and conjectures swirled as well, as demonstrated by an old wino begging for change in front of a graffiti littered liquor store in Los Angeles. "Fuck whatcha heard. That nigga got murked," the drunken wino managed to slur before taking a swig of beer from a warm can of 211. "I saw the body on the news. He took a slug to the face," he added to the conspiracy, followed by a loud burp.

Pastor Dickens attempted to comfort the multitude with soothing tales of me being with God in a better place. Even he knew he was lying. Why do preachers do that anyhow? Mentioning only the positive attributes in their eulogies and omitting the sinful characteristics and reckless lifestyle that caused that person to die a violent and sudden death in the first place.

I didn't deserve the good words this man of the cloth was speaking of me, nor was I worthy of the sorrowful screams and groans coming from the beautiful woman hugging my casket, not wanting to let go. A river of tears fell from behind the tinted lenses of her Dolce & Gabbana sunglasses. Black streaks of mascara covered her sad face. I didn't deserve the salty tears that rolled down her cheeks and caressed her lips; however, I didn't deserve what happened next either.

No African-American funeral is without drama, but the unspeakable abomination that transpired at my funeral was morally reprehensible. Just as the deacon pried the grieving woman away from my casket, the church's double doors crashed open. All heads swiveled to face four masked men standing in the doorway. Closely trimmed haircuts and square jawlines were concealed under their ski masks. Black army fatigues hid their chiseled muscles and tattoos. They were Los Cinco Diablo's soldiers.

Two ushers angrily rushed from the pews to confront the uninvited intruders. The first was smashed in the face with the butt of an assault rifle. He slumped to his knees and covered his face with both hands in a fruitless attempt to stop the flow of blood and teeth that gushed from his mouth. The second usher reconsidered and stopped in his tracks. The infrared dot on his chest made his Superman S disappear. The menacing intruders stepped over the body of the would-be hero and moved methodically down the middle aisle of the church.

"This is the house of the Lawd!" the pastor proclaimed in a deep Southern drawl. "Leave us in peace, now!" he demanded, attempting to regain control and assert his leadership.

One of the intruders answered with a three-round burst of .223 slugs into the air. The bullets from his AR-15 defaced the Jesus mural on the ceiling and caused the pastor and those attending the funeral to scream and scramble towards the nearest exit as chunks of plaster crashed to the floor. In the midst of the chaos, the quartet of heavily armed gunslingers remained calm and determined. They were professionals.

They marched toward the casket paying no regard to its beauty or the holiness of the sacred temple. The tallest and deadliest member of the murder squad snatched the lid of my coffin open. There I lay, I looked nothing like the handsome man in the gold-framed picture that accompanied my closed casket. The mortician did his best to repair my once handsome features; however, *Max Factor* makeup and craftsmanship is no match against the voracity of 12-gauge shotgun pellets.

The tall leader snatched my body from the Maybach coffin. His muscular biceps rippled under his fatigues. He held my arms while another intruder grabbed my legs. They marched toward the broken double doors. Their accomplices stood guard with their weapons aimed and ready, daring anyone to try and stop them. Once outside on the church steps, they dropped my body on the cold slab of concrete. My corpse landed with a thud.

The shocked spectators couldn't believe what they were witnessing. My body was doused with gasoline. The pungent odor tainted the crisp September air. The leader lit a match and watched it burn. The glow from the flames made his masked features look even more sinister. Witnesses would later say that he looked like a shark smiling as he let the match fall. My body instantly burst into flames. The embalming fluid helped fuel the fire. A deafening silence enveloped the crowd. Even the sound of approaching sirens seemed miles away.

Next, the intruders did the unspeakable evil. They unzipped the front of their black uniforms and pulled out their dicks. The mortified bystanders gasped as yellow streams of urine splattered what was left of my custom-tailored Armani suit, dousing out the flames. In the end, my burnt corps looked like smoldering charcoal in a BBQ pit and smelled like stale piss.

After admiring their destruction, they calmly walked away. The crowd parted like the Red Sea as the merciless mercenaries strolled past. As if on cue, lightning crackled in the dark clouds above, the Gods angrily protesting the desecration of my grave. As the crowd dispersed, one pedestrian stood alone fuming, watching, and plotting revenge. To understand how my life ended, you have to know how my life began. *Here's my story.*

The Streets Made Me

Chapter One

The Beginning of the End

Hollywood – June 2, 1988

"Push! Push, baby, you can do it!" Mama Merl coached the pregnant young lady in labor.

"Awww, hell nawl! Y'all bet not mess up my fuckin' seats," Prince grumbled while glancing in the rearview. He caught a glimpse of his reflection in the mirror and held his own gaze. Pimps are arrogant by nature, and Prince was no exception. He smiled at the pretty yellow nigga that glared back at him and mashed the accelerator.

His Fleetwood floated in and out traffic like a spaceship as the trio sped down the Sunset Strip frantically searching for Kaiser Permanente Hospital. Prince had already blown through three red lights and avoided two collisions. His urgency, however, was not for the safety of the young lady and her child. He was only concerned about his new leather seats.

"I swear fo' God, y'all get one drop of blood on these seats and I'm gon' flip the fuck out!"

"Just drive and keep yo' eyes on the damn road," Mama Merl snapped.

She was the only person on earth who talked slick to him. Mama Merl had been rocking with Prince for close to ten tumultuous years. She blessed him with everything he knew about the game. Because of this, he tolerated her occasional back talk, but even she knew her limits.

"Push! Push, Monica, I can see the head."

The young lady lay sprawled across the backseat, her beautiful face contorted in pain. Her legs were wide open, which caused her skirt to rise above her voluptuous thighs. Beads of sweat formed on her forehead, but she was brave and tenacious. She bit her bottom lip and pushed.

Mama Merl performed like the perfect midwife. Nothing was new to her. She had been around the block a few times and had seen it all and done it all. She was a dark-skinned, heavyset woman and not that attractive. However, where she lacked in beauty, she excelled in street smarts. She was a boss bitch—a bonafide money maker with a vagina that was wetter than octopus pussy. Add those attributes to her unwavering loyalty and one could see why Prince made her his bottom bitch.

"Oh no, Daddy, something ain't right," Mama Merl announced.

"What's the business, did she have the damn thang yet?" Prince inquired.

"The umbilical cord is wrapped around the baby's neck!" Mama Merl shouted.

"The what?" He heard her clearly the first time but wanted to be sure.

"I said the umbilical cord is wrapped around the baby's neck, and it's choking him."

Prince shook his head from side to side. He regretted ignoring his instincts. When he first spotted Monica walking bare feet down Figueroa Street, a gut feeling cautioned him against running game to her. But just as it's a scorpion's nature to sting, it's a pimp's nature to mack. A seasoned pimp can smell vulnerability. It's as if they have a built-in sensor that detects a woman's weakness. Monica was cold, hungry, and had black dirt on the bottom of her feet when he slid up on her, yet he knew that her innocence and ebony skin would be a hit with the white tricks. His goal was to turn her out, but she was turning him into a different person.

"What's wrong with my baby?" Monica asked, her voice quivering with concern.

"Just relax, it's gonna be okay," Mama Merl's soothing words were not for the young girl. She was reassuring herself.

They pulled into Kaiser Permanente Hospital, and the Cadillac's whitewall tires screeched to a halt in front of the emergency entrance. Two nurses and a doctor rushed Monica onto a gurney. Prince and Mama Merl tried to follow the team into the triage unit but were instructed to wait in the visitor's lounge.

2

The Streets Made Me

Prince anxiously paced back and forth in the waiting area. To him, time was a precious commodity. Time was money. He checked the face of his *Oyster Perpetual* and expelled an impatient sigh. Observers thought he was simply an anxious first-time father. He wondered what they would have thought of him if they knew that several women called him Daddy but certainly not because of his parenting skills. People branded him a pimp, but he preferred to think of himself as a coach, a protector, and a pussy manager. He liked the sound of the last title.

Prince knew that the baby wasn't his. He wasn't that foolish. The last time he got a chick knocked up, he fought the paternity case like a dope charge. When he met Monica eight months ago, she was already pregnant by a country square. She met the biological father during her freshman year at Mississippi State University and let him sweet talk her out of her panties. When she missed her period, she bought a home pregnancy test and was excited when the line turned blue. Her joy, however, was short-lived.

The father denied that the baby was his and avoided her on campus. She eventually cornered him in the study hall and reminded him of the spot of blood on his dormitory sheets after the first time they had sex. There was no denying that she was a virgin, so he tried to reason with her. He explained that they both needed to get their education and that neither of them was ready for a kid. Although he made perfect sense, she refused to abort her child.

Monica's parents offered no condolence. Her mother chastised her, calling Monica a whore and a slut. She even threatened to cut off all funds if Monica didn't wise up and have an abortion. Her mother's harsh words ripped through her heart. She sought empathy from her usually understanding father, but he averted his eyes in disappointment. She was all alone.

She decided to pack her bags and head west. With her beauty and talent, she was confident that she could make it as an actress in Hollywood. She quickly discovered that dreams are for those who get caught sleeping. She was robbed at gunpoint within hours of arriving in L.A. Having no money, friends, or anything else to lose, she took off her high-heels and started walking. That's when she

3

met Prince. She was so naive that she didn't even realize she was wandering down one of the most infamous hoe strolls in America.

Prince was tugged from his ruminations. A doctor approached, he appeared subdued with sagging shoulders. Prince sensed something was amiss.

"Good evening, sir. I'm Dr. Griffin." The physician shook Prince's hand and then escorted him and Mama Merl to a quiet corner. "I'm afraid I have some bad news."

Prince disguised his relief with a look of concern. He was hoping that the baby wouldn't make it. Monica was a potential moneymaker, but a kid would only slow her down, he reasoned. He almost licked his lips and rubbed the palms of his hands as dollar signs appeared in his eyes.

"I hate to be the messenger of bad news, sir, but your wife did not make it—" he paused before continuing. "The baby, however, is fine—a healthy boy, ten pounds, eight ounces."

****

Prince changed dramatically after Monica's death. Months after the funeral, he still wouldn't eat and his face grew noticeably thin. His tailored suits and expensive furs no longer hugged his muscular 6'2" frame. His meticulous grooming took a nosedive and his eyes remained bloodshot red from drinking or worrying or both.

"You need to pull it together, Prince. People are starting to talk about you." Mama Merl massaged his frail shoulders.

"Let the haters talk," he replied bitterly.

"The girls are starting to second guess your mackin', Prince. Money is coming up short and the vultures are starting to circle."

She didn't want to go into too many details, but things had gotten bad. She felt it was her duty to pull his coat. She loved Prince. She met him when he was young, hungry, ambitious, and didn't know a damn thing about pimping. She groomed him into a powerful street player, but now his crown was in jeopardy. She couldn't understand why he had become so emotional in the first place. The first lesson she taught him was that a pimp must possess

4

a narcissist personality. Being cold-hearted isn't enough. A boss, pimp must be heartless.

"Why you trippin' so hard anyway?" she asked. "Hoes die deaths ten times worse than how Monica went out. Remember, Coco?" she reminded him. "A trick cut her up and put her body in a trash dumpster. And what about sticky fingers, Mercedes, remember what that crazy trick did to her?"

His mind drifted back to Mercedes. She spoke with a German accent and had a pussy that purred like a foreign car. He spent hours schooling her on how to steal a man's wallet, watch, and heart without him even noticing. She had caught a date in Malibu with a rich white trick. He pulled his BMW into a secluded area, reclined the front seat, and pulled his pants around his ankles. Mercedes deep throated his small pink dick and stroked it with one hand while removing several large bills with the other. She stealthy replaced the wallet as she drained him dry.

The trick was so happy and satisfied with her fellatio skills that he went into his wallet to give her a tip. He immediately realized that his money was missing. Anger consumed him. His fist crashed into her face with the force of a wrecking ball. The cartilage in her nose and cheekbones shattered under his knuckles. He continued to pummel her face until she was unrecognizable, then dumped her body along the Pacific Coast Highway.

"Prince, nigga, do you hear me?" Mama Merl's words jolted him back to reality.

"How could I not hear yo' loud country ass?" he snapped. "You screamin' in my damn ear."

Mama Merl rolled her eyes and twisted up her lips. "Well, I'm just tryna' put you up on game."

"Bitch, did I ask for your advice?"

"No, but—"

"But nothing," he cut her off. "Stay in a ho's place and out ah pimps face fo' I put a size thirteen alligator shoe up yo' ass sideways."

His anger was misdirected. He was more frustrated with himself than Mama Merl. She was giving him the game in the raw, but a

5

pimp never gives the hoe the satisfaction of knowing she's right. Monica did have potential, but she never lived up to his expectations. She even caused rifts between his other girls because he never actually turned her out.

When he took Monica on her first date, he made sure it was with a regular customer in a luxurious hotel suite. He wanted to break her in easy and give her a false illusion of what the game was really about. Ten minutes later, however, Monica came running through the lobby half-naked with her wig on sideways and tears in her eyes.

"What happened?" Prince cranked the engine and reached in the stash for his heat.

"I couldn't do it," she mumbled and slid beside him. She sat noticeably close.

"Look here, bitch. This is how I eat," he explained. "Don't fuck with me or my money!"

"I know honey, just give me another—"

"And don't call me honey," he interrupted. "Ain't nothing sweet about me. Save that sweet talk for them tricks, ya dig?"

They drove in silence. Raindrops, thunder, and the swoosh-swoosh sound of the windshield wipers gliding back and forth served as their soundtrack. "I'm sorry, I just couldn't do it. He was pale and flabby and his dick was all shriveled up. Ugghh!"

Her voice was soft and innocent. It was a vast difference from the callousness Prince was used to. He laughed as he made a left onto Vine Street. "Don't laugh at me." Monica flashed her million-dollar smile. "I'm serious."

Prince laughed even harder. Monica reached over and tickled his ribs, and Prince giggled like a baby. "Oh, the big bad wolf is ticklish, huh? Let me find out."

Prince liked Monica's innocence and ability to make him smile. She was also intelligent. He absorbed everything she told him about the microeconomics and finance courses she had taken in college. Monica was astonished by his ability to remember formulas and calculate large numbers in his head. She often told him that he was better than the path he had chosen and that he was capable of accomplishing great things. Prince exposed a side of himself to Monica that he would never reveal to the other women in his stable.

As if reading his thoughts, Mama Merl checked him. "That hoe got your nose wide open," she accused with disgust. "You've been slippin' ever since you brought her up in this piece."

"What the fuck you mean slippin'?"

She stopped massaging his shoulders and walked around the recliner to confront him. "You got soft around the edges." She pointed her finger like a machine gun. "You haven't been paying attention to what's been going down in your own domain. Remember the rules, be aware of your surroundings."

"Bitch, I made the rules!" he barked and lit a Newport. He inhaled, then blew a ring of smoke in her face.

"No, I made you!" she snapped back. "Everything you see around this muthafucka is because of me, from the whip you drive to the expensive clothes on your back."

Prince stood up, his intimidating frame towered over her. "Silly, hoe, pimpin' gotta be in you not on you." The old Prince was back. Mama Merl could feel the heat rising from his skin.

The commotion caught the attention of the other women who were in the kitchen having breakfast. Candice who he named Candy, Sharon who he called Sugar, and Bunny, a 6'0 tall white girl with blond hair and sea blue eyes, watched Prince with anticipation. They could feel the ship sinking. Other pimps openly approached them on the track offering a better life and better opportunities. How Prince demonstrated in this situation would seal his faith.

Prince could feel the thick tension in the air. Everything was on the line—his manhood, his livelihood, his future. He knew that he had to make Mama Merl an example. Even she knew it. It's what she had taught him.

"Dig this, get out my limelight and getcha mind right before you get fired, hoe."

Mama Merl stood her ground. "What she do pussy whup you?" she asked sarcastically.

Prince balled his fist and clenched his teeth. "You pushin' it, Merl."

"What she do? Tell you that you were smart and you could do great things? And you actually fell for that square shit? Hoes tell every trick that. You ain't gon' never be shit but a half-ass pimp."

Prince lost it. The first powerful blow connected with Merl's left temple with a sickening crack. Her vision blurred and her knees buckled. The second blow struck her in the jaw. Flashes of pain shot through her body. Her legs surrendered, and she collapsed.

"Funky bitch! You wanna test a player?" His foot slammed into her stomach. "I got something for that ass." He grabbed each of her ankles and spread her legs into a V. Using all the might he could muster, he viciously kicked her in the pussy like he was punting a football. Merl screamed in agony and used her hands to protect her crotch area.

Prince grabbed a fist full of her hair and dragged her across the carpet and into the master bedroom. He screamed profanities while savagely kicking her swollen vagina again and again and again. His face was skewed into a menacing frown. His silk robe parted open and his long penis swung free. Candy, Sugar, and Bunny looked on in horror.

Reaching into the closet, he pulled out a wire hanger. He twisted the coiled hook until it unraveled and became one long piece. Pimp sticks, as they are called, are lethal weapons used to discipline whores. Merl held up her hands to plead with him, but her petition landed on deaf ears. Prince folded the hanger in half and proceeded to beat Mama Merl until she was unconscious.

Candy, Sugar, and Bunny huddled in the doorway looking on with disgust. Tears trickled down their cheeks and hatred flared in their hearts. Prince was a mad man. He had gone too far. Just when it seemed as though the beating would go on forever, the baby started crying. Although Mama Merl and Monica didn't see eye to eye, Merl was very nurturing to the motherless child.

"Somebody better get that muthafucka, fo' I throw his crying ass out the window," Prince threatened. No one moved. They were paralyzed with fear. "Did I stutter, utter, or mutter? Somebody get his little ass!" He was sweaty, his chest puffed in and out as he sucked in air trying to catch his breath.

The Streets Made Me

"You good for nothing hoes!" He lunged towards them. They scattered with high pitched screams, ran into the bathroom, and bolted the door. "I don't need y'all lazy asses. Y'all need me."

Prince turned his attention back to Mama Merl. "Gon' get up, baby girl. I ain't mad no more." Mama Merl's body lay curled up in the fetal position at the foot of the waterbed. "Com'mon now, I ain't got all day, lil' mama. I'm finna put them hoes back on the track and keep ten toes on they back." He looked over to the crying child, then back to Merl.

He got on his knees and shook her limp body. She didn't move. Prince panicked. "Merilyn!" he shouted her government name. She was unresponsive. "Oh, no, please be okay, lil' mama! Please be okay!" He rolled her over onto her back. Her glazed eyes stared straight forward she was dead. Prince pulled her lifeless body close to his chest and cried for the first time in years.

Officers from the Hollywood Police Department found Prince sitting in his favorite Lazy Boy chair with the twelve-week old baby cradled in his arms. He had named the child Najee in memory of a black revolutionist who was gunned down by the LAPD during the Watts riots. Najee sucked on a pacifier as his big brown eyes smiled up at Prince. Prince intuitively sensed that those same loving eyes would one day harbor insatiable hate.

An officer pried the baby out of Prince's arms and gave him to Sugar. The baby immediately started crying. Sugar looked at the crying child as if she had been handed a ticking time bomb.

"I don't want him," she protested and roughly shoved the newborn to Candice.

Candice held the baby with a perplexed look. She didn't know what to do but took pride in knowing that the infant instantly stopped crying when she held him. Najee's beautiful, innocent eyes studied her features.

Prince was cuffed and hauled away. Detective Brooks, the lead investigator handling the homicide, approached the women. He pulled an ink pen from behind his ear and flipped open a small notepad. "So, let me get this straight, no one saw or heard anything?" He watched each of them closely.

Candice was tempted to speak up but decided against it. She hated Prince for what he did to Mama Merl, however, she respected the code of the streets. Silence was the key to survival in the asphalt jungle, and when this was all over, she still had to eat.

"I'll take that as a no," Detective Brooks scoffed and stuffed the notepad into his breast pocket. "Well, somebody at least tell me this. Who does that baby belong to?"

There was a long, awkward silence. The women didn't want the child to enter the system, yet they didn't want to claim him either. Something deep within Candice compelled her to speak. "He's mine," the lie easily slipped off her tongue.

Chapter 2

Street Life

Standing at 5'7, Candice had a thick waist and a beautiful girl next door face. Prince had named her Candy because she had a sweet soul and smooth chocolate skin the color of a Hershey's bar. She was wise for her twenty-five years, yet naive to the streets.

She met Prince while she was working at Red Lobster and attending nursing school at L.A. Trade Tech. She was initially impressed by his charm, good looks, and generosity. He left a $100 dollar tip at the edge of the table, however, when she unfolded the money, she discovered that the bill was ripped in half. His phone number was scribbled on the c-note along with a flirtatious note encouraging her to call him once her shift was over if she wanted the other half.

She dialed his number as soon as her shift was over. He told her that all she had to do in order to get the other half of the hundred-dollar bill was talk to a friend of his for twenty minutes. It was the fasted $100 she never made. Prince kept both halves of the c-note but promised to take care of all her needs if she pledged her loyalty to him. She had gotten turned out and didn't even realize it.

One would think that having custody of an infant child would have slowed Candy down. Motherhood, however, only pushed her to grind harder. She wanted to provide Najee with a better life than the miserable upbringing she endured as an adolescent. The baby was her motivation—her inspiration to get in them streets and get down for her crown. Her goal was to stack up some bands and then return to nursing school.

By day she was a nurturing mother. She showered Najee with gifts and sincere love. At night she would throw on her platinum-colored wig and transform into one of the baddest chicks on the track. Her stilettos agitated the concrete as she swayed her wide hips, enticing men of every background to open their wallets in exchange for her open legs. Often, the Johns just wanted conversation. She charged double for that.

As the sand trickled through the hourglass, her reputation as a stomp down money maker echoed throughout the ghetto. Every pimp and bonafide player wanted to recruit her. She was a number one draft pick, but, she refused to choose-up. Ultimately, her reluctance sparked drama and conflict.

"Hey beautiful, lady, slow down and holla at a playa!" a deep voice called from a passing vehicle.

Candy walked faster, she had been ignoring Boulevard for weeks, but he continued to pursue her. His persistence was irritating. In the past few days, he had started to come on stronger. When it was obvious that his game wasn't live enough, he resorted to Gorilla tactics. Candy ignored him and kept her high heels clicking.

"Ay, bitch, you hear me talking to you. I'm in hot pursuit of a prostitute, don't ignore this pimpin'!"

Candy rolled her eyes and kept it moving. She was a renegade and wasn't about to come home every night with sore feet and a sore pussy just to hand over her hard-earned cash to a slick-talking con man. Been there done that, she had plans for her future, and they didn't involve a pimp.

Boulevard's Cadillac sped up. He maneuvered the whip with one hand on the steering wheel while leaning over to talk out of the passenger side window. The game he ran landed on deaf ears. As Candice approached Sunset and Highland, she recalled a survival tactic that Prince had taught her. He always instructed his girls to walk with the flow of traffic, as she was currently doing, not against it. Doing so allowed a trick to easily pull up beside them and negotiate a price without causing her to break her stride. It also allowed her to shake any unwanted attention by simply turning around and walking in the other direction. She decided to put the theory to test.

As Boulevard drove with the flow of traffic attempting to put his bid in, Candy did an about-face and turned in the opposite direction. She looked over her shoulder and smiled when she saw confusion on the pimp's face. The Cadillac couldn't stop or turn around. There was too much traffic behind him.

12

Candy assumed she was safe, however, a bulky figure stepped from the shadows and slammed a fist in her face. Pain shot from her eyelashes to her toenails. Candy stumbled and landed on the pavement. She clutched the cement on her hands and knees while desperately trying to escape her attacker. Ice-cold fear surged through her veins. "*Run!*" Her body screamed for her feet to move, but she was paralyzed with terror. The shadow's rock-solid fist connected with her cheek. She felt a bone shatter in her jaw. Blood dripped on the sidewalk. "*Run!*" There was that voice again, it urged her feet to move.

"Where the money at?" the raspy-voiced attacker demanded.

"I ain't got no money!"

He repaid her lie with a blunt blow to the back of her head. Candy balled up into the fetal position to protect her face as the attacker repeatedly slammed his foot into her midsection.

"This ain't no game, lady. Where that money at?" He reached down and grabbed a handful of hair. Candy's platinum blond wig came off instead. This is where she stashed her cash when she was on the grind. A large wad of green bills fell onto the ground.

"Run!"

Candy realized that the voice wasn't in her head. Sugar dashed across Sunset zigzagging through heavy traffic with a sharp blade in her grip. "Get away from her!" Sugar swiped the knife at the assailant.

"You don't want these problems, ugly bitch." He dodged the knife and punched Sugar.

Boulevard crept up and blindsided the crook with a powerful roundhouse to the temple. The attacker fell to one knee and held up his hands to surrender. Boulevard ignored his pleas and stomped him out with a colorful alligator shoe. Sugar helped Candice up and led her limp body to the Cadillac. After placing Candy in the backseat, she hopped behind the wheel prepared to be the getaway driver.

Boulevard removed his burner from the small of his back and pressed it against the attacker's forehead. His eyes got bigger than high beams on a UFO. "Hold up, Boulevard. You acting this out a little too far."

"Shut the fuck up, dope fiend ass nigga!"

"I'm just doing what you paid me to do, nephew."

Boulevard slapped him with the pistol. "I said scare the bitch, Willie, not beat her senseless. You damaged the merch."

"My bad, playboy. I thought—"

"Don't thought—think nigga! Think!" Boulevard lectured. "What am I supposed to do, huh?" He delivered another blow with the butt of the gun. "How is she gon' make me some bread all broke up, huh?" He swung the pistol again, catching the assailant on the temple. "Do it look like I got time to play doctor, dumb nigga. Do it look like I run a shelter for battered women?" He completed his reprimand with another strike.

The incompetent dope fiend didn't get a chance answer. Pulling the hammer back with his thumb, Boulevard popped him in the kneecap. The fiend hobbled away spewing profanities. Boulevard tucked the strap in his waistband, fixed his ruffled up attire, and calmly strolled away. It was just another day in the life.

****

Candy woke up groggy and in pain. It felt like there was a demolition crew doing construction in her head. Realizing that she wasn't in the comfort of her own bed, she abruptly sat up.

'*Where the fuck am I?*' she wondered. The last thing she remembered was a bulky figure wearing a black hoodie. Panic gripped her soul as she recalled the brutal attack.

The bedroom door opened and a familiar face came in holding a breakfast in bed tray. The omelet with cheese, Canadian bacon, and English muffin with peach marmalade smelled scrumptious, but it was the glass of orange juice and bottle of Tylenol that appealed to her appetite.

She swallowed four aspirin and let out a sigh. "What happened? Where am I?" she had a ton of questions.

"Relax, beautiful, you're safe now that you're rocking with me."

Candy stiffened. The long scar across Boulevard's face gave her the chills, and she wondered what hidden message lay dormant behind his words. She sat up to leave, but the pain in her abdomen caused her to plop back down on the fluffy pillows.

"Like I said, just relax, baby. I got you," Boulevard assured smoothly. His left eye twitched involuntarily.

Determined to leave, Candy tried to get up again but failed. "I gotta go, I need to check on my baby."

At that moment, Sugar walked in holding Najee's small hand. Even as a one-year-old, his legs were strong and he was mature for his age. He was accustomed to being in the company of strangers and no longer cried when Candy left him for long periods of time.

Najee spotted his mother and joy and excitement filled his spirit. He ran to the bedside with a smile on his face. Despite the agonizing pain, Candy reached down and lifted her pride and joy into her arms.

"I love you, mommy!" his words melted the layer of ice surrounding her heart.

She finally had someone who loved her unconditionally. A teardrop formed at the corner of her swollen eye. She tried her best to check her emotions. She didn't want to appear weak. On the callous streets of Los Angeles, tears were as annoying as a dripping faucet. Despite that ugly truth, tears seeped from her eyelids. Her chest convulsed, exposing her human vulnerability to a ghetto full of heartless monsters.

She embraced her surrogate baby closely and whispered promises in his ear. "I'll never leave nor forsake you like my parents abandoned me. I will never use or abuse you like these streets have violated me. I will never be dishonest or disloyal to you like my so-called friends have bamboozled me. I'm gonna do big things so that you can be a giant, I promise."

Boulevard watched the scene from a distance. He casually leaned against the door frame and lit a Kool King cigarette. He inhaled the menthol-flavored tobacco and exhaled smoke rings toward the ceiling. A feeling of calmness swept over him. The streets were working his nerves. He was going through a pack a day.

15

After a few patient minutes of letting the mother bond with her child, he interrupted the reunion. "A'ight, let's break this soap opera up." A smile appeared on his lips, but his tone was dead serious. "Sugar, fix him a plate, then let him open those new toys I copped for him. I need to holla at Candy alone for a minute."

Sugar rolled her eyes at Candy and reluctantly left the room. Boulevard sat on the edge of the bed and looked at the cold bacon and eggs. His left eye had a habit of twitching when a scheme hatched in his mind.

"What's the business; you don't like my cooking?" he joked.

Candy eyed the tray. She had to admit that the food looked delicious, but her stomach felt queasy. "You make all of this?" She made a sweeping gesture with her hand.

"Yup!" Smoke eased from his nostrils.

"Stop playin'." She smiled. "Did you really buy my kid some new toys?"

"Fa' sho'," he confirmed. "It ain't no thang, baby girl. You with me now, I gotcha back." His left eye twitched again.

Candy let the comment slide. She knew the rules of the game. Inequality existed in the streets just as in the corporate world. Eventually, she was going to have to choose-up. The game didn't favor a woman getting paid solo. It was only a matter of time before the predators devoured her alive. She shivered as she thought about the attacker. She owed Boulevard her gratitude, and the fact that he was being nice to her son was a plus.

She never second-guessed taking on such a great responsibility. Najee was her motivation for transformation, a reminder that her true aspirations were better than what she had become. She didn't plan on making a career out of hooking. She was caught up and believed that her body was the only commodity she possessed. Had she placed more emphasis on her self-worth, she would have realized that there were other alternatives. She could have used her brains instead of her pussy to get ahead in life. But such thoughts were for squares and those who still clung on to the possibility of hope.

She had lost hope long ago and had to get it how she lived. She clung to the stark reality that in order to get somewhere in this life you had to do it by any means necessary. Her vagina was her toolbox and she planned on using it to build a better future.

She glanced at Boulevard out of the corner of her eye as he talked, schemed, lit another cigarette, and sampled the cold bacon all at the same time. She was impressed by his ability to multi-task and still stay on point.

Boulevard was thirty-five years old and on top of the game. He didn't fit the stereotypical description of a pimp. Where others had long silky perms, he rocked a smooth bald head and a rough beard. His skin was the hue of a black olive, and people often said he resembled Isaac Hayes. He rocked expensive clothes but no flashy, colorful suits. He thought those chumps looked like clowns and were putting a black eye in the game. His GQ attire made him look like he was about to hit the golf course.

He only stood 5'6, but his powerful presence bought the animal lust out of women. He used his eleven-inch Mandingo to control their bodies and his cunning words to control their minds. When neither of those worked, he used his fists. His reputation as a Gorilla pimp caused the hoes and other players to shy away from him. He didn't give a fuck, though. Above all things, he kept it, gangsta.

Boulevard pulled a cigarette from behind his ear, passed a Bic lighter to Candy, and leaned forward. "Are you serious?" she pouted. "Light your own damn cigarette!" Boulevard gave her that look. He was setting the tone for their relationship. Candy got the message and complied.

Satisfied, Boulevard kept on mackin'. "Like I was saying, baby girl, I see your potential. If you link up with me, the sky's the limit. I'm talkin' 'bout space age pimpin' type shit. I'm talkin' eating crab legs and lobster with aliens on Mars type shit."

He brought a rare smile to Candy's lips. She had already chosen him but was enjoying the effort he put in. They continued to chop it up, mainly about his habit of putting his hand on women. His eye twitched as he vehemently denied the rumors. She would soon find out which version was the truth.

****

Boulevard allowed Candy and to rest up for two weeks, then vacation was over. He worked her, Sugar, Bunny and his other two women until they had blisters on their feet. Bunny got the worst treatment. Boulevard was bitter at her because she had once left him to work for his archnemesis, Prince. The worst blow to a pimp's ego is losing a girl to another player. Bunny came running back once Prince got snatched up on a manslaughter charge. Although Bunny stole all Prince's jewelry and brought Sugar along with her, Boulevard was still salty.

His stable was in check and churning like the gears in a well-oiled machine. He kept one foot on their necks and the other on the gas pedal. Even when Bunny came on her period, he didn't let up. As the girls got dazzled up to hit the strip, Bunny was slow dragging as usual. Boulevard liked to hit the track and drive around in his shiny new whip while flossin' his women and success. The envious glares he received from other pimps and the admiration he received from young, up and coming players energized him. It also gave him the opportunity to check the temperature of the block. If vice was too hot, he took his hustle to another part of town. Now Bunny was fucking up his flow and testing his patience.

"Wus the business, Bunny? Let's groove, we late, baby?"

Bunny was sprawled across the leather couch watching T.V. She had on the same halter top, tight boy shorts, and footsies she'd slept in the night before. "I'm on my period, Daddy," she whined. "Let me stay in tonight."

Boulevard cocked his head to the side and looked at her like she was crazy. "Bitch pleaseee, get yo' lazy ass up, get dressed, and screw yo' wig on tight. Money don't wait."

The other ladies snickered and laughed. Bunny thought she was special. They took pleasure in seeing her get checked.

"I'm serious, I'm having bad menstrual cramps. Besides, what can I do on my period anyway?"

18

"I don't see nothing wrong with your mouth or yo' asshole. What you gon' tell me next, that you got a toothache and hemorrhoids, too? Get cho' ass up!"

Bunny leaped off the couch with her pouting lips poked out. She rolled her eyes at the other women as she passed by. They returned the shade, then busted out laughing when Bunny angrily slammed the bathroom door.

Later that night as Boulevard counted his money, a smile formed on his lips. Counting cash was better than having sex. The silky feel of hundreds and fifties excited him more than ass and titties. He rubberband the stacks of dirty money, then placed the loot into his floor safe. He spent the combination wheel to secure the lock, then leaned back and fired up a Kool King. After taking a toke off the cancer stick, he expelled smoke through his nostrils and reflected on the events of the past year.

There is only room at the top for one, and after Prince slipped on a banana peel, Boulevard took over the track. He was nominated Player of the Year for the very first time and was looking forward to making an eloquent acceptance speech at the Annual Players Ball. He rubbed the long keloid scar on his cheek, courtesy of one of Prince's hoes during a bar fight.

"Fuck 'em both." He chuckled victoriously.

Mama Merl was dead, and Prince's fool ass was locked up for killing her. '*What irony,*' he thought.

He did have to salute mack buddy for the jewels he had laced Bunny, Sugar, and Candy with while they were under his management. Now Boulevard was the benefactor of all the game they learned. Bunny was bringing in double the paper, and his other girls had learned how to pick-pocket a trick or steal the Rolex off his arm without him noticing.

Things were definitely looking good. They shopped every day, splurging on jewelry, fly clothes, and expensive shoes. Boulevard graduated from a Cadillac to an oyster grey *Bentley GT* with cranberry guts. He slapped on some 24-inch Lexani rims and had *Bitch Pleeeze* was stitched into the leather headrest, but that wasn't good enough for the women. They eventually wanted to see their man in a Rolls-Royce.

Boulevard took another drag off his square as he tried to dissect the psychology of the game. He could never fully comprehend why a woman would risk life and freedom selling her goodies on a dark, dangerous street corner just to hand over her money to a pimp. It didn't make sense to him, but he was glad that such a phenomenon existed.

Candice pulled Boulevard out of deep contemplation. She stood in the doorway holding a bottle of red wine and two glasses. She wore the long, white mink coat that Boulevard had recently purchased. The slit was open, revealing her curvaceous thighs and shaved pussy. Her chocolate nipples stood erect and were the size of Hershey Kisses. Boulevard understood why they called her Candy. His anaconda came alive in his slacks. His heart raced with lust, but he kept it nonchalant. He was a player. Candice sat in his lap and poured wine into both of their glasses.

"Here's to space-age pimpin'!" she joked, and they clicked glasses.

Boulevard downed his glass and crushed out his cigarette. He grabbed a small mirror containing a mountain of cocaine off the table, then used a trick's stolen credit card to divide out four lines of coke. He used a gold straw to vacuum two lines of the potent powder with each nostril. He passed the straw and mirror to Candy. Candy used a finger to press in one side of her nose, then used the straw to sniff a line of the crystalline powder in one smooth stroke.

When she leaned forward to do the other line, she noticed her reflection in the mirror. She paused and glared hard at the image. She barely recognized the person staring back at her. Her innocence was lost, and her schoolgirl features had become hardened by the life. She was still beautiful, but the streets were taking their toll.

Boulevard sensed her mood change. "What's good, Candice?" he questioned while running his hand between her legs. He found her phat clitoris and rotated his middle finger in a circular motion. She was slick and wet.

Candice liked it when Boulevard called her by her government name. It made her feel special. She sniffed the second line of blow and licked the residue off the mirror. The Columbian drug numbed her tongue as well as her soul.

She sank to her knees, unzipped his slacks, and removed his throbbing dick. It looked like it got bigger and bigger every time she saw it. She stacked both of her small hands on his pole and squeezed. The head swelled and leaked pre-cum. She placed her mouth over the head and took him into her mouth. Even with her superior skills, she was only able to deepthroat half of it. She choked and removed it from her mouth, leaving it shiny with saliva.

Lifting the mink coat around her waist, she straddled his hips with her back against his chest; reverse cowgirl style—her favorite position. She worked the huge head into her moist opening slowly tormenting her lover. She looked over her shoulder and smiled. She knew she was about to put it on him. She lowered herself inch by black inch until she felt him deep in her stomach. The intense pleasure and exquisite pain made her juice box wet.

Candy bent over and grabbed her ankles, working three more thick inches into her pussy. An animalistic moan escaped Boulevard's lips. "Yeah, baby, take all this big dick!" he encouraged and pushed his middle finger up her asshole. Candy bounced and rolled her hips on his huge pogo stick as if it were a mechanical bull.

Sugar was rudely awakened by the distinctive smell and sounds of raw, raunchy sex. Bunny was knocked out snoring, and she knew Boulevard wouldn't dare stick his dick in any of the other trifling hoes. She came to the conclusion that Candy was the culprit eliciting moans and grunts from Boulevard. Jealousy sparked like a forest fire in her heart.

She felt that ever since Boulevard played captain save a hoe and brought Candy and her trick baby into the house, they were getting all of his attention. She was the boss bitch and didn't appreciate Candy stepping on her toes. She put her pillow over her head in a futile attempt to block out the lustful moans. It didn't work, so she did the next best thing. She woke up Najee.

****

Boulevard couldn't take it anymore. The pussy looked too good and felt too good. He watched his pole disappear in and out of her tight kitty cat for a few more strokes before grabbing Candy's hips and flipping her over. He hooked both of her sexy legs over his broad shoulders and plunged all eleven-inches deep into her vagina.

This time it was Candy who threw her head back and moaned. "Ooohhh, yes. Hell yes! Get this pussy, Daddy, it's yours."

"It's my turn now," Boulevard whispered. He held her ankles and beat the pussy up like she'd stole a mule. Candy's acrylic nails raked his back. She tried to tap out, but Boulevard kept long stroking her with deep, powerful thrusts until her pussy gushed cum.

****

The blade of the butcher knife glistened in Najee's small hand. Someone had shaken him out of his sleep. When his eyes adjusted to the dark, he realized that his mother's bed was empty. He heard moans, his mother was in immediate danger. His intuitive instincts told him that he needed to protect her, so he climbed out of bed in his Spiderman underwear.

Seeing a man on top of his mother making her cry put rage in his heart. He ran up on Boulevard while the pimp was in mid-stroke and plunged the sharp knife into his left buttocks.

"Aaaahhh!" Boulevard screamed in pain. His ass cheek was on fire.

"That's right, kill this pussy, Daddy." Candy thought that Boulevard was on the verge of busting a nut. He pulled away in agony, but she hugged him and pulled him closer.

"Aaaahhh, shit!" he groaned as the tip of the blade penetrated his thigh.

"Get off my, Mommy," Najee demanded.

He stood strong and defiant. He held the knife over his head and charged. "Leave my mama alone!" He aimed for a kidney, but

Boulevard backed kicked him in the chest just as the blade swung downward.

In one motion, Boulevard rolled out of the pussy and snatched his snub-nose .38 off the table as Najee tumbled to the floor. He pulled the hammer back and aimed at the shadow.

"Noooo!" Candy yelled and jumped between her son and the barrel. "He thought you were hurting me."

Boulevard's pupils focused in the darkness. He spotted Najee bravely wielding the bloody knife. He lowered his gun and hobbled on his good leg to the bathroom in order to check the severity of his wounds. Sugar stood in the door frame wearing a mischievous grin. That was Najee's first taste of blood, it wouldn't be his last.

Chapter 3

Hustle Muscle

The game moves fast, making time a fleeting commodity. Boulevard woke up one morning and found grey hairs in his chin. Over the years many hoes came and went, but Candy and Sugar held it down. The first few years were lucrative, but the hustle has unpredictable ups and downs. The game was rapidly changing. The Hollywood vice squad was coming down hard on prostitution because of the growing number of HIV and AIDS cases. Thanks to Kingpins like *Freeway Ricky Ross* and *Felix Wayne Mitchell*, crack cocaine and inexpensive Heroin had the ghetto under siege.

To compound matters, the D-Boys had all the juice. Ready rock and vials of H controlled the hoes, and the pimps were pushed to the back burner, rapidly becoming a rare breed and an endangered species within the hustler hierarchy. The perms were exchanged for bald fades, French braids, and dreadlocks. The colorful suits and alligator shoes were replaced with designer jeans, Nike Air Max, and platinum jewelry. The gun became mightier than the mouthpiece.

There were still die-hard macks yelling pimpin' ain't dead. However, Boulevard wasn't one of them. He was a visionary and saw the drought on the horizon. Too many stomp down hoes were getting turned out on dope. Getting high became their motivation for selling their bodies, not lining a pimp's pockets. He even witnessed pimps get strung out and start selling their asses on the corner for a bag of dope. The game had gotten pathetic.

It was time to switch lanes. He had Candy and Sugar operating his trap houses by day and stripping at an upscale gentlemen's lounge near LAX at night. He moved wherever the money called. He was grinding hard but hated being a two-bit, low-level drug dealer. As with everything he did, he wanted to be the best. His supplier kept promising to introduce him to the connect, but that never came to fruition.

Boulevard remained undeterred and kept on hustling. When Najee wasn't in school, Boulevard made sure he was riding shotgun. He didn't have any kids of his own and grew to love the little soldier. He sensed that Najee was destined to do big things if the ghetto didn't swallow him first.

****

Boulevard looked over to the passenger seat and smiled at Najee bobbin' his head to *Curtis Mayfield*. He was an old soul. Boulevard was making a drop in Hawthorne, a small city trapped between the beach on one end and South Central on the other. Against Candy's wishes, he decided to let Najee ride shotgun. She preferred to shelter him from the dirt they did in the streets, but Boulevard was a realist. He knew that as a black man living in an unfair society, there was a strong probability that a street nigga is all Najee would ever be, so it was best to bless him with the jewels to the game while he was young.

Besides, Najee had gotten kicked out of school again for fighting. Candy wasn't available to scoop him up, so Boulevard did. The other reason for taking Najee along was so that he could hold the package of cocaine that Boulevard was either picking up or delivering. If he got pulled over, the jakes wouldn't frisk a kid, Boulevard rationalized. The game is cold but fair.

After dropping off four and a split in Hawthorne, Boulevard grooved to Inglewood to meet his supplier, a Hispanic and black cat named Cheddar. He planned to cop another half brick of fish scale and ask Cheddar about meeting the connect.

Boulevard flipped through radio stations while waiting impatiently in the parking lot of the indoor swap meet on Market Street. Cheddar was always late. Boulevard began to believe that he was doing the shit on purpose. Just as his anger started to boil, a cherry red 6-Deuce Impala recklessly swooped into the parking space next to the lowkey Maxima.

The driver hit one of the 16-Hydraulic switches and the low-low's front end popped in the air. Another flick of the switches and

26

the frame lowered all the way to the ground. Najee watched in amazement.

Cheddar jumped out of his low rider like a cowboy dismounting a horse. He rocked a pair of white Chucks with fat red shoestrings and a crispy wife beater that showed off his bulging muscles and prison tattoos. His tan Dickies sagged, revealing red boxers and a Taurus .9mm. He was a hot-headed Damu from the Eastside, but the Inglewood Family Bloods and the Neighborhood Pirus showed him love. They gave him the green light to hustle on their turf as long as he plugged the shot callers with guns and dope.

Before Cheddar got into the Maxima, Najee crawled into the backseat while Boulevard laced him with street knowledge. "We ain't even got down to business yet and this clown has already made three crucial mistakes. Can you tell me what they are?"

Najee grinned. "Never ride flashy when you're riding dirty. Never do a transaction in somebody else's car when somebody is posted in the backseat. Oh, yeah, and never be late." He looked at his mentor for approval.

Boulevard gave him some dap. "My man, my brand. You're catching on quick. Tonight, I'ma teach you how to shoot dice."

Cheddar slid in the front seat and the two men shook up. Cheddar reached into his pants and pulled out a large clear bag stuffed with large chunks of coke fresh off the brick. Boulevard examined the contents, then handed over a brown paper bag containing fifteen bands for the 18 zips. The men conducted business in silence. Once the transaction was complete, Boulevard hit Cheddar up for a better ticket on the work.

"Awww man! Here we go with that shit again!" Cheddar exaggerated his complaint. "I dun' told you I'm doing the best I can on the price."

"Well, introduce me to yo' connect then. I could move a lot more work if the number was right."

Cheddar shook his head. "Hell no! Look, Blood, Benzo Al ain't tryna' meet no new niggas." The name of his connect tasted bitter on his tongue. He instantly knew he had made a crucial mistake.

Larry D. Wright

Boulevard played it off and acted nonchalant like the name meant nothing to him, but his soul cheered inside. Benzo Al was a rising star within Los Cinco Diablos. Los Cinco Diablos are one of the deadliest and most profitable criminal cartels in the Western hemisphere. Los Cinco Diablos translates into The Five Devils. It received its name because the members had their hands into everything from narcotics, human trafficking, gambling, counterfeit goods, and money laundering. Just as a human hand has five fingers, Los Cinco Diablos has five board members, each with equal authority. Thanks to an elaborate network of tunnels, most of the yayo smuggled from Mexico to California and distributed across America had their stamp on the seal.

Benzo Al frequently visited the Airport Lounge where Sugar and Candy stripped. He was known for making it rain, buying out the bar, and buying black pussy. He also had a sick fetish and paid top dollar to get his rocks off. The Latino Kingpin had been pestering Candy to come back to his mansion, but she always kindly declined. Her stomach would knot up just thinking about squatting over him and pissing on his chest. Sugar, however, was all game. She would even drink a pitcher of water before his limo arrived to pick her up.

Boulevard drove back to the trap enjoying the dense L.A. smog. He knew just how to get at Benzo Al. His left eye twitched as he weaved through the heavy ghetto traffic. As soon as they entered the spot, Candy was waiting with a thick leather belt wrapped around her knuckles. Najee knew what time it was. This was the second time this semester he got suspended from school for fighting. One more incident and they were going to kick him out of the district.

Candy lashed out, connecting with Najee's legs, back, and arms. The leather strap caused his skin to welt. Candy chastised him during the beating attempting to knock some sense into his hard head.

"Didn't I tell yo' black ass not to get into any mo' trouble?" The belt swished through the air. "All I do for you, have you lost yo' damn mind?"

28

The Streets Made Me

Swish!

Najee stood silent and defiant, trying his best not to cry. He bit his bottom lip and accepted his punishment like a man. His blatant defiance fueled Candy, she lashed out harder. She needed to teach him a lesson before the white man did. If she didn't intervene now with tough love, his fate was death or jail, she reasoned.

The beating was getting too intense. Boulevard approached Candy from behind and gently held her waist. He wrestled the belt from her grip and kissed the nape of her neck to calm her down. Najee appreciated being rescued. He respected Boulevard like a father.

"That's enough, baby girl, he gets the point."

Candy wiggled from Boulevard's embrace. "He ain't gonna get it until he's lying on his back on a bunk in prison or lying on his back on a cold table at the morgue." She got in Najee's face. He could smell Taco Bell on her breath. "Do you know why I whoop you all the time?" she asked. Najee remained mute. "You hear me talkin'? Answer me, damn it!"

He knew the answer well, he'd heard it often. "You whoop me because you love me," he professed through clenched lips.

Candy kissed him on the forehead and hugged him tightly. It was at that moment he began to associate pain with love.

Southern Cali

The beautiful California skyline was breathtaking. The egg yolk yellow sun sank into the deep blue Pacific Ocean creating a kaleidoscope of colors. Boulevard's new connect chose Venice Beach as their meeting spot. They had been juggin' for a year. For every kilo Boulevard copped at sixteen-five, Benzo Al fronted him one. The business arrangement was lucrative for both parties.

After Cheddar slipped and name-dropped his connect, Boulevard put his plan in motion. He knew Benzo Al was a boss freak. He also knew that ballers were not used to hearing the word no. Men with expendable cash believed that currency could resolve any problem.

29

The more Candy rebuffed his advances, the more paper Benzo Al rained on her when she danced on stage. She was a challenge. She made the chase exciting. After completely ignoring him for a few weeks, Boulevard instructed Candy to make Benzo Al believe that he had won her over. She made up a lame ass excuse about her money getting stolen from her locker at the club, and that she was in a jam. Benzo Al put on his cape to save her, not knowing that he was the prey. After they linked up a couple of times, she made the introduction.

Boulevard was linking up with Benzo Al to pick up four more bricks. He was paying for two of them, and the other two were on consignment. He had sixty-six bands stuffed in a leather Gucci duffel bag. Half of the money was payment for the last batch of coke he was fronted.

Benzo Al arrived on time in a new S-Class. He had a different color Benz for everyday of the week. Today's color was appropriate for the occasion; cocaine white. The hustlers welcomed each other with a firm handshake.

"Cómo está usted, señor Benzo Al?" Boulevard greeted in Español.

"Muy bien, gracias."

Boulevard handed him the duffel bag. Benzo Al unzipped it and quickly glanced at the rubber band stacks. Satisfied, he tossed the bag on the backseat. He made a call, and within minutes, a black Chevy Tahoe pulled in next to the Mercedes. The driver was flamed up, rocking red attire from head to toe. Boulevard nodded his head what up to Cheddar, but the cold-hearted Damu greeted him with a frozen stare.

"What's good with that nigga, Benzo?" Boulevard returned the frown.

"Ignore his fool ass," Benzo Al suggested. "He's salty because he got demoted to runner."

"On what?" Boulevard chuckled.

"On everything. That vato is a liability." Benzo Al gave the signal and Cheddar got out of the Tahoe holding a chrome briefcase.

30

The Streets Made Me

Boulevard felt the temperature inside of the Mercedes drop. Benzo Al was usually cordial, but when it was time for business, he meant business. One does not ascend that high in the illicit drug trade without possessing an evil streak.

"Listen compadre," Benzo Al began in a serious tone. "I put a little sump'n extra in this shipment. You been moving that perico so fast, I gotta meet you two or three times a week. I don't like taking risks like that. Plus I'm moving up in my organization. That means I'll be spending more time in Nogales, Mexico—" he paused to make sure he had Boulevard's full attention. "So, dig this, amigo, I will front you ten kilos at dieciocho G's. Get at me when you got the hundred and eighty racks. I know the ticket is higher, but you ain't gotta put no money down. Entienden?"

The men shook up to seal the deal. Boulevard was geeked about the new arrangement. He was gonna flip ten into a hundred and a hundred into a thousand. After that, he would retire, he told himself. No more pimpin', pandering, or drug handling.

Before he exited the vehicle, Benzo issued a stern warning. "Cheddar is mi familia. When he fucks up, I charge it to the game. But if you fuck up—" he allowed his words to linger as he lifted his silk shirt and revealed the pearl handle of his foe-nickel.

Boulevard overstood what was being implied. He got out of the Benz and grabbed the briefcase. As he turned to leave, he locked eyes with Cheddar. Cheddar glared at Boulevard with murderous contempt in his eyes. For the first time in a long time, Boulevard was shook.

****

As Boulevard made his way back to the stash spot, Candy hit him on the hip. He looked at the screen and saw her code 304, hoe spelled backward. He didn't want to draw any unwanted attention from the jakes, so he hit her back and placed the call on speaker. Candy answered on the first ring in a frantic voice.

"Hold up! Slow down, woman, you talkin' too damn fast."

"Najee got suspended from school again. Can you pick him up, Papi?"

He wasn't about to take a detour into a school zone with ten bricks carpooling with him. "Naw, lil mama, I'm in traffic. Lock up the trap house and go handle yo' business."

"But the spot is crackin'. I'm tryna get this paper."

Boulevard laughed. Candy loved chasing that check. He didn't prescribe to the philosophy of love, but he did have a warm affection for her and a fond attachment to Najee. Deviating from his plans, however, was too risky. She was on her own. "Lock the joint down and go pick his badass up. I will personally talk to him tonight."

Candy grabbed her thickest leather belt and threw it into her camel-colored Birkin bag. She stormed out of the house determined to teach Najee a lesson he'd never forget. He was doing excellent academically but failing miserably socially. She wondered why he couldn't get along with the other kids at school because at home, he was an angel.

She did everything in her power to keep him happy. Every weekend they cashed-out at the Fox Hills Mall or the Beverly Center. She kept him laced with the flyest gear and all of the hottest video games. But that was about to change, she promised herself. She wasn't going to keep rewarding his bad behavior.

She arrived at Hawthorne Intermediate School just as class was ending. The *click-click* of her expensive high heels echoed in the hallway as she marched towards the principal's office. Faculty members, parents, and students gave her funny looks. She returned the shade but noticed what she was wearing. In her rush, she forgot to change into something more appropriate. She wore a pair of red peek toe Prada shoes and a black spandex jumpsuit that showed off her curves and camel toe. She was relieved when she finally made it to Principal O'Neal's office.

Najee sat on the wooden bench with his head down, dreading the punishment he was going to receive when he got home. He didn't have to look up to know that his mom was standing there, he felt her presence.

The Streets Made Me

Principal O'Neal stood up to greet Candy with a lustful smile. Although his salt and pepper hair was thinning and brown age spots discolored his white skin, he was tall and extremely fit for a sixty-three-year-old man. "How are you doing today, Mrs. Howard?" His eyes stayed on her breasts.

"I could be doing better," she replied dryly and popped her gum before grabbing Najee by the ear and hauling him out of the office. Mr. O'Neal ran his tongue across his lips and watched that phat ass wobbled out of view.

Candy cussed Najee out as she dragged him to the car. All his peers witnessed what was happening. Some snickered while others watched with concern. Everyone was happy that he gave the school bully a taste of his own medicine during fifth period.

Once in the parking lot, she pulled out her belt. Najee's eyes widened. The beatings made him feel like a runaway slave. Candy swung, but he caught the belt in midair. She attempted to snatch the belt away, but his grip was too strong.

"Boy, if you don't let go of this damn belt!"

"Mama, please don't hit me. I'm too old for whoopins."

"You ain't never too old for me to beat some sense into yo' black ass. Now let go of his belt," she ordered.

Defeated, Najee released his grip. His shoulders slumped and a tear slowly trickled down his cheek. This was not him. He usually stood tight lipped and contemptuous, showing remorse yet feeling no pain. His current demeanor made Candy's heart melt with sorrow. Tears streamed down her own face as well.

Candy lifted Najee's chin with a French tip fingernail. "What's wrong, baby? Why are you crying?"

Silence!

"Talk to me, son. Don't block me out like this," she pleaded. "How can I help you if you don't tell me what the problem is?"

Silence!

Candy grew frustrated and lashed out. "I take you in and treat you like my own, and this is how you repay me? By fighting and getting kicked outta school every other week? I shouldn't even waste my time. I should've let you go into the system." She regretted her words as soon as they escaped her lips.

Najee sniffled. Too much weight had been placed upon his young shoulders. Too much hurt had been inflicted on him. For the first time, he struck back. "I fight all the time because of you, mama!"

"Me?" she asked incredulously. "What did I do?"

"The kids at school tease me and call you a prostitute. They say the only reason you can afford to buy me nice things is because you be selling your body and that you got an old, white sugar daddy," his words dug into Candy like a dull machete. "Please tell me what they sayin' ain't true, mama! Please don't let it be true."

Perplexed, Candy fell silent. She had told him long ago that she would never be dishonest or disloyal to him. She intended to keep that promise. She couldn't shelter the truth from him any longer. It was now or never. She decided that now was the best time to put him up on game.

They drove a few short blocks to Eucalyptus Park, located on 120th and Inglewood Ave. They sat on a bench and she told him everything about her past. Layers of shame and guilt peeled off as she talked about her lost dreams and ambitions of becoming a nurse. She became physically shaken and emotional as she talked about meeting Prince and getting turned out to the streets.

She told him how she watched the heartless pimp brutally beat Mama Merl to death and how Prince was responsible for putting the ugly scar across Boulevard's face during an altercation at a bar regarding a gambling debt. Najee instantly disliked Prince. He didn't even know the man, but hatred for him became a malignant cancer hibernating in his heart. He knew that one day their paths would cross.

Candy let out a deep sigh and finally told him about Monica, his real mother. Najee sat silent and completely numb, absorbing all of the heavy shit that was just placed on his young mind. To Candy's surprise, when he did speak, he wasn't angry or bitter.

34

"You're my only mother, no matter what." He reached out to hug her tightly and thanked her for making sacrifices in her own life to make his life better.

His reaction to the news pleased Candy. As an inquisitive child, he always asked about his father. She knew that telling him about his biological father also meant revealing that she wasn't his biological mother. She intentionally avoided those conversations, but today she knew she couldn't hold anything back, no matter how painful.

"There's something else you need to know about your real mom," she insisted.

Najee held up his hands. "I'm good, I don't need to know nothin' else. You are my real mother."

"Prince killed your mother!" she blurted out quickly. It was like a heavy stone had been lifted off her shoulders.

Najee's features formed into a scowl. "Wha—what do you mean killed? You just said she died while giving birth."

Candy put her hands in her palms and cried. When she composed herself, she told him the truth. It took a while for the streets to put the story together, but Boulevard told her that on the night he got slashed in the face, he went to see the voodoo lady in Watts to stitch him up. She was well known in the hood for treating everything from stomach aches to gunshot wounds. When he arrived, he spotted Prince and a washed-up pimp named Godfather quickly leaving the projects. He didn't think nothing of it and ducked low until they mashed out.

On a separate occasion when she and Boulevard went to the medicine women for some antibiotics and treatment for his stab wounds to the thigh and buttock, the mysterious lady divulged that she had given Prince a powerful white pill that was effective in inducing labor but deadly if taken with a carbonated beverage.

Candy tried to lighten the mood by playfully reminiscing about Najee attacking Boulevard with a knife while wearing Spiderman underwear. Najee's mind, however, had been swept to a faraway place. A place where revenge was painful and calculated. A place where Prince's mutilated corpse was buried face down in a shallow grave. No matter how long it took to track him down, Prince would pay for his transgressions, Najee vowed.

CHAPTER 4

Business Is Business

Boulevard pulled up to his trap house on 56th and Figueroa, deep in the bowels of South Central, Los Angeles. This condemned part of the ghetto was controlled by the notorious Five-Deuce Hoover Criminals. Although their roots started with infamous Crips, the Hoovers become so large, powerful, and hated that they changed their gang colors to orange and declared war on both the Crips and the Bloods.

OG's like Big Sniper, Big Twin, Gangsta T, and Fat Rat gave Boulevard their blessing to operate on their turf. In exchange, Boulevard plugged them with automatic weapons and drugs. It was a win-win situation for both parties.

Boulevard got out of the whip and nodded to Bam and Roscoe who were lifting weights and sipping 40-oz. They ripped the labels off the bottles to show disrespect to their arch enemies, the Rollin' 40's. Boulevard could never understand that gang culture shit. The only color that was important to him was the shade of green.

He knocked on the window with a special knock to announce his arrival, then used his key to enter the black bar gate and door. He stepped inside and was disappointed to find Sugar in her bra and panties sitting on a rundown couch with two crack heads. The blinds were closed, the air conditioner was broken, and the spot smelled musty. A roach strolled across the dingy wall. Displeasure was scribbled across Boulevard's face. The hypes got the point and quickly scattered out of the front door.

"What the fuck is hap'nin' up in this piece? Didn't I warn yo' triflin' ass about letting customers up in the trap?"

Sugar waved him off. "That's just Lamont and Teresa, they harmless."

Boulevard opened his mouth to fire back with something slick but decided against it. Sugar was seeking attention, and he was tired. All he wanted to do was dump off some of the new yayo and pick up his paper. He had moves to make and laws to break. Neither could be accomplished by arguing with Sugar's silly ass.

He ignored her comment and got right down to business. "Let me get that cash up out of you. I got other runs to make."

Sugar avoided eye contact. "It's been slow, I ain't made no money yet," she stuttered.

"Slow, huh?" he repeated in a skeptical tone.

"Yeah, man. Plus, the jump out boys been sweatin' the block."

Boulevard reached back and smack fire out of Sugar. The blow caught her off guard, almost snapping her head off her neck. He caught her by a dingy bra strap and held her up before she could sink to the ground.

"Did you forget that it's the first of the month? People got their EBT at midnight, and the mailman ran three hours ago."

While holding her up, Boulevard was able to examine Sugar for the first time in a long time. She felt thin and frail. Dark rings encircled her cheerless eyes, and her mouth twitched uncontrollably. She was addicted to dope. He felt betrayed.

"Bitch, have you been dippin' in that shit?"

"Hell no!" she objected with indignation. "Are you calling me a crack whore?"

"Yeah, that's exactly what I'm calling yo' ass." Boulevard grabbed her by the face. "If you don't have my money, then that means you should have the four and a half zips I left."

The first sign of addiction was denial. Sugar had already done that. The second sign of substance abuse is theft. A dope fiend will steal from their own mama in order to get that fix. Even if it's nailed down, welded shut, or in a vault guarded by two killer clowns, they will find a way to take it regardless of the repercussions. Sugar had to have that glass dick. It was an obsession, and the pain from withdrawal was more vicious than any injury Boulevard could inflict.

Boulevard shook his head in disgust and released her chin from his grip. Sugar sank to the ground and hugged his ankles, begging for forgiveness through a mist of sniffles and tears. Boulevard looked down at the lump of useless flesh and felt no pity. Their relationship was over. He shook her off his leg and marched toward the door.

Sugar charged at him. "Muthafucka, you, can't leave me!" She hawked a wad of saliva in Boulevard's face.

Boulevard peeled a hundred-dollar bill off his bankroll, wiped off the spit, and threw the crumpled C-note at Sugar. "I should break my foot off in yo' ass, but I don't want to scuff up my shoes, bitch. Don't let me catch yo' punk ass around here no more."

****

Candy and Najee sat under the spring sun for another hour having a mother and son conversation. She promised to stop stripping at the club and use the free time to pursue her dreams of becoming a registered nurse. He promised to stop getting kicked out of school. He also vowed to go to college and become a software engineer so that she wouldn't have to work anymore. They sealed their deal with a pinky handshake. He deliberately left out the part about hunting Prince. A fire was kindling in his heart that could only be extinguished with the blood of the man who made him an orphan.

Candy's phone vibrated. The screen read: *007*. It was Boulevard's code. She didn't want to get her new line hot, so she and Najee walked across Inglewood Avenue to a 7-11 convenience store. Najee went inside to buy a Big Gulp and some snacks while she used the phone booth.

When Boulevard answered, she could hear the depression in his voice. "What's good, papa? You don't sound too hot." A white man in a 750 BMW pulled up on her, but she rolled her eyes.

"You ain't gon' believe this shit, Bae. Sugar is a mufikin' crack head."

"Tell me something new," she retorted and gave the driver of the BMW the finger. She could spot an undercover from a mile away.

Boulevard lit a cigarette. "How come you didn't put a playa up on game?"

"I thought you knew. Look at her, she's only ninety pounds soaking wet. Besides, I ain't no snitch. Sugar is your problem, not mines."

She was right, Boulevard didn't see the obvious and vowed to keep a closer watch on his organization. He was about to expand and do some grown man shit. Any little mistake could mean prison or the cemetery.

As she hung up the phone, a homeless man limped toward her and extended his dirty palm for some change. His thumb was burnt and callous from flicking cigarette lighters and holding the flames to glass pipes for long periods of time. He looked familiar, but she couldn't put her finger on where she knew him from.

"Do I know you?" She dug into her designer bag and pulled out a twenty-dollar bill, knowing that he would spend it on drugs. That was cool, Boulevard controlled all the dope in that area anyhow, so the money would come back to her.

The homeless man looked at Candy with lifeless eyes. He was zoned out for a moment, then a flicker of recognition appeared on his face. He smiled and revealed two missing front teeth. "My name is Willie, and yeah, I remember you. Youz wuz one of Prince's hoes. Uh, excuse me, I meant one of his ladies."

Candy cringed, she had been called worse things in life; however, the name he mentioned sent chills down her spine. She glanced over her shoulder, making sure Najee was still inside the store. "That was a while ago. Have you heard anything about, Prince?"

The hype scratched his crotch, then smelled his fingers. "Last I heard, he wuz up in the joint pimpin' out faggots for cartons of cigarettes and dumb shit like that."

Candy absorbed the info, relieved that Prince was still doing a long bid. The homeless man was eager to leave. The money was burning a hole in his palm.

"I gotta go, good looking out. And I'm real sorry for what I did to you back in the day. I wuz high off that angel dust and got my wires crossed. Boulevard told me to scare you, not beat you up," he sincerely apologized.

The Streets Made Me

She cocked her head to the side, confusion shrouded her face. What are you talking about? You sure you got the right chick?"

"Yo' name Candy, right?" He looked her up and down. "I might forget a face, but I'll never forget a body like that. Youz wuz a renegade back then, and Boulevard wanted me to put the fear of God in you so that you'd choose-up with him," his words were like strong hands wrapping around her windpipe, suffocating her with the truth of Boulevard's betrayal.

The homeless man limped off just as Najee came out of 7-11. He spotted some of his homies across the street. He had hung out with his mom enough and was anxious to link up with his friends from Eucalyptus Mob. Eu-Mob was a rising Crip set that dominated the city of Hawthorne.

Candy, however, had other ideas. "Remember when I told you that one day soon things would change?" she asked in a serious tone. Najee nodded his head in confirmation. Candy grabbed him by the hand and hailed down a passing taxi cab. "Well, today is that day. We're never going back to the house on G-Block. I'm leaving Boulevard's ass for good."

As they checked into a rundown hotel on Imperial, Candy told him how Boulevard had played her, tricked her, and robbed her out of her dignity and dreams. Najee had been hit with a ton of grown people shit in one day, but he was strong and mature for his age. He hugged his mother and reassured her that everything would be alright. He loved Boulevard like the father he never had, but he loved his mother even more. Because of that, Boulevard had to pay restitution for his sins. A clever plan hatched in his head.

****

Boulevard's whip moved low key, avoiding potholes and floating through the ghetto back streets like a yacht. He made dropoffs and pickups on 101st and Vermont, 63rd and Crenshaw, 75th and San Pedro, and finally 118th and Eucalyptus in the city of Hawthorne. He was happily headed back to the spot Candy operated on 120th and Gale, known to the locals as G-block.

41

Larry D. Wright

To all his worker's surprise, he dropped off a brick at each location, double what they usually saw. The briefcase was quickly being emptied of coke and filled with dead presidents. He had forty-eight stacks on him, and six kilos left, more than enough incentive to forget about the sour move Sugar pulled. He was relieved that he only kept four and a split at the spot on, Figueroa. Them niggas off Fig were unpredictable. Anything could pop off and usually did.

As Boulevard was moving up 118th Street, he spotted crack head Willie limping up the block. He was tempted to pull over and shoot him in his other kneecap for being such a fuck up, but he had business to tend to.

A long line of loitering dope fiends greeted him when he pulled up on G-Block. You would think the house was a food pantry giving out free cheese. Boulevard wondered what was going down. He drove to the carport and jumped out with the briefcase securely tucked under his armpit. He rushed inside and found an empty house. He peeked through the blinds and observed the impatient crowd. He had just talked to Candy, so where the fuck was she? He pondered.

Something didn't feel right. He rushed to the stash spot in the freezer. Relieved that a fat knot of gwuap was still stuffed inside the hollow cavity of a frozen turkey, he opened the kitchen cabinet and grabbed two cans of fake Raid roach spray. He unscrewed the false bottom to the first one. Cool. He unscrewed the second one and found a zip of hard. He relaxed a little. Everything was accounted for.

He chopped the zip of hard into chunky fifties and dubs. Next, he pulled the triple beam from under the sink and measured out four and a half ounces from one of the new duct taped bricks. Opening the black security bars on the front door, he scanned the crowd for Charlie, a washed-up ex-drug dealer who started getting high off his own supply. Although the game had gotten the best of him, he was still the best cooker on the West Side. His whip game was on point. He could make the work bounce back double and still be butter.

Charlie stood over the stove with the Pyrex and water whipping the work. Boulevard broke him off an eight ball and thanked the

42

crowd for not coppin' elsewhere. To reward their loyalty, he announced that he was giving out double-ups, two for the price of one. The crowd damn near cheered. The new work that he cooked up was superior quality and gone in under an hour. Boulevard texted Candy a gang of times but got no reply. This wasn't like her, he began to worry.

Word spread across town that Boulevard was selling double-up. The trap was jukin', but he opted to close up shop. He needed to find Candy. He contemplated leaving Charlie to run the spot but wisely decided against it. He had learned his lesson about letting hypes handle dope unsupervised. That was like letting Dracula run a blood bank. He locked the spot down, then hit the bricks in search of his woman.

****

The tan, single-family house near the corner of 56th and Figueroa was dark and smelly inside. The living room was bare except for an old leather couch, a wooden table with a wobbly leg, and a small television playing a rerun of Miami Vice. The setup was typical of the many trap houses that populated the urban landscape.

Sugar looked through the dingy blinds for the thousandth time that day. Stray dogs and feral cats roamed the streets, cars on chrome rims sped by thumpin' loud hip-hop music, young black men hugged the corner, and young black women strutted up the block wearing tight booty shorts and cheap flip flops. Occasional gunshots and blaring sirens completed the dysfunctional backdrop. It was just a normal day in the hood.

Satisfied that aliens were not coming to get her, Sugar sat on the worn couch and placed a white rock into her pipe. The long glass tube had a small piece of brillo screen stuffed in the tip. She placed the end of the glass dick between her chapped lips and flicked the lighter. Flames shot up, illuminating her frail features. She took a blast, exhaled, and began to cry. Out of frustration, she threw the glass pipe at the T.V. It shattered on a scene of Crocket and Tubbs arresting a major drug dealer. At that moment, a sinister plot formed in her head.

"That punk bitch Candy gon' pay for turning Boulevard against me," she mumbled to herself. "And that hoe ass nigga Boulevard gon' get his, too." In her feeble mind, the world was against her. She was bitter, and misery hated to be alone. She wanted others to feel her hurt. Resolved to inflict pain on the world, she racked a slug into her .380 and headed to G-Block.

CHAPTER 5

Evil Side of Innocence

It had been six months since Boulevard had last seen Candy. He looked for her all over South Central and stalked their old stomping grounds in Hollywood. No one had seen or heard from her. He also checked Najee's school only to find out that he had been transferred at the request of his guardian. They couldn't provide him with any further details.

Boulevard's worry morphed into anger when he returned to the spot on, G-block and sadly discovered that all the money and dope was gone. He had been double-crossed. There was no way he could pay Benzo Al the hundred and eighty bands he owed him. Boulevard was fucked! He closed his eyes and contemplated what went down.

After bending corners looking for Candy all over the city, he decided to head back and wait for her at the spot on Gale Street. Maybe she lost her phone or something, he tried to convince himself. When he returned, the house was securely locked up just as he left it, but as he entered the living room, he immediately sensed that something wasn't right.

He checked the six copper rounds in his revolver, thumbed the hammer back, and cautiously proceeded toward the bedroom where he had stashed the briefcase. It was gone, stolen. A sudden migraine squeezed his cranium. He checked the freezer. Without even sticking his hand inside the hollow cavity of the frozen turkey, he could see that his fat knot of gwuap was missing. Rage seized his soul.

He sprinted out of the house in search of Charlie, the ex-drug dealer who water whipped the work. He was the only other person who knew about the briefcase and the only person foolish enough to steal from him. He had to be the culprit. Boulevard knew just where to find him.

Boulevard's Benz swerved into the parking lot of Lakers Liquor Store with the headlights off. Charlie and crack head Willie were posted up out front sharing a bottle of yak concealed in a brown paper bag. They didn't notice Boulevard slither up gripping a snub nose trey-eight until the blue steel barrel was pointed at their faces.

He wanted to blast Charlie on the spot but being reckless wouldn't reunite him with his money and dope. He held his anger in check and pressed the cold metal between Charlie's bushy eyebrows.

"Whoa!" Charlie and Willie simultaneously stuck their hands in the air.

"Where my muthafuckin' merch at, nigga?" Boulevard demanded.

"Hold on, nephew, what merch you talkin' 'bout?"

For Charlie's foolish reply, Boulevard kicked Willie in his bad knee. The dope fiend buckled in pain. "I'm only gonna ask you one mo' time, negro. Then I'm gon' splatter yo' ass all over Imperial Highway." He held the thumper sideways to add emphasis.

Charlie's reddened eyes widened. "C'mon, nephew, I'm dumb, but I ain't stupid enough to steal from you. This gotta be some kind of mistake. At least tell me what I'm supposed to have you yours," he pleaded.

Boulevard looked at the two trembling men and lowered his gun. Even if they glued both of their brains together, they still weren't clever enough to pull off a $200,000 lick. He tucked the heat and mobbed off. Inside his ride, he put his head down on the steering wheel trying to clear his thoughts. Benzo Al's goons were on his heels, and his life was in imminent danger.

Crack head Willie knocked on the window, interrupting his ruminations. Boulevard rolled down the glass. "If you ask me for some spare change, I swear fo' God I'ma run yo' ass over."

Willie scratched his crotch, smelled his fingers and said, "I don't know if this means anything to you, but I ran into that chick Candy today."

Boulevard sat up straight. "Where you see the bitch?"

"At the store this afternoon 'round three or foe o'clock."

"Which store, nigga?" Boulevard hissed impatiently.

"The 7-11 by Eucalyptus Park."

46

Boulevard rolled up the tinted window. It was official. Candy had fucked him over. He was in denial thinking that Charlie hit the spot. She was right around the corner from the crib but wasn't answering her phone. She was probably somewhere laughing at him right now, Boulevard tortured himself.

That was six long months ago. Since then he had been dodging Benzo Al's calls and looking over his shoulder. The last text message he received from the Latino Kingpin read 187, the California penal code for murder. Boulevard took the few dollars he had saved up and moved to Van Nuys, the armpit of San Fernando Valley, he blended right in.

His plan was to lay low. Candy could hide, but Najee was the key. He had been kicked out of almost every school in the district for fighting. There were only a few schools he could attend. Boulevard fired up a Kool King and grinned knowing that is was only a matter of time before he had Candy's neck in his grip.

****

Candy was frustrated with her job at Red Lobster. Her swollen feet ached from standing on her legs all day, and her shift supervisor was an asshole. The customers were nice, a little too nice. She was propositioned for sex more times as a waitress than when she danced at the strip club, but she quickly learned that most restaurant patrons are lousy tippers. In fact, she made more money in an hour shaking her ass than she made all week taking orders.

When her shift was over, she would rush home and soak her feet in Epsom salt, vowing never to return. Her tenacity, however, helped her keep on pushing. The big picture was more important than any small inconvenience.

Her joy came when she loaded her backpack with heavy textbooks and headed to school. She had enrolled in El Camino Community College and was enjoying the learning experience. Between long shifts at Red Lobster, submerging herself in her studies, and networking with likeminded people, her past was eroding away into a distant memory. The only residue leftover from her former life was Najee. He was a blessing and a reminder that she had conquered the concrete jungle.

****

Najee sat in the back of the classroom trying his best to avoid eye contact with his ninth-grade math teacher, Mrs. Olsen. He was one of her brightest students. He was also the sauce amongst his peers. Standing at 5'7, he was short in stature but made up for his height in other ways. He was dark-skinned and handsome, dressed Dougie, had a slick mouthpiece, and always kept a pocket full of money courtesy of his parent's illegal activities. Although he was laid back, there was something untamed and unpredictable about his persona. This mystique made the girls love him.

Being smart didn't hurt Najee's cause either, but he was afraid to display his intelligence. In the ghetto, to be smart was considered being a geek, and in a predatory environment, geeks were perceived as weak. So, when Mrs. Olsen wrote a difficult math equation on the chalkboard, he slumped deep in his seat. He could have easily calculated the problem in his head, but like many young black men, he had been duped into believing that it was better to be the class clown versus the class valedictorian.

Mrs. Olsen turned to address the class. "Can anyone give me the answer to this equation?" Her eyes roamed the room. The blank faces of hardened teenagers stared back at her. "Okay then, I guess I'll have to pick a volunteer. Let me see." The teacher searched the classroom for a candidate. Everyone sunk deeper in their desks trying to avoid her radar. Her gaze landed on Rio, a tall Puerto Rican kid who had recently transferred from a school in the Bronx. "Mario, would you like to give it a shot?"

"Why you pick me? You already knowin' my dumb ass don't know the answer." The class roared with laughter.

To Rio's relief, another student eagerly raised her hand. Angel Thomas was the prettiest girl on earth, at least that's what Najee thought. She scribbled on a piece of scratch paper, and then eagerly gave her answer. "The hypotenuse of A squared plus B squared is fifty square feet," she offered with confidence.

Mrs. Olsen smiled her approval then wrote the answer on the board. "Very good, Angel. As a bonus question, can you explain the Pythagorean Theorem?"

Angel was on stuck, she didn't know the answer. Her confidence was deflated. Snickers came from the other females in the class. Angel's silence was becoming uncomfortable and embarrassing.

Najee stepped in to rescue her. "A Greek philosopher and mathematician discovered a special relationship among the sides of a triangle. Today we call this discovery the Pythagorean Theorem. Basically, you can find the length of any side of a right triangle if you know the lengths of the other two sides," the words oozed from his lips like a Harvard professor. The male students and haters snickered until Rio and Najee grilled them with frowns.

After class, as Najee was headed for the door, Mrs. Olsen pulled him to the side.

'*Now what,*' Najee thought, as he watched the other energetic students filter into the hallway.

"You're a very intelligent young man, Najee. I've been doing this for a long time, so I know why you don't volunteer more often in class. You don't want to look like a nerd in front of your boys, but there's nothing wrong with being an intelligent black brother," she preached.

Najee wanted to roll his eyes. "Not another Malcolm X speech," he mumbled under his breath.

The concerned teacher continued, "Society wants you to have an inferiority complex, and most young black men feed right into those false stereotypes. I want you to think about breaking that cycle, okay?" After kicking knowledge, her stern features transformed into a pleasant smile. "And I see those little love notes you pass to, Angel Thomas. You two make a good couple but stop letting her cheat off your homework."

When Najee stepped outside, Angel was waiting for him, all 5'5 of her. Najee tried his best not to cheese, but his lips betrayed him.

49

Larry D. Wright

The haters looked on in jealousy as he handed her his heavy textbooks to carry. They couldn't believe that he had the finest girl in school eating out of the palm of his hand. The girls called him Romeo because he always had a sweet comment in the chamber, but in actuality, he was simply regurgitating all the game he heard from Boulevard and the other colorful street players he was exposed to over the years. The lessons he learned and the things he observed while riding in the passenger seat of Boulevard's ride would become priceless gems in the near future.

"Why do I have to carry your books? You should be carrying mines," Angel pointed out. "And why do I have to use my allowance and lunch money to pay for everything? You the one with all the drip." She looked even sexier when she got mad.

Najee laughed as a toothpick bobbed in the corner of his lips. "Cuz I'm a pimp, that's why!"

She hated when he talked this way. "Boy, stop! You ain't no pimp and probably never met a real mac daddy in your life."

Najee's mood grew serious. He never talked about his family's past, so he changed the subject. "You look beautiful today, baby. Sorry I didn't tell you earlier. I just got a lot of shit on my dome."

It was moments like these when the facade faded, and glimpses of his vulnerability shined through that drew her to him like a moth to a flickering flame. Or was he the actual flame, she often questioned? She would soon learn that playing with fire will get you burned, but for now, she was infatuated with the bad boy.

Angel moved closer to Najee. "Thank you for seeing me for who I am. And good looking out for slipping me that note with the answer to today's math problem. You're so smart."

"Thanks," Najee said dryly. He worried about his mother.

"I'm serious, you're smarter than you let on, but you think you're slick, and that's what's gonna get you in a lot of trouble."

"Whateva!" Najee wasn't trying to hear that. He pulled her into his arms and gently kissed her lips.

Angel melted in his embrace. He cupped her big round booty as their tongues clashed. Najee was determined to hit that. He played nice and carried her books, something he never did. As he was

50

trying to talk up on the pussy, he noticed a blue Chevy Suburban. That was the third day in a row he had seen the SUV. The tinted windows prohibited him from seeing who was inside. He hadn't said anything to anyone before, but he decided to mention it to his mother when she got off work tonight.

****

Boulevard sat in the Chevy Suburban with the windows rolled up and the air conditioner on full blast. He fired up a square and observed Najee from a distance. He smiled proudly when he peeped the cute female stand on her tippy toes and give him a sensual kiss. He had been following the two teenagers for a week undetected. He knew where Najee lived but hadn't seen any signs of his real target, Candy. He decided that if he didn't get a visual on her tonight, he would snatch the kid and make her come to him.

Boulevard was so absorbed in his own thoughts that he did not notice the money green SS Monte Carlo slowly trailing him. The passenger flicked a half-smoked cigarette out of the window, then inserted red shotgun shells into the guts of his sawed-off pump. The driver drove cautiously while speaking with Benzo Al.

"On Bloods, we can catch this hoe ass nigga slippin' right now. How you wanna do this, big homie?"

"Hold off for now but follow him closely, Ese. We need him to lead us to the fetti. Entiendes?"

"I think we should murk this nigga, right now." He made a left onto Avalon.

"That's why I don't pay you to think. Just stay on that vato and don't get caught slippin'. I want Boulevard, that chica, and my dinero."

Benzo Al hung up the phone feeling better than he had in months. Being promoted within Los Cinco Diablos didn't come with all the perks he expected. Instead, the extra responsibility only caused more stress. He was already making catastrophic mistakes. His hot temper had sparked a war with the Sinaloa Cartel, and one of their drug smuggling tunnels in Arizona had been compromised.

He looked down at the female between his legs sucking his dick and wondered who in the hell gave her the name Sugar. There was nothing sweet about her. The streets had sapped all her youth, and the crack pipe had stolen her dignity. He regretted talking business on the phone in her presence. She couldn't be trusted.

Sugar stroked Benzo Al's dick and licked his balls. "Do you want me to do that little thing you like to do?" she offered. "My bladder is full, Papi." She held both of his balls and massaged them while waiting on an answer. At one point, she used to charge him a stack to fulfill his perverted cravings. These days she would do anything for a nickel bag.

Benzo Al's erection instantly deflated. "Puta, are you loco? I wouldn't let you piss on me if I was on fire. Get the fuck outta here." He pointed at the door. "Now!" He grabbed her by the weave, pulled her off her knees, and shoved her into the hallway.

Defeated and detested, she picked herself and her pride up off the floor and stumbled away on a broken high heel. She paused in the hotel lobby and stared at her image bouncing off of the double glass doors. She reached out to touch the reflection but withdrew her hand as if she had touched fire.

"Where did I go wrong?" she mused. She promised herself that she would check into rehab, just not today. She reached into her pocket and fished out the gold, presidential Rolex belonging to Benzo Al. Rehab and redemption were put on hold. Today she was about to get high as giraffe's pussy.

****

Najee loved California nights. A crisp, cool breeze blew off the Pacific Ocean and the stars twinkled in the sky, offering the illusion of hope. The house phone rang, but he didn't rush to pick it up. He didn't want to seem too anxious. Angel usually called at 7:00 o'clock, and they would chop it up until the wee hours. After the fourth ring, he cleared his throat and answered in his best Barry White voice.

"What it do, baby? Your pretty little feet were just tiptoeing through my mind."

Candy busted out laughing. "Boy, if you don't take some of that bass out of your voice, so help me God!"

"Oh, hi, mama." Embarrassed, he turned down the R&B music.

"Don't hi, mama me. You thought I was one of your little hot in the ass girlfriends, didn't you?" she teased. "I'm gonna go out after my last class, so don't wait up for me."

"Who you going out with? I need to screen ole boy to make sure he ain't no stalker. And don't you have some homework to do?"

Candy chuckled at his overprotectiveness. "You just make sho' you do your homework and don't stay up too late. I gotta go, Mister Lover Man."

She hung up before he could tell her about the suspicious Chevy-Suburban he spotted three days in a row. The thought troubled Najee until the phone rang again. His heart skipped a beat, it was Angel. He picked up and greeted her with a well-prepared line. Her voice was sexy and brought a smile to his lips. Angel was a biracial, yellow-bone with bright, hazel eyes and kinky-curly hair. She ran track, which made her thighs thick as oatmeal, and her booty killed every pair of jeans she owned.

Najee had been trying to crack that egg and make an omelet ever since the first day of class. Even though she lived on Townsend Street, deep in the middle of Blood hood, he risked his life on several occasions just to dry hump. He chilled on his bed, phone to his ear, imagining that it was Angel pictured in his *Lil' Kim* poster wearing a skimpy bikini with that phat monkey.

"My momz ain't home. You gon' sneak over here or what?" Najee asked.

"Why does your mother always leave you home at night by yourself?" she probed curiously.

"Why do you ask so many questions?" he rebutted.

"I'm just worried about you, Bae. You only smile to hide whatever pain you're feeling inside, but your eyes say it all."

"There you go on that bullshit again, actin' like you know a nigga."

"Don't call yourself that. And I don't know you; that's the problem. You won't let nobody in."

Najee contemplated her words, she was right. His existence was shrouded by secrets. He never had a chance to be a regular kid. He felt himself becoming hardened on the inside, and Angel just confirmed that his exterior was becoming just as callous.

"Come over, baby. I wanna introduce you to the real me," Najee coaxed.

Angel knew what he was hinting at. He had been pressuring her for sex ever since everybody and they mama found out her best friend Keisha was giving it up. Her body was ripe, but her mind just wasn't ready to take it to the next level.

Angel made sure her nosey little sister wasn't around, and then lowered her voice into a conspiring whisper. "I'll give you some head, but I'm saving my virginity for my husband."

Najee belched an audible sigh. "That don't make no damn sense. You will suck my dick, but you won't let me fuck?"

"Ugghhh, don't say it like that! You make it sound all nasty."

Najee decided to change tactics. "I love you, Angel, and I will be your husband one day."

Angel took the bait. Najee did a quick two hundred push-ups and cleaned up his room while Angel hopped on the bus. He didn't have time to take a shower, so he took a quick hoe bath, and splashed on a couple of dabs of Polo cologne. Once complete, he took some of the flowers his mother's new boyfriend had given her and spread the rose petals all over his bed. Despite all the machismo, he was still a virgin as well. This would be a special occasion for both of them.

Najee paced nervously until he heard a hard bang on the front door. It didn't sound like Angel's knock, but when he looked through the peephole, he saw her standing there in the short DKNY mini skirt he bought from the Slauson Swapmeet. Making sure his own swagger was on point, he wiped off his Jordan's, brushed the lint off his blue Polo shirt, and opened the door. His mood immediately soured.

Boulevard stepped from the shadows and pushed the muzzle of his trusty .38 to the back of Angel's dome. He shoved her into the house.

"I'm sorry, Bae," Angel apologized through tears. "He came outta nowhere and said he was gonna kill me if I didn't knock on the door."

Najee protectively placed her behind him and faced Boulevard. It had only been six months since he had seen the ex-pimp, but the hard lines in his face from worry and stress made him appear years older.

Boulevard held the pole firmly in his rubber-gloved hand and pushed his way into the apartment. He was expecting them to be living large and lavish off his stash, but the unit was sensibly furnished.

He pointed the muzzle at Najee's chest and nodded toward the house phone. "Call yo' triflin' ass mama and tell her it's an emergency, and she needs to hurry home."

"No!" Najee replied defiantly.

"*No!* You tellin' me no, little nigga?" Boulevard raised the banger and smashed the butt against Najee's skull, causing his ears to ring. He lost his equilibrium and dropped to one knee. "Call your mama, and tell her to get her black ass here in the next few minutes or I'ma—"

"Or you gon' what?" Najee stood up and faced Boulevard.

Boulevard grabbed a fist full of Najee's shirt and viciously slung him into the entertainment system. Najee groaned, then charged Boulevard, but the ex-pimp snatched Angel by the neck and placed the burner against her right temple. Tears caused her mascara to run.

"Pick up the phone and start dialing, or I'm gonna splatter this little pretty bitch all over the wallpaper," Boulevard promised.

Angel tried to wiggle free, but Boulevard's clutch was too tight and too determined. Her eyes begged for help. "Who are you? Why are you doing this to us?" she asked.

"Why am I doing this?" Boulevard asked rhetorically. "Najee, tell this young bitch why I'm doing this."

"He thinks my momz took his money and dope."

"*Think*! Nah, lil' nigga, I know for a fact she got me!"

"You wrong, Boulevard, I took it," Najee confessed. "I flushed the poison and gave the blood money to that shelter in Hollywood for homeless kids called the Covenant House."

"I don't believe you!" Boulevard screamed, pushing the barrel of the gun tighter against Angel's skull. "You lying to cover for yo' mama. Call that thieving winch, now!" He held Angel in a headlock and pointed the weapon at Najee's face.

Boulevard's trigger finger trembled. He examined Najee's demeanor and knew the teenager was telling the truth. He wanted to shoot him even more now. Not because he stole the merch, but for his youthful stupidity—for putting all their lives in grave danger.

Boulevard lowered the gun and released Angel. His anger dissipated, and his voice swelled with compassion as he asked, "How could you do this to me out of all people, Najee? I raised you."

"You're wrong again, Boulevard. The streets raised me."

Boulevard opened his mouth to respond, but someone pounded on the door. It was hard and firm like one of those distinctive police knocks. "Shhh, don't nobody say shit." He gave the teenage couple a stern look, then crept towards the front door. He looked through the peephole. It was Candy. A flood of emotions rushed through his veins and a thousand questions tumbled in his head.

As Boulevard's hand twisted the doorknob, he subconsciously wondered why she wasn't using her key. A pistol aimed at his chest offered an answer. His eyes met with Candy's. Shock and confusion registered on their faces.

Plew! Plew! Plew!

Stepping from the shadows, Cheddar squeezed off three rounds into Boulevard's torso. The silencer twisted onto the barrel suppressed the sound of gunshots. Cheddar's accomplice, Lil' Wack, shoved Candy into the house as Boulevard's bullet-riddled body fell backward.

Candy crawled to him. "Boulevard!" she screamed. She cradled his head in her arms and watched helplessly as his body fluids leaked onto the carpet.

Lil' Wack cocked the sawed-off and pointed the barrel at Angel and Najee. Angel opened her mouth to scream. Lil' Wack crammed the barrel in her grill, cracking her two front teeth. Najee flexed up, but Lil' Wack swung the 12 gauge in his direction. Najee felt helpless. This was his fault, he blamed himself.

Cheddar stood over Boulevard's body with a satisfied look. The image of Boulevard on his back, wheezing through collapsed lungs for one final breath was gratifying. Lil' Wack, however, didn't share those sentiments.

"Damn, Blood! You wasn't 'posed to smoke the nigga. Benzo Al said get the money and the yayo first," he reminded Cheddar.

"Fuck Benzo, we doing this shit my way."

Cheddar had his own plan brewing. His intention was to get the money and dope, get rid of the bodies, and then get out of town. Portland sounded good. There were a lot of Bloods up them ways. He was tired of living under Benzo Al's shadow and constant scrutiny. Using the money from ten bricks, he could go from being a D-Boy to being the main man wherever he set up shop.

His accomplice was a disciplined soldier and wanted to stick to the script. He kept a watchful eye on the vics while Cheddar placed the muzzle of his heat to the back of Candy's unfortunate head. She was supposed to be on a date, but it turns out that her new boyfriend had a new wife and newborn son. Disappointed, she came home early only to be ambushed by the two thugs.

"We gon' make this shit real simple, Candy. Tell me where that paper and that work at, and you get to stay alive," he explained. "Try to run game on me and I'm murkin' everythang in this bitch, straight up."

"The money is in the freezer. Take it and leave."

"Get up and show me," Cheddar demanded.

Lil' Wack kept the shotgun trained on Angel and Najee as Cheddar led Candy to the refrigerator. Her hands shook uncontrollably, but she managed to open the freezer door and pull out a box of fish sticks.

Cheddar frowned. "What the fuck is this?" He dumped the contents onto the kitchen table. Frozen fish and a large bankroll fell out. The wad of money turned out to be five, tens, and singles—tip money that Candy was saving. "You gotta be shittin' me. Where the rest?"

"That's all I got to my name. Take it and get the fuck out of my house!"

Cheddar swung the butt of his pistol and knocked blood from Candy's lips. Before the pain registered in her brain, he reeled back and hit her again. The kitchen table caught her fall. Najee sprang into action. He pushed Lil Wack off balance and charged Cheddar. Lil' Wack regained his composure and aimed the strap at Najee's back. He was about to squeeze off, but Angel screamed and ran toward the front door. He couldn't allow her to get away. He slugged her over the head with the pump just as she reached for the doorknob. Her body slipped into unconsciousness.

Najee picked up a vase and smashed it against Cheddar's skull. The glass shattered on impact, causing dark red blood to trickle down his face. Stunned and visibly impaired, Cheddar squeezed off reckless shots.

Four bullets silently whisked through the air. Two of them struck Candy in the back as she reached for a butcher knife. The first slug burrowed into her flesh and chipped two of her ribs on exit. The second hollow point moved at a high velocity, striking her sixth dorsal vertebrae and snapping it in half. If she survived, which was highly doubtful, she would be a quadriplegic.

Najee caught Cheddar with a right hook, knocking him backward. He squared up in a boxer's stance and followed with a one-two punch combination to the chin. All his life he had fought to defend his mother. Tonight, was no exception. He delivered blow after crushing blow. The bigger man stumbled against the stove, regained his balance and popped off four hasty shots. They missed Najee's dome by inches.

Lil' Wack moved into position with the swiftness of a panther. Two people were already dead, he didn't want to hinder their getaway by letting the shotgun bark loudly. Besides, if he was going to shoot anyone, it would be Cheddar for fucking up a sweet lick. Now the two people who were most likely to know where the money and dope were stashed, were slumped in puddles of blood. He couldn't wait to holler at Benzo Al.

Lil' Wack ran up on Najee holding the shotgun like a baseball bat and swung, connecting with the back of his cranium. Najee's eyes went blank, his legs resigned, and he collapsed into a pool of his mother's warm blood. The hard-fought battle was over.

Cheddar grabbed an oven towel and wiped the blood from his stinging eyes. "Yo, Blood, go pull the whip around the front while I tie this little nigga and his bitch up."

Lil' Wack rushed outside while Cheddar used the kitchen sink to run cold water over his face. He kicked Najee in the ribs, then staggered into the living room.

Boulevard gasped for air. "You ain't dead yet, nigga?" Cheddar stomped his Chuck Taylors on Boulevard's larynx. The body stopped making indecipherable noises. Boulevard was dead.

Cheddar tucked his pistol in his waist and admired his handy work. He looked over, saw Angel, and grinned. Her short skirt rose above her curvaceous thighs. She wasn't wearing any panties, and her neatly trimmed pubic hair aroused him. He licked his lips like LL Cool J. "You's a little freak, ain't you?" he mocked the semiconscious girl.

Lil' Wack ran back inside out of breath and tripped over their entangled bodies. Cheddar had Angel's legs over his shoulders and his face buried deep in her young pussy. He was eating her out like a watermelon. Anger boiled in Lil' Wack's veins.

"*This fool ass nigga gon' get us popped off,*" he scoffed. Just as he was about to voice his opinion, Cheddar snapped on him.

"Don't just stand there and watch me, go tie homie up. You gon' get yo' turn, Blood."

"Nigga what? You trippin'." Lil' Wack dashed to the kitchen and secured Najee's hands, legs, and mouth with duct tape. As he finished, he heard the girl scream. He dragged Najee's unconscious body into the next room to investigate.

Cheddar carried Angel over his shoulder and tossed her onto Najee's rose petal covered bed. He fell on top of her and pried her struggling legs open like a crowbar. Angel's sharp nails raked

59

across his face. Cheddar retaliated with a swift backhand to the jaw. Lil' Wack entered the room just as Cheddar pulled out his hard dick. It was the first one Angel had ever seen in real life. Sheer terror washed through her.

Najee groaned as he came to. The tumor sized lump on the back of his head leaked blood down the nape of his neck, staining his Polo shirt. As he shook off the grogginess and caught his bearings, he heard Angel whimper. The will to fight flared up in him, but he couldn't move, couldn't yell, couldn't defend his loved ones. Tears of rage rained from his eyes as he crashed onto the floor trying with all his might to break the restraints. His determination was futile.

Cheddar laughed at his efforts and stroked his penis, making it harder and longer. Najee's watery eyes locked with Angel's. He tried to encourage her to be strong, but she turned her head away in shame.

"Ay, Wack; you wanna go first, homie?"

"Nah, I'm good, Blood." He declined and looked at the face of his watch. "We need to bounce."

"Stop acting like a mark and come fuck this bitch while I run up in her booty," Cheddar insisted, and flipped Angel onto her stomach.

"Let's go, Blood! We gotta raise up!" Lil' Wack demanded firmly.

Cheddar ignored him and positioned himself on top of Angel. He opened her ass cheeks, but as he was about to penetrate her anus, he heard a distinctive sound that stopped him in his tracks.

Chic! Chic!

Lil' Wack pumped the sawed-off. "On Damu, I said let's ride out before I smoke you, nigga!"

Cheddar glanced over his shoulder and saw the street sweeper pointed at his back. He knew his accomplice was a rider and wouldn't hesitate to pull the trigger. He had witnessed him put in work on several occasions. Lil' Wack was a dedicated soldier on a mission that was commissioned by a major shot caller, so it was strictly business, nothing personal.

60

Cheddar understood this and zipped up his pants. "Ol' cock blocking ass nigga," he teased and aimed the banger at Angel's dome. Without warning, he fired two shots into her grill at point-blank range. Chunks of bone and brains splattered the headboard and stained the white pillowcase. Next, Cheddar spun around and squeezed off two more rounds at Najee. The thumper jerked in his hand.

The slugs rocked Najee's body. Najee closed his eyes and held his breath. The only way to stay alive was to play dead. The pain was excruciating, but the thoughts of vengeance helped ease the agony. He vowed to deliberately inflict injury on those responsible for this senseless act. Before he fell unconscious, the names of Prince, Cheddar, Benzo Al, and Lil' Wack were permanently engraved into his memory.

****

Bad news travels fast through the arteries of the ghetto. Just twenty-four hours after Rio went looking for Najee and made the gruesome discovery, rumors of the quadruple homicide made its way to the chow hall in San Quentin State Prison. Prince shook his head, then went back to eating the tray of tasteless beef casserole. After almost fifteen years in the belly of the beast, the names Boulevard and Candy had become distant memories of a past life he was desperately trying hard to forget.

****

In South Central, students from Locke High School hung teddy bears and flowers on the light pole outside of the apartment where the bodies were discovered. The makeshift shrine included white candles and R.I.P posters signed by all of Najee and Angel's friends and a few empathetic strangers. The story made the front page of the L.A. Times. As usual, opportunistic politicians pushed for stiffer gun laws.

Inside Martin Luther King Jr. Hospital, Najee slept peacefully in a deep coma. It would be three months before he regained consciousness. When he did, all hell broke loose.

CHAPTER 6

Martin Luther King Jr. Hospital
Los Angeles, CA.

Najee's eyes slowly opened. He lay on his back hypnotized by the bright florescent lights on the ceiling. A digital clock read, 3:05 a.m. The hospital was quiet. He looked around attempting to gather his surroundings, wondering where he was. His memory was foggy. It wasn't until he called out for his mother for help that the images of the bloody murders exploded in his head.

He tried in vain to get out of bed. He was restricted by tubes in his arms and nose. He ripped the IV out of his forearm and snatched the electrocardiogram patches off his chest. The life support machine flatlined, setting off alarms and sending text messages to the doctors and nurses who were on call.

Najee struggled out of bed and stumbled when his bare feet met the cold tile floor. His legs were weak, but he was determined to make it to the door. He shuffled down the sterile corridor holding the wall for support. The blue hospital gown left nothing to the imagination. His buttocks were exposed for the world to see. As he searched for an exit, two nurses followed by a police officer rushed off the elevator.

The hospital personnel tried to coax Najee back into his room, but he struggled and fought them with all of the strength he could muster. One thing was on his mind. He needed to retaliate. He needed to taste the aftertaste of mayhem.

Two orderlies dressed in crisp white uniforms arrived, brought Najee to the floor, and subdued him. They held his thrashing arms and legs while a nurse stuck a long needle in his arm. Najee could feel the tranquilizer squirting into his vein, circulating through his system, and rocking him to sleep.

He awoke that afternoon and looked at the heart monitor. The beeping sound of the machine confirmed his worst fear. He was still alive. He felt as though he didn't deserve to breathe. Guilt chewed through his soul like a colony of termites. His Fam was slaughtered because of him. He stared at the machine wondering why God had spared him, not knowing that there was a diving plan for his life.

A tall white man interrupted his thoughts. Najee took in his well-pressed suit and neatly trimmed grey hair. His scent was familiar. He smelled like a cop.

"Good morning, Mr. Howard. I'm Detective Brooks," he introduced himself and sat on the edge of the bed without an invitation. "I heard you were feeling better, so I thought I'd stop by and ask you a few questions." Najee turned his head and gazed out of the window. It was raining. "Listen, son," the detective began. "I know you've been through a hell of a rough time, but it's important that you tell me all you know. You're the only witness. The people who did this are dangerous, and we went through great lengths to protect you."

Najee remained mute and thought about the irony of pouring rain followed by the beautiful rainbow that now arced over the city. Detective Brooks decided to switch tactics and offer a little info.

"One of my informants told me that some two-bit pimp was searching around town for your mother. Something about a large amount of money and drugs was stolen from a spot in Hawthorne. Do you know anything about that?"

Najee ignored the question altogether. He needed some answers of his own. "When are they having the funerals? I want to see my mom one last time before they bury her."

"Jesus Christ, you mean you don't know?"

"Know what?" Najee sat up.

Detective Brooks placed a sympathetic hand on Najee's shoulder. "You've been in a coma. Your mother, Angel Thomas, and Robert Allen were buried a couple of months ago. I'm sorry, son."

Najee burned with rage. He took his anger out on the investigator. "I ain't your son, white muthafucka! And why are you sorry? Did you know her?" He lashed out. "Nah, I didn't think so. Just leave me the fuck alone. You're never gonna find the people who did this because I plan on finding them first."

Offended, the detective reached in his breast pocket and flicked a business card on the bed. On his way out, he stopped to speak to a pretty redbone nurse. She was coming to check Najee's vitals.

The nurse illuminated the dreary hospital room. She had been praying for Najee and was happy to see that his condition had stabilized. She examined his sutures. The stitches had healed well. The .9mm bullet penetrated his back and went through and through, chipping a lower rib but missing all major arteries. Still, he had lost a lot of blood, and it was a miracle he was still alive.

Satisfied with the progress, the nurse gave Najee a sisterly kiss on the forehead and placed a pocket-sized Bible on the nightstand. As she turned to leave, she informed him that he had another visitor.

Najee wondered who it could be. There was a courtesy knock, then the door swung open. Sugar walked in holding a *Get Well* card and a bouquet of colorful flowers. She sat on the edge of the bed and gave Najee a kiss on the cheek. Her lips were cold. For the next hour, she fussed over him making sure he was comfortable. Najee wasn't new to the game and wondered what her agenda was.

As they spoke, however, his suspicions dwindled. He had known Sugar since he was a baby, and even though his mother and her had their personal beef, she was the only family he had left. He watched her moves. She looked healthy and vibrant, not irritated and jittery as he last recalled. She told him that what happened to Candy and Boulevard was a wakeup call, so she checked herself into rehab shortly after.

"Never mess with drugs, baby boy," she warned. "Don't sniff it, don't smoke it. Matter of fact, don't even sell it because one way or another, it will fuck up your life. Real talk." Najee stored her words in his memory bank. "And another thing, baby boy," Sugar stated excitedly. "You're coming home with me next week. I've already started the paperwork with the Department for Children and Family Services to become your legal guardian. There's no way in hell I'm gonna let them put you in foster care."

Later that evening as Najee was dozing off to sleep, a breaking news segment caught his interest. He propped two pillows under his back and listened. A late modeled SS Monte Carlo had been set ablaze near Fremont High School. When the fire was extinguished, investigators found the burnt remains of a male victim in the trunk. Heinous incidents like this were a common occurrence in Los Angeles, but the victim's mug shot in the corner of the screen demanded Najee's attention. He could never forget those cold eyes. He grinned and clicked the off button on the remote. As he drifted to sleep, he checked Lil' Wack's name off his mental hit list.

Najee was released a week later. The pretty young nurse laid hands on him and prayed for his safety and salvation before he was discharged. Najee wasn't feeling all that Jesus stuff, but ole girl was hella fine, he admitted.

Rio and the rest of the clique threw Najee a big homecoming party. The spot was lit and surprisingly lasted until 3:00 a.m. without the po-po sweating the joint. After the party disbursed, Najee and his homies loitered in a dark alley and politicked. Baby Bandit pulled a can of orange spray paint out of his backpack and wrote his hood on the wall. They passed a bottle of Hennessy and a blunt of loud while putting him up on what had been jumpin' off in the hood. Kev was in juvy for grand theft auto. Flossy was ballin' outta control. E-Bow was on the run. Jodi with the sleepy eye was pregnant. Same old ghetto shit. The bottle and the weed rotated to Najee, but he passed. Sugar's warning echoed in his head.

Sugar lived in Manual Arts school district, but Najee checked into Hawthorne High instead. After losing his whole family, he wanted to be close to his old classmates. He made the freshman football team and excelled as the first string middle linebacker. His pent up frustration came out on the field, and he was hitting hard. He earned a reputation for putting players on opposing teams flat on their backs.

He also excelled academically. He could no longer afford shopping sprees and name brand gear, so he used his intelligence to stand out versus trying to fit in. Rio even improved his grades. They made being nerds look cool. The fact that he had a slick mouthpiece also worked in his favor. He made hearts flutter and panties moist with his clever lines and smooth compliments. Chicks were on his dick, but his eyes were on Tomboy Tammy.

Tammy used to run track and hang out with the fellas, but she had recently developed into a sexy young woman. Standing at 5'9", she was taller than most women, and her long chocolate legs looked like two Twix bars merging into a round booty and a pair of perky breasts. It seemed as though Tomboy Tammy had transformed into Tammy the Stallion overnight. She and Angel used to be tight, plus Rio was feeling her, so Najee fell back. Their playful flirting, however, eventually evolved into passionate kisses on the low.

School was going well for Najee, but his home life sucked. Sugar had abandoned drugs and picked up another habit, drinking. When she was drunk, she became a different type of monster. The abuse started shortly after he moved into her dilapidated house on 56th and Figueroa. From the jump, she had an ulterior motive for taking him under her guardianship. She thought he had access to the ten kilos of dope and money that Boulevard had stashed.

The pieces began to fall in place when she was bossing Benzo Al. As she sucked his dick, she ear hustled on his conversation concerning fronting Boulevard ten bricks. Her assumptions were confirmed when she threw the crack pipe at the T.V., and then rushed to Hawthorne in order to confront Candy and drop a dime on Boulevard. As she sat in her car soaking in her own desolation, she witnessed Najee running from the spot on G-block, clutching a chrome briefcase. When Candy and Najee disappeared, she had no doubt as to who hit the lick.

After learning that Najee had survived, she put her plan into play. She was confident he could lead her to the money. She filled out the appropriate paperwork to become his legal guardian and played the nice guy. Her kindness, however, was short-lived. After a couple of months of being badgered, Najee revealed what he had actually done with the dope and the loot. It hurt to talk about the possible cause and motive for the merciless slaughter of his loved ones. The guilt stalked his conscience.

What stung, even more, were Sugar's bitter words. They sliced through him like a chainsaw. At times, he wished she would just hit him, but Sugar was a different type of abuser. She used verbal jabs to inflict pain.

"Yo' ugly black ass ain't never gon' be shit but a thug!" Sugar's venomous barrage of insults would begin as soon as Najee returned home from school. "Yo' stupid momma should've swallowed you like a good hoe instead of letting that trick run up in her raw!" She would finish with a cruel laugh.

Sugar's disparaging comments cut Najee to the core, and he began to believe that his life would never amount to anything. Sticks and stones break bones, but words break the spirit and leave permanent scars. Ironically, Najee grew to care for her. He learned long ago to equate pain with love, so he started to blame himself and make excuses for her abusive behavior.

As the school year dwindled down and summer rapidly approached, constant rejection at home pushed Najee into the only place that happily accepts the wounded, broken, and unforgiven, the streets. The Hoover Criminals embraced him in South Central, and the Eleven-Eight Eucalyptus Crips welcomed him in Hawthorne. He even played a pivotal role in convincing the two ruthless gangs to form an alliance. Everyone was digging his new gangsta swag except Tammy.

"Slow down, Tam Tam. Why you walking so damn fast, baby?" The bell rang and Najee jogged a few paces to catch up with his high school sweetheart. Tammy rolled her eyes, clutched her books to her chest, and kept it moving with her nose in the air. "C'mon, mami! I know you ain't gon' front on me like this? Are you trippin' because I was hollering at that cheerleader at lunch? That was nuthin'," Najee stated convincingly.

Tammy smacked her lips and walked past the metal detector. She could feel Najee's eyes watching her big booty. He usually walked her home from school, which she enjoyed. She loved holding his hand as he philosophized about life, politics, and all the amazing places he wanted to see, but ever since he started bangin', an entourage of orange and blue bandannas followed him everywhere. They were loud, obnoxious, and banged on anyone who looked like the opposition.

Najee laughed when she pointed out the sudden changes in his character, but she began to fear for his life. Worrying about him caused her grades to decline. Her parents disliked Najee the moment they met him and blamed the thug for their daughter's recent attitude change.

Rio watched with envious eyes as Najee tried to get Tammy's attention. "Don't chase her ugly ass, Cuzz. Let that bitch walk home by herself," he remarked, as he chunked up the hood to a passing Range Rover gliding on chrome twenty-eights.

Najee ignored the comment. Rio was salty because Tammy didn't choose him. Najee knew that the minute he was out of the picture, Rio would be all up in her face trying to dirty mack.

Najee actually liked when Tammy got mad. In a strange way, it turned him on when she played hard to get. He walked up behind her and held her firmly by the waist, gently kissing the baby hairs on the nape of her neck to calm her down. He had watched Boulevard do this to his mom on many occasions.

"Don't be mad at me, my Earth," he whispered sweetly. "I don't mean to bring these negative vibrations into your universe. Give me another chance to get it right."

Tammy melted in his embrace but didn't want to give in too easy. "You're not the Najee I used to know. You've changed since—" her words were caught in her throat.

"Since what? Say it." Najee let go of her waist. His anger went from zero to a hundred. "Since I watched my mother get murdered? Since I watched Angel get blasted in the face at point-blank range? Or do you mean since I was laid up in the hospital with bullet holes in my body? If that's what you're referring to, then you mufuckin' right I changed!"

Tammy could hear the pain and anguish in his voice. She reached for him and apologized, but he slapped her hands away. Before he turned to leave, she thought she saw a tear in his eye. She was left standing alone with confusion in her young mind and a dagger in her broken heart.

Rio placed a comforting arm around her shoulders. He was as helpful as a wolf coming to the aid of a wounded rabbit. "Fuck that nigga, baby. He trippin', I'll walk you home," he offered and grabbed her textbooks. A wicked smile formed at the corners of his cunning lips.

****

Ghetto streets seem darker at nightfall than in suburban neighborhoods. Najee dodged shadows and made it home just after dusk. He twisted the doorknob slowly, then tiptoed quietly into the house. Sugar was asleep, and he wanted to keep it that way. Every night she drank to numb whatever pain haunted her. If Najee was around, she used him as a verbal punching bag. Her venomous words would sting his ears for days.

To his delight, she was passed out drunk on the futon. Two bottles of Captain Morgan were drained dry, and an ashtray full of half-smoked Newport 100s had been knocked onto the floor. The ashes blended into the dingy shag carpet. Najee paused for a moment and listened to her breathe peacefully. He felt a jolt of compassion as his eyes trailed the hard lines and wrinkles crisscrossing her face. She looked older than forty years. He remembered a time when she was one of the baddest bitches on Sunset Boulevard. Now he hardly recognized the lonely, old lady passed out in her own vomit.

He placed a blanket over her incapacitated body, collected the empty bottles, and picked the cigarette butts off the floor. There was nothing he could do about the yellow stained walls and roaches. He had gotten used to them, but something deep within told him that life shouldn't be this difficult.

He turned on the kitchen lights and more roaches scattered. He lost his appetite, besides, the refrigerator was empty. Like so many disenfranchised youths, Najee was slowly falling prey to the concrete jungle. He could never understand why the slums were glorified in rap songs and romanticized in movies. He hated the ghetto. Hated the rat traps Sugar made him set up behind the refrigerator. Hated the pissy hallways and trashy alleys.

He especially hated to see people so defeated that they've lost the will to live. He wanted to do something to empower young black faces like his own, but what could he do? He felt powerless.

A noise at the kitchen entrance startled him. He was still jumpy and shell shocked from the shooting. Looking over his shoulder, he was relieved that is was only Sugar. He nodded hello. She replied by firing up a cigarette. The embers on the tip glowed orange when she inhaled.

She wore a short, silk kimono robe with nothing underneath. She purposely let the front slip open, exposing her nappy pubic hair. Najee's eyes involuntarily traveled to her hairy triangle, but he quickly looked away embarrassed. Sugar laughed. She had been trying to give him some pussy since he was little and got a kick out of making him feel uncomfortable.

"You act just like yo' mama, you know that?" Sugar commented. "Not that scheming ass heffa, Candy. I'm talkin' 'bout your real momma, Monica."

Najee's shoulders tensed up, but he kept his composure and poured some Dawn dishwashing liquid in the dirty sink.

Sugar flicked her ashes on the floor and continued her drunken, verbal assault. "Yeah, y'all both got those dreamy eyes and big ideas in those small ass brains." She chuckled. "And both of y'all think you're smarter than everybody else. Ha! Smart my ass. Look where it got that bitch?"

Her speech was slurred, yet her fiery vocal arrows hit the bull's eye, piercing Najee's soul. He remained silent, not wanting to give her the satisfaction. His strength and resistance fueled her burning gloom even more. She tried harder to push his buttons.

"You think you all that too, but you ain't shit but a trick baby." She saw his shoulders stiffen. "Don't act like you didn't know yo' mama was a ten-dollar hoe. All those lies about her getting pregnant in college is a bunch of bullshit. She got her degree from the University of South Central, and her major was sex education." She paused to relight her cigarette on the stove. "If it was me, I would have gotten an abortion."

Najee frowned and bit his bottom lip. Seeing him down lifted Sugar's spirits. Feeling better about herself, she turned and sashayed away. Her cellulite ass cheeks jiggled under the thin robe, but no one was watching. Najee wanted to lash out and hurt her like she hurt him, yet he felt sorry for her as well. She had lost everything—her looks, her dignity, and her soul. He was all she had.

Najee stormed into his room and flicked on the bedroom lights. Roaches scattered for shelter. He had a can of Raid on the dresser but said fuck it. This was their hood. He immediately noticed that his drawers had been rummaged through. He looked under the bed for the only thing of value that he possessed. He was saddened to discover that the Nike shoebox containing pictures of his mother and old love letters from Angel was gone. Sugar was the culprit.

Frustrated, he punched his bedroom door leaving a fist print in the thin plywood. Rage consumed him. He marched to the living room. Sugar lounged on the lumpy futon drinking Captain Morgan straight from the bottle. Marvin Gaye's hit, *What's Going On* drowned out the sound of passing police sirens.

As Sugar raised the bottle of rum to her lips, Najee smacked the liquor out of her hand. The bottle flew from her grip. Startled, she jumped up to save her drink, which was rapidly soaking into the carpet. She held the bottle up to the light to see how much liquor had been wasted. Half the bottle had spilt.

She glared at Najee through bloodshot red eyes. "Negro, is you crazy?" She cradled the bottle like it was a newborn.

"Where my pics at, Sharon?" Najee asked, using her government name.

Sugar ignored him and took a long swallow of her drug of choice. Najee moved closer to her. "I said where are my muthafuckin' pictures?"

"Boy, you better check yo' self and watch who the fuck you yelling at!"

Najee's jaws were clenched, and his fists were rolled tight. He could feel his fingernails digging into his palms. "I want my shit back," he demanded. "Those pics and those letters mean everything to me."

Sugar laughed bitterly in his face. Her silk robe slipped open and revealed a pair of saggy breasts that hung down to her belly button. The nipples looked like two shriveled up raisins. "I ain't got yo' shit," she stressed with a hand on her wide hips. "I ripped them up and flushed them just like you did to all that good dope. Now you know how it feels to lose something." She paused to take a swig of liquor and then continued spewing hate. "I hope one of them Rollin' Sixties blow yo' fuckin' head off."

When one blanks out, darkness is all you see, fire and rage is all you feel. Najee snapped, his open palm met her cheek. He slapped the taste buds off her tongue. Before she could collapse, he grabbed her by the throat. Her toes came off the ground as he lifted her up and squeezed tighter. He looked into her eyes and saw fear. It felt good to be feared. It made him feel bigger, better, more powerful.

Her eyes rolled into the back of her head before he finally released his grip. Sugar crumbled to the floor, trembling as she hugged herself tightly and rocked back and forth.

Najee snatched up the bottle of Jamaican rum and took a long swig. The liquid fire burned his throat. He looked at Sugar one last time and stormed out of the house, slamming the door behind him. He felt free, he felt liberated. He felt like shit. The light drizzle hid his tears as he roamed the streets in the rain. When his anger subsided, remorse kicked in. Sugar had lost everything, and so had he. In a complicated way, all they had were each other.

In his haste to leave the house, he forgot his cell phone. Locating the nearest phone booth, he checked his watch. It was close to midnight. He wondered if Tammy was still awake. He hit her line and tried to stay warm. Tam Tam picked up on the fourth ring. She wasn't too excited to hear from him.

"Wassup, my Earth, it's me. I was thinking about you and—"

"Hold up a sec—" She rudely cut him off and clicked over to the other line. A second became a minute, then two. Najee was feeling some kind of way and wondered who she was bumpin' her gums to this late at night. Finally, she clicked back to him. "Okay, now what were you saying?"

"Never mind that. Who you caking to this late at night?" he interrogated.

"Oh, are you mad 'cause I wuz talking to that basketball player. That wuz nuthin', baby." She mocked him in his own voice, retaliating for the line he hit her with earlier that day.

"So that's how it is, huh?" There was hurt in his voice. "I'll holla at you later, I got shit to do anyway."

As he was about to slam the phone on the hook, Tammy stopped him. "Wait! If you hang up in my face, I'm gonna be heated."

"I thought you were already mad."

"I am, you call me your Earth and all this other sweet shit, yet you neglect me. You don't even go to football practice anymore. All you care about is reppin' yo' hood and putting in work. I want my old Najee back."

"I feel you, Bae, but my homies need me."

"Trust me, you don't have any real homies. They smile in your face but really want to take your place. You know Rio tried to holler at me."

"Whatever! What up with us tho'? I'm trying to come through and hit that."

"Is that right?" Her vocals dripped with sex appeal.

An automated voice prompted him to insert more coins. He patted his pockets but was out of loose change. "Why are you at a phone booth in that neighborhood at this time of night anyway?" Tammy asked.

"It's a long story." He didn't feel like regurgitating the incident with Sugar. "You gon' let me come through and smash, or what?"

"Yeah, just be careful when you get on my street."

"Why, what's crackin'?" The operator terminated the call before she told tell him that she spotted some Bloods patrolling her block.

CHAPTER 7

Bowen Homes Projects: Bankhead

In a different dysfunctional household in a different part of the ghetto, two opposing forces clashed. "Get cho' fuckin' hands off me!" Marcus shook off the strong fingers gripping the collar of his shirt. He was tall for a sixteen-year-old. He stood nose to nose with his abusive foster father. His skinny arms and frail frame camouflaged the fire and strength within his heart.

"Sit the fuck down, Marcus! Don't ever disrespect me in my own damn house!" The cognac and cigar smoke on his guardian's breath was heavy. His huge black fist resembled two bowling balls.

"I hate you!" Marcus snapped back. "You run around screamin' all the time and treating everybody like shit. Your scare tactics may work on them but not me. Not anymore."

Marcus Fischer glanced over his shoulder. His foster mom and adopted sister were cowering in the corner of the kitchen with fear and tears in their eyes. He felt pity and empathy for them. His foster mother was thirty-five but looked fifty-five. Stress had accelerated the aging processes, and the caked on Revlon makeup barely concealed the purplish-black bruise under her swollen right eye.

The ten-year-old foster girl's back and legs were covered with puffy, red, welt marks from an extension cord. The plan was to unite and confront their abuser together, but when the shit hit the fan, Marcus was all alone. He was used to being alone, so tonight he wasn't taking a stand for himself; he was doing it for them.

"Sit yo' black ass down!" the foster father ordered firmly. "As long as you live under my fuckin' roof, you gon' abide by my rules. You don't like it, you can get the fuck out. Do I make myself clear?"

Marcus answered the ultimatum by stepping closer, testing the boundaries of his foster father's authority. The tension in the air was thicker than wet cement. He couldn't take the verbal lashings and physical abuse any longer. His soul ached from the constant beat downs.

The foster father backed up and stumbled into the dinner table as Marcus approached. He knew he could take the younger man. Even at the ripe age of 45, his construction job kept his 6'3" frame in excellent shape. Something in Marcus' eyes, however, was different tonight. He could feel the steam rising off the troubled teen's skin. He couldn't punk out though. Not in his own domain. One of them had to go, and it wasn't going to be him, he determined.

"Pack your shit and get the hell outta my house!" he demanded while pointing a shaky finger at the front door.

Thirty minutes later, Marcus stood on the sidewalk with his shoulders slumped in defeat and all of his worldly possessions stuffed inside of a black trash bag. His plan had backfired. His best friend Bones swerved next to the curb in a weather-beaten box Chevy Caprice. The rugged voice of Scarface and the aroma of potent weed engulfed Marcus when he opened the passenger door.

Bones turned down the music, leaned over, and offered Marcus the blunt. "What it do, Fam? You gettin' in or not, whoady?"

Marcus looked back at the rundown projects that Child Protective Services had placed him in six years ago. His antagonist stood in the doorway with his arms folded across his broad chest. Sosa had two choices, stay in the frying pan or hop in the fire. He grabbed the neatly rolled spliff from Bones and dove headfirst into the flames.

CHAPTER 8

Innocence Lost

Najee hung up the phone with Tammy feeling a lot better. The rain had subsided and the dark clouds that seemed to be hovering over his head evaporated. He grooved on the back streets of South Central for safety while sippin' on the remainder of Captain Morgan. The strong rum flowed through his bloodstream making him feel like the Incredible Hulk.

He was tipsy by the time he made it safely to a Hoover Criminal hang out on Budlong Street. There was always either a fight or a party going on at the tan, single-family house. Najee shook up with some of the little homies who were on security, then mobbed inside. Music was blasting but the mood was somber. There must have been a fight.

Hoova Kim was twisting a Swisher Sweet and Pebbles was taking a collect call from her homegirl Smokey. They were just the two people Najee wanted to see. Most niggas want a whole tank full of gas just to run you around the corner, but his homegirls did it out of love. Plus they were happy to have an excuse to get out of the hood.

The rain had washed most of the ghetto filth into the gutter and traffic was light. Najee sat in the backseat of the '62 Impala protectively clutching the bottle of alcohol like a wino. Hoova Kim maneuvered the low-low down the 110 Harbor Freeway as Pebbles used the cigarette lighter to spark the Swisher. The gangster rap pumping through the 15" woofers elevated his buzz.

Pebbles hit the weed and held the THC in her lungs for as long as possible. Finally, she hacked and coughed, exhaling a thick cloud of Kush smoke. When she composed herself, she high-fived Kim. "Whoa, you wasn't lying! Blue got that fiyah ass weed!"

"I dun' told you, bitch." She laughed, hit the ganja, and passed it Najee.

"Nah, I'm good."

"Stop frontin' and hit this fire, Groove. You seem like you got some deep shit on your mind. This will help you relax."

Sugar's warning ricocheted in his head. It was the best advice she had ever given him, but the drink had him intoxicated, the herb gave him a contact high, and the peer pressure was too convincing. Najee accepted the Mary Jane and held it between his two fingers like he had seen so many others do in the past. He took two puffs and held the smoke in his throat like Pebbles did. His virgin lungs couldn't take it, and he hacked and coughed.

His chest was on fire. His eyes watered, and his mouth drooled. In a matter of seconds, he was high. The coughing was replaced by giggles, and the tension in his muscles relaxed. The high-grade Cali bud transported his mind to a state of ideal perfection. *Utopia*! He placed the spliff between his lips again and took another pull.

The girls politely put him up on weed smoking etiquette. "Damn, nigga, puff, puff, pass!" they said simultaneously. All three of them busted out laughing.

By the time they pulled in front of Tammy's house, Najee was faded and his swag was turned all the way up. "You got any condoms, Groove?" Hoova Kim asked.

Najee looked embarrassed. He wanted to keep his little rendezvous a secret. Reaching into her Coach bag, she pulled out a Magnum condom. "Here you go. I know you tryna' get some coochie, so don't even try to front. Only some pussy will make a nigga walk through a dangerous hood in the rain, and then drive all the way out here."

Najee accepted the rubber. It was about to go down. As he was about to exit the whip, he saw the curtains in the house move. It was probably Tammy, but his spider senses started to tingle. He hesitated for a moment, becoming aware of his surroundings. Since the shooting, he had become more alert.

"I need to borrow some heat?" Najee expressed. "I don't ever want to get caught slippin' again." The words came from a deep, dark place in his heart.

Kim went back into her oversized leather bag, moving aside lipstick, mascara, and tampons. When her hand emerged, she was

78

holding a nickel-plated .380. She wiped the weapon down with a blue bandana and pushed it towards Najee with a stern warning.

"Listen, little homie," she began in a serious tone. "That's not a toy, and this street shit is not a game. Never pull a burner on anybody unless you're absolutely prepared to use it. Feel me?"

The only thing Najee was feeling was himself. The street veteran's attempt at handing him precious jewels to the game fell on tone-deaf ears. He had already tucked the steel in his waistline and was strolling up Tammy's walkway. The gun made him feel so big and powerful that he had to duck in order to fit his ego through the door frame.

****

Tammy greeted Najee at the door in a pink Victoria's Secret bra and a matching pair of tight, boy shorts that hugged her ass and showed off her puffy pussy print. She smelled good and the aromatic candles added to the romantic ambiance. The home was decorated in an African motif. Najee was especially feeling the bamboo warrior spears. Tammy pointed to a menacing looking yet, beautifully crafted African mask.

"My dad smuggled that one from Nigeria. The Igbo people used masks in religious rituals, festivals, and secret society initiations."

Najee absorbed the knowledge and inquired about a naked Ebony sculpture. The voluptuous statuette had wide hips and perky breasts. "Who is she?"

"That's Venus, the Goddess of Fertility."

"Did your pops bring that back from Africa, too?"

Tammy giggled. "Boy, bye! My momma bought that from the Slauson Swap-Meet."

They both laughed, then a thick silence engulfed them as they gazed deeply into each other's eyes. Their small talk on the couch turned into long kisses. Their tongues wrestled as Najee rubbed the wet spot between her thick legs. She unhooked her bra, revealing her sexy breasts. Like the rest of her body, they were firm. Najee took one of her tits into his mouth and twirled his tongue around her large brown areolas. Tammy's head went back, and she expelled a low moan of pleasure. Najee repeated the process, alternating from nipple to nipple while two fingers breached her boy shorts and pushed into her phat monkey. Tammy came on his knuckles.

She was hot and ready. She grabbed Najee's hand and led him to her bedroom. R&B music played in the background. Once in the privacy of her room, she became the aggressor. She lifted Najee's shirt over his head and stroked her long fingernails up and down his chiseled six-pack. Her touch made his toes tingle.

She pushed him on the bed and climbed on top of him. "Relax," Tammy whispered. "I don't bite unless you want me to," she added with a lustful smile.

Najee folded his hands behind his head while she planted soft kisses on his neck and chest, slowly working her way down the trail of hair on his stomach.

She kissed the bullet wound on his torso. It turned her on. "I thought you got shot in the back?" she asked and licked his belly button.

"I did, the bullets went through and through, missing my kidney, bladder, and everythang. Real talk, I'm blessed to be alive."

Like a freak, she unbuckled his belt with her teeth. She reached into his boxer briefs and freed his rock hard dick. His manhood was stiff and pointed towards the ceiling fan. Smiling her approval, she stroked him up and down. It grew another inch in her palm. Her small hands barely fit around his thick shaft. Tammy licked the pre-cum from the tip, then took the mushroom-shaped head into her warm mouth. Najee wanted to explode, but she squeezed the base of his throbbing dick, prolonging his orgasm.

She took him deeper into her throat until her nose met his pubic hair. Najee moaned. Tammy gagged and came up for air. A string of saliva was connected to her bottom lip and the tip of his dick. In one smooth motion, she pulled her boy shorts to the side and sat on his rigid pole.

"Damn, big daddy!" she moaned as his thick cock stretched her tight cunt and pussy juice dripped on his big balls.

"Hold on, baby. Let me strap on a rubber," Najee insisted.

Tammy ignored the request and placed his hands on her big, smooth booty. Najee held her ass cheeks wide open as she bounced on his dick, making sure her clit rubbed against him. Her big titties flopped and smacked Najee in the face. He caught one of her erect nipples in his mouth. The sensation spurred her on. Tomboy Tammy put up an innocent front, but she knew how to fuck. Her moans became screams, and on one final downstroke, she coated Najee's chocolate stick with her creamy juices and collapsed on his chest.

Najee was still on rock. He rolled her over and placed her legs over his strong shoulders. He slid balls deep into her. Tammy tried to run, but he held onto her slim waist and tried to crawl into the pussy. Grabbing a hand full of her big booty, he pulled her to him and pounded her tight pussy without mercy. No one had ever beat it up this hard before. The headboard slammed against the wall, and Tammy's nails dug into his back.

Suddenly, his mouth opened wide and his body went rigid. From experience, Tammy knew that he was about to cum. "Pull out, don't nut in me," her words went unheard. Najee dove deeper, pounding into her kitty harder. Tammy pushed on his chest. "You better pull out, I ain't playing either!" she demanded.

Najee kept beating the pussy up until her complaints became sensual moans. "This pussy belongs to you and only you," she promised as she nibbled on his ear.

Najee looked deep into her eyes, and instead of pulling out, he pushed deeper and coated her sugar walls with streams of cum. She could feel him shooting into her. Tammy's tight vagina contracted, squeezing and milking his dick dry. Minutes later, he recovered and slid into her doggy style.

"Do me dirty and fuck me hard!" Tammy encouraged.

He slapped her ass cheeks and pulled her weave as he stroked long and steady into her juice box. Her cell phone rang and fucked up the vibe.

Najee stopped mid-stroke and looked at her alarm clock, it was 1:30 a.m. "Who the fuck is that?" He was feeling some type of way.

"I don't know, and I don't care. Just keep giving me this good dick, Bae," she moaned and backed her booty up on him.

"Answer it and find out!"

"Why you trippin'?"

"Because ain't nothing open at this time of night except legs and the drive-thru at Jack-N-The-Box." He snatched his dick out of the warmth of her silky vagina and reached for the phone. Tammy attempted to wrestle it out of his grip. "Hello!" Najee made his voice sound deeper, tougher. There was silence on the other line. The caller didn't expect her nigga to answer the phone.

After a moment of awkward silence, the caller finally spoke. "Let me holler at, Tammy," a male voice requested.

"Who is this?"

"Nigga, who you?" the caller's voice was equally aggressive.

"This is Tammy's husband! Whatchu' wanna do, bitch ass nigga?"

"Whatever, Najee. Check ya' bitch, not me. Matter of fact, tell my boo, I'll holla at her later."

The line went dead. Najee threw Tammy's cell phone at the wall, sat on the edge of the bed, and put his underwear and socks back on. The first heartbreak is the one you remember most. Najee's insides turned hard as Mason's stone. He vowed to never trust a bitch again.

Najee was almost dressed, but Tammy grabbed his Levi's and urged him not to leave. They each held a pants leg, playing a game of tug-of-war. In one final, angry yank, Najee snatched the jeans out of her grip. The ominous .380 fell out of his back pocket. The instrument of death looked as poisonous as a coiled-up rattlesnake.

"Are you serious? Why do you have a gun, Najee?" She sat on the end of the bed and put her head in her hands. Najee silently slipped on his pants, then tucked the thumper in the small of his back. He owed her no explanation.

"Answer me, baby." Tears leaked from her concerned hazel eyes. "I thought you were smarter than that? Violence only leads to more violence."

Najee ignored her pep talk and grabbed his Pelle Pelle jacket and Houston Astros hat off the couch. Tammy clung to his arm, pleading with him to stay, but he brushed her off and stepped

82

outside into the darkness. A cold chill penetrated his bones. Evil was in the air. He could feel it, almost taste it when he inhaled.

After having his pride wounded and his heartbroken, Najee braved the elements and made the six-block trek from Tammy's house near Hawthorne Boulevard to 118th and Eucalyptus. It had been a shitty day. Eucalyptus Street was lit twenty-four-seven. The drugs, women, and booze were plentiful. Najee knew he could get in rotation on a bottle and a blunt with no problem. Sugar's warning was shoved to the edges of his mind. He smiled, however, when he thought about Tammy. She was a thot, but the pussy was fire, he admitted. He smelled his fingers, then wrinkled up his nose. They smelled like fish, better yet, octopussy. He laughed at his own joke as his homies from Eu-Mob greeted him.

As anticipated, lost black boys and girls loitered outside of an apartment building passing bottles of Belvedere and Philly blunts. Najee jumped right into rotation. By the time recently released Kev and Rio pulled on the scene in a stolen SS Camaro, Najee was faded.

Kev gave Najee a shoulder bump and a brotherly hug, but Rio remained distant. He stood by Stretch, Roscoe, and Big Dana as the three street soldiers plotted their next big money scheme.

Najee felt the shade coming from Rio and decided to address the issue. Rio was bigger and known for throwing them thangs, but Najee was a goon with more heart. It was only a matter of time before the two Titans clashed.

Najee stumbled into the circle of thugs. Stretch, Roscoe, and Big Dana showed him mad love as they shook up, but Rio stuffed his hands in his pocket.

"What it do, my nigga?" Najee asked. Rio nodded his head what up, then turned his back. Najee felt disrespected. He wondered why Rio was acting like a mark. "I said what it do, Cuzz?"

Rio turned to face Najee. "You tell me? I hope you didn't kiss that bitch, Tammy? Cause she been sucking my dick!"

Swoosh!

Najee threw a powerful haymaker. Rio ducked the blow and countered with a right hook to the rib cage. Najee winced in pain just before a left hook smashed into his temple, causing him to stagger. Najee regained his balance and threw a one-two punch combination. Rio sidestepped the punches and countered with a left, right, left to the face. The weed and the drank put Najee at a disadvantage, but even sober, he was no match for Rio's superior boxing skills.

Blood oozed from Najee's nose and seeped into his mouth. The salty fluids energized him. He lowered his shoulder and charged forward like a linebacker stalking a quarterback on third and long. His broad shoulder collided into Rio's stomach and knocked the wind out of him. Rio fell on his back. The concrete caught his fall.

Najee pounced on top of him and delivered vicious blows to his face. Rio's mouth gushed blood. Najee saw the blood and blacked out. Grabbing two fists full of Rio's cornrows, Najee smashed the back of his head on the concrete over and over again.

"You killed my mama!" Pain was in his heart. "You killed my mama!" Tears were in his eyes.

Big Dana dove in to break up the fight. "Somebody help me get, Cuzz!" the big homie shouted. "Najee blacked out. He thinks he's fightin' somebody else."

It took five people to pull Najee off Rio. "Get off me!" He snatched his arms free. Upon seeing his best friend curled up on the ground, he came to his senses. Dropping to his knees, he cradled Rio's head and profusely apologized. "My bad, cuzzin. I must've snapped out, I'm sorry." His regret was genuine.

Rio felt the sincerity in his voice. "We best friends, bruh. We shouldn't be fighting over no bitch. Tammy tryna' play you, my nigga, just like she tryna' play me." Rio opened his shirt and revealed the dark red hickeys on his neck and chest—passion marks courtesy of Tammy.

Najee and Rio shook hands and hugged it out. Having no more drama to see, the lost black boys and girls who cheered the fight from the sidelines went back to the weed and drank. It was just another day in the hood.

****

The liquor and the bud had Najee turnt up and feeling himself. Tammy had broken his heart, and he had a sudden urge to confront her punk ass. Rain drizzled as he made the six-block journey back to her love nest. While walking there, he contemplated his unfortunate life. He had survived through a lot of tumultuous tragedies and calamities that no teenager should have to endure. He felt hopeless but had no way of knowing that the harsh lessons he had learned so far would become essential survival skills that he would grow to appreciate.

Najee turned the corner onto Tammy's block and froze. His heart thumped in his left pectoral. He could never forget Cheddar's cherry red six-deuce Impala. He still remembered being mesmerized by the hydraulic pumps and the tatted-up Damu who used to serve Boulevard in the parking lot of the Inglewood Swap-meet.

The low-low sat under a cedar tree in front of Tammy's duplex. Najee spotted the silhouette of a stocky man in the driver's seat and the orange glow emitting from the tip of his blunt.

Najee's heart rate increased, beating faster as the pace of his feet slowed down. His conscience pleaded with him to get off these wet, deadly streets, but the evil side of innocence urged him on. He placed his hand inside his Pelle coat pocket, feeling for the pistol. Although the steel was cold, his palms became moist from fear and anticipation. He was so nervous; he damn near dropped the gun.

Chic! Chic!

He composed himself and racked the metal slide. A Teflon coated slug slid into position. He inched closer to the Impala. He wanted to make sure the driver was Cheddar. Who knows, he could've sold the whip a long time ago, the sensible side of him reasoned.

Cheddar had the bucket seat reclined, his eyes closed, and his head laid back. A young bitch he had met at World on Wheels was swallowing his dick. She deepthroated him with ease and smacked her lips like she was devouring a BBQ rib. As he blew on the weed and enjoyed her talented tongue, he tried his best to remember her name.

"Tina, Tanya, Tamera? *Damn, what ole gurl say her name was?*" he wondered as he shot cum down her throat and into her stomach. The nameless chick swallowed and kept sucking, eagerly draining his dick dry.

Najee pulled his New Era hat low over his eyes and approached the driver's side window with his hand concealed in his jacket pocket. He lightly tapped on the window, hoping that it was a case of mistaken identity. The knock startled the man. They looked into each other's eyes. Najee's heart jumped out of his chest, it was Cheddar. The scratches from Angel's long fingernails had healed but left dark blemish marks across his face.

Najee hesitated, his Air Max sneakers stuck to the concrete. Talking about retaliation was easier said than done. He didn't have the heart of a killer. He was an honor roll student, a star athlete, and a young man who had struggled through misfortune, affliction, and adversity, not a murderer.

He turned to walk away, but a flash of metal stopped him. He looked down the barrel of a .44 magnum with a red flag wrapped around the rubber handle.

Blocka! Glass shattered, with his hand still concealed in his coat pocket, Najee squeezed off five more rounds. *Blocka! Blocka! Blocka! Blocka! Blocka*! The loud pops pierced the tranquility of the residential street.

The female passenger screamed. Chunks of Cheddar's brain splattered on her face. She could taste his blood in her mouth. Cheddar died with his eyes open and his limp dick sticking out of his zipper.

He'd did it, he made his first kill. Porch lights came on and dogs barked. Najee ran hard and fast towards Eucalyptus Street. He had no way of knowing that the gang task force and the jump out boys were sweating the block. A female dispatcher frantically announced the shots fired call. Walkie-talkies crackled, and the officers scrambled into action.

Nearby units were cautioned to be on the lookout for a male suspect wearing dark blue clothing. The assailant was young, black, armed, and extremely dangerous. Screaming sirens and swirling red and blue lights illuminated the night.

Najee heard the blades of the ghetto bird chomping through the sky. The sirens edged closer. He looked over his shoulder. The coast was clear. He was out of breath but pushed harder. Three squad cars suddenly screeched around the corner. Najee turned and sprinted in the opposite direction. More police cars raced past Tammy's house. They had him sandwiched in.

He dashed across the street and hopped over an old wooden gate, wrong move. A large German shepherd viciously barked his disapproval. The K-9 charged at Najee with sharp snapping teeth. He was inches from ripping into Najee's leg, but the leash binding the dog to a strong tree snatched his collar.

Najee tumbled over a chain-link fence and stumbled into the next-door neighbor's backyard, another bad move. Motion sensor lights lit up the lawn, leaving him exposed. Jumping over a tall, black metal gate, he ripped his jeans and landed hard on his knees as he tumbled into the trash littered alley. Will power urged him to move. He stood up on wobbly legs and limped away.

The police helicopter circled in the air like a vulture. The bright searchlight shining from the underbelly hunted for prey. Walkie-talkie chatter and the thump of heavy boots rapidly approached. Najee had nowhere to hide. The perimeter was locked down.

Thinking quickly, he tossed the pistol over a picket fence into a patch of tall grass, then he dashed in the opposite direction while removing his leather Pelle jacket. The pocket had six bullet holes burned into the material. He stuffed the incriminating evidence in a garbage can and covered it with trash.

The ghetto bird hovered above. The spotlight pointed at him like an accusing finger. A convoy of squad cars smashed through the alley from both directions, boxing him in. Najee put his hands in the air and surrendered his freedom and future to become another statistic in the perpetual cycle of black youth incarceration.

Larry D. Wright

CHAPTER 9

San Quentin State Prison: East Block

Prince sat cross-legged in his cramped maximum-security prison cell eating a bowl of corn flakes as he read the Los Angeles Times. His inquisitive eyes scanned the headlines and stopped on an article detailing the city's most recent gangland slaying. An unarmed man had been ruthlessly gunned down while sitting in his vehicle talking to a female companion. Authorities believed the incident was gang-related. The victim, twenty-nine-year-old Antonio Williams, was wanted for questioning for his possible involvement in several homicides. The article went on to state that a juvenile male was in custody. No weapon was recovered from the scene.

Prince slurped the leftover milk out of the bowl and shook his head. So many people he knew were dying. He felt blessed to be alive even though he had spent the last sixteen years behind bars. He knew that Cheddar worked for a major drug supplier named Benzo Al. They were checking a bag, so their names constantly came up in prison yard gossip. Benzo Al owed Prince several favors for the protection Prince supplied when Benzo came through the joint for a parole violation. He planned on looking the drug runner up as soon as he hit the bricks.

He was due to be released soon, but that didn't stop his jailhouse hustle. For the last decade, Prince had been pimpin' the punks and supplying the junkies with the poison of their choice. There was no shame in his game, he was a career criminal and stayed about his coins. He tossed the newspaper aside, grabbed his shank, and hit the upper yard. Business was calling.

Larry D. Wright

****

L.A. County Jail

Consequences

Najee read the letter for the third time. It was the only piece of correspondence he had received from the free world in five months. None of his so-called homies bothered to write him or put money on his books, and Sugar put a collect call block on her phone. Even Tammy had abandoned him. He heard through the gossip mill that she was pregnant but didn't know who the baby daddy was. The possibility that he was the father added to his stress.

He sniffed the sweet, smelling fragrance on the envelope, then examined the sender's name. Renee Brooks. The kite was from the compassionate nurse who took care of his gunshot wounds while he was in the hospital. She offered him encouraging words and suggested that he read Psalms 51. She closed her letter by giving him the green light to call her and to look for her warm smile at his next court date.

The delicious smelling letter lifted Najee's spirit. The cramped cell didn't feel so small anymore, and the thin mattress didn't feel as hard. He placed the envelope on his chest and folded his hands behind his head. He drifted off to sleep reminiscing about Renee and her soft, luscious lips that kissed his forehead.

He awoke in the middle of the night to the sad sound of a grown man crying. His sorrow came from somewhere deep within his soul. Najee couldn't get back to sleep. After the thoughts of Renee wore off, the mattress and the metal slab that supported it seemed harder.

Feeling restless, he hopped off the top bunk and grabbed his cellmates, King James Bible. He flipped through the thin pages looking for the book of *Psalms*. He had never read the Bible before or stepped foot in a church. The streets made him, and the only deity pimps, whores, and drug dealers worshipped was the almighty dollar.

He found the book of Psalms, licked his finger, and flipped to chapter 51. His cellie had already marked the passage with a yellow highlighter. Najee stood by the door under a thin sliver of light to illuminate the pages. The first two verses penetrated his spirit.

"Have mercy upon me, O God, according to your loving-kindness; according to the multitude of your tender mercies, blot out my transgressions. Wash me thoroughly from iniquity and cleanse me from my sins."

Najee was intrigued. It was as if the writer was reading his mind, saying all the things he wanted to say to God but didn't know-how.

"Create in me a clean heart, O God, and renew a steadfast spirit within me."

Najee repeated the verses under his breath, committing the sapient scriptures to his memory bank. As he was about to continue reading, his cellie rolled over. "My bad, old-timer. Sorry, I woke you up," Najee apologized.

"Don't sweat it, young blood," the old-timer stretched his stiff limbs, sat at the edge of the bottom bunk, and slipped his calloused feet into a pair of shower shoes. "That's a good book you reading, by the way."

Convicts can get territorial when another inmate touches their property. Najee looked at the book in his hands and regretted not asking for permission. "My bad, I would've asked, but you was knocked out."

"Stop apologizing, youngsta! Sorry is something you say to your girlfriend when you cum too fast."

Najee was about to fire back but admitted that the old-timer had a valid point. For the next three hours, the convict blessed Najee with jewels.

"If you don't belong to something, you will belong to someone," he spoke while fishing a line down the tier.

He broke down the game, prison politics, and even opened up about his crime. "Them people tryna give me double digits for running up in Wells Fargo. It was supposed to be a sweet lick, but the shit went bad from the jump. The teller slid me a stack of money with a dye pack hidden in the middle and it exploded as soon as I left the bank. To top that off, my get away car stalled-out in the parking lot—" He paused to contemplate his misfortune, then continued, "Anyhow, what them peoples snatch you up for? Your secrets are safe with me."

Desperately wanting legal advice and to get everything off his chest, Najee opened up as well. He laid out how his family was killed and described the events leading up to him airing out Cheddar. He even told the old-timer where he had tossed the murder weapon. He fell asleep relieved that he finally got it all off his conscience.

He hit up Renee early the next morning. He was nervous as he punched in her digits. *What did a beautiful, older woman have in common with a young thug?* he questioned as the operator connected the call.

"Hi, Najee! I'm so glad you called. How are you doing, my brotha?" Her voice sounded sweeter than German chocolate cake.

"I'm straight, just chillin'." He was already fucking up by talking slang. He caught himself and cleared his throat. "I mean, I'm maintaining despite the circumstances. How is a beautiful lady like you doing today?" he asked in the deepest, smoothest voice he could muster.

"I'm blessed, just busy with work, school, and the ministry at church."

There she go talking about church again. He didn't feel like hearing a sermon, but as long as Renee was doing the preaching, he was willing to listen. Turns out she had just turned twenty-four in June. They were both Geminis. She was working towards becoming a plastic surgeon and was doing a residency at Martin Luther King Jr. Hospital.

The conversation took a serious turn when she asked about his case. The whole situation had him scared and depressed. He tried his best to block the incident out of his mind, hoping the charges would somehow disappear. So far, that wasn't happening. His bail was five-hundred bands, and because of the severity of the crime, he was being charged as an adult. To compound his troubles, he took the advice of his public defender and foolishly waived his preliminary hearing.

"What charges are they holding you on?" Her concern was authentic.

"First-degree intentional homicide."

Renee thought she heard a trace of macho pride in his voice but didn't press the issue. "Do they have any evidence against you?"

"Nah, they don't have any physical evidence. No murder weapon and no gunshot residue on my hands because they failed to do a GSR test."

"Then why are they still holding you?" she wanted to know.

"Supposedly somebody picked me out of a lineup."

Renee sighed. The last piece of information deflated her hopes. "Did you do it, Najee?" Her sexy voice was almost a whisper.

He didn't want to start their friendship off with a lie, so he diverted the question. "I don't wanna say too much over the phone, feel me? But I do appreciate you being here for me. Hopefully, I'll be able to repay you one day," he said humbly.

"Don't worry about it. My reward is stored in heaven. Keep reading your Bible and pray because prayer really does work. Do you need any money?"

Najee couldn't answer. "Phone check, crab ass nigga!" A slim, dark-skinned thug with long French braids pressed his finger on the silver phone hook. The line went dead.

Najee was hip to the rules. If he let one person disrespect him and didn't defend his rep to the fullest, he would be easy prey for the rest of his stay. Najee was trained to go. He turned around and curled his fingers into tight fists, but the sight of four goons bigger and older than him forced him to hesitate.

The slim thug with nappy cornrows twisted to the back had a tattooed teardrop under his right eye and CK on the other. The initials MSB were branded into his chiseled bicep in Old English letters. Najee immediately knew what time it was. Cheddar repped Mad Swan Bloods.

"What set you from, little nigga?"

It didn't matter. A fist as solid as a cement block connected with his jaw. Najee stumbled and crashed into the phones. More powerful blows connected to his face, ribs, and back. He put his head down and started swinging wild haymakers. He struck one of the oppositions in the mouth and drew blood, but a stiff punch blindsided him. Najee caught the blow on the chin. His knees buckled and he crashed to the concrete floor.

He balled into the fetal position to protect himself from the barrage of vicious kicks. The mob of angry gang members spit thick, slimy saliva in his face and yelled derogatory statements as they brutally stomped him out in retaliation for their fallen comrade.

"Yo, blood! Here comes one-time!" their lookout warned. The four hoodlums calmly walked away.

Later that night, Najee sharpened the handle of his toothbrush by scraping it back and forth on the rough cement floor. He refused to get caught slippin' again. He filed the plastic down until the tip was sharp. The shank wouldn't kill anyone, but it could definitely put out an eye or two.

The weekend went by without incident. Najee had court on Monday. It was still dark outside when they rudely woke him. He was fed the bare minimum to keep him alive and then led to the funky holding tanks in the Annex Terminal. After three hours of inmate complaints, ghetto gossip, and occasional fistfights, the offenders were chained together and led through a long tunnel.

"Shut the fuck up, keep a straight file line, and follow the tape on the floor," a Sheriff Deputy ordered. His shirt was two sizes too small.

The color-coded lines on the ground led to a convoy of black and white transport buses. Najee remained silent and stuck to himself. He was still sore from the beating but sported the black eye like a badge of honor.

His left wrist was cuffed to a heavyset, talkative Crip from Compton. Every time someone told a story, he had to top their tale with one that was more elaborate, outrageous and unbelievable. The other prisoners knew he was just jackin' and welcomed the entertainment. On the contrary, Najee wished he would shut the fuck up. He was trying to concentrate on his case and find a way out of the deep pile of elephant shit he had stepped in.

When they arrived downtown at the Los Angeles Superior Court building on Temple Street, everyone simultaneously became quiet as the bus pulled into a dark, underground garage. Game time was over. Each man drifted into his own thoughts, consumed with his own worries. Najee had never spoken to God before, but he desperately needed His help. He recalled what Renee said about prayer and wondered did it really work. Bowing his head for the first time in life, Najee made a heartfelt petition to God.

"Dear Lord, I know I fucked up but please forgive me for my sins. If you get me outta this shit, I promise to go straight and change my life for the better. In the name of Jesus, Amen! Oh yeah, one more thing God. Tell my momma and Angel that I said hello." Although his prayer was neither long nor eloquent, his heart was sincere, and that's what matters most.

Two deputies held Najee securely by the elbows and led him into the courtroom. The tight ankle shackles dug into his flesh as he took small steps towards the oak table where his attorney, Thomas Monroe, was seated. Najee's eyes searched the crowd of spectators for a familiar face. He had no family, and none of his friends came to support him.

His gaze landed on Renee. Her long, frizzy hair was pulled back into a ponytail, and she dressed professionally in a navy-blue Alexander McQueen jacket and knee-length skirt. She smiled warmly and gave him a discrete wave. Najee didn't smile back. He frowned at the young, handsome, white guy sitting close by her side on the wooden court benches. The deputies shoved him into an uncomfortable chair and locked his ankle shackles and handcuffs to a steel loop.

"All rise!" A Sheriff Deputy commanded in a loud, baritone voice.

Najee shifted uncomfortably in his blue county jail uniform as Judge Hobbs entered the courtroom from his chambers. He was a light-skinned black man with a large distinctive nose, short salt and pepper hair, and a dignified appearance. He exuded wealth, power, and respect.

Najee became nauseous. The court clerk opened a thick manila file and read the case docket. Judge Hobbs shuffled through the pile of papers in front of him before speaking. "Does the defense have any pre-trial motions?"

Mr. Monroe was caught off guard. "Oh, umm, not at this time, Your Honor," the government-appointed lawyer nervously announced. He was fresh out of law school and suffered rejections from all the prestigious firms. As bills piled up and his student loans drifted into default, he dropped his pride and accepted the only job offer on the table, Public defender. The judge glared at the second-rate attorney with contempt and turned to the prosecution. "ADA Clark, any motions on behalf of the state?"

Ms. Clark was a shark in the courtroom. "Yes, Your Honor, several in fact." She stood up and smoothed down her tan Donna Karan skirt. "The first would be a 186.22 gang enhancement. The defendant is reportedly a member of a large Crip organization. The motive for the homicide may be gang-related. There was a red bandanna recovered from the unarmed victim. The law states—"

"I know what the law states, Ms. Clark. You stated that the motive *may* be gang-related. You don't sound too sure. Can you tell me which Crip gang he is a documented member of?"

"Well, uhh, not at this time. I'm still—"

He cut her off again. "Let's move to your next motion."

The judge didn't seem like he was in a good mood, so she abandoned the notion of asking for the death penalty and requested a protective order for the key witness instead. "Your Honor, the defendant was positively identified by the female occupant of the vehicle. Her life is in imminent danger. The State moves to have her identity redacted from the discovery documents."

Judge Hobbs remained in deep thought for a moment. Perspiration soaked Najee's underarms as the judge looked down upon him from his mahogany throne. "The defendant has a constitutional right to confront his accuser and cross-examine any adverse witnesses. So, the State's motion is denied. I will, however, grant the penal code 186.22 enhancement. The crime took place in Crip territory and the defendant was wearing gang attire synonymous with that organization."

The judge set a court date for December and banged his gavel. Najee was snatched up and escorted back to the bullpen without getting a chance to talk with his attorney. He was beginning to see how unbalanced the system was, yet he was confident that he could beat the case. The prosecution didn't have a motive or murder weapon, and the identity of the only witness was in the packet of legal papers he received from the bailiff. He couldn't wait to comb through the discovery documents.

When he got back to his cell, he was surprised to see that the old-timer was not there. His sheets and blankets had been hastily removed from the thin mattress and his books were gone. The only trace left behind was the scotch tape where his pictures once were. Najee didn't lean on it. Nigga's were moved, transferred, and released from the county jail on a daily.

He sat on the empty bottom bunk and scarfed down a bag lunch consisting of a dry bologna sandwich, a warm carton of 1% milk, and a withered apple. He wiped the crumbs off his mouth with the back of his hand, then read through the legal papers and criminal complaint. The police reports described the crime scene and the chase. The autopsy report outlined where the bullets had struck Cheddar. There was nothing there to incriminate him. His hopes of an acquittal swelled to an all-time high.

Finally, he flipped to the document titled Witness Statements, and his heart dropped out of his chest and hit the floor. His hands visibly shook. He licked his dry lips and wiped the moisture off his forehead. The address of the only witness jumped out at him in 3D. He dropped the papers, grabbed his homemade shank, and ran to the phones on the tier. He needed to call Renee.

He tapped his feet impatiently waiting on Correctional Billing Services to connect the call. "We're sorry, your call was not accepted."

Fuck! He slammed the phone on the hook. The thoughts in his head moved with urgency. The witness needed to be dealt with quick and swiftly. A tap on the shoulder startled Najee. He spun around with his fist up prepared for battle.

"Whoa! Calm down, little nigga. It's just me."

Najee dropped his hands. Hoova Blue from 52nd Street embraced him in a brotherly hug. He had arrived a few days ago on a bogus homi charge. Although Najee didn't wish jail on anyone, he was glad to have a fellow young gunner on the unit with him.

Blue was all smiles. "I got a D.A. reject, Groove. Them peoples didn't process the case."

"On what?"

"On everything, bruh!"

Najee was genuinely happy for Blue. He was beginning to realize the disparaging number of Latino and African-American men who were disenfranchised and locked behind bars. The two street soldiers shook hands and gave each other a shoulder bump.

"Ugghh! Ouch!" Najee groaned and rubbed his shoulder.

Blue looked on with concern. "I heard about that little situation you got into. Niggas said you fought back though. That's what's up. Them fuck boys gon' get dealt with. In the meantime, you gotta stop ridin' 'round this bitch solo. Shit ain't sweet! If you go to the joint, make sure you got somebody on S when you in the shower, on the yard, and especially when you on the phone. Feel me?"

Najee nodded, while thoroughly examining the faces of the other captives. Even though they were playing dominos and cards, jail was not a game. Danger lurked behind every grin.

"If there's anything I can do for you, just holla, and I got you," Blue offered.

"Matter of fact, I just might have some action for you."

Blue quickly scoured over the discovery documents. There was legal jargon that Najee didn't understand, so Blue translated the legalese. Both young men knew how important it was to neutralize the state's key witness. Najee got a slip of scratch paper and began to scribble the witness's name and address, but Blue stopped him.

"Don't worry about a thang, Groove. I got it all written down up here." He pointed to his temple. "Tammy Washington, 11918 Birch Street."

The Streets Made Me

****

For the next two days, Najee blew up Renee's phone but didn't get an answer. That same Thursday, he got some bad news. The police recovered the gun. His fingerprints were on the handle and trigger. Ballistics matched the slugs taken from Cheddar's corpse. He was up shit creek.

The new discovery documents also stated that a confidential source revealed the location of the murder weapon in exchange for a favorable plea bargain in an unrelated crime. A no-contact motion had been granted, and the confidential informant's identity had been redacted.

Najee threw the papers at the wall, and then angrily swiped everything off the small metal desk. He sat with his face in his palms and his teeth clenched tight. The paperwork identified the snitch as CI-One, but Najee knew that it was the old-timer. He was the only person who knew where he had stashed the burner. Najee was young and naïve to prison politics. He broke rule number one, which is never talk about an open case.

He desperately needed to reach the free world. He dialed the only number he had. This time Renee answered. "Where you been, gurl?" he interrogated without saying hello.

"Ah, excuse me? Where do you get off questioning me in that tone about my whereabouts?"

Najee had learned from Boulevard not to argue with a woman. You'll get a migraine before you get a straight answer. "That doesn't answer my question."

"You are a hot mess, King Najee," her voice lightened. "I've been at work, school, and church."

Najee felt foolish. He realized that her world didn't revolve around him. Individuals struggling with the hardships that come with imprisonment sometimes forget that their loved ones have lives of their own.

"I'm sorry, Renee. I've just been under a lot of stress. Excuse my language, but this shit ain't easy."

Larry D. Wright

"I can only imagine how hard it is in there, especially with the latest piece of bad news."

"Hold up a sec. How did you know I got some bad news?"

"I heard it from the lead investigator on the case, Detective Mark Brooks, he's my dad."

She had dropped a bomb on him. He was speechless. Renee spoke first. "Before you start trippin', he's only out to help. He knows how much I care for you. All this may seem like a coincidence, but I truly believe that God placed you on my floor at the hospital for a reason."

Najee let it all sink in. Renee put a bookmark in her Bible and continued speaking. "And don't be mad, but I talked to a friend of mine who's an attorney. He agreed to take your case pro bono. I saw your current lawyer, there's no way I'm letting you go to trial with that loser."

Najee had no idea what pro bono meant, but he was glad that someone was looking out for his best interest. He expressed his sincere gratitude and even made Renee laugh before the time expired.

Early the next morning, a deputy notified Najee that he had a visit. He was already awake. Between his bad dreams and the sorrowful sound of a grown man crying, he did not sleep well the night before.

The visiting room was simply a strip of small cubicles. A thick sheet of plexiglass separated the inmates from their visitors. Najee was directed to booth 12. He walked slowly to the visiting station. *Who could this be?* He turned the corner and was surprised to see the handsome white guy who was sitting close to Renee in court. He wore a navy-blue Michael Kors suit with a deep purple tie. His expensive attire and chiseled jawline emanated power. Najee remained stoned face as he picked up the phone.

"Good morning, Najee. I'm attorney David Shapiro Esquire. Ms. Brooks has told me a lot about you."

"Good morning, sir." Najee decided not to be a hater. If the guy wanted to help, then so be it, because shit wasn't looking too good.

Mr. Shapiro got right down to business. "I got some good news for you. Tammy Washington recanted her story. Yesterday she called the D.A. and stated that maybe it wasn't you who she witnessed shoot, Antonio 'Cheddar' Williams. It was dark and rainy, and she was preoccupied if you know what I mean." He winked his left eye.

Najee was relieved, he knew Blue would come through for him. A heavy boulder was lifted off of his shoulders.

Mr. Shapiro adjusted his tie and continued. "But even with her sworn affidavit, they still have the murder weapon with your fingerprints on it. That's a difficult hurdle to overcome."

Najee's smile melted. "So, give it to me raw. What are my options?"

"I'm two steps ahead of you." He popped open the gold-plated locks on his leather briefcase. "Assistant District Attorney Cathy Clark owes Renee's dad a huge favor. And it just so happens that I play golf with the judge."

"What does all of that mean for me?" Najee inquired.

The slick lawyer placed an official looking document against the glass. "The state is willing to reduce the charges and is offering you a deal for ten years in prison in exchange for your guilty plea. I advise you to take it!"

Najee's eyes became glossy, but he didn't cry. He was permanently out of tears. "Tell the D.A. I'll take it!"

Larry D. Wright

CHAPTER 10

San Quentin State Prison: Receiving and Release

The prison industrial complex is a profitable enterprise that never suffers from a lack of clientele. When one inmate is being released, another is handcuffed and shuffled through the system. It's a never-ending cycle of mass incarceration disproportionately built on the backs of impoverished African-Americans and Latinos.

As Prince slipped into his release clothes, Najee was handed his prison blues and a bedroll. The two mortal enemies passed each other several times in the receiving and release area at San Quentin but didn't know it.

The fifteen new inmates were hurdled into a large dingy holding tank like cattle headed to the slaughterhouse. They were fed and then ordered to strip naked. The seasoned convicts knew the drill and complied with no complaints. The newbies, however, mumbled their protests.

Take away a man's freedom and all he is left with is his dignity. Strip away a man's dignity, and he becomes an animal. Two stoic C.O.s stood guard with their arms crossed. The younger of the two barked out a command.

"Line up against the wall quietly and stop bitching! This ain't the place to start complaining. If you can't do the time stop snatchin' purses from old ladies, scum bags!" he sounded like a country boy from Alabama.

As Najee undressed, he sized up his oppressor. The arrogant Caucasian officer wore his blond hair in a military-style buzz cut, and his well-pressed Department of Corrections uniform was two sizes too small in order to make his skinny biceps appear bigger. He was weak, you could see it in his eyes, but the badge gave him the protection of a ruthless regime.

The inmates lined up against the wall and were searched.

"Open your mouth, lift up your tongue and lift up your nut sack. Now turn around and face the wall. Let me see the bottom of your left foot, now your right, bend over and spread your ass cheeks, now squat and cough." Everyone coughed simultaneously. Najee was shocked to learn that convicts keester dope and knives up their asses.

He and several other inmates were giving a delousing agent and forced to take a cold shower and lather their bodies with the crab and lice shampoo solution. Feeling degraded, he positioned himself with his back against the shower wall and stayed fully alert. He took the opportunity to read the tattoo graffiti that permanently stained the skin of the other captives. He realized he was surrounded and outnumbered by the opposition. SUR 13, Aryan Brotherhood, East Coast Crips, Mad Swan Bloods. They were all potential enemies. The alarms ringing in his head gave him a migraine.

After the showers, the offenders had two photos taken. As the C.O.s escorted them in a single file line deeper into the dark bowels of San Quentin, Najee's heart thumped in his chest. He tried his best to keep his head straight forward, but his nervous eyes frantically scanned the unfamiliar terrain.

The concrete plantation was cold and decrepit. Signs reading *No Warning Shots* were posted at every turn. To compound matters, North Block was adjacent to the condemned prisoner unit, better known as death row. The dim-lit strip of prison cells with chipped paint on the iron bars was depressing. The cages were so small, you could spread your arms out and touch both sides of the walls.

Najee was visibly tired. The long bus ride shackled on the grey goose combined with the fear of the unknown had him physically and mentally exhausted, but sleep didn't come easy. As the sun melted into the horizon and the lights went out, the prison walls came alive.

The sad sound of remorseful men crying, the agonizing screams of men plagued with nightmares, and the haunting moans of men making love to other men vibrated the steel bars. This was only the first day of his ten-year stay. He understood that in order to survive, he needed to man up and quickly adapt to prison life.

Off top, he fashioned a piece of metal into a lethal shank by vigorously grinding the tip on the coarse cement floor. Satisfied with his handy work, he plopped on his thin plastic mattress and folded his hands behind his head. A lonely tear escaped from the corner of his watery eyes and journeyed down his cheek. He was the youngest inmate in the institution, but the cruel world made his soul feel old.

****

The pages fell off the calendar faster than Najee expected. It had been five turbulent years since he pleaded no contest to second-degree reckless homicide. Renee's letters fell off once he hit the joint. In her final scribe, she told him she was happily engaged to a lawyer. It didn't take much to figure out who that lawyer was. Najee didn't sweat the news. He had matured a great deal and reasoned that you can't lose something you never had.

Sugar got hooked on a new drug—Heroin. After hearing about several overdoses from dope coming from a spot on Sunset and Hobart, she took an Uber to the location in search of the ultimate high. She figured if people were OD'ing, then it must be some bomb as boy. The paramedics found her decomposing body three days later in an abandoned building on Franklin Street. The H was laced with fentanyl.

Najee avoided the gumps and gossip, but he couldn't avoid the violence. In the dungeons of confinement, confrontations were unavoidable. During his first few years, he had to chin check a few haters and use his blade during race riots between the blacks and the Mexicans. The hole became his second home.

It was during these days, weeks, and months locked in solitary confinement that his mind, body, and soul began to transform. To defeat boredom, he read anything he could get his hands on. Authors like Malcolm X, Marcus Garvey, and Na'im Akbar became his cellmates. He also adopted a daily workout routine to conquer stress and depression. By the time he was placed back into general population, the muscles in his body and brain were noticeably bigger.

As part of his transformation, he exercised his spirit as well. He studied the Bible and the Qu'ran. He attended Protestant church

105

services with the Christians on Sundays and Jumu'ah with the Muslims on Fridays. During the other days, he held Ciphers with the Five Percenters building knowledge of self. Although he had made dramatic changes in his life, his nightmares remained the same. When he closed his eyes, loud gunshots exploded in his head. The image of dark red blood seeping from the twisted bodies of his loved ones caused him to wake up every night in a cold sweat.

Candy's words echoed through his mind, plaguing his peaceful thoughts. *"Prince killed your mother! Prince killed your mother!"* The voice haunted him. He came to the conclusion that the only way for him to live peacefully was to kill violently, Prince and Benzo Al had to go.

Ironically, during a trip to the library, he came across an old book with worn edges. The title captured his attention. He picked it up and read the spine. *The Prince* by Niccolo Machiavelli. He checked the book out and meditated on the lessons like a Buddhist monk. He intuitively knew that one day he would use the author's cunning tactics to save his own life.

From that moment on, he studied all of the military greats from Sun TZU to Genghis Khan. He had a plan, a vision, a desire to empower young African-Americans and help them avoid the deadly pitfalls that blacks encounter every day in the slums. In order to fulfill his mission, however, he needed money and lots of it. He had a good idea where he could get some. He just needed to put together his own militia. A team of dedicated soldiers who were willing to ride or die for the cause.

Najee didn't despise drug dealers. He overstood that most hustlers hustled out of necessity, but he despised their ways and their greed. They never gave back to the broken communities they preyed upon or helped rebuild the blocks and project buildings they destroyed.

They bought foreign cars and jewelry for bitches but never purchased computers for inner-city schools. They toasted with champagne but ignored the thirsty souls in the ghetto. All of that was about to change when he hit the streets, he promised. Benzo Al's clandestine organization would be his primary target.

106

"As-salaam Alaykum," one of the brothers from Black Guerrilla Family greeted Najee in Arabic.

"Wa Alaykum al-salaam," Najee returned the blessing. They performed their daily constitution consisting of ten sets of pull-ups, ten sets of burpees and five hundred push-ups. When they finished, they walked the track on the lower yard and tested each other's Arabic and Swahili.

Larry D. Wright

CHAPTER 11

Club iCandy: Atlanta, Georgia

Club iCandy was the hottest spot in the A. The club owners had transformed a dilapidated warehouse into a lavish, two-story party palace. Celebrities, socialites, and members of the underworld politicked in the VIP and shared pills and lines of blow in the restrooms.

Sosa stood up and tapped the side of a bottle of rose gold Ace of Spades with a fork. His commanding presence demanded everyone's undivided attention. "I propose a toast." Bottles of champagne were raised in the air. "Here's to BBE, Block Boy Empire till death do us, or the Feds unglue us!" The entourage of hood rich D-boys cheered and clicked bottles.

Sosa flossed for the spectators and tossed a fist full of blue faces in the air like confetti. Several half-dressed strippers scrambled for the C-notes like bridesmaids fighting over a wedding bouquet. The club's VIP section was turnt up. Although it was Sosa's twenty-sixth birthday party, everyone had a reason to celebrate. Product was moving fast, gwuap was being stacked, foreign cars were being purchased, and the women were exotic. BBE was on top of the food chain. All the other squads were shark bait.

Sosa leaned against the bar and took a long swig of champagne directly from the bottle. The liquor and the loud pack had him bopped. His droopy yet watchful eyes scanned the room taking in everything in a single sweep. He liked what he saw. The machine was in motion.

Just five years ago, Sosa was living out of a black trash bag and making small hand to hand transactions at the Texaco on Custer Avenue and Bouldercrest. Now he was the patriarch of a ruthless drug syndicate. He recalled his resurrection from the low bottoms to his current zenith like it was yesterday. He tilted the bottle up and guzzled more of the expensive champagne as he reminisced about his humble beginnings.

Larry D. Wright

****

"Y'all niggas acting like pussies!" Sosa's right-hand man Bones declared while strutting back and forth in the tiny living room. They were pumping yay out of a hype's house in Zone 6. Bones had nominated himself as the crew's enforcer. The high school dropout was stocky, dark-skinned, and sported an uneven afro that was as course as his rough demeanor. "I say we mob down the block and air them Baton Rouge niggas out! We need to let them fuck boys know they servin' on our block. Straight up."

One of the young men at the impromptu meeting nodded his head in agreement. He was just as young, dumb, and ready to get buck. Sosa remained silent. He sat on two stacked milk crates thinking deeply and sippin' on syrup. The movie Scarface rolled in the background. The blunt rotated to him and he took two pulls, allowing the purple dro to get acquainted with his lungs.

Finally, he spoke. "Why do we fuck with Blue exclusively on the weed tip?"

Bones stopped pacing, spun around, and looked at Sosa like he was crazy. "What the fuck, Marcus? These out of town niggas short stoppin' our custies and you worried 'bout some punk-ass weed?"

Sosa took another puff and passed the cigarillo to Bones, deliberately skipping Dejuan who was next in rotation. He didn't trust Dejuan and detested his presence. "Bear with me for a minute, mane. Just think about it. Why do we shop with the same weed man all day every day?"

Bones reflected on the question as the ganja burned his chest. On the flat screen, grimy drug dealers forced Tony Montana into the shower and revved a chainsaw. Bones allowed the smoke to escape through his nose and replied, "Cause he got that fiyah!"

All three men laughed and nodded in agreement. Blue had that loud pack coming through Fed-Ex from Cali. His sacks were fat and didn't have any seeds, stems, or irritating sticks. Because of his high-quality merchandise, competition was non-existent.

Sosa continued, "Big facts, nobody wanna smoke that Bobby Brown, so the whole East Atlanta fucks with him."

110

Dejuan reached for the doja, but to his dismay, Bones bypassed his fingers and gave it back to Sosa. "I still don't see what that has to do with the price of tea in China?" He was gassed up off Scarface and ready to air something out.

Sosa got off the milk crates and held out his hand. Two off white crack rocks rested in his palm. "Look at their work compared to ours. Their dimes are bigger than our dubs." Bones and Dejuan stepped closer to examine the ready rock. "Going to war with them will only make the block hot. When you fight fire with fire, you end up with ashes. The way to shut them studs down is to sell a superior product, that butter. We gotta stop putting so much baking soda on our work and start giving out fatter sacks. And y'all stop calling me, Marcus. From here on out call me, Sosa."

Bones liked the sound of the new name, it fit him well. The young thugs shook up and chanted, "BBE till death do us or the Feds unglue us!"

Sosa was right, the improved product made the block juke, but his assumptions about putting the competition out of business were incorrect. The out of town studs saw a lucrative opportunity and swarmed the drug-infested neighborhood like killer bees. There was enough money for everybody, so neither side declared war.

Instead, Sosa came up with an ingenious plan. He allowed the Baton Rouge cats to grind on their turf as long as they shopped with Block Boy Empire. His squad sat back and collected the bulk of the profits while the opposition did all the work and took all the risks. Sosa was enterprising and no longer cared about street corners. He wanted to corner the market.

Although Sosa tried to stay off the radar, his name was ringing. Outsiders took notice of his success and ambition. The haters loved to hate him, the gold diggers were diggin' his swag, and the narcotics task force was raiding his spots on a regular. The workers were expendable, however, finding a reliable coke plug proved to be a difficult task.

His Dominican connect from Spanish Harlem cut him off. Marco felt that the Block Boy's reckless and flamboyant nature was making the city hot. Even worse, he also felt that Sosa had a snitch *in his midst. Sosa tried hard to persuade Marco that the heat would eventually die down, but Poppy still wasn't fucking with him. Sosa was down and out, but his luck soon changed.*

A white Mercedes Benz limousine cruised slowly down the block. It looked out of place amongst the poverty-stricken Zone 6 residents who sought shelter from the blistering summer sun. All eyes were on the luxury automobile as the heavily armed Hispanic driver slid up to the curb and stopped in front of a rundown two-bedroom flat.

Sosa sat on the porch between the legs of a mocha-skinned female. He munched on a bag of hot flaming Cheetos while the sexy chick greased and braided his thick hair. His expensive Gucci fit was in stark contrast to his dingy surroundings.

Bones stood on the rickety steps gripping the butt of his Draco with an extendo clip. He squinted his eyes and tried to peer through the dark tinted windows. "Who you think that is, mane?" he asked Sosa and Dejuan. Neither had a clue.

Behind the limo tint, Benzo Al pulled a sweet-smelling cigar from his inner breast pocket. He ran the tightly rolled brown leaf across his top lip and savored its rich aroma. The high-yellow, distinguished gentleman sitting next to him respectfully produced a lighter and lit the cigar. Benzo Al nodded his gratitude and looked towards the three young black men hanging out on the stoop.

A frown found his lips. "I don't like these vatos. They look like a bunch of low life porch monkeys to me." He was more interested in the thick sista with her legs cocked open.

The well-dressed black man stiffened but let the racist remark slide off his shoulder. "Sosa is the brotha getting his hair braided. He's smart, loyal, and hungry. I think you should let him shoot his shot. I vouch for him with my blood."

Sosa had no way of knowing that the two criminals inside the limo were discussing his future, but he remained cool and stared at the tinted glass as if he knew his destiny waited on the other side.

Benzo Al stroked a string of wooden rosary beads. Like many Latino drug dealers, he practiced Santeria and hoped that the African deities and Catholic saints would bring him good fortune and protection. As he focused his attention on Sosa, he acknowledged that there was something raw and electrifying about the ambitious hustler's humble yet confident appearance.

"Call him over here. Let's see if he really about that life."

The window slowly rolled down. Reacting quickly, Sosa dropped the bag of chips and upped his tool. Bones crouched low and aimed the Draco. Dejuan bitched up and was ready to run. "Whoa! Put them thangs away, young blood. It's me," a familiar voice called from the backseat.

The three youngsters instantly recognized Prince who on occasion would wow them with fascinating tales of the pimp game. They mobbed over to the stretch Benz and paid their respects with enthusiastic handshakes and sincere admiration.

Prince slid over on the leather seat. "Hop in, young blood. There's somebody important I want you to meet." Bones shoved Sosa and Dejuan aside and stepped forward. "Nah, youngin', he only wants to holler at him." Prince pointed at Sosa.

Feeling crushed, Bones reluctantly moved aside, and Sosa climbed into the backseat. It was his first time in a limousine. His mind worked overtime as his eyes took in the luxurious interior. The old player made the introductions. "Benzo Al, meet my main man Sosa. Sosa, meet Alonzo Guzman, the boss of all bosses."

Benzo Al passed Sosa a shot glass from the minibar. "Tu drinka Tequila, no?" His Mexican accent was thick and syrupy. His diamond pinky ring glistened.

A dead worm floated in the 100-proof liquor, but Sosa readily accepted the challenge. He tossed his head back and bravely downed the Tequila and liquor-soaked worm in one swallow. The strong booze scorched his stomach but was better quality than the Patron he was used to. Sosa smiled and held out his glass for another shot.

Benzo Al laughed his approval. "Muy bien, mi amigo! You have balls. Me and you, we do business for a very long time."

The driver placed the limo in neutral, flicked on the high beams, and pressed the button on the emergency brake. A hidden compartment carved into the armrest opened. It held a duct-taped

113

square block. Benzo Al used the tip of his pocketknife to puncture the package. When he pulled the knife out, a small lump of crystal white cocaine was on the blade.

"Here you go, amigo. Taste this pure sugarcane from Bogotá, Colombia."

Sosa used his middle finger to rub the crystalline substance on his gums. Within seconds, his entire mouth became numb. "I can't feel my face!" he said while rubbing his cheekbones.

Benzo Al belched out a devilish laugh as if Satan himself had told a funny joke. He poured up more shots of Don Julio, and the three villains cooked up an illicit get rich scheme.

****

"Sosa! Yo' Sosa!" Bones' raspy voice yanked him out of his trance. Sosa looked around the packed club and wondered how long he had been zoned out reminiscing about the come up.

"What it do, my nigga?" The two ballers gave each other dap on the fist.

Bones pulled Sosa by the speakers so that no one could hear their conversation. "Dig this you were right about that fuck boy, Dejuan. He working with them peoples."

Sosa shook his head. "Damn, I bet he the reason we lost that Dominican plug back in the day. You brought him in, so you gotta delete him. Just do it discreetly."

"Say no more. They found his body this morning stankin' up in an abandoned warehouse on Howell Mill Road. Word on the street is that he was wearing a wire and had a backpack full of marked money."

Sosa let out a low whistle. "That was a close call. I was supposed to meet him tonight to pick up that gwuap he owed. From here on out, no talking on the phones or flashing money on social media. And we gotta establish code names for the drop off spots and the stash houses. It ain't over. The Feds are gonna try to flip someone close to me." He would soon find out how true his words were.

CHAPTER 12

San Quentin State Prison: Receiving & Release

The last five years of Najee's bid moved at a snail's pace, but he kept his mind occupied and stayed firmly on his square. Renee wrote him occasionally, usually on his birthday and Christmas. She had achieved her goal of becoming a plastic surgeon. He even heard from Tammy once or twice. He appreciated the love, but he didn't write either of them back.

Finally, after 120 months of pain, struggle, and growth, he was being cast back into society. It was one of the happiest days of his life. He divided his books, girlie magazines, and electronics between the soldiers he rocked with during the decade he spent in the bowels of the penal system and promised to go out there and go hard.

On the day he was leaving, Kev and Hoova Blue were arriving. The revolving door of the Department of Corrections never stops swinging. They shook up and gave each other shoulder bumps.

"Treach from Naughty by Nature lookin' ass nigga! What they been feeding you, steroids?" Blue joked.

Najee flexed his penitentiary muscles, making his chest bounce. "Nah, homie, I been lifting yo' fat ass baby mama."

The two long lost friends slap boxed until a C.O. ordered them to stop horse playing. "On the reals though, how you been holding up, bruh?" Najee inquired.

"This bald spot should say it all, I've been stressin'," Blue admitted.

Kev added his two cents. "They caught him dead bang this time, he burnt up." Blue and Najee gave him a shut the fuck up look. Kev got the point and shrunk into the background.

Najee put his hand on Blue's shoulder and looked him squarely in the eyes. "I didn't forget what you did for me, Fam. Anything you need, just holla, I got you."

Blue pulled him to the side. "Check this out, bruh. I was trappin' hard down in the ATL but needed to come back to re-up with my whiteboy connect who owns a weed dispensary in West L.A. I copped fifty pounds of loud and as I was taking the shit to that Fed-Ex depot by LAX, the detects fucked around and pulled my black ass over. They found the work in the trunk and hit me with an intent to deliver charge. I can't even get a decent lawyer because all my paper is tied up in the streets."

Najee absorbed the info. "Just let me know what you need me to do and it's done," he promised.

Now that he had stepped in dookey and was knocked out of the game, those who owed him money were dodging his phone calls. He wanted Najee to pay them a special visit and keep half of the dough for his troubles. Najee gladly accepted the mission. It would become the first of many violent shakedowns.

****

Venice Beach, CA: The Come up

It was a perfect night for a homicide. Blackness covered the sky like Batman's cape, and dense fog tiptoed from the shoreline. Najee put away his night vision binoculars equipped with thermal imaging and rolled the foot of a tan nylon stocking over his head and face. The thin fabric smashed his nose down and made his handsome features look evil and intimidating.

He avoided wearing ski masks made out of cotton because they were breeding grounds for DNA. In prison he read that hair follicles could get stuck in the woven material, and they absorbed sweat.

While contemplating the lessons he learned in gladiator school, he pulled a .38 caliber from his waistline and examined the six copper-coated slugs. Snub nose revolvers were the tools of assassins. Their short barrels made it difficult to run ballistics, and no bullet shells were ejected. He put the binoculars back up to his eyes and watched the red and yellow body heat emitting from the two figures partying inside of a lavish penthouse overlooking Venice Beach.

"That's what it do, mami. Pop that thang for daddy!"

116

"You like, Papi?" a sexy Dominican stripper teased as she twerked her round booty to the thumping trap music.

"You already knowin' I like it. Now turn around and let me see that phat monkey."

Twan was short and chubby with skin that was blacker than motor oil. He resembled Big Worm from Friday and used his intimidating glare to pump fear into his workers. He leaned back on the soft, butterscotch leather sofa and enjoyed the show. In fact, he was enjoying life. He had an Aston Martin parked in the carport, a bad Latina bitch shakin' her moneymaker in his living room, a bottle of rose gold Moet in his left hand, and a thick moonrock blunt in the right.

From the jump, he had no intention of paying back the twenty-five racks he owed Blue. Instead, when Blue came back from Atlanta, he got him jammed up by secretly calling the jakes with an anonymous tip about a Hertz rental car transporting fifty pounds of high-grade THC stashed in the spare tire.

Once he confirmed that his benefactor was stuck in the L.A. county jail on a parole hold and a pending trafficking charge, he found a new distributor and flipped the money. For the last few months, he played the role of a stomp down hustler, but in reality, he was simply a runner and a send-off. He had no idea that his good fortune was coming to a screeching halt.

The stripper washed down a Percocet with a swallow of Moet and continued dancing without even missing a beat. She made each of her ass cheeks pop, then she dropped it low and did the splits. Twan damn near lost his mind. He stood up on drunken legs and started to dance. His flabby belly hung over his YSL belt buckle. He did the two-step unconcerned with how ridiculous he looked. In a matter of minutes, he was breathing heavy and sweating profusely.

"I'm finna beat that pussy up," he bragged and grabbed a handful of the stripper's ample backside. "That's on me, I'm gon' tear that monkey up all night long and have you walking bowlegged in the morning," he promised. His pudgy palms went to her breasts.

"Yeah, right!" the stripper mumbled under her breath and rolled her eyes.

She played along with him though. She sweetly stroked his ego while rocking him to sleep. Before following him into the master bedroom, she secretly took the chain off the hinge and unlocked the front door. It never ceased to amaze her how gullible niggas were.

Twan flicked off the light switch and let his designer jeans fall to his ankles. His short penis poked through the hole in his boxers. He pushed the stripper on the bed and climbed between her open thighs. The mattress sagged under his heavyweight. Placing her thick yellow legs over his shoulders, he slipped into her ocean and damn near drowned in the process. The pussy swallowed him, and with just three pumps, his body stiffened, and he squirted a huge load of cum in her sugar walls.

Satisfied and exhausted, he rolled over and reached for the half-smoked joint in the astray. He even had the nerve to ask, "Was it good, Mami?"

"Hell no, it wasn't good, estupido! Pinche pendejo! I told you not to cum in me, puto." Twan laughed and lit the joint as she cussed him out in Spanish on her way to the bathroom to wash her kitty.

Najee patiently waited fifteen minutes after the lights went out before quietly creeping into the spacious penthouse with his weapon drawn. He had paid the stripper, slash hairstylist, slash babysitter, slash all around scandalous bitch two bands to set Twan up. He twisted the brass doorknob and a surge of relief and a rush of excitement shot through his veins. He waltz right in and paused a second to allow his pupils to become acclimated to the darkness. He pressed his ear to the door expecting to hear sounds of sex, but the room was silent.

The toilet flushed and put him on alert. He swung around and aimed his iron at the bathroom. He hoped there was not a third person in the house. Beads of sweat trickled down his face as he waited for the door to open. When it did, calmness circulated through him. The stripper stood in the door frame vigorously scrubbing between her legs with a wet washcloth. He lowered the gun and called for her.

"Psst, psst, Katrina!" he whispered trying to get her attention.

She turned towards him with wide eyes. At first, he thought he had startled her with the mask over his face, but her frantic eyes were focused on something behind him. Najee swiftly turned around. He was confronted by a dark shadow barreling towards him. Before he could react, Twan swung the bottle of Moet. The thick champagne bottle smashed into Najee's skull and sent him tumbling backward. Twan held the bottle of Moet high in the air and swung again.

The bottle shattered when it connected with Najee's forehead. He stumbled and held onto the wall for balance. Blood gushed from a three-inch laceration and soaked the nylon stocking.

The shadow became a fuzzy blur. Najee raised the gun to blast, but a Nike shoe kicked his wrist and sent the banger across the room. It was time to panic. He scrambled on his knees to retrieve the weapon. His fingertips were inches away, but Twan grabbed him roughly by the ankles and snatched him back.

He lifted Najee onto his feet by the collar like a rag doll. Najee was surprised by Twan's strength and agility. The leaking blood stung his eyes. He was disappointed in himself. He had botched up his first lick and was about to end up dead, or even worse, back in the joint. Neither outcome sounded appealing.

Twan grabbed a fist full of Najee's leather jacket and slammed him against the drywall. His back made a deep impression in the sheetrock as he groaned in agony. His eyes begged the stripper for help, but Katrina was too busy going through Twan's wallet, which he had left on the coffee table. Najee was on his own.

"Bitch ass nigga! You tryna' creep up on me?" His thick, calloused hands tightened around Najee's throat as he spoke. "I never slip, boy. I'm king muthafuckin' kong!" he declared and squeezed his Adam's apple tighter.

Najee's eyes rolled into the back of his head. He was seconds from passing out, but the primal instincts of survival kicked in. In a last moment of desperation, he spit a mouth full of blood and saliva into Twan's face. When Twan released his death grip, Najee followed up with a Timberland boot to his scrotum. Twan doubled over in pain. Najee dove for the gun.

Loud gunshots echoed throughout the penthouse like a muffler backfiring. Three hollow points struck Twan in the shoulder, chest, and stomach. He clutched at the air for leverage and then collapsed in the narrow hallway facedown. An eerie silence enveloped the penthouse.

He did it, he killed again! Najee stared at the lifeless body without blinking. He marveled at how easy it was for black people to delete each other from existence.

Katrina scrambled by him and the dead man and quickly gathered all her belongings from the bedroom. She returned with her clothes, Hermes bag, and red Prada heels spilling out of her arms. Najee sat on the floor with the smoking pistol in his hand locked in a cationic daze. The sound of the stripper's movements jarred him out of hypnosis.

"Vamos, Papi! We gotta go." Katrina rapidly put her clothes on, then searched through the penthouse with urgency. She opened and slammed drawers and flipped over couch cushions. Najee followed her lead. He searched for a safe in both bedrooms and behind the expensive oil paintings on the wall. He struck out in each location. They met back up in the hallway.

"Did you find anything?" he asked. Katrina shook her head. "Damn, me either."

"That nigga one of those broke D-boys. That's all he do is fuck his bag off on cars, clothes, jewelry, and panocha. The other night, dude had the nerve to ask me for a lap dance on credit. Can you believe that shit, Papi?"

Najee left her rambling to herself and rushed into the kitchen. He rummaged through the refrigerator. Nothing! He checked the dishwasher. Dirty dishes but no dirty money. Next, he opened the food cabinet and pulled down a box of Captain Crunch. Jackpot! The cereal box was filled with rubber-banded stacks of gwuap. His heart pumped with excitement, but there was no time to celebrate. He put the four boxes of cereal into a brown paper bag and dashed to get Katrina.

"I got the money, let's ride out!" he announced with enthusiasm.

When he rushed into the hallway, he stopped in his tracks. Katrina was kneeling down removing Twan's pinky ring. She held it to the light to appraise the diamond quality, then dropped it in her purse. Najee watched in silent disbelief as she removed his platinum chain and icy Audemars.

When she started to unscrew the backs of his huge diamond earrings, Najee stopped her. "What the fuck you doing?"

"What it look like? I'm getting paid," she affirmed bluntly and stuffed one of the earrings inside of her oversized bag.

"Naw, fuck that jewelry, let's ride out."

Katrina let out a cruel, heartless laugh. "No, nigga, you ride out. If you gon' be out her stickin' doughboys, you better lose those feelings, Papi. They're gonna get you killed. These streets are cold. The players are ruthless and calculating. Every smile conceals a hidden agenda, and that firm handshake could hold the knife that stabs you in the back. Comprende?" She unscrewed the other diamond stud.

Najee looked down at the murder apparatus clutched in his grip. It still smelled like smoke and gunpowder. She was right, he admitted. It was a cold world indeed.

"Okay, cool. It is what it is. Just don't sell none of that shit to these local niggas. They might put two and two together and come after you. Understand?"

He instructed her to wipe down everything she might have touched. He didn't want to leave behind any DNA. He quickly put the soiled sheets, broken Moet bottle and champagne glass that had her lipstick around the rim into a black trash bag. They slipped out of the penthouse unnoticed and melted into the shadows. Authorities found Twan's badly decomposed body three weeks later after a concerned neighbor reported smelling a suspicious odor. The homicide investigators quickly closed the case and attributed the shooting to a drug deal gone bad.

That was five years ago. Since then, Najee had put together his own squad of street warriors. Each person specialized in a different skill and was willing to kill for the drip. They pledged their allegiance to Najee. When their lives and careers were swirling down the drain, he showed up with a lucrative proposition.

His team was a turbulent typhoon. Their deadly reign swept through hoods from coast to coast, leaving a string of top-level drug distributors either murdered or moneyless. In some cases, both. They became known as the Body Snatchers. No street hustler was immune. No organization was exempt. If you were checking a bag, there was a strong possibility that you might get snatched out of your sleep with a high caliber firearm in your mouth or a red dot on your forehead.

Rumors about them circulated through the ghetto like Chlamydia. In a matter of months, they were the topic of conversation in every barbershop, bodega, and crime syndicate meeting. Benzo Al's cartel took most of the losses. Votes were cast and decisions were made. The anonymous stickup kids were bad for business, they had to go.

THE END OF THE BEGINNING

"I will render vengeance to mine enemies and will reward them that hate me." Deuteronomy 32:41

Larry D. Wright

CHAPTER 13

Southern California: 2019

"Team-one, are you ready?" The walkie-talkie crackled.

"Affirmative, Sir."

"Team-two, are you in position?"

"Yes, Sirrr!" the deep voice responded, imitating Jay-Z.

"Dig this, we move on my command," Najee, the team leader stated. "Team-one will enter through the front entrance, and Team-two will take the rear. Nella and I will secure the perimeter. Any questions?" he asked after giving each unit their assignments.

Just as anticipated, there were no questions. The Body Snatchers were the best. He handpicked each of them when he got out of the joint, and they had been puttin' it down ever since.

Juice was the team's weapon expert. Handguns, assault rifles, improvised explosive devices, you name it, he could get it. The ATF had kicked in his door, accusing him of being an Al-Qaeda sympathizer because of the angry anti-war messages he frequently posted on Islamic blogs. They found a 3D blueprint machine, homemade silencers, and the drafts to print a 3D gun. He was placed on the enemy combatant list and lost his job as a youth counselor. When he met Najee at a shooting range in New Jersey, he was depressed, deranged and planning a Columbine-style attack. Linking up with some more crazy muthafuckers was right up his alley.

Yung Zay was the youngest member of the Body Snatchers and had the most swag. He specialized in communications and countersurveillance. He once made headlines for secretly planting listening devices and webcams in several dorm rooms at Spelman College.

His website was clocking a million hits per week, however, the lucrative site was shut down, and Yung Zay was threatened with invasion of privacy charges after a prominent African-American Senator logged on to jackoff but was disgusted when he saw his own daughter taking a steamy shower with another female. Najee had some dirt on the politician and the charges mysteriously went away. It's not about who you know, it's what you know about them that's important. Yung Zay was on Team-one with Juice.

Maceo acted as the chief technology officer, or simply put, computer hacker. When it came to gaining illegal access to a company's network, he was the shit. There was not a firewall he could not penetrate or code he could not crack. He met Najee at a gamer's convention in Las Vegas. He wasn't in any trouble, but Najee convinced him that gangsters get more pussy than geeks. That's all it took, he was in!

He was on Team-two with Rio, the resident thug. Rio was straight up gutter and loved to fight. Once a ruthless gang member and prized mixed martial arts competitor, he was known for brutalizing his opponents with Muay Thai and Brazilian Jiu-Jitsu. His signature move was called the Ghetto Blaster, which eventually got him banned from the UFC for life. He and Najee went way back. They went to the same school, fucked the same girls, and repped the same hood, so it was only right that Najee put him up on a money makin' caper.

Finally, rounding up the elite group was the lovely Nella. Born in France on an American military base, the armed forces were all she knew. She grew up as a tomboy, but couldn't hide her sexy figure. She eventually followed in her father's footsteps and entered the Air Force Academy. She learned how to fly everything from spy drones to fighter jets. Her promising career ended abruptly when she was court-martialed for leaking confidential military documents to WikiLeaks. She received a dishonorable discharge but offers from military contractors such as Black Water and Halliburton poured in. She rejected their offers and chose to head up transportation and logistics for Najee's elite crew. He had proven to her that crime does pay and pays very well!

"Everybody move in!" Najee commanded. Team-one crashed through the large, expensive front door. Their weapons were cocked, locked and loaded.

"DEA, nobody fuckin' move!" Juice shouted and tossed a smoke bomb. The device exploded with a bright flash.

"Hands in the air!" Yung Zay yelled, waving the infrared on his AR-15.

The three Mexicans sitting at the poker table looked confused and didn't know whether to freeze or put their hands in the air.

"Hands in the muthafuckin' air, now!" Juice and Yung Zay both demanded. Six hands flew in the air like fans doing the wave at a football game.

Maceo's Nextel crackled, "The rear of the compound is secure, Sir."

"Any collateral damage?" Najee wanted to know.

"No Sirrr, just one prisoner. He gotta couple of lumps on his head, but he's alive."

"Cool, meet Team-one at the front of the compound, I'm on my way in. And y'all niggas stop calling me, Sir, it makes me feel old."

"Yo' ass is old!" Juice joked, causing everyone to laugh.

The compound was a large Victorian mansion situated in an exclusive part of Escondido, California. Escondido is 150 miles away from the Mexican border. It is known for its sunny weather, private beaches and proximity to military bases; a perfect place for wanted drug cartel members to hideout.

Najee strolled through the front door with confidence. He had come a long way since his first lick. Nella was on his heels. Her weapon was aimed and ready, welcoming any drama.

The other crew members became alert when their leader entered. He had handpicked each one of them when they were at their lowest points in life and made them wealthy just as promised. They owed him their lives.

"Good job gentlemen," he complimented their work. "Let's make this quick," he said and brandished a nickel-plated .40 cal.

"Where's the money?" The prisoners were lined up on their knees. No one volunteered the information.

Blocka!

Sparks flew from the barrel of his weapon. The scorching hot slug smacked the goon who was guarding the rear entrance in the middle of the forehead. Blood and brains splattered the walls as he sank to the floor like a slinky. Smoke rose from his dead body.

"Okay, who's next?" Najee calmly pointed his pistol at the next person in line.

"Me no speak English!" the oldest of the three remaining prisoners blurted out. His hands were still in the air.

"No problemo, puto, I just happen to speak Español." Actually, he had taught himself Spanish, Arabic, and Swahili but didn't have the patience to play games.

Blocka!

More fire spit from the tip of Najee's banger. The bullet burned a nickel-size hole in the vic's temple and turned his brains into mush.

"Okay, okay, I tell you, I tell you," a heavy set Mexican with a thick salt and pepper beard volunteered. He had seen enough.

"Callate, pendejo!" his partner warned him. "Don't be stupid. We're already dead. If they don't kill us, Alonzo will!" His statement was true, but the petrified, heavyset Mexican decided to take his chances.

"Move the table, there is a trap door under the rug."

"You heard the man, move the table," Najee instructed.

Yung Zay and Juice each grabbed an end of the thick, oak table and moved it to the side. Nella leaned down and rolled up the Persian rug. Just as promised, there was a trap door expertly carved into the floor.

Rio kept his weapon drawn on the prisoners as Maceo and Nella pried the trap door open. Two big blocks of shrink-wrapped money was in the hole. The faces of dead presidents stared back at them. They removed the money and discovered one hundred bricks of Los Cinco Diablos cocaine wrapped in grey duct tape. Each package had a sticker with a cartoon character who had a goofy smile and big ears. Upon closer inspection, you could see that the character was Donald Trump. The cartels had been taunting the U.S. government like this for years, blatantly telling America that the border patrol was a joke.

"Whew!" Rio whistled. "That's worth about two mill tickets on the streets!" His eyes grew greedy.

"Probably so, but we're not drug dealers," Nella reminded him.

128

"Last time I checked, we wasn't saints either," he shot back.

Nella and Rio stayed at each other's necks. They had a love-hate relationship.

"Both of y'all chill out for a second." Najee raised his hand for silence. "I'm tryna' think."

They were on an inside job. Najee had a connect within law enforcement that provided him with sensitive information about criminals who were under surveillance. He used this information to rob the targets before authorities took them down. That's how he knew there was supposed to be at least a million dollars in the mansion. From the looks of it, they only had about 250 racks. A light clicked on in his head.

"Something ain't right," he informed his team. "There was supposed to be more money than this, which means somebody is late dropping off their taxes and picking up their weekly supply of dope. Let's bounce before we bump heads with 'em."

"What about the coke, B?" Juice asked.

"Burn it!" Najee said bluntly. "Maceo, Nella, pull the vehicles into position."

"We're on it." They quickly jumped into action.

"Yung Zay and Rio, tie these two clowns up."

The two surviving prisoners had confused looks on their faces. "You can't do this," the older Mexican protested in clear English.

"I can do whatever I want. I'm the F-B-muthafuckin' I!"

"I thought you were the DEA?"

"And I thought you couldn't speak English," Najee shot back. "Make sure you duct tape this one's mouth up real good. He's a potential problem. Juice, grab one of these bundles of cash and let's get outta here."

"Hold up a sec. So, we're gonna torch all this yay? Do you know how much paper we're missing out on?" Rio asked in disbelief.

"I don't like repeating myself." Najee looked Rio directly in the eyes. "Our mission is to empower the youth by putting this money back into the hood, not flooding the block with poison. Now let's move out before this stash house is crawling with Diablo soldiers."

"What about these two?" Yung Zay pointed at the hostages.

"They come with us. They're worth about a quarter of a million," Najee replied while checking the minute hand on his watch.

"We're gonna hold them for ransom, B? Who would pay that type of bread for these two lames?" Juice asked with a puzzled look in his eyes.

Najee smiled. "The U.S. Government, that's who. Both of them are on the narco's Top ten most wanted list. We'll hand them off to my connect."

The crew rushed out of the house and roughly shoved the two cartel members into the back of a white cargo van. They gently loaded the shrink-wrapped blocks of money, then split into three groups. Rio and Juice took the van. Yung Zay and Maceo hopped in an inferno red Charger and Najee and Nella climbed into the silver SRT Dodge Challenger.

The older, feisty narcotics trafficker was the infamous Ismael Zambada. He was suspected of smuggling tons of cocaine into the United States. Juan Guzman, the heavyset Mexican, was passive but extremely dangerous. He was wanted for the gruesome assassination of three border patrol agents. Rio drove while Juice kept his chopper aimed at the gaffled up prisoners.

As they pulled off, a black Ford F-150 pulled up. Two Los Cinco Diablos drug runners jumped out of the truck. Each of them carried a heavy suitcase. Just as Najee suspected, they were late dropping off the cash and picking up their weekly supply of narcotics. Najee contemplated doing a U-turn and laying everybody down but decided against it. Greed will send you to hell if you get shot or jail if you get caught. He watched the two men enter the mansion through his rearview mirror then smashed his black Timb's on the gas. The Hemi engine roared like a ferocious lion.

As they made their getaway, Nella couldn't help herself; she kept stealing quick looks at Najee out of the corner of her eye while he gripped the steering wheel, deep within his own thoughts. She wanted to reach out and run her soft hands up and down his hairy forearms and chiseled biceps. She wanted to feel his smooth bald head between her legs and his full lips exploring her body. Just thinking about him made her pussy moist. Of course, she didn't let him know this. For now, sneaking sips of his handsome features was quenching her thirst.

Najee weaved in and out of the heavy 405 freeway traffic headed back to Los Angeles. Although the strong and silent type turned Nella on, she was getting bored. She was tired of streaming her playlist, and the silence was driving her crazy.

"What are you thinking about, Najee?" she asked, breaking his concentration. Her speech was proper. She sounded like a white girl.

He took his eyes off the road and looked over at her. She resembled Lisa Raye. His smile made her panties melt. "Actually, I was thinking 'bout you."

"Oh, is that right?"

"Yeah, I remember when my homegirl Hoova Kim introduced us. You winked and told me that your name rhymes with Vanilla. I liked you off top because you had a slick mouth."

Nella playfully punched him in the arm, "My mouth ain't slick!"

"Ouch gurl, you hit like Mike Tyson!" he teased while laughing.

"More like Layla Ali. Now tell me what you were really thinking. Because if you were thinking about me, you would've had a big smile on your face instead of a frown."

Najee stiffened and remained silent for a moment. He didn't like people trying to get all up in his head; however, he was impressed at how observant she was.

"What are you, some type of mind reader?" he asked.

"No, I read body language. I can tell when a man has some heavy shit on his mind. Look how stiff you are. And those deep lines in your forehead are a dead give-away. What type of demons are haunting you?"

For an answer, he worked the gear shift, switched lanes, and weaved in and out of traffic until he came to a freeway exit in South Central, Los Angeles. The gloomy scenery paled in contrast to the

131

cool breeze and green palm trees of Escondido. The Victorian mansions were replaced with shabby apartments and dingy project buildings. The European automobiles were replaced with broken down hoopties and low riders. There was more concrete than grass, and the smell of poverty polluted the air. They came to a stop at a red light on Florence and San Pedro, a few blocks from where the L.A. riots kicked off. Najee laughed as Nella locked the passenger door and cocked her .380. The slums reminded her of Iraq.

"This is what I had on my mind," he finally spoke. "Look around and tell me what you see?"

Nella looked around. Nightfall hung over the city like a dark shadow, yet there was still a lot of traffic and activity. People of all ages moved to and fro like army ants. Each of them was on their own mission but shared the same look of despair on their faces.

"I don't see anything except a bunch of boarded up businesses and some broke Latino and black people," she answered.

"That's right, and I want to help change that. I'm not hittin' all these licks for nothing. There's a method to my madness, but it takes money. The government wouldn't give me grants so I took matters into my own hands and started robbing Benzo Al's stash houses."

"Then why don't we just take the dope and the money. We left over a hundred kilo's back at that house. Rio is right, we could easily make two million. And that's not even including all the drugs we left on those other stick up's."

"Rio don't know what he's talking about. He wants to give out dope packs, I want to give out jobs. His intentions are good, but we can't pump poison back into the hood, feel me? Let me show you something else."

The light turned green. Najee drove up San Pedro, made a left on a back street and drove deeper into the Eastside. It was like they had suddenly stepped into a different world. This was *New Jack City* meets *Boyz-N-The-Hood*. Gang bangers, crack whores and Heroin addicts littered the sidewalks.

"See shorty over there?" Najee pointed at a youngster who couldn't be more than twelve years old.

The Draco in his waistband made his pants sag. "Tomorrow is a school day. Why do you think he out here huggin' the block so late?"

"His mama and daddy probably don't care!"

"His so-called daddy was never there from the jump. His mother ain't shit either. There she is over there." He pointed to a figure across the street stepping from the shadows.

Nella looked just in time to see a tall, dark-skinned woman with hardened facial features leaning into the window of a parked Audi A6. Her cellulite ass cheeks hung from under her short, black leather mini skirt, and her lips moved fast. When she opened the door to get in, the interior light came on. The middle-aged, married white male pulled out his wallet. Nella shook her head in disgust as she watched the prostitute's wig disappear into the man's lap. Within minutes, she got out of the car and spit a wad of saliva and cum on the curb while simultaneously stuffing a fist full of crumpled bills into her bra. The trick drove to the suburbs with a satisfied grin on his face and the woman shuffled across the street to buy $20 worth of Heroin from her son.

Nella was shocked. "Did you see that?"

"Yeah, I saw it, but you're supposed to be watching everything. God gave you two eyes, learn to use both of them. You'll start seeing the world from a different perspective. There are a thousand more brothas just like him. I do this shit for them."

She followed his advice and looked at the foreign terrain from every angle. She noticed that there was a calculated order to the chaos like army ants moving with a purpose. Transactions of every type were being conducted on every corner. This was commerce at its best. The street entrepreneurs operated like graduates from the University of Harvard. Buying low, selling high, scheming and scamming, all in an effort to make a dollar out of fifteen cents.

"So, now can you tell me why lil' homie out here holding it down?"

Nella was speechless, she couldn't believe her eyes. He wasn't the only shorty huggin' the block. Young black faces laid in the cut camouflaged by darkness. They were baby soldiers abandoned to survive on their own.

After they left, the couple went to Johnny's Pastrami off of Crenshaw and Adams. Nella had the best double-dipped pastrami sandwich she'd ever tasted. She was so amazed at all the car clubs and street vendors selling everything from fake Gucci purses to bootleg DVDs. She felt comfortable and protected in Najee's presence. Young hustlers ran up to him to shake his hand, and the O.G.s saluted him with a head nod as they bounced by in their Chevys. They appreciated what he was doing for the hood with his non-profit organization aimed at helping at risk youth. He was a ghetto celebrity, a mascot for the streets. The blacktop was the color of his skin, and the lines in the middle of the road were his veins.

Najee and Nella talked and laughed some more until they found themselves parked outside of her condo in Marina Del Rey. Deep inside, neither one of them wanted the night to end.

"You coming up?" she asked in her sexiest voice.

"Nah, I gotta catch up with the fellaz and arrange for my inside connect to pick up those cartel members."

"Business as usual, huh?" she had rejection in her voice.

Najee felt her body temperature go from steamy hot to icy cold. Nella was just his type, but he didn't want to get attached to anything or anyone he couldn't walk away from in thirty seconds or less. That's the complicated lie he told himself. The truth was simple, he was afraid of love!

Before he left, he leaned over and gently kissed her on the lips once, then twice, then three times. She responded by pushing her tongue into his mouth. The heat coming from their bodies made the windows fog up. His hands were drawn to her phat monkey like a magnet. Just as he suspected, she was moist! Her curious fingers found their way to the growing lump in his pants. Just as she anticipated, it was big!

Najee leaned over, reclined her seat, and removed her Coach tennis shoes. "Damn, even yo' feet pretty!" He licked her pinky toe, and she giggled. He sucked her big toe, and she moaned. He unzipped her snug-fitting Emilio Pucci jeans and pulled them down

134

to her ankles along with her thong. Her shaved pussy looked sweeter than Godiva chocolate.

Najee kissed between her thighs and slowly worked his way to her wet spot. She could feel his warm breath on her vagina. He put her clitoris into his mouth and sucked it like a Jolly Rancher. Each time his tongue swiped her throbbing clit, the sensations shot to her nipples.

"Ohh, yes, right there—right there!" Nella placed her sexy feet on the dashboard, held the back of Najee's smooth bald head, and gushed cum on his lips and goatee.

He wiped the sweet feminine juice from his chin and placed his middle finger in Nella's mouth. Her eyes rolled into the back of her head as she tasted her own pussy. She tore his shirt off and frantically unzipped his jeans. Najee's Zulu spear sprang free. It was long, thick, and hard as granite. Placing her curvaceous legs over his broad shoulders, he slowly and deliberately pushed his dick into her tight cunt. He looked deep into her eyes as he stroked to the left, to the right, and all up in the middle. Nella held his gaze, it was as if he was double penetrating her pussy and her soul.

Their lovemaking grew intense. The windows fogged up and the shocks squeaked. Najee pushed Nella's legs back so that her plump ass lifted off the seat and her kneecaps were by her ears. This position gave him direct access to her pussy. "You my, Beyoncé," he whispered into her ear as he pounded her box with long, powerful strokes.

Her pussy was so wet he needed rain boots. She took the dick and savored every inch. Najee's body went rigid as Nella's cunt contracted and milked his pole. They both moaned as they came simultaneously. Their lips stayed locked in a sensuous kiss until Najee's cell phone vibrated. It was Rio.

"You know I gotta take this call right?"

"Call him back later." She leaned over and took his dick into her mouth. She squeezed the base, then licked the drop of cum that bubbled at the tip.

Her throat was hard to resist, but business came first. He had to answer it. "I'm diggin' you baby, but you can't come between me and my business. Go upstairs and get some rest. I'll call you in the morning."

"Oh, it's like that?" Nella rolled her neck. Najee simply looked at the minute hand on his Hublot. Frustrated, Nella dressed in silence, got out of the car, and slammed the door extra hard. She felt stupid for throwing herself at him like that. "*You should know better*," she thought out loud.

Najee watched her thick thighs and big booty bounce as she walked away. "Man, I handled that all wrong. Boulevard taught me better than that," he chastised himself before hitting the call back button.

Rio picked up on the first ring. "We got a situation, bro."

"Wassup, holla at me."

"Bad news, Fam. The hostages are dead."

"What?" Najee pulled the phone away from his ear and stared at the screen with a disgusted look on his face. When he finally spoke, his voice was calm, but his blood was boiling. "How in the hell did that happen?"

"See—what happened wuz—the old man offered us twice the amount of money if we let them go. He said he had some loot stashed at a safe house in Oakland. But shit got twisted."

"Who gave the green light on this bright idea?"

"I did," Rio admitted.

"Finish, I'm listening."

"Well, like I was saying, when we—I mean, when I untied them, the fat one pulled a strap from his ankle holster and caught me slippin', but Juice was on point and sprayed them both with the chopper."

"What about the fetti? Did you at least find out where the stash house was at first?"

Rio paused before answering, realizing his own stupidity, "Naw Cuz, the shit popped off so quick, I didn't get a chance to." He knew he was in the wrong, but he still didn't like the way Najee was coming at him.

Annoyed, Najee made a quick right turn, then looked in his rearview mirror. The suspicious headlights that had been following him since he left Nella's condo turned down the dark street. He put his loaded pistol on his lap and kept a watchful eye on the vehicle as he spoke to Rio.

"Don't even trip, it is what it is. Dump the bodies, torch the van, and lay low." He hung up without waiting for a reply.

The driver of the suspicious vehicle slid up to Najee's rear bumper and flashed the high beams on and off, waited five seconds, then flashed the bright lights on and off again. Najee slowed the Dodge Challenger down and relaxed his grip on his gun. He didn't recognize the car, but he had a good idea who the driver was. He pulled into a vacant lot and let the Hemi engine idle.

The midnight blue 750Li BMW came to a stop next to him. Both men stepped out of their vehicles and faced each other. The driver of the BMW was an older white gentleman of medium height. His broad shoulders stretched the material of his well-pressed suit. He was dressed like a businessman but smelled like a cop.

"You're slippin', Najee. You led me directly to your girlfriend's house."

Najee smirked. "I never slip, I didn't lead you to my people's house; I led you into a death trap. Look behind you."

The older gentleman shifted on nervous legs, then looked back to scan the dark, vacant lot. When he turned back to Najee he had a chrome pistol pointed at his nose. His lips parted with a smile.

"Good one, son. Good one!"

The two men laughed and gave each other some dap and a brotherly hug. They were happy to see each other. Najee tucked his burner into his waistband and pulled a thick yellow envelope from his back pocket. He tossed it to the older gentleman who wasted no time fanning the stack of big faces with his thumb. Satisfied, he reached into his breast pocket and pulled out a thumb drive.

"Here you go, two new names."

Najee accepted the device. "How heavy is surveillance?"

"That I don't know, but I can tell you that the Fed's want both of these guys bad."

Najee raised an eyebrow. "Who are they?"

One is Alonzo Guzman! The other is just a link in a long chain. You know how it goes, we indict the whole crew, the leader flips and takes us higher on the totem pole." He watched Najee's demeanor to see how the information affected him

Najee knew that Benzo Al's elusive head was on top of the totem pole, but the boss was virtually untouchable. He was insulated by layers of faithful captains, lieutenants, and street soldiers. The only way to hurt him was to hurt his pockets. Najee was robbing his workers and using the funds to promote his non-profit organization.

The grey-haired Caucasian turned to leave, but had a question, "Why are you only interested in organizations that get their supply from Alonzo Guzman? I have intel on a list of wealthy drug dealers, con artists, and gun runners, but you're not interested. Why are you so obsessed with Benzo Al?"

Najee's face went blank. He ignored the question and reached for the door handle. The older gentleman stopped him with a firm hand on his shoulder.

"Son, I know what you're up to, but does your team? If this is some type of personal vendetta for your slain family, please let it go. Trust me, you don't want Los Cinco Diablos as your enemy."

Najee looked down at the concerned hand touching his shoulder but hardened his heart. He shook the hand off and jumped behind the wheel and sped off. His selfish thirst for revenge was clouding his better judgment.

CHAPTER 14

Secure the Bag

A week after the Escondido lick, the Body Snatchers gathered together at the Lab. The Lab was a non-descript two-story warehouse located near Santa Monica, California. The area was chosen for its breathtaking view of the Pacific Ocean, privacy, and buildings with no characteristics. The commercial property that they were meeting in was a renovated seafood plant. Although the outside of the warehouse was not appealing to the eyes, the inside boasted a high tech interior complete with fiber optics, an impenetrable surveillance system, an underground bunker, tasteful art, and contemporary office furniture. They were meeting in the East conference room.

Najee dumped the contents of an overstuffed duffel bag onto the conference table. Thick stacks of hundred-dollar bills spilled out into a neat pile. He separated the money six ways, giving everyone in the clique forty-two bandos each. This wasn't their biggest caper by far. However, it was enough to pay the bills and still be able to stash away a few racks for a rainy day. Everyone was satisfied except, Rio. He shook his head in disappointment while scraping the money off the table and into his leather Gucci backpack. Najee watched Rio's body language out of the corner of his eye but didn't speak on it. The last lick didn't meet his expectations either, he was ready to move on to bigger and better things.

"I know this ain't a lot of loot."

"Damn right it ain't," Rio mumbled under his breath. He was ready to break off from the Body Snatchers and do his own thing.

Najee ignored the comment and continued to speak, "But if you haven't been blowin' yo' dust, then you should have at least a ticket tucked away. But I know some of you have been trickin' off on cars, women and fancy jewelry."

He paused and looked directly at the twin platinum Jesus pieces sprinkled with diamonds dangling from Rio's neck. Each chain was appraised at $75,000 a pop. Najee didn't rock a lot of bling. The rapid flutter of a money counter machine was his drug. The smell of currency was like a line of Peruvian coke transporting him to euphoria.

"Anyways, like I was saying, we got one last lick to hit, and then we're moving on to bigger and better things. We're about to put an end to corporate greed. When we're hitting our list of fortune 500 companies, Wall Street is gonna be shook! I'm talking about computer scams, credit card fraud, identity theft and any other high-tech crimes we can think of. Are y'all with it?"

Hell yeah, they were with it! The tension in the room lightened and Najee moved on to the next two items on his agenda.

"Juice, what's up with those fullies equipped with silencers those A-Rabs were talkin' about?"

"It sounded too good to be true dawg, so I passed on 'em. I got another plug in Wisconsin at Badger Guns, though. They seem solid."

"A'ight cool, stay on it. And speaking of Wisconsin, did you upload the footage of my debate with the mayor of Milwaukee?" His question was directed toward Yung Zay, their computer guru.

"We global, my Nig! The video is going ham on the Gram! We already got over one million views. Our Twitter account and Facebook page is buzzin' too. We're receiving hundreds of friends requests every day. Tavis Smiley wants to interview you next, and I just got a tweet from Al Sharpton. He's pissed that the government won't help fund Alive365."

Najee was pleased. The world had no idea that he was responsible for the string of deceased drug dealers poppin' up in boroughs from L.A. to the Bronx. Their social network campaign was going viral and his message was being accepted by politicians and other community leaders. There was one more important item he needed to check on.

"Nella, how are we looking on the Alive365 project?" Najee asked.

Nella flipped through her notes. "Everything is Gucci. We are on schedule and below budget," she reported proudly.

Alive365 is a non-profit organization that Najee set up with proceeds from his illicit capers. The goal of the foundation is to help inner-city youths transform their at-risk behavior into positive characteristics. His belief was that teaching them conflict resolution would reduce violence. Self-awareness would teach them to respect and protect their bodies, therefore, lowering the teenage pregnancy rate and HIV epidemic that has plagued the urban community.

He knew all too well the pressure and disadvantages inner-city kids faced. They were not equipped academically nor prepared mentally to compete in today's workforce. From the womb to the tomb was a harsh reality that the ghetto comfortably embraced. Najee wanted to change that. By far, he was no modern-day Robin Hood. He just wanted to give back to the hood. To fulfill his ultimate mission, he needed cash.

Satisfied with the progress of his most important project, Najee moved on. "Who is our next target from the new list?"

"Marcus Fischer, also known as Sosa." Yung Zay flipped through his notes.

"What type of intel do we have on him and his organization?"

"Enough to knock him at any time. He's a flashy nigga fa' reals."

"Pull up any images you have," Najee directed.

Maceo tapped a link on his iPad and the four large LCD monitors that were mounted to the wall instantly came alive. He swiped right and images of Sosa and several exotic automobiles appeared. The collection was quite impressive.

"That's him on the left," Maceo stated.

Rio's mouth watered at the sight of all the colorful European eye candy. "Now that's what the fuck I'm talking about."

Irritated, Najee said, "Let's move on!"

"Here are the two stash houses," Maceo informed the team. "They call them the White Castle and the Blood Bank."

"Let me guess, the White Castle is where they keep the coke and the Blood Bank is where the cash is stashed at?"

"That's correct, according to the DEA files both of these spots are hotter than fish grease, but I can't tell. Those niggas party like rock stars every night!"

"Do the Feds have a live feed?"

"Of course! There are wireless cameras covertly mounted in several palm trees surrounding the compound. I just hacked in."

"Zoom in on the Blood Bank."

"Why the Blood Bank, Cuz?" Rio interrupted. "If we hit the dope spot, we can flood the streets and double our profit."

"You're absolutely right," Najee agreed. "But you never want to hustle twice. Besides, we've been over this already."

Rio waited for further clarification, but no explanation came. The seven monitors lit up with colorful images of a beautiful suburban mansion. Each camera was mounted at a different angle giving them a 360 view of the magnificent compound.

"Do we have live feed of the streets?" Najee asked. Maceo manipulated the touch screen device and images of the streets and well-manicured lawns appeared. "Take us up the block." The high-resolution camera had an optical zoom feature that was capable of reading a license plate from a thousand yards away.

"Stop right there." Najee pointed to monitor number three. "See that unmarked car?" he asked without expecting an answer. "And see that lady walking her dog?"

Everyone focused their gaze on the middle-aged white woman walking a small Pomeranian. She wore blue yoga pants and Beats headphones over her ears. To the naked eye, she looked like a regular housewife walking the family dog. To the trained observer, however, there were obvious tell-tell signs.

Nella spoke up first, "See how she's looking around without actually looking around?"

"You're right," Yung Zay chimed in.

"And where is her pooper scooper?" Nella observed. "These uppity white people would cry bloody murder if they knew that mutt was taking a shit on their well-kept lawns."

As if on cue, the golden Pomeranian lifted his hind leg against the palm tree and marked his territory. The woman took this

142

opportunity to casually glance over her shoulder to take in any activity going on, then spoke into her shirt collar to relay a message.

"The Feds!" Rio sat straight up in his chair.

"That's correct and I bet if we bring up footage from yesterday, we'll see the same unmarked car parked in a different location." Najee pointed out. He finished with a smile and a quick wink. His full lips parted to show off a beautiful set of pearl white teeth.

Nella felt warm inside. Something about Najee's swag turned her on immensely. His walk, the way he talked, his Ralph Lauren cologne and his intelligence caused her to admire his style. However, it was his gentle mannerism, mixed with his bad boy image that made her panties wet.

"Keep it together girl!" she told herself.

"So, what do we do now?" Maceo asked. "We can't knock him without the Feds knockin' us."

Rio and the others shook their heads in agreement. Getting in and out with bags of cash would be a difficult task alone and far too risky with a government agency clocking every move.

Najee had an idea. If he could flip Sosa, he would be one step closer to murkin' Benzo Al. The corner of his lips formed into a sinister smile. "Instead of robbing, Sosa, I say we let him know that the Alphabet Boys got him and his organization under surveillance. We can tax him for all the intel we have. What boss wouldn't pay a few racks for the names of the snitches within his crew?"

The team ordered Chinese food from PF Chang and ate while calculating their next caper. Between bites of steamy shrimp, fried rice and orange chicken, they formulated their plot.

Sosa was a young, handsome, walking bankroll. Through a relentless hustle, business savvy and a lot of luck, his humble street corner operation quickly grew into a nationwide criminal enterprise. Like the Italian Mob, his black mafia was a close-knit family. For years they operated under the cloak of secrecy and reaped enormous profits from cocoa wrapped in grey duct tape. The street talk was that he didn't even know how to calibrate a scale. This was probably true, seeing that there was no need to break the bricks down. He was strictly wholesale, moving bundles of white product through coded conversations on his cell phone.

His flamboyant behavior, however, would ultimately lead to his demise. Just as the streets were talking, the streets were watching, and Sosa gave the people exactly what they wanted to see. The team would exploit this chink in his armor and use it to their advantage.

"So, let me get this straight," Nella addressed the group of men. "We walk up to this Sauce guy, or whatever his name is, and tell him that while we were watching you, we discovered the Feds were watching you as well?"

"Sure," Najee answered nonchalantly.

"And we want you to reward us with a large sum of cash for spying on you," she continued.

"Sounds good to me."

"And just who is going to be the one to tell him?" All eyes were on her.

"Oh, hell no, you got me fucked up!" A look of bewilderment fell upon her face.

Najee placed both hands on her shoulders and looked her directly in the eyes. "He has a weakness for exotic cars and beautiful women," he reassured her. "You're perfect for the job."

The Streets Made Me

CHAPTER 15

Club iCandy: Hot-Lanta, Georgia

The first-class flight from LAX to Atlanta airport was relaxing and uneventful. As the Boeing 747 floated above the clouds, each member of the team fell into their own thoughts. From Najee's position on the plane, he was able to examine the members of his elite crew. He methodically studied each person closely.

Juice, the weapons expert, was nodding his head to the rhythm of his favorite hip-hop artist, *Jai-Swift*. His dreads were dyed red on the tips and hung in his face. His Ralph Lauren suit hugged his 6'0 athletic frame. The yellow, silk tie complimented the hue of his golden, brown skin. At the young age of twenty-five, his innocent looks and boyish charm often caught his opposition off guard. Although he was susceptible to peer pressure and easily influenced, Najee loved him like a brother. Besides, when it came to weapons and artillery, Juice knew his shit.

Najee's gaze shifted towards Yung Zay. He was typing on his laptop, probably updating his profile on one of the many social networking sites he visited on a regular. Mature beyond his twenty-one years, he had an uncanny knack for espionage and countersurveillance. He was constantly introducing the team to new spy gadgets. Because of this, he was the butt of many 007 jokes. His similarities to *James Bond* did not end there. He was also handsome, suave and quite the ladies' man.

Maceo had a window seat next to the exit. He did not like flying. As the Boeing jet prepared to land, the green and brown square patches became visible outlines of a busy metropolitan area. As Maceo focused on the tiny objects below, his mind was no doubt concentrating on computer hacking or a complicated string of code. Standing at 6'2 with broad shoulders and muscular arms, he looked more like a linebacker than a computer genius. A stewardess passed by with a tray of refreshments, and Maceo's eyes openly followed her sexy hips. Najee watched with a smile as they flirted with one another. Every man has a weakness!

Having that thought in mind, he looked toward Nella. She looked like sleeping beauty as she snored lightly. Her silky black hair was pulled back into a bun, and she wore little to no makeup. She was very light-skinned with cute freckles on her nose and a pair of full, luscious lips. Being the product of an African-American father and Dutch mother, she had the ability to take on the identity of a white woman or Creole by simply changing her accent. Make her mad, however, and all the nigga would come out of her in a hot second.

As Najee watched her angelic features, he thought about how he had hardened his heart after they made love. It was for the best, he convinced himself. Although he was falling for her, he knew the importance of keeping things professional. He needed her mind to be clear and focused. He was counting on her for the current mission and there was no room for errors or distractions.

"What's on your mind, Cuzzin'," Rio interrupted Najee's thoughts.

If Najee was caught off guard, he did not let it show. "Not much, my man. Just going over the plan in my head."

"Think it will work?"

"I don't see why not. We give Sosa an envelope with the names and identities of the confidential informants within his crew, along with the other inside information we got from our connect at the Drug Enforcement Administration. In return, he gives us a briefcase stuffed with cash, simple as that!"

"Are you ever gonna tell me who this secret DEA insider is? And what about, Nella? If thangs go wrong, she'll be in the direct line of fire." Rio pointed out.

"She's a big girl, she can handle herself. Besides, I have a backup plan."

"And what's that?"

"Put your seat belt on Loco we about to land. I'll fill you in later." Najee looked at Rio out of the corner of his eye and wondered why he was asking so many questions lately.

Rio fastened his seat belt and brought the reclining leather chair upright. Even at 6'3, the first-class accommodations gave him more

146

than enough room to stretch his long legs. As the planes large rubber tires met the tarmac and taxied to the landing terminal, Najee meditated on his relationship with Rio. They had known each other longer than the other crew members and fought side by side on many occasions like soldiers.

Although they were completely opposite of each other, they were inseparable. Rio was tall and lanky and Najee was short and stocky. Najee was the brain. Rio was the enforcer. Najee had dark, chocolate skin and a smooth bald head. Rio was Puerto Rican with shoulder-length cornrows. Rio's only flaw was that he wanted to be the leader.

They were flying to Hot-Lanta for Sosa's birthday bash. He was turning thirty-one. Many entertainment heavyweights would be in attendance along with major figures of the underworld. Sosa was known for throwing extravagant parties. This would provide the perfect cover for the team.

Before leaving Los Angeles, Nella had coordinated the flight and ground transportation with her plug at 404 Exotic Autos. When they landed, the vehicles she reserved were waiting for them. A tall Somali heavy hitter with curly hair and a beak nose handed over several sets of keys. Nella tossed him a large manila envelope. He quickly flipped through the blue big faces and flashed his yellow teeth with a smile of approval. While openly admiring Nella's curvaceous figure, he licked his dry, chapped lips and asked was there anything else he could do for her.

"Sure," she responded. "You can start by biting on a tic-tac." Everyone, including the Somali gangster, roared with laughter.

"Okay, everybody, let's smash out," Najee said.

Yung Zay chose the Lamborghini Huracán. He lifted the Lambo doors and was greeted by a tan Nero leather interior with red piping and a carbon dash. Maceo walked up to the Porsche 911 GT2 RS and rubbed his hand along the smooth contours of the body. Even sitting idle, the car looked fast. Juice opted for the Audi R8. The glossy black paint complimented by black Asanti rims gave the vehicle the appearance of a stealth bomber. Rio hopped into the inferno red Alfa Romeo. He pushed the start engine button and the

Capristo exhaust system growled like a lion. He looked at the top speed on the dash and grinned. Today was a good day.

"What it do, where's my whip?" Najee asked.

"Relax, you're riding with me," Nella informed him.

"That's cool, but what are we rollin' in because I don't see a Bugatti or anything else slick?"

"We're rolling in that." She pointed to a large, menacing vehicle that resembled a Hummer on steroids. It was midnight black with dark tinted windows and a large, metallic letter K mounted on the front grill.

"What the hell is that?"

"It's a Knight XV, made by Conquest Inc. I saw one in the DuPont Registry and fell in love. It has more security, luxury options, and amenities than any other handcrafted armored vehicle."

Najee shook his head from side to side. "That's all good. But you mean to tell me that everybody else got a fly whip, and you got me driving a Knight Fifteen armored truck? How lame is that?"

Nella smiled. "Correction, I'm doing the driving."

The entourage of expensive vehicles raced each other on the 285 freeway. The adrenaline rush was a natural high as they avoided accidents and eluded the law. This was the first time in a while that the crew had had some fun. Najee would constantly remind them of the dangers of splurging and spending large sums of cash. Today, however, keeping a low profile was not on the agenda. He decided to let his elite group unwind, relax, and live a little, but just a little.

****

When they pulled up to club iCandy, the party was turnt up. The parking lot was jam packed with foreign automobiles sitting on oversized chrome rims and dripping House of Kolors candy paint. The line to get in stretched around the block and only the prettiest women with the shortest skirts were granted entrance through the velvet ropes.

Nella maneuvered the Knight XV through the crowd. All eyes were on them as the string of exotic cars made their way to the secured, valet parking lot. Only the sexy and important were permitted in this area. They flashed their exclusive VIP passes to a large security guard wearing a black T-shirt that read BBE in large white letters. After waving a metal detector wand over each person, they were led through a side door marked private. Once inside, they were greeted by another goon sporting a black BBE T-shirt and a large caliber weapon tucked into a leather shoulder holster. He quickly pat searched each of the males, while a female hostess peeked inside of Nella's Salvatore Ferragamo bag, scanning for contraband.

"What's with all the extra security?" Najee asked.

"There are a lot of hip-hop artists in the house tonight. Most of them are studio gangsters, so the amped-up security helps them feel safer," the large bouncer chuckled at his own joke.

The hallway was soundproof, however, as soon as the bouncer ushered them through the large double doors, the loud beat pounded on their eardrums. The bass served as an aphrodisiac as everyone swayed from side to side in a trance to the sounds of Grammy Award Winner, The Pancake Man exploding through the speakers. Lavish gold metallic bottles of Armand de Brignac champagne flowed freely.

On the first level of the club, *Nene Leaks* from, *The Real Atlanta Housewives* was arguing with *Kim Kardashian* about who's the biggest reality TV star. Upstairs in the lounge area, Larry Wright, the CEO of Baller Belly Entertainment was pitching a movie idea to *F. Gary Gray*. The Body Snatchers were clocking everything and everybody.

"Plenty of celebrities are up in this bitch!" Yung Zay was star struck.

"On my word, this nigga is hotter than, P-Diddy!" Juice said with admiration.

Najee was not impressed. "Get off his dick and let's get focused," he reminded everyone.

Rio scanned the room. He spotted Sosa and his goons lounging in the VIP area. Two hulking guards blocked off the entrance.

"There go Sosa over there," he informed the team with the nod of his head. He dared not point in their direction.

"How am I gonna get close enough in order to deliver our proposition with all those groupies surrounding him?" Nella asked nervously.

A group of scantily clad women invaded the VIP area competing for attention as Sosa made it rain with crispy one-hundred-dollar bills. Each member of his entourage was drippin' with flawless diamonds and had their own bottle of expensive champagne.

"You're not going to approach him. Just do you and he will make the initial contact," Najee said with confidence.

The crew split into two separate teams while leaving Nella on the dance floor. She looked very sexy in a pair of white, leather booty shorts that hugged her hips and matching white, leather Salvatore Ferragamo boots that came up past her knees and wrapped around her thick red-bone thighs. Her low-cut blouse showed off her 36DDs.

As the two teams melted into the crowd, the male vultures swooped on Nella. They came at her with compliments and every pick-up line in the book. Sweaty palms groped at her voluptuous figure as she made her way to the well-stocked bar. She found a stool and observed the crowd.

"This is bullshit. I was about to break that fool's fingers for grabbing my ass!" Nella complained into her communication piece.

Yung Zay had equipped the entire team with small two-way devices that fit snuggly behind the earlobe. Unlike Bluetooth devices, the data that was being transferred was encrypted and could not be intercepted with a packet sniffer.

"You're doing just fine," Najee offered as encouragement. "Just keep throwing the bait out there, and the big fish will bite."

"Oh, that's what I've been reduced to, huh—bait?"

"Not just any bait—sexy, deadly bait!"

The sound of Najee's deep voice coming through her earpiece made her smile. He was warm, caring and protective. "Keep talking like that, and I'm gonna put this thang on you again."

"Stop it, I had you runnin' from this dick like you were a track star!" Najee teased.

Juice hacked as if he was coughing, "I think I'm gonna throw up."

"Y'all need to get a room," Yung Zay joked.

"Nella, somebody from Sosa's crew is approaching you now. He's an older cat. Look over your left shoulder," Rio alerted her in a serious tone.

A very tall, handsome, and distinguished gentleman made his way through the crowd of partygoers. For a moment their eyes locked. The staring contest ended when Nella broke eye contact and looked away. His intense gaze seemed to penetrate her soul. She felt vulnerable. Something about the stranger's demeanor oozed money, power, and danger. In a strange way, it turned her on.

His lips curled into a smile before he spoke. "Hello beautiful young lady, may I buy you a drink?" he asked politely.

Before Nella could respond, a sexy, dark, chocolate hostess approached the couple balancing a tray with a bottle of chilled Ace of Spades and two champagne glasses. As she poured each of them a drink, the stranger extended his hand for Nella to shake. She was hoping he would also introduce her to Sosa.

"I hope I'm not intruding," he said as slippery as a snake.

"No, not at all," Nella replied while shaking his hand.

The hard lines in his face told a story of a rough past, but the palms of his hands were smooth and soft as if he never worked a day in his entire life. "Do you have a name?" he inquired.

She gave him a flirtatious smile. "Call me, Huny."

"That sounds delicious, but I'd rather call you, Peanut Butter."

"And why is that?"

"Because those legs look like they'll spread for some bread!"

"Oh, no you didn't go there!" She laughed and rolled her eyes playfully. "That is the cheesiest pick-up line I have ever heard!"

"But you must admit I got you to smile." He was a smooth talker.

"And what's your name?" she asked over the loud hip hop music.

Using a quick flick of the wrist, the stranger produced a professionally designed business card. He leaned in to whisper in her ear. "My name is, Prince!"

Before he could finish his introduction, there was a loud commotion coming from the VIP section. Bodies and elbows were being slung everywhere as small patches of scuffles and altercations broke out.

"He got a gun!" someone yelled.

The sea of partygoers erupted into pandemonium. The music went off and the lights came on. A stampede bum-rushed the nearest exit, trampling bodies as they rushed to safety.

The crew immediately sprang into action. "Team-one make sure Nella is safe," Najee instructed. "Team-two, we're gonna grab the target. We still have a mission to accomplish!"

"Let's ride out!" Rio replied.

Team-one consisted of Juice and Rio. Najee, Maceo, and Yung Zay made up Team-two.

"I don't see Nella anywhere! We can't locate her!" Rio informed the team.

"Have you checked by the bar?" Najee asked through his communication piece.

"We at the bar now, Loc."

"Shit, she could be anywhere!"

"I've tried to contact her through her earpiece but didn't get a response," Juice added.

"Keep looking, but stick together," Najee instructed Team-one. "We're gonna check outside. Meet us by the vehicles in ten minutes."

Even with the lights on, the panic and chaos ensued. D.J. K-Slay attempted to calm the crowd over the PA system to no avail. Everyone rushed to the exit and the violence spilled outside. Juice and Rio continued to search for signs of Nella as Najee, Maceo and Yung Zay pushed their way through the VIP private exit. As soon as they stepped into the valet parking lot, they spotted Nella. She kicked and screamed as two large men dragged her toward a waiting cargo van.

She broke away momentarily and kicked one of the assailants in the balls. He crouched over in pain and clutched his scrotum. Nella followed up with a knee to the chin. The attacker slumped over and hit the asphalt.

The second assailant grabbed her from behind. His arms were like a thick python wrapping around her throat. His hot breath stunk like he had been eating shitty baby diapers and washing it down with cheap liquor. If she didn't die from him squeezing her esophagus, she would surely pass out from the smell of his breath. Thinking quickly, Nella angrily bit his hairy forearm. Her sharp teeth sank into his flesh.

"You bitch!" he spat before he released her.

She followed with a roundhouse kick to the head but missed. As the second assailant dodged the heel of her Ferragamo boots, the driver quietly stepped from the van. He crept up behind Nella and slugged her over the head with a blackjack. Her eyes went blank. She oozed to the ground like a limp noodle.

"We don't have all damn day. You two clowns get her in the van, pronto!" The large bouncer that escorted them through the VIP entrance earlier that evening ordered. The white BBE initials on his black T-shirt glistened in the dark night.

They threw Nella into the back of the cargo van and sped off just as Team-two arrived to assist her.

Juice and Rio ran up behind them moments later. "You mind letting us in on that so-called back-up plan?" Rio asked sarcastically.

Najee ignored him. Something that Nella dropped had captured his attention. He walked over and picked up a small object. It was a business card. It read: *iCandy Entertainment. Chief Executive Player, Prince.*

"The plan is to get Nella back safely by any means necessary," Najee declared through clenched teeth. "Let's hop in the Knight Fifteen, we can still catch them!" He did not tell the team that the man named on the business card was a ghost from his past.

The five courageous men piled into the Hummer on steroids. Najee was behind the wheel. "Let's see what this thing is made of." The V12 engine growled to life.

They pulled out of the parking lot just in time to catch a glimpse of the cargo van's rear taillights as the kidnappers turned onto Peachtree Street. Najee pressed the pedal to the metal in hot pursuit. They were quickly gaining ground.

"Everybody brace yourself," he warned seconds before ramming into the back of the van.

The sound of metal clashing against metal echoed in the night air. The passengers in the van were startled by the collision. Before they could gain their composure, Najee rammed into them again. The driver's neck snapped back as the passengers in the rear held on for dear life. Nella's unconscious body rolled on the cold metal bed of the van. Her hands and legs were tied. A black bag covered her head.

"Don't just sit there, shoot them muthafuckers!" the driver shouted over his shoulder.

The rear double doors of the van flew open. Both goons braced themselves on one knee as they aimed their fully automatic weapons. Their faces twisted into evil frowns as they squeezed off.

Rat! Tat! Tat! Tat! Tat!

"Watch out!" Rio shouted from the passenger seat.

Sparks from the barrel of both guns flashed in the dark. Several deadly bullets smacked against the windshield, however, they bounced off like rubber. The crew collectively let out a sigh of relief, grateful to Nella for being so thoughtful.

Juice pulled out a Glock .9mm from the stash and rolled down his window. "It's on and poppin'."

"Tuck that heat, my nigga. Nella is in there, too," Yung Zay reminded everyone.

"I have an idea." Najee maneuvered the vehicle like Dale Earnhardt. "I'm finna pull on the side of the van, then I want you to air them fuck boys out."

"That could be dangerous," Rio warned.

154

Najee looked over at Rio. He was right, however, desperate times called for desperate measures. "We don't have any other choice." Najee switched lanes and mashed on the accelerator. Both vehicles ran the red light at high speeds.

The Knight XV picked up momentum and inched along the driver's side of the van. The driver counter maneuvered and swerved to the left. The van smashed against the Knight XV aimed at the tires. The .9mm was knocked from his hand and landed in the middle of the street.

"Aww, hell naw. Now it's really on and crackin'!" Juice pulled an even bigger burner from the stash box. He cocked the Desert Eagle and squeezed off several shots into the driver's side door.

The driver of the van temporarily lost control and veered into oncoming traffic. With blatant disregard for his own life or the lives of others, he drove even faster on the wrong side of the street. Several cars blew their horns and flashed their headlights, desperately trying to avoid a head-on collision.

"Stay with them, don't lose 'em, Cuz!" Rio stated the obvious.

Najee gripped the steering wheel tighter. "I got this," he replied. He wanted Nella back in one piece more than anyone else. He smashed on the gas and drove with determination. Whoever was behind this would pay with their life.

"Oh shit, we got company!" Maceo informed the team while looking out the back window.

Najee looked into the rearview mirror. Four police cars with flashing red lights and loud sirens were on their tail.

"Pull the vehicle over, now!" a boisterous police office demanded over the bull horn.

"Yeah, right!" Najee made a hard left and the Knight XV tumbled over the cement island that divided the lanes. They were now on the wrong side of the street as well and dodging oncoming traffic. Two more squad cars joined the high-speed chase. Their sirens were blasting as the red and blue flashing lights on the roof illuminated the darkness.

The two goons in the back of the cargo van let off another burst of slugs from their fire breathing weapons. Even though the crew

155

was protected by ballistic grade armor, Najee's reflexes still caused him to swerve in order to dodge the barrage of hot metal. The stray slugs sprayed the lead squad car instead. The bullet-riddled vehicle spun out of control and did a 360. The young officer's brains splattered the headrest. The procession of police cruisers that trailed behind smacked into each other like falling dominos.

Najee watched the horrible episode unfold in slow motion through the side rearview mirror. Tonight was not going his way and was about to get worse. When he focused his attention back on the road, they were headed for a head-on collision with a semi-truck. The fully loaded 16 wheeler bullied the road like a freight train. The chubby white driver's eyes gleamed as if he loved a good game of chicken.

The Knight XV was no match for a 30-ton semi overflowing with cargo. Najee yanked the steering wheel. The vehicle veered to the left. Then he yanked the wheel to the right desperately trying to avoid hitting a parked car. He miscalculated, and the left fender smashed against a parked vehicle. The Knight XV skated on two wheels before finally rolling over and crashing violently on its right side.

Sparks flew as they slid on the asphalt for a few meters before coming to a halt. A cloud of white smoke floated from the engine. Diesel fuel leaked from the tank. More police cars, fire trucks and an ambulance carrying emergency medical personnel descended upon the scene. The local media intercepted the action on their scanners and were en route. The cargo van disappeared into the night.

"Is everybody okay?" Najee grunted. He had somehow ended up in the backseat. Pain shot through his entire body.

"I'm good!" Rio responded first.

Juice rubbed the swollen lump on his forehead, and then looked at the palm of his hand to see if there was any blood. "I'm good, too."

Maceo tried to move, but a searing pain shot through his right arm. "I'm straight, I just busted up my arm."

Najee pried the rear driver's side door open and climbed on top of the Knight XV. "Let's ride out," he commanded. "This bitch about to be crawling with the fifties!"

He reached down to extend a helping hand to Maceo as Rio kicked the front driver's side door open. He and Juice climbed out and jumped down. A crowd of pedestrians started to form.

"Let's ride out, Yung Zay," Najee looked around. "We're running out of time."

Yung Zay did not move or respond. He was cramped in the backseat laying in the fetal position. The smell of gasoline filled the air.

"Yung Zay, are you okay?" Panic gripped Najee's soul. "Yung Zay!" he called out passionately. There was no response from the crew's youngest member. Najee quickly jumped back inside the SUV. He was a true believer of no man left behind.

"Whatchu' doing?" Rio asked. "We gotta get the fuck out of here!" he added and started to back away.

"Then go!" Najee yelled. "Can't you see I'm tending to a wounded soldier?" He gently cradled Yung Zay's head in his arms, then placed two fingers against his neck to check for a pulse. His efforts were useless. Yung Zay was gone. Nella was gone. Tears flowed from Najee's eyes. A trickle of blood oozed from Yung Zay's head wound. This was war.

No matter how much the remaining crew members reasoned with their leader, they were unable to pry him away from the fallen soldier. Reluctantly, Juice, Rio, and Maceo made their escape as the streets lit up with police lights, news cameras, and curious bystanders.

The SWAT team had the perimeter secured and the Knight XV surrounded. Najee did not see or hear an ambitious officer draw his service weapon and yell, "Freeze nigger!" He didn't need to freeze, his soul was already frozen. Revenge would be served the same way.

Larry D. Wright

CHAPTER 16

Caught Up

The dilapidated warehouse on Howell Mill Road was cold inside and smelled like musty mildew. Prince hated being there. He had a distaste for getting his hands dirty with the physical work of the organization. He also disliked the scent the building left on his expensive suits.

"This damn place is probably filled with asbestos," he mumbled out loud and brushed a fallen paint chip off his shoulder as if the crusty flake was fire.

Nella was in an isolated part of the worn-down building. She was sitting in a metal folding chair with her hands tied tightly behind her back. The coarse rope cut into her wrists. She was fully conscious but remained silent. Despite the awful pain pounding in her head, her survival skills kicked in.

Prince admired her shapely body from afar. His dark eyes traveled from her leather boots to her diamond heart-shaped belly ring, to her melon sized breasts, up to the black blindfold that covered her head.

"Remove the blindfold," he instructed the driver of the cargo van.

The driver stood directly behind Nella with his huge arms folded. He stepped forward and snatched the black cloth bag from over her head.

Nella was not prepared for the bright lights after becoming so accustomed to the darkness. She squinted her eyes for a moment while her pupils adjusted to their surroundings. When she became focused, she felt a sense of relief after seeing Prince's comforting smile. He was very nice to her at the night club, and she felt he would be an excellent ally in getting down to the bottom of this escapade.

"Prince, what's going on?" she asked, "What am I doing here?" she was trying to be brave as possible. It wasn't working.

"You tell me!" he responded dryly.

"I don't have a clue. You and I were talking, and the next thing I know, I woke up with a headache."

Prince stepped forward and lifted her chin with his index finger and carefully examined the lump on her head. While doing so, Nella looked into his eyes. Her body stiffened. She remembered making direct eye contact with him when they first met and how his intense gaze seemed to penetrate her core. Now those same eyes seemed smaller, darker and more dangerous than before. Once again, she looked away.

Without warning, he grabbed her by the throat! Her face turned pale as his huge hands squeezed her larynx. Her heart pounded in her chest, trying to break through her skin. Just as quickly as he choked her, he released his grip. Nella gasped for air. A red handprint branded her neck.

"I'm gonna ask you some questions, and you're gonna answer them truthfully. Do I make myself clear?" Prince asked.

"Baby, I don't know any—"

"Bitch!" he cut her off. "I'm a grown-ass man! Do I look like a baby to you? Now, what the fuck was you doing at my club tonight?"

"It's not what you think." Relief began to settle in again.

"What was I thinking?" Prince countered. "That you'z an undercover agent? Which branch of the Alphabet Boys do you work for, the FBI, DEA, ICE?" he continued with anger in his voice.

"Baby, I ain't no cop! I was there because—"

Smack!

Prince reached back and pimp slapped the lipstick off her mouth before she could finish her statement. Salty blood trickled from the corner of her bruised bottom lip.

"I dun' told you about calling me out of my name!" he admonished. Reaching into the breast pocket of his tailored suit, he pulled out her communication earpiece. Nella's eyes widened. She had forgotten all about the device. "What is this?" he held the small gadget in his palm.

"Oh, that, it's just the Bluetooth for my cell phone," she lied.

"Nah, bitch, I ain't going! Neither Sprint nor Verizon has anything this sophisticated on the market, or else I would have one my damn self. This here is government-issued." He slammed the device on the cold concrete and smashed it with the toe of his Mauri gator shoes. "Now start bumpin' yo' gums, hoe, or I'ma feed you to the wolves."

The goon that she kicked in the scrotum was standing off to the side. At hearing Prince's words, he rubbed his crotch. Lust gleamed in his eyes.

Nella started talking fast, "You got it twisted. We work against the government, not with them."

"Who is we, bitch?" he interrupted her.

"Look, I'm not gonna be too many more of your bitches and hoes!" she insisted defiantly and braced herself for another blow.

"Would you rather me call you, Petronella Jackson?" he asked with a slippery smile. "Checked your fingerprints!" he added. Nella cringed at hearing her birth name but didn't let her emotions show. "As I was saying, my organization doesn't work with them, people. In fact, I was there to deliver an important message to, Sosa."

Prince raised an eyebrow. "What kind of message?"

Nella hesitated, she knew that information was a commodity, and if she was going to get out of there in one piece, she needed to hold her cards close to her vest. She decided to stall him.

"How did you know I wasn't who I said I was?"

"Easy, when I leaned in to whisper my name, I noticed that strange-looking device behind your ear."

"Is Sosa your boss?"

Prince popped his collar. "Pimps don't have bosses!"

She was about to ask another question, but he held up his hand to stop her. "Enough questions, I want answers!"

Nella let out a deep sigh while collecting her thoughts. Prince thought she was an undercover agent. In order to escape unharmed, she decided she needed to level with him and come clean.

"My people found out that there is an informant within your organization. Right now, there is twenty-four-hour surveillance on all the stash houses. The Feds have cell phone conversations, pictures, and a chart depicting the hierarchy of the Block Boy Empire criminal enterprise." She paused for a moment to allow him to digest the critical information.

"And how did you find all of this shit out?" he questioned.

"We have our resources."

Prince gave her that funny look, prompting Nella to continue talking. "Okay, I'll tell you. Just stop it with the eye thing. It creeps me out! Anyhow, we have a person on the inside that provides us with accurate information. Don't ask me who he or she is. I've never met them, no one has. Everything is done electronically."

This intrigued Prince. "So, I take it that my picture is not on this organizational chart or else you would have recognized me?" This was more of a statement than a question.

"Oddly enough, your picture wasn't inside the file. Why is that?" The gears were spinning in her head.

Prince ignored her question as he nervously paced back and forth. "So, how do you and your people benefit from all of this?"

"Money is the motive."

"It always is," he agreed.

"I belong to an elite group of street soldiers. We rob drug dealers. Sosa was a target on our list but he is a hot boy. So, instead, we decided to barter our inside information in exchange for cash."

A light clicked on inside Prince's head. He had been hearing rumors about a group of jack boys robbing drug dealers and ballers. They moved fast and were ruthless, so the streets started calling them the Body Snatchers.

Benzo Al had a million dollars bounty out on their heads. Recalling what his goons had told him earlier about the bulletproof SUV, he looked over to the smashed communication device, then back to Nella. He could barely contain his excitement. Lady Luck was finally smiling down on him. Just hours ago, he had a meeting with Sosa and his supply of cash had been shut off because of too many bad business ventures.

Bitterness flared up in his heart. While Sosa was lecturing him about burning too much loot on failed investments, he was busy playing Mr. Big Shot and throwing blood money at filthy whores.

For the life of him, Prince could not understand this new concept of it ain't trickin' if you got it. Just the thought of young niggas giving money to ho's made him want to get completely out of the game. He shook his head as if to clear the ugly images out of his mind like Etch-a-Sketch.

Prince had a plan brewing. He already knew everything that Nella knew, which meant she knew too much. "And fuck Sosa," he said to himself! He had introduced him to the game, now Sosa was powerful and didn't need him anymore. That fact infuriated Prince. Sosa would never know about this little conversation with Nella, Prince decided. His goal was to lure Nella's crew into a trap, and then turn them over to Benzo Al.

He probed Nella for more information. "So, let me see if I got this straight. Your plan was to wear those tight coochie cutters to my club because you knew Sosa was having his birthday bash there, correct?" he probed. Nella nodded her head in agreement. "And you were gonna tell Sosa that while you and your friends were casing his spots in order to jack him, you realized that y'all were not the only ones watching him, and now y'all want some of his bread?"

"That about sums it up."

"Who the hell thought of that silly ass plan?" Prince chuckled. His goons joined in, and the abandoned warehouse echoed with laughter. Nella squirmed uncomfortably in her seat. The rope binding her wrists dug deeper into her flesh. '*He has a point*,' she thought. The plan was ridiculous but sounded good at the time. She whispered a silent prayer for Najee to save her.

"So, enlighten us. Who is the snitch?" Prince gave her the evil eye.

"His name is, Princeton Reidel," she revealed, not knowing that she had just revealed his government name!

****

Prince stiffened, but not because the first and last name belonged to a confidential informant. He knew that his name would be revealed one way or another. The Feds used you. They suck you

163

dry of your manhood and loyalty, then leave you swimming in a cesspool of humility and dishonor when your information becomes useless. He knew the game all too well, yet hearing his government name brought back memories, painful memories. The last time he heard his name spoken out loud was in federal court. His mind drifted back to that dreadful day.

****

"Your Honor, my client would like to enter a guilty plea," the $500 per hour federal defense attorney out of Chicago announced.

"Counsel am I hearing this correctly?" the U.S. District Judge asked.

"Yes, Your Honor. The Assistant U.S. Attorney, along with the Department of Justice has offered my client a downward departure deal in exchange for his cooperation in an ongoing investigation to bring down a ruthless, nationwide prostitution ring."

Judge Martins raised his head from his notes and looked down on Prince from his wooden throne. The authority of the white judge and the power he possessed made Prince want to sink under the oak table. His ankle cuffs and body chains rattled as he shifted positions in his seat.

"Do you fully understand that any plea negotiations are between you, your legal representation, and the U.S. District Attorney and that this court is not bound by the results of those negotiations?" the silver hair judge quizzed.

What the judge was saying was that the court did not have to go along with the recommendation offered by the D.A. Prince knew the risks involved but felt the odds of getting off with just a slap on the wrist were in his favor. After all, he was saving the government money by accepting responsibility for his actions and not wasting their time going through a lengthy trial, but more importantly, he was cooperating with law enforcement officials.

The word cooperate left a bitter taste on his tongue. It went against every principle he stood for and the street code he faithfully abided by for so long. 'But fuck it,' he thought to himself. 'Better them than me!' Self-preservation was the only code in the jungle. He couldn't afford going back to prison again. He had already served a fifteen-year sentence for manslaughter.

"Yes, I understand, Your Honor." He had crossed over there was no turning back now!

"Your Honor," the seasoned District Attorney spoke for the first time. "We would like to hold off on sentencing and adjourn until the Special Victim's Task Force can meet with the defendant. We believe that once he debriefs, we will know the inner workings and key players involved in this sophisticated prostitution ring that preys on young women." He paused for effect, before continuing, "Mr. Riedel's cooperation will be essential in gathering sufficient information for the affidavits and applications for arrest warrants."

"I see," the judge replied while looking directly at Prince again. His neatly pressed black robe was the new attire of the KKK. "The court accepts your guilty plea, Mr. Riedel. You will be released on your own recognizance while you assist the Task Force. However, you will be on a very short leash. Do I make myself clear?" Judge Martins asked sternly.

Prince hated the way the judge looked at him, hated the way he pronounced his name, and hated becoming a rat. Yet he managed to shake his head in agreement and muttered, "Yes, Sir!"

Indictments were handed down and pimps from Oakland, Vegas, Milwaukee, and St. Louis were snatched off the streets. In the end, all of Prince's assets were confiscated and he was left penniless. But at least he had his freedom, or so he thought.

There is no escaping the Feds once they pierce your soul with their tentacles. As soon as that assignment was over, special agents from the High-Intensity Drug Trafficking Area Task Force were pulling his Dodge Magnum over, and searching the vehicle. The HIDTATF is a joint effort between local law enforcement, the DEA and the Office of National Drug Control Policy.

"Well, well, what do we have here, Prince?" Detective Donald Smith asked with a sarcastic grin. He held up a kilo of cocaine. "What happened, can't find any more little girls to pimp on?" He tossed the brick to Prince. Prince's reflexes caused him to

automatically catch the shrink-wrapped package. Common sense caused him to drop it like a hot potato. It was then that he noticed that the detective was wearing white surgical gloves. Detective Smith laughed. "You dun' fucked up. You know that, right?"

"This is bullshit!" Prince yelled angrily. "That ain't mines. You planted that shit in my trunk!" He smelled foul play.

Detective Smith's partner, Federal Agent Walker walked up to face Prince nose to nose. "Your fingerprints are on that brick, not ours, asshole! You work for us now! Or maybe I might find a weapon with an unsolved homicide under the driver's seat!" he said coldly while pulling a rusty Colt .45 out of a plastic evidence bag. "There's no telling how many bodies this piece has on it."

It was clearly a setup, but there was nothing Prince could do. When Dejuan was found dead in an abandoned warehouse, the DEA's investigation of Block Boy Empire came to a halt. They needed a new CI on the inside. His heart sank as they briefed him on his next assignment of ultimate betrayal. Help bring down Sosa!

****

"*Princeton Riedel,*" Nella repeated. "Does that name ring any bells?"

Her voice snapped Prince from his thoughts. He wondered how long he had been reminiscing. He had been living a double life, caught between the lure of the streets and the tight grip in which the government clutched his soul. In the beginning, he was tormented by what he had become. Sosa was closer to his heart than anyone knew or could imagine. However, after the cancerous cells of jealousy and envy became malignant, his tasks became easier to live with. Like a snake shedding skin, he put on a new layer of deception.

"So, can I go now?" Nella crossed her fingers behind her back, wishing for the best.

"I'm afraid not, bitch!" his response deflated her hopes. "I have other plans for you!"

One of the goons placed duct tape over her mouth and covered her head with the blindfold. As Nella struggled to break free of her restraints, the room became pitch black. The last thing she heard was the chilling sound of a solid metal door being slammed shut and heavy breathing. She held her own breath for a second and remained stiff while she listened. After a brief moment, her fears were confirmed. She was not in the room alone!

Larry D. Wright

CHAPTER 17

Atlanta Police Department – 3:00 A.M.

The 1st District Precinct is the headquarters of Georgia's finest men and women in blue. Located on the Westside of Atlanta, the station was also known for well-publicized scandals and corruption. It was rumored that the interrogation room doubled as a torture chamber. Najee was being held in cellblock 5-A. It was a large holding tank where new inmates were held while they were fingerprinted and booked into the system.

Najee sat isolated in the corner taking in his surroundings. The tank was made of solid brick and painted tan. It stunk like stale piss and funky feet. There was a stainless-steel toilet in the far corner, but he doubted anyone ever used it. The pool of urine in the corner confirmed his thoughts. Graffiti littered the walls.

There were several other prisoners besides Najee. Some sat on the cold slab of concrete while others lay sprawled out on the floor. All of them were deep in their own thoughts trying to get their stories together.

Najee needed to get to a phone, and quick! His fake driver's license was valid enough to pass a routine traffic stop, however, he had just been fingerprinted and it was only a matter of time before the Automatic Fingerprint Identification System revealed his true identity. He looked at the black ink on his fingertips and decided it was time to make a move.

"Officer—Officer, let me holla at you for a minute!" he shouted through the bars with urgency. The nightwatchman simply ignored him.

"I know you hear me! I need to make a call. I know my rights, I'm entitled to one phone call!" his plea's landed on deaf ears. The jailor flipped to the sports section and continued reading his newspaper.

"Keep that muthafuckin' noise down, nigga!" A drunken inmate slurred while standing up. "You ain't the only one that needs to call his baby momma!" The smell of Hennessey seeped through his pores.

"Actually, I need to call my lawyer. But to each his own," Najee shot back.

"You tryin' to get slick, nigga? I will smash you! Do you know who the fuck I—"

Smack!

Before he could finish his sentence, Najee landed a right hook to his jaw! His words were replaced with blood. The drunk stumbled backward on wobbly knees and landed with a thud onto the pissy floor. Just as quickly as the fight started, it was over. The crowd dispersed with a newfound respect for the winner. No one even bothered to help the loser as they stepped over his body.

"Mr. Madlock, please step forward," a black, chubby detective with a gold badge clipped to his hip called out. He was standing with a tall, white officer who wore a wrinkled dress shirt and brown slacks. He also possessed a gold shield, however, his badge was on a chain that hung from his neck.

Najee didn't have to travel far, he was already standing at the bars. "I'm Mr. Madlock," he repeated the alias, relieved that the national database had not returned his government name.

"Place both of your hands through the bars. I gotta cuff ya before we take a walk-n-talk."

Najee extended his hands to allow the Detective to place handcuffs on his wrists. As he did so, the black detective continued to speak. "I'm detective Donald Smith, Atlanta Police Department. My colleague here is, Special Agent John Walker, FBI." He pointed to his partner. Najee nodded his head to acknowledge both of them but remained silent. "Open Five-A" Everyone stood back while the electronic doors slowly slid open.

Once Najee stepped out, master control immediately closed the bars. They escorted him to a sterile interrogation room and uncuffed him. Unlike the movies, there was no two-way mirror or light bulb swinging from the ceiling.

"Cigarette?" Detective Smith offered while lighting a Newport 100 for himself. He inhaled deeply, then blew the smoke at Najee.

170

"No thanks."

"Coffee?"

"I'll pass."

"Well, how 'bout I read you your rights?"

"That won't be necessary, I already know my rights. Miranda vs. Arizona, besides, I have nothing to say."

Detective Smith leaned back in his chair and folded his arms over his big belly. Agent Walker shifted on his feet. Both of them were irritated and had no time for games.

Agent Walker walked over and sat next to his black partner. He placed a thick manila folder on the table and pushed it toward Najee. "Look, I'm gonna level with you," Agent Walker stated while chewing a stick of Double Mint gum. "We know exactly who you are. Intelligence ran your prints through AFIS. They came back thirty minutes ago."

Najee sat still and kept his facial expression blank, however, his mind was moving a mile per minute. *"I'm sure I can beat whatever charges they throw at me. Just remain calm and keep a poker face,"* he told himself.

"Look, you can play the tough guy role all you want, smart ass. We're here to help you help yourself," Agent Walker reasoned. "You're facing a lot of time."

Najee laughed in their faces. "This good cop, bad cop routine won't work with me."

"Who said anything about being good cops?" Detective Smith countered. "We're both as bad as they come." He meant every word.

Agent Walker opened the manila file sitting in front of him as if it was Pandora's box. He pushed several incriminating photographs, invoices and official documents across the table. A condescending smile formed on his lips.

"The shootout tonight on Peachtree is the least of your worries, Mr. Howard." He pronounced Najee's real last name slow and deliberate. "We figure you and your boys tried to rob Sosa at the club and all hell broke loose. That's what you and your crew do right, rob drug dealers?" he insisted with a smug look.

171

Although the temperature in the interrogation room dropped a few degrees, Najee felt beads of sweat forming on his forehead. He did his best to remain calm, cool and collective while the gears in his head worked overtime.

Agent Walker pushed the crime scene photos towards Najee. Even in black and white, the brutal slayings looked gruesome. "Here's what we have so far," he hinted while tapping his trigger finger on a picture of a lifeless body. "Major drug dealers are popping up dead everywhere. Two of Supreme McGriff's guys in upstate New York, three men connected to Vicki Stringer's old crew in Ohio, a couple of Haitians in Miami, four bodies found in a Blues club on Beale Street in Memphis, and most recently, two of Alonzo 'Benzo Al' Guzman's drug carriers murdered in cold blood at a Los Cinco Diablos stash house in Escondido, California." He fanned the photographs out. "What do all of these crime scenes have in common? You!" he answered his own question.

"Me?" Najee asked innocently as possible. "How in the hell does a few dead scum bags involve me?"

"From what Mario Delgado tells us, everything!"

"I don't know anybody named, Mario." He didn't sound convincing.

"Sure, you do! Here are the two of you leaving Roscoe's Chicken and Waffles in Los Angeles." Agent Walker passed Najee an 8x19 surveillance photo. "And here are the two of you at a construction site in Wisconsin."

Najee was holding a picture of him and his best friend Rio standing at the groundbreaking ceremony for the Alive365 community center located on the north side of Milwaukee. The picture was only two weeks old. Anger swelled up in his heart, however, he was not going to take a pig's word over the bond he and Rio shared. Sure, Rio had been asking a lot of unusual questions lately and had been spending more time away from the crew, yet his allegiance was unparalleled.

Detective Smith lit another cigarette and poured himself a second cup of coffee before he jumped back in. "I know it's hard to believe that someone so close to you is a snitch, but it's true! I see this type of shit all the time in my line of work." He blew a smoke ring in Najee's direction.

Najee watched the cancer cloud float to the ceiling. It was symbolic in a way. Everything was going up in smoke. "All you have is a bunch of pics and a theory," Najee stated frankly. "There's no physical evidence connecting me to any crime!"

"True, but the circumstantial evidence is just as damaging." Detective Smith took a drag on his Newport. "Two bodies pop up in Jamaica Queens. A lot of half-burnt drugs found but no cash. Same thing in Columbus, Miami, and Memphis, a lot of coke and blood but no loot. Tell me what's wrong with that picture?"

Najee shrugged his shoulders. Experience taught him that it's best to keep your jaws clenched and your ears open. Anything you say can and most definitely will be used against you.

Detective Smith continued, "I'll tell ya what's wrong, after each of these brutal slayings, a substantial amount of cash would be deposited into the accounts of a non-profit organization called, Alive365. The money would then be funneled to a construction company called Wright Way Industrial. We know that Wright Way Industrial is a shell company owned by Demetrius Wright, another one of your aliases."

He paused to let the information sink in while stubbing his cigarette out on the table. Both law enforcement officers were confident that they had Najee where they needed him. Special Agent John Walker decided to put the nail in the coffin. He took a sip of strong black coffee before speaking.

"Mario Delgado has been making deals behind your back. Instead of leaving the cocaine behind like you reportedly instruct your crew members to do, he stashes three or four kilos and makes an extra 80 to 100 G's on the side. Pocket change in comparison to the amounts you're getting from these dead high rollers, but at least he doesn't have to split it six ways. Greed is the root of all evil and the beginning of the end."

Najee put on his poker face. "I still don't see what any of this has to do with me." He wanted to know how well the dots were connecting.

"It has everything to do with you. Mr. Delgado sold three kilos to an informant while the two of you were in Milwaukee. He was set up. The DEA followed him from the 618 Night club on Water Street to a stash house on 54th and Burleigh. From there, they trailed him a few short blocks to Sherman Park where the exchange was made. When we took him down, he had sixty-thousand dollars in marked bills and a stolen firearm equipped with a silencer. He was facing a mandatory minimum of twenty years. He buckled under pressure and agreed to debrief his involvement in several homicides in exchange for immunity."

The incriminating information was damaging, but something wasn't adding up. *"Why are they willing to divulge all of this confidential evidence?"* Najee questioned himself. He decided to probe the two for as much 411 as possible. "So, why hasn't the U.S. Attorney presented this testimony before a grand jury and sought a Rico indictment against me?" Najee probed.

"Because we want in!" Detective Smith stated bluntly. "I don't give a shit if Sosa rots in prison or rots in hell. We have been trying to build a case against that bastard for several years, yet he always manages to slip through our grip." He lit another Newport and let it dangle from the corner of his mouth as he continued to speak. "I'm tired of watching assholes like that live like kings while my alimony and child support payments drain me dry. And why did my wife leave me in the first place?" he asked while flicking his ashes on the floor.

"I'll tell ya why! Because all day I'm filling out affidavits, and all night I'm stuck in a cramped surveillance van with a pair of binoculars watching these fuckin' drug dealers cook crack and crack lobsters. And what do I get out of it?" He hit the Newport, took a sip of coffee, and answered his own rhetorical question. "I'll tell ya what, nothing! Unless you count a nagging ex-wife, high blood pressure, and a son who's a lazy piece of shit."

Detective Smith went on a tyrant for another five minutes before Special Agent Walker interrupted him. It was clear that both officers were as crooked as Don King's afro. A modest salary and a handsome pension following retirement would not accommodate their greed. They wanted more and were willing to abuse the authority of their badges to accomplish that objective.

Agent Walker stood up and motioned with his hands for his partner to be calm. He then looked Najee directly in the eyes. "You have two choices. One, we torture a confession out of your black ass and you spend the rest of your life mopping floors in federal prison. Or, you get that gang of bandits you control to rob Sosa for us. If his head happens to get blown off in the process, that's a bonus!"

Najee was caught off guard. Two veteran law enforcement officers who were sworn to protect the public were attempting to blackmail him into robbing and killing another man. Greed truly was the beginning of the end.

He sat back and contemplated their clandestine offer. The Feds obviously did not know his true intentions. It was not his lifelong mission to rid the world of drug dealers. Sosa was merely a step up the ladder toward the ruthless kingpin responsible for the senseless slaughter of his loved ones. The killings so far were done out of necessity; however, after witnessing Nella get abducted and cradling Yung Zay's lifeless body in his arms, a murderous fluid pumped in his veins. More bloodshed was on the menu.

Despite an insatiable thirst for revenge, he wasn't going to allow two crooked pigs to pull his strings like a puppet, no way. A smile crept across Najee's lips as he formulated a plan. "I'm all in!" he agreed with a mischievous grin.

Najee was transferred to another holding tank. This bullpen was designed similar to cellblock 5-A except there were two phones mounted to the wall, and it did not have the stench of urine. Several men were sitting across a wooden bench. Each prisoner was suspended in solemn silence swimming within their own pools of misery. A drunken wino snored peacefully in a corner.

Najee went directly to the first available phone. Even at this late hour, he was confident he could reach his lawyer. He made the collect call and after waiting patiently for the computerized voice to warn him that all calls may be monitored and recorded, he was connected to his Jewish attorney.

Larry D. Wright

"About time you called!" a gruff voice said through the receiver.

"I apologize for calling at such an inconvenient hour, Mr. Meyers, but it's an emergency," Najee stated.

"No problem, sir. In my line of business, sleep is a delicacy."

"Have you heard about what happened?"

"Yes, Juice sent me a text. You have my condolences. Yung Zay was a brave and loyal young man," he expressed with sympathy.

"Make the arrangements for the funeral, and make sure his family is straight as well, spare no detail."

"Done!" he assured his client. "How are you holding up?" Both men were well aware that the phone call was being closely monitored. They finished the conversation using prearranged code talk.

"I'm okay, however, Rio is very ill. I need someone to take him some medicine as soon as possible," Translation: *I'm okay, however, one of my crew members is out of line. I need some goons to teach him a lesson ASAP.*

"How serious is the sickness?"

"He has an incurable case of cancer and is in a lot of pain. He's tossing and turning in his bed." Translation: *I can't forgive him for this. I want him to feel a lot of pain. He flipped on me and is in bed with the Feds.*

"I understand," Mr. Meyers confirmed after a brief moment of reflection. He cleared his throat, then asked, "Who shall I send?"

"The Somalis!" Najee said coldly. The line went dead. No translation was needed!

Detective Smith and Agent Walker listened to the short phone call between Najee and his lawyer. When the line went dead, they looked at each other puzzled. They could not decipher the hidden message embedded within the conversation.

"What do you think that was all about?" Agent Walker asked.

"I don't know, but we're gonna find out." Detective Smith pressed the rewind button to replay the digital recording. They listened to the conversation again, determined to break the code.

176

CHAPTER 18

Military Minds

Rio, Juice, and Maceo posted up at the Hilton Hotel. A breaking news segment abruptly interrupted the late-night movie marathon on NBC. Their eyes became glued to the flat screen as the news reporter chronicled the events of the chaotic evening. Images of the bullet-riddled police car and the mangled Knight XV flipped on its side filled the 60-inch flat-screen.

The police spokesman declined to give a comment, other than stating that this was an ongoing investigation, and the city of Atlanta's hearts go out to the victims and their families. The anchorman concluded by informing the viewers that one suspect was in custody and provided a 1-800 number for those who were foolish enough to provide additional information.

Maceo turned off the television and threw the remote out of anger. "I can't believe this shit!" he grumbled as the device smashed against the wall. He couldn't phantom the thought of losing both his best friend and his mentor on the same night. To add salt to his open wounds, Nella was still missing. "Why we sittin' around? We should be out there bending corners." Maceo preached to no one in particular.

"I just texted Christopher Meyers, the attorney," Juice informed while picking up the pieces to the broken remote. "He will handle everything on the legal side. I will call Yung Zay's mother and baby momma as soon as I get my head right. I'm fucked up."

The crew members were obviously in pain. Losing Yung Zay in such a tragic way was like losing a limb. They were all parts of the same body. When the foot hurts, so does the hand.

"Maceo is right, we need to be making them streets bleed." Rio was anxious to make a move. "There's nothing we can do for Najee. So, let's focus on getting Nella. We find her, we find the cowards responsible for Yung Zay's death."

A thought popped in Juice's mind. "Yo', Maceo, are those communication devices equipped with GPS?"

"I don't think so, dawg," Maceo replied and passed the doja to Rio.

"Why, what did you have in mind?" Rio asked curiously, took a puff, and passed the loud to Juice.

"I was thinking we could track her movements through the device," Juice responded and flicked the ashes off the blunt.

Maceo's eyes lit up. "You might be on to something. The communication pieces may not contain a GPS locator, but it may be possible to track her iPhone."

Rio scratched his head. "How can we do that?"

"Cell phones continuously communicate with the towers of their service providers. We can locate her up to a one-block radius by triangulating the longitude and latitude of the cell tower her phone is bouncing a signal off of."

"Can you repeat that in English?" Rio asked with a confused look on his face. He was not computer savvy.

Maceo removed his Android phone from the leather case attached to his belt. He tapped on the touch screen, and the colorful menu icons appeared. "See these four bars right here?" He pointed to the upper right-hand corner of the screen. "Well, these little bars indicate signal strength. My cell phone provider has a tower somewhere in the vicinity. If I was to use my phone, they could tell exactly where the call originated."

"I highly doubt that a group of kidnappers would allow her to make a phone call," Juice pointed out.

"She doesn't necessarily have to make a call," Maceo replied. "Law enforcement has been tracking criminals like this for years. Most people think that if you turn off your cell phone, you're safe. However, even if the device is powered down, the signal is still being beamed to the nearest tower. You have to remove the battery completely in order to disable the signal locator." He accepted the blunt from Juice, took two deep hits, and then passed the bud back to Rio.

"I'm confused, but fuck it, time is running out. We need to get you in front of a computer and find some wheels quick," Rio suggested and stubbed the weed out in an ashtray.

The Hilton Hotel was equipped with a mobile business center that was reserved especially for their executive clientele. Located on the first level conveniently adjacent to the conference rooms, the business center was equipped with all the latest amenities a traveling CEO needed, including a computer with internet access.

The night clerk glared at the trio of men suspiciously as Maceo swiped his key card to gain entrance into the privileged area.

"We're just putting some finishing touches on a presentation that's due tomorrow," Rio assured the desk clerk with an awkward smile. The last thing they wanted to do was raise eyebrows. The nosey clerk responded with a phony smile of his own.

Once inside the room, Maceo went directly to the nearest computer workstation. He quickly typed in the room number and the fake name the suite was registered in. On the next screen, he was prompted to enter a credit card number.

"You gotta be fucking kiddin' me?" Juice began to rant. "As much as they charge per night. You would think they would at least throw in some free internet service?"

Maceo ignored his complaint and remained focused on the task. He punched in a sixteen-digit Visa number that was popular among the hacker community and was granted instant access. From the desktop, he pulled up a command prompt and typed in the IP address to a primary domain name controller belonging to a company named Telligent GPS Systems. He was prompted once again to supply a username and password.

Maceo quickly typed the name of the CEO's family pet and his daughter's birth date. He was granted full administrative privileges. It never seemed to amaze him how easy it was to penetrate even the most sophisticated networks using the simplest methods. Most computer users are burdened with the task of having to memorize multiple passwords, so they typically use phrases and numbers that are easy to remember. This lack of security made it easier for hackers.

Maceo expertly navigated through the maze of files until he located the program he was looking for. He doubled clicked a file marked SatelliteProg.exe to launch the company's global

179

positioning satellite software. A few more taps on the keyboard and he was at the screen he desired.

"We're in!" Maceo announced proudly then blew his fingertips as if they were smoking pistols.

He typed in Nella's area code and phone number and pressed the enter key. Rio and Juice eagerly watched over Maceo's shoulder as an outline of a map generated on the computer monitor. Once completed, Maceo jotted down the X and Y coordinates of the cell phone tower Nella's iPhone was recently near.

"Man, all I see is a bunch of numbers! How do we find a physical location using that information?" Juice asked with confusion in his voice.

"First off, stop breathing on the back of my neck, your breath is hot," Maceo joked, trying to ease the tension in the room. "Secondly, watch the master work his magic."

Maceo logged onto Google Maps and typed in the longitude and latitude as search criteria. When the web browser refreshed, they were presented with an aerial view of the warehouse district in Bankhead.

"I'm familiar with this area, I used to have a third shift gig as a forklift driver in one of those factories," Juice stated while pointing to the monitor. "There are at least twenty large warehouses in this radius. They could be holding Nella in any one of them." Disappointment settled in.

Maceo quickly typed on the keyboard with expert precision. After browsing several websites, he opened Microsoft Excel and formatted a spreadsheet. He then copied and pasted bits of information from two of the websites onto the spreadsheet. Once satisfied, he used the search and compare feature to filter out any unneeded data. The results of the query yielded two addresses, both on Howell Mill Road.

"Bingo!" Maceo pointed at the monitor.

"What's the business, did you find anything?" Rio asked.

"I was able to narrow down our search area by cross-referencing city hall records with the Georgia Power Company to see which of these factories is shut down but still using a modest amount of electricity. I came up with two locations on the same street!" They printed a copy of the map and the results from the Excel spreadsheet.

Maceo was the first to make it outside. He quickly scanned the area for police cars. As his eyes expertly swept back and forth, a black Cadillac Escalade sitting on 26-inch Forgis recklessly swerved up in front of the hotel. The driver was obviously drunk. He slid from behind the wood grain steering wheel and balanced himself before wobbling around the vehicle to open the door for his beautiful passenger.

'*Chivalry isn't dead after all,*' Maceo thought to himself. The white female passenger was pissy drunk as well.

When the door swung open, so did her legs. She was not wearing any panties. The night air caressed her shaved pussy. Giggling like a bimbo, she pulled down her tight-fitting mini skirt to cover her goodies. She stumbled from the Escalade, breaking the heel of her $2,700 red bottom Christian Louboutin shoes in the process.

The man finally noticed Maceo standing in front of the glass entrance of the hotel. "Good evening, son!" he slurred in a drunken Southern drawl and extended his right hand.

Maceo politely extended his arm as well. He thought the man wanted to shake his hand, but the arrogant drunk slapped his car keys into Maceo's palm instead, mistaking him for the valet parking attendant.

"Make sure you take good care of my baby," the vehicle owner ordered as he dug into his pocket and peeled a crisp $20 off his gold money clip.

"Thanks, I guess!" Maceo replied with a mischievous grin. The issue of transportation was solved.

Maceo was waiting behind the wheel of the luxury SUV when Juice and Rio made their exit. He rolled down one of the dark tinted windows and waved for them to get in.

"On my word, how did you come up with this, B?" Juice asked. He was surprised to see the keys jingling in the ignition.

"I told you I had magic, my nigga!"

Rio jumped in the backseat. Juice rode shotgun and punched one of the addresses located on Howell Mill Road into the in-dash GPS. Each man drifted deep into his own thoughts as the computerized voice guided them into their next battle.

****

Inside the warehouse, Prince slammed the heavy metal door and slid the deadbolt in place to secure the entrance. He was anxious to get out of the dank smelling abandoned building. A goon named Low Down had been purposely locked inside to keep a close eye on Nella. Prince turned toward the two goons in order to give them specific instructions.

"K-Roc, I want you to guard the door. Nobody comes or goes without my permission. You got that?" Prince asked firmly.

"Yeah, I got it covered boss, nobody comes or goes without checking with you first," K-Roc repeated with confidence.

Prince turned to face, Mac the driver of the cargo van. Out of all of his comrades, he trusted Mac the most. "I need you to post up on the first floor. Stay on point and blast anything that looks suspicious. If my feelings are correct, we haven't heard the last from her friends," he warned.

"I got you covered, you can count on me," Mac said reassuringly.

Once outside, Prince lifted his sleeve to check his Breitling watch. The time was 3:00 a.m. To the colorful figures of the underworld, it was still early. The night had just begun. Prince believed that when you're awake, you should be hustling, and when you're asleep, you're on call. Despite his own philosophy, he let out a long yawn. Today had been a long day. He reached into his coat pocket and pulled out a small glass capsule.

After twisting the yellow cap open, he dabbed some of the crystal white contents on the back of his hand. Like an expert, he sniffed an equal amount into each nostril. The cocaine exploded in his brain, sending tingling sparks of euphoric ecstasy throughout his body. Now he was alive, now he was the man. He felt invincible!

182

Seconds later, a small rat scattered from its hiding place and found refuge under a pile of old cardboard. Prince got spooked from the noise and damn near jumped out of his skin. When he noticed that it was only a small rodent, he let out a nervous laugh.

"Muthafucka' you blew my high!" Prince blamed the rat for increasing his paranoia.

He removed the capsule again and tooted another jab of blow. He licked the residue off the back of his hand and used moisture to wipe any traces of coke left on the tip of his nose. His features changed immediately. The whites of his eyes got as big as two hard-boiled eggs, and his mouth became dry as cotton, he was high.

Prince chirped the alarm and the automatic start to his jet-black Bentley GT. He stood back a few feet, just in case the car exploded. '*I watch way too many gangsta flicks,*' he thought to himself. The combination of potent drugs frying his brains and the shiesty deeds he had done to others in his past, caused him to become constantly paranoid. Better safe than sorry was his mantra.

Satisfied that there was not a bomb under his car, Prince laid his head back on the soft butterscotch leather headrest. He needed to collect his thoughts before calling Sosa. Even though he was not involved or had a clue about how the fight at the club jumped off, there was no doubt in his mind that Sosa was going to blame him for the confrontation that ruined the extravagant birthday bash.

No matter how hard he tried, he just couldn't please Sosa. As he scrolled through the contact list on his prepaid cell phone, he contemplated telling Sosa about Nella and the devious plot hatched against him. He highlighted Sosa's name and pressed the call button. While the phone rang, a clever thought came to his mind. His decision would kill two birds with one stone and make him seem like a hero.

He decided to tell Sosa that the Body Snatchers attempted to rob them at the club, but he fucked up their plans and a fight and gun battle ensued. He would deliberately leave out the parts about abducting Nella. He had other plans for her.

Sosa's line rang several times, then rolled to voicemail. "Aww, shit, answer the phone player!" He hung up and hit him back, but once again, he was prompted to leave a message at the sound of the beep. "I know damn well this nigga see me calling! He probably somewhere tricking off."

He placed the Bentley in drive and smashed off. The low-profile Pirelli tires left their imprint on the asphalt. In his hast to leave, Prince did not notice the black Escalade pull up and park down the street.

****

A few miles outside of Atlanta, several luxury cars lined the quiet suburban streets on Glenridge Lane. Behind the tall iron gates of a large, tri-story mansion, the after-party was in full effect. The lower level boasted a twenty seat movie theater. The hood classic *State Property* played on the huge screen as several sexy women and a hand full of thuggish looking young men passed around thick Garcia Vegas stuffed with lime green doja.

The professional size pool table was black instead of the traditional green. There was a large white BBE logo in the center. All the pool balls were black as well with the words, Block Boy Empire stamped in green. A small group of half-naked women lingered around the pool table admiring the two players who were betting ten stacks per game.

Upstairs inside the marble-floored master bathroom, Sosa soaked in his large Jacuzzi filled with bubbles. He took a long hard puff of a neatly rolled grape Swisher Sweet blunt and blew a ring of thick grey smoke into the air. The room was suddenly filled with the herbal aroma of Kush.

The triple stack he popped earlier had him feeling amped up and horny. The high-quality weed rushing to his temples made him feel mellow and relaxed. The slits of his eyes were so low, he looked Chinese. He felt great!

A call from Prince temporarily interrupted his bliss. He deliberately ignored the call and took another pull on the blunt. He held the smoke in his lungs for an extra second or two before blowing out the smoke. He hacked and coughed for a moment. He was smoking good ganja!

He became irritated when the phone rang again. "Damn, this nigga sho' know how to fuck up a wet dream!"

The phone kept ringing, this time interrupting Sosa's exotic looking sex partner while she was underwater sucking his rock hard dick. When she came up for air, her shoulder-length wet hair made her look like an Egyptian goddess, water dripped from her perky brown nipples.

She wiped her juicy lips with the back of her hand and said, "Turn your phone off, Papi. I can't concentrate," her foreign accent added to her sex appeal.

Sosa ignored the request and roughly pushed her head back under the water. She was starting to get on his nerves. Not because she wasn't attractive or didn't fulfill his every desire, but he just didn't trust her kind. In his world, beautiful faces and firm handshakes camouflaged ugly agendas. For that reason, he had *Trust No Bitch* tatted over his left eyebrow and *Trust No Man* tatted over the right.

It was getting harder and harder for Sosa to trust those around him. Lately, he found himself looking at each of his workers with scrutiny. He studied their movements to see if their eyes revealed any signs of betrayal. So far, he had come up with nothing, he knew from experience that a person's handshake doesn't always match their smile. He was determined to stay on his square and stay alert.

The Egyptian goddess came up again to fill her lungs with air, then plunged back underwater. She sucked his 11-inch dick with no hands, expertly massaging his stiff pole with her luscious lips and warm tongue. She deep-throated him as far as her mouth would go. She gagged and her eyes watered as the mushroom-shaped head pressed against her tonsils. Her motivation was the designer leather bag and matching heels she saw on display at the Gucci boutique in the mall. She could care less about whose dick she had in her mouth. All ballers were tricks in her opinion.

Sosa tried his hardest to concentrate on the bomb head he was receiving, but his mind kept drifting back to Prince. "Maybe he had something important to tell me?" he second-guessed himself, regretting not answering the call. He quickly pushed the guilt to far junctions of his mind and frowned. "If Prince had something important to report, he would be here with the rest of the empire and not somewhere trickin' off," he reasoned.

He thought back to the bad yellow bitch he saw Prince mackin' to at the club right before the fight broke out and wondered who she was. He had to admit that Prince had mad game. He was capable of getting any woman he wanted with his slick mouthpiece. Sosa had the handsome looks, however, he wished he possessed the natural charm and self-confidence that Prince displayed.

Sosa was good at trappin', not mackin'! The streets were his stage, and every time he performed, the block gave him a standing ovation. Yet under all the designer name tags, foreign cars, and sparkling jewelry, he was shy. Even as a youth coming up in the game, his palms would sweat, and he would stutter while introducing himself to the opposite sex. After his heart became callous from the constant rejection, he adopted the hustler's creed: *Money Over Bitches*! Every night he would hit up Magic City and rain thousands of dollars on stage causing the women to trip over their thongs trying to get next to him. '*Who needed small talk anyhow,*' he rationalized.

A few crisp big faces stuffed inside a stripper's thong was all the conversation he needed. Nowadays, he saw more pussy than a gynecologist. However, he would never be able to muster up the courage to approach a sexy thoroughbred stallion like the one Prince was caking to at the bar. Just thinking about the way her tight leather shorts hugged her ass and showed off her phat monkey made his manhood grow harder. The warm mouth engulfing his long thick pole worked overtime in a zealous attempt to coax his edible fluid to the tip. Just as he was about to cum, his phone rang.

"Damn!" he lost his concentration, lost his erection, lost his high! He snatched up the burner cell phone without looking at the caller ID and barked his displeasure into the receiver. "Damn, Prince, can't you see ah nigga busy? Shit, mane!"

"Mira tu tono de Vos, amigo! Watch your tone of voice, my friend," the voice on the other end cautioned in a thick Mexican accent.

Sosa sat up straight in the Jacuzzi and put his finger to his lips, silently telling the Egyptian goddess to shush.

"What's wrong baby, don't you want me to finish?" She rubbed his broad shoulders and chest affectionately.

He covered the phone with his hand and spoke in a low voice. "Give me a little privacy, bae, I gotta take this call."

"But baby, I—"

Sosa cut her off. "Not now, this is business!" he warned and swatted her away like a fly.

Becoming angry, she splashed bubbles everywhere as she got out of the Jacuzzi with an attitude. She stormed out of the bathroom dripping wet and slammed the door. Sosa made sure she was gone before he spoke into the phone.

"Benzo Al, what's good, poppy?" Sosa asked with respect.

He really admired how the fat Mexican handled business. It was Benzo Al who saw something unique in Sosa amongst an overcrowded pool of street hustlers. Against his better judgment, Benzo Al took Sosa under his wing and opened the flood gates of cocaine to his exposure. Now he was one of Benzo Al's most profitable apprentices. The calculated risk the cartel boss took in the beginning had now transformed into a lucrative investment.

"Feliz cumpleaños!" he wished Sosa a happy birthday in Spanish.

Sosa smiled, "Gracias, señor!" He had picked up a few words of Español while spending time with his connect in East L.A.

"I don't like phones, so I'm gonna get straight to the point, estás muy caliente. You're too hot. In this business, we move in silence, not arrive at parties in helicopters, entiendes? Do I make myself clear?"

Sosa was surprised at how fast news traveled on the streets. He knew that his plug wouldn't approve of the extravagant birthday bash, but his desire to do it big overruled his common sense.

"How did the fight break out?" Benzo Al asked.

"It wasn't my people. As soon as the fist and bottles started flying, we moved around," Sosa answered honestly.

"Keep a low profile and your ear to the streets. I was informed that an officer got murked during a high-speed chase with some of your partygoers, so expect the policiá to have a lot of questions. Ones you need to be prepared to answer."

Sosa did not like being lectured or chastised. He decided to change the subject. "I got things covered on this end, don't worry about me. Worry about those jack boys who have been sticking up yo' spots!" He intentionally tried to strike a nerve.

"The penalty for crossing me is death! Their graves are already dug!" the connect replied with mayhem in his voice.

"So, are we still on?" Sosa inquired, referring to the next large shipment of cocaine.

"Of course, amigo! Same time, same place, same price!" He hung up without waiting for a reply.

Sosa was about to say something else into the phone but wisely decided against it. Now was not the time to ask for a lower price. After all, he was only paying $12,000 per brick of Grade A, uncut cocoa with the Cinco Diablo's seal on the wrapper. He could step on their dope with ProCentra or Inositol and still have a more superior product than his competitors.

Every week, a late model Toyota Camry would be parked at the Kroger grocery store. The door would be unlocked and the ignition key under the floor mat. One hundred keys of compressed cocaine, equivalent to a life sentence in the Feds, would be tucked in hidden compartments throughout the vehicle. In the same parking lot, there would be another nondescript rental car with the door unlocked and a single ignition key under the floor mat. $1.2 million dollars with the faces of deceased presidents would be secured in a stash box hidden under the removable backseats.

Shooters would be nearby, but neither Sosa nor Benzo Al would be present to personally swap it out. That task was reserved for their most trusted and loyal runners. This set up isolated the two bosses from the scrutiny of the law.

188

The Streets Made Me

On the surface, the gears of their well-oiled operation had been churning smoothly for years. However, Sosa sensed that the walls were bound to collapse soon. He took another puff from his blunt and exhaled the smoke. For the first time in his criminal career, he contemplated getting out of the game, taking the money he had stashed, and squaring up.

Maybe being a year older and a year wiser caused him to think this way, or maybe it was the Cali weed and molly making him emotional. Either way, he was finally realizing the consequences and dangerous risks associated with the life he was living.

As he soaked in the Jacuzzi philosophizing with himself, there was a soft knock on the door. "Sosa are you coming to bed, baby?" the sexy voice on the other side asked.

Sosa rolled his eyes and exhaled a long groan. Ughh! He was trying to relax and she was fucking up the vibe. He stepped out of the Jacuzzi butt naked and grabbed his silk Hugh Hefner robe. When he opened the door, his frown instantly became a big Kool-Aid smile. The Egyptian goddess was waiting in the archway rubbing her clit. An equally beautiful and thick stallion sucked on the Egyptian goddess' erect nipples. Sosa recalled seeing the chocolate-flavored hostess serving champagne at the club.

His manhood came alive under his robe. The new chick noticed first and reached for his penis. She gripped him in her hand and dragged him to the king-size bed by his dick. All thoughts of leaving the game evaporated from his head. He chuckled to himself and laughed at how foolish he was for even considering retiring.

This was the life for him. As the two females gave his entire body a tongue massage, he yelled out, "I'ma ball 'till I fall!"

The Egyptian goddess cupped his cum filled balls in her hand while her luscious lips slurped noisily on his throbbing pole. Her ass was in the air, giving the chocolate-colored hostess full access to her pink vagina. She used her fingers to spread open those puffy pussy lips and then buried her face deep in the Egyptian goddess' shaved cunt. She licked her pussy from the back like she was at a pie-eating contest, making sure her tongue devoured all of the cream filling. Sosa took turns laying pipe to both of them all night, bringing them to the highest point of sexual excitement.

CHAPTER 19

Streets on Lock

Najee paced back and forth inside the cramped holding cell located inside the 1st District police station. A shadow of concern cloaked his handsome facial features. His mind was focused on all the events that had recently occurred. Just hours ago, he was in the comfort of his high-tech headquarters in Santa Monica, and in the company of his handpicked crew. A sudden thought of regret rushed through his heart as he recalled the bright smile on Yung Zay's face as the youngest member of the clique chose the Lambo to be his whip for the day when they arrived in Atlanta.

Killing those responsible for his untimely death was going to be a pleasure, in order to get the revenge he desired he needed to locate Nella first. Another surge of pain shot through the core of his heart. He tried everything in his power to conceal his feelings for her, but the radiant smile on his lips when she was around betrayed his efforts. Now he wished he had never put her in the line of fire.

He stopped pacing for a moment to observe two black youths sitting close together on the bench. They looked familiar. Their heads hung low and their self-esteem looked deflated. They reminded him of himself at that age. He was young, defiant, mad at the world, and possessed a steel exterior, but on the inside, he was vulnerable and subjected to be another sad statistic of the ghetto. The callous surface was just a disguise to obscure the truth.

The reason he started Alive365 was to help marginalized African-Americans like them avoid the traps and pitfalls of the system. Najee decided to give the young men some encouragement, but before he could approach the two young men and kick some knowledge.

One of them spoke first. "What tha' fuck you looking at, nigga?" the taller of the two young thugs demanded. Both of them jumped to their feet with their fists clenched. Years of struggling in the ghetto taught them to protect and depend on each other for survival. They were more like Najee than he realized.

191

For instance, Najee's concern boiled into anger. He didn't like the way the youngster disrespected him. He could have easily broken his spine, however, the curriculum of his non-profit organization taught men to resolve conflict in a non-violent manner whenever possible. Najee realized that he was not perfect and that his own life was full of contradictions, yet he had a strong desire to give back to the communities that he gained so much from. He decided to let the comment slide.

"My bad, lil' homie, you just look familiar. What do they call you?" he asked, easing the tension.

"My name is, Jezz, and this is my little brother Dee," the taller and older one stated.

Najee instantly recognized their names. "I knew y'all looked familiar. I know your pops. His name is Blue, right? He used to show me your pictures and talk about y'all all the time!"

Both of them had big ears like their father, but that's where the physical similarities ended. You could tell they shared the same struggles but had different mothers.

"For real?" the younger and slightly shorter youth named Dee asked with excitement. "Where you know my dad from?"

"Me and him use to—"

"We ain't got no daddy!" Jezz interrupted. You could hear the hurt and bitterness in his voice. "Fuck that nigga! He ran out on me and momz when I was just a baby. I barely even know him!"

"Maybe he had a good reason," Dee came to his father's defense.

"Don't take up for that nigga, ain't no excuse. Besides, he did the same thing to your momz, too!" Jezz pointed out. Dee nodded his head in disagreement.

Blue started out as the father of the year. The undeniable love for his seeds was clearly evident, but like many black men, somewhere along the line, he lost his way. The hard knock life and the long corridors of state prison ate away years like locust, leaving behind generations of fatherless children. Najee couldn't judge Blue nor make excuses for him either, but he could help these young men avoid taking the same destructive path.

"This penal system—" Najee took in the dismal holding tank and made a sweeping gesture with his hands. "—stole you father away from you."

Jezz immediately smacked his lips in skepticism. "The system? You tryna blame his absence on the white man?"

Najee sat between the two hardened young men. "Nah, of course not! Every man is responsible for his own actions, but empirical research shows that there are a number of socioeconomic issues that affect impoverished, inner-city communities and that puts black men like you, me and your pops at a disadvantage."

Dee interrupted Najee's spill. "Hold up a second, big homie. What the fuck does empirical mean?"

"Empirical means based on observation, not on theory. For instance, you can go into any hood from Watts to the Bronx and observe the faces of disadvantages, fatherless children. Shorties without a positive role model in the home are five times more likely to live in poverty compared to kids raised by two parents. Fatherless children also report higher rates of physical abuse, delinquency, teenage pregnancy, and drug abuse—" He paused to let the data from the U.S. Department of Health and Human Services marinate. Jezz and Dee clung to every syllable as Najee continued kicking knowledge. "Fatherless children are twice likely to drop out of high school, become under or unemployed and ultimately resort to a life of crime. With all that against them, it's not surprising that fatherless shorties also have higher rates of incarceration. Think about it, the joint is packed with brothas who grew up without a father figure.

Jezz stood up and leaned against the bars. "That's deep, but even if all that is true, just because you grew up without a father doesn't necessarily mean that failure and jail is your destiny."

"That's true," Najee agreed. "There are numerous resilient single black women who raise successful black men, but that ain't the reality for niggas like you and me, is it? Your dad spent the majority of his youth in and out of prison, and from the looks of it, y'all are perpetuating the same cycle and headed down the same destructive path."

The truthfulness of his ominous words punched Jezz and Dee in the gut. They were in and out of the Fulton County Jail.

Jezz returned to the concrete bench as Dee asked. "How do you know all those numbers? Are you one of those conscious niggas?"

Najee chuckled. "I'm woke, but I chase that bag. So, I'm far from a poor righteous teacher. I read a lot while I was in the joint. A cold book called *The New Jim Crow* by this sista named *Michelle Alexander* opened my third eye to a lot of shit. *The 48 Laws of Power* also a must-read if you want to play the game of life and win."

The young men were like birds picking up seeds as they absorbed the supreme lessons.

Time ticked by as the three men held a cipher in the holding tank. The conversation reminded Najee of a scene from the movie *Belly* where the rapper *Nas* was kicking game to a young thug while they sat on a project bench.

It was against protocol to ask another prisoner what they were in jail for, however, Najee asked anyhow. "I'm not tryna' get all up in your business or nothin' like that, but I was wondering what charges are they holding y'all on? I might be able to help."

The two men eyed Najee suspiciously. It wasn't too often that a stranger was eager to help them, but there was something authentic about Najee's swag and street cred that made him trustworthy.

Dee smiled as he boasted about their arrest. "Those punk-ass bouncers wouldn't let us in the club. They sweated us because of our dress code or whatever. So, we tore that muthafucka' up!" He high fived his partner in crime and they both laughed.

Najee was jolted back into reality. Speaking with the two young men allowed him to temporarily escape his worries, but the mention of an incident at a club caused his mind to race with curiosity. He needed to know more.

"What was the name of the club?"

"It's a new spot called, iCandy," Dee answered. "Some ballin' ass nigga was throwing his birthday party there, and security was trippin'."

The pieces of the puzzle quickly came together. Najee was grateful for the encounter. The world was small indeed. "The party was for, Sosa. I know you heard of him?"

"Yeah, he's the man down here. He got the streets on lock!" Jezz stated.

Najee thought about the business card that Nella dropped in the club's parking lot. He hoped they could help him connect the dots.

"Do you know anything about a cat named, Prince?"

"What do you need to know?" Dee offered.

Jezz elbowed his younger brother in the ribs, urging him to remain silent. Najee noticed the exchange and fully understood Jezz's reaction. In the hood, you kept your mouth closed tight and your eyes wide open. He decided to approach the subject from a different angle.

"I gotta keep it one hondo with you. I was at Club iCandy tonight, too. Me and my clique got into it with security just like y'all did, except my situation ended in some major gunplay!" Najee let the seriousness of his voice marinate before continuing. "A police officer got murked, and one of my soldiers died when our SUV flipped over. On top of that, them Block Boy Empire niggas kidnapped my girl! I need your help."

He did not notice that he had called Nella, *his girl*. Unconsciously, his strong feelings for her were rising to the surface. Dee looked at his big brother Jezz and waited for his approval to continue speaking. He felt no loyalty towards BBE.

"You didn't hear this from me," Jezz whispered while looking over each shoulder to make sure no one else was listening, "But word on the street is that Prince is Sosa's, right-hand man. The club is just a front."

"I kinda figured that the two of them were tight. Do you know where I can catch them slippin'?"

Jezz scanned the holding tank in a paranoid manner before replying in an even lower tone of voice. "You tryna' get us murked, bruh? If we give you the four-one-one on them cats, our life will be in danger!" he whispered.

"My people are already in danger!" Najee pointed out through tight lips. "I need your help. Are you down with me, or not?"

Jezz rubbed the stubble on his chin. He was caught between a rock and a hard spot. The Block Boy Empire gang was a deadly group of individuals with money, power, and influence. They were well known for dishing out a lethal brand of justice to their enemies.

Dee spoke up, "Man, fuck them, niggas! We don't owe them shit! They wouldn't even let us in that punk-ass club!" Jezz was about to protest, but Dee spoke over him, "Prince is elusive. He changes whips and spots like a chameleon changes colors, but Sosa has a crib somewhere on Glenridge. They call it the Blood Bank or some shit like that. You can't miss it. It's the biggest house on the block."

Just as Dee finished speaking, master control opened the iron bars of the holding cell. A female officer who looked like a dike stood in the entranceway with a yellow slip of paper in her ashy hands. It was movement time.

The cell became quiet as everyone waited to see whose name was called. The police station was a revolving door. Offenders were detained and booked throughout the night. If you were lucky, your name was called in order to be released. The unfortunate inmates were shackled and transferred to the dreadful county jail.

"Mr. Madlock, step forward. You're being released!" the officer yelled like a drill sergeant. The remaining detainees were disappointed that it wasn't their name being called.

Najee, Jezz, and Dee shook hands with enthusiasm and gave each other a shoulder bump. They exchanged phone numbers and promised to keep in touch.

Before parting ways, Jezz leaned forward and offered one more piece of advice, "Look, man, those BBE cats got the streets on click-clack. I don't know what you got planned but be extremely careful. It's gonna take an army to bring them down."

"Let's go, Mr. Madlock," the female officer barked. "I don't have all day."

Najee stepped through the open bars and looked back with an ominous grin. He did have an army, better yet, a navy.

196

CHAPTER 20

Blood for Blood

Nella was being held hostage at an old aluminum recycling factory. Not too far in the distant past, the sound of machinery radiated throughout the building. Now the factory was in a state of despair and decay. Each time Nella wiggled in the uncomfortable metal chair the coarse rope tied tightly around her wrist sliced deeper into her skin. The abandoned building was ice cold. Goosebumps covered her arms and legs as her body shivered uncontrollably in her skimpy outfit.

She regretted leaving the hotel suite with her ass cheeks hanging out and most definitely regretted accepting Najee's mission. The sound of Prince openly mocking their scheme to blackmail Sosa did somersaults in her mind. She couldn't get his tormenting laughter out of her head. Nella knew she had to make a move, and quick.

The hostage keeper lit a *Black-N-Mild* cigar while leaning against the wall. The champagne, the blunts, the high-speed chase, and the adrenalin from the shootout had him feeling cocky and confident. He had a lust for violence. The BBE soldier looked over toward Nella. The room was dark, however, a slither of moonlight trickled in from a window. This allowed him to admire Nella's body. His eyes traveled from her sexy boots to her thick thighs and rested upon her breasts.

"Damn, she got some big ol' titties!" he chuckled.

Even with the blindfold on, Nella could sense the goon undressing her with his eyes. His glare made her feel naked and vulnerable. The restraints made her feel trapped and helpless. It was now or never, she decided to make her move. Despite the excruciating pain, Nella wiggled in her chair to get the goon's full attention. She also tried to talk to him, even though she knew the duct tape would smother her words.

"Whatchu say? I can't understand you." He stepped closer.

Nella continued to speak, but the duct tape caught the words coming out of her mouth like a fishing net. "Uhmm go-hmm-he!" she said in a muffled voice.

"What? I can't understand a word you sayin', dumb ass bitch!"

"I gotta-go-he-he," Nella repeated again.

"Oh, now I understand you." His face lit up with recognition. "You said, you gotta go pee-pee?"

Nella shook her head up and down, confirming his words. She crossed her fingers once again, and whispered a silent prayer, hoping to God her plan would work.

"You want me to untie you so you could use the bathroom?" he asked as nicely as a piranha could.

Nella nodded her head, her hopes were inching higher.

"If I untie you, will you try to escape?"

Nella shook her head from left to right, indicating no. '*This is too easy,*' she thought. '*Too good to be true!*'

The goon dropped his cigar and used the toe of his Yeezys to extinguish the flame. He approached Nella from the rear and placed both hands on her shoulders. Nella cringed, his touch repulsed her.

"If I let you go to the bathroom, can I watch?" He ran one of his calloused fingertips up and down her arm. The hair on the back of her neck stood alert like sharp thorns on a rose.

She wanted to scream out, "*Hell no you can't watch, you sick bastard*!" Instead, she played nice and shook her head up and down enthusiastically, agreeing to play his perverted game.

The BBE foot soldier knew it was a bad idea to unbind her. Prince would have a fit if he found out. The devil on his shoulder urged him on, but the voice of reason whispered sound advice to his conscience. In the end, lust prevailed, his freakish nature outweighed common sense. He wanted to see that phat monkey, even if it cost him his life.

He yanked the blindfold off Nella's head and snatched the duct tape off her lips. The pain was unbearable, but she was relieved. The stale air was refreshing to her lungs. The goon wanted reassurance. He asked Nella to promise that she wouldn't do anything stupid, like try to escape.

"I'm harmless," she lied. "But, if it makes you feel better, call one of your friends in, they can watch, too." Even before she suggested the idea, she knew he didn't want an audience. He wanted her all to himself, pussy made niggas dumb! She could literally see the blood rushing from his brain to his penis, impairing his ability to think clearly.

The kidnapper unexpectedly pulled his gun from the small of his back and cocked it. This was not anticipated. The gun turned the odds against her. The goon pressed the barrel against her temple. "Like I was saying, I'm not falling for no slick tricks, so don't get yo' sexy ass murked." He stood Nella up roughly and held the pistol under her chin as his eyes roamed across her body. "Damn, you thick!" his compliment was unwelcomed.

Nella tried to pull away, the kidnapper grabbed her tightly by the arm. "Don't move slut!" He pulled her body close to his. She could feel his erection throbbing in his pants. His breath smelled like tobacco and alcohol. He grabbed her face in a firm grip and squeezed her cheeks with all his strength. "Give me a kiss, baby!" he asked as smooth as sandpaper.

Nella knew she had to tranquilize him with kindness before he got completely out of control. She puckered her lips and submitted to his request. She wanted to vomit in his mouth. Their lips touched, she twirled her tongue around his until he released her face and relaxed the hand holding the gun. A small groan of pleasure escaped from his throat. She had him exactly where she wanted him. Without warning, she bit down on his tongue. She took all her pent-up frustration out on his flesh.

"Who's the dumb bitch now?" she wanted to say.

Shocked, he tried to pull away, but that made the agonizing pain worse. The taste of his salty blood urged Nella on. She clamped down harder. Her fangs pierced his tongue like raw meat. In a last-minute effort, the goon snatched his mouth away from hers and collapsed on the floor traumatized. He looked up at Nella with a mixture of fear and rage in his eyes. He tried to scream but couldn't, his vocals cords failed him.

"Oh shit!" he thought.

Nella spit half of his tongue at him, blood and mucus splattered on the floor. He put his hands to his mouth and damn near fainted once he realized it was his own flesh lying in a puddle of blood.

Nella kicked the gun out of his hand. It hit the floor and slid into a dark corner. He crawled on his knees, desperately searching for the weapon like a dope fiend searching for crumbs of crack on a rug. Nella ran to the window. Because her hands were tied behind her back, she used her forehead to head butt the glass. The window didn't budge. She banged her forehead again and again, still nothing. She looked over her shoulder and saw the kidnapper frantically searching for his pistol in the darkness. Whoever succeeded first would win the battle.

Nella drew her head back once more, then lunged forward with all her might. The glass shattered and cut her face. Blood trickled from her eyebrow to her lips, mingling with assailants DNA.

She quickly turned around so that her back was facing the window. She used the jagged edges of the broken glass like a saw as she tried to cut the rope. The kidnapper fanned his hands in a sweeping manner, groping the floor in darkness. He was getting warmer, Nella needed to move faster.

She was in an awkward position, but willpower encouraged her on. She moved her bound hands up and down, faster and faster until the glass finally cut through the stiff rope.

Her hands were now free. She turned around and looked out the window. "Ain't this about a bitch!" she groaned out loud. They were on the second floor, too far up to jump. She needed another plan. Nella turned around and came face to face with her attacker. She was staring down the deadly barrel of his Glock-9, game over!

****

Rio, Juice, and Maceo watched Prince get into his Bentley GT and mash off. Maceo was about to open the driver's side door and get out, but Juice stopped him. "Hold up a sec, B." He grabbed Maceo's arm and pointed up the street. "On my word, I see two heads in that parked car."

Just as the words left his lips, the second car slowly pulled away from the curb. They professionally trailed the Bentley at a safe distance. The men sank lower in their seats until both pair of taillights turned the corner.

"That was close. Who do you think was in the second whip?" Maceo asked.

Rio answered him from the backseat, "Definitely wasn't for security. I think that was them, peoples."

They scanned the block for more action but didn't notice any movement or unusual activity. This was the perfect part of town to run a clandestine operation. There were low traffic and high buildings.

Rio relaxed. "I don't see the van, but I bet there's a loading dock on the other side."

Juice racked a foe-five round into his weapon. "There's only one way to find out." He eased out of the passenger's seat and slipped into the night.

The Body Snatchers were back in full military mode as their silhouettes merged with the shadows. A battle in the concrete jungle was no different than guerrilla warfare in a third world country. Add a few dedicated soldiers, gunpowder, and a noble cause, and you had the recipe for destruction.

They made it to the back of the building without being observed and was thankful that there were no surveillance cameras. Whoever was in charge of security needed to be assassinated.

Maceo noticed the van first. It was backed against the loading dock doors as Rio had suggested. He touched the hood. The engine was still warm. Juice gazed at the gaping bullet holes from his Desert Eagle lodged into the driver's side door. He wished he would have aimed higher.

Rio saw a flash of movement in one of the windows on the second floor. "Everybody take cover, we got activity! Third window from the right." He pointed upwards.

They crept behind the cargo van. From their vantage point, they had a clear view of the window. It wasn't long before the flame of

201

a Bic lighter illuminated the face of the bouncer that was at the club earlier. He lit a Black-N-Mild and faded into darkness.

"That must be where they're holding Nella," Juice whispered.

"The old man left in the Bentley," Maceo stated. "That leaves the three studs with the BBE shirts."

Rio nodded his head. "I agree. They probably spread out on each floor. We gotta come up with a plan." He rubbed his knuckles while deep in his thoughts.

"I wish Najee was here. He would know exactly what to do," Maceo offered. He missed the mentorship of his leader.

"Well, he ain't here, so fuck it," Rio snapped. "I'm in charge now!"

Juice and Maceo stared at each other with bizarre looks on their faces but remained silent as Rio went on a tyrant about Najee.

"If it wasn't for him, Yung Zay would be alive, Nella would be safe, and we wouldn't be hiding behind this fuckin' van like cowards. That nigga ain't telling you the whole story. Think about it. Why do we always go after Benzo Al's workers? Najee is chasin' ghost from his past. He's on some revenge shit. He don't give a fuck about us! If he did, we would be filthy rich by now. We could have the streets on lock." Rio had his own idea of how the crew should be ran.

Rio's words soaked into Juice's heart. He began to second guess their leader's motives and intentions but was going to remain loyal until he sorted things out. "I'm feeling you, bro'. I hate leaving all that dope behind, too, but my allegiance is with him."

They both looked at Maceo waiting for him to speak. "I'm not the captain of the yacht, but at least I'm on the boat. I know how to play my position," Maceo said with conviction. "I'm still ridin' with, Najee."

Rio was infuriated but did not let his emotions show, snakes never do.

A loud bang infiltrated their awkward moment of silence. They looked up towards the window. Someone banged their head viciously against the glass. Moments later, the window shattered. A female looked out of the window, and then suddenly turned her back to them. It was Nella!

They silently cheered for her as she used the sharp edges of broken glass to saw away the rope restraining her wrists. Finally, the twisted fibers gave way and her hands were free. Nella stuck her head out the window to look around as if she wanted to jump. She looked down directly in their direction, however, the crew members were camouflaged by darkness. She could not see them or the bulky figure approaching her from the rear. By the time she turned around, it was too late. She had a gun pointed at her face.

****

Nella's brain sent signals to her feet, commanding her to run, but she could not move. The kidnapper looked like a monster. Blood dripped from his mouth and his face was distorted into an evil snarl. She watched in slow motion as his index finger pressed harder on the trigger.

Bang!

A single gunshot pierced the silence of the night. Nella ducked and covered her eyes with her hands as if her fingers could somehow stop the velocity of a .9mm slug. It took a second for her to realize that she wasn't dead. She peeked through her fingers and saw the goon fall over sideways. His heavy body slammed to the floor. He was dead, blood and puss oozed from the deep gash in the center of his forehead.

Nella stood up. '*What the hell just happened*,' she thought as she looked out of the broken window. Maceo stood on the roof of the cargo van. Smoke flowed from the barrel of his gun.

K-Roc was throwed off dirty Sprite, a mixture of soda and codeine. The lean had him chopped, but the loud crackle snapped him out of his daze. He was posted outside of the room where Nella was being held captive. He jumped out of the old chair where he was nodding off and placed his ear against the metal door. It was quiet, too quiet. His phone vibrated on his hip. Mac's name appeared on the caller ID.

"Did you hear that gunshot, my nig?" Mac asked immediately.

"Yeah, I heard it, fam!"

"Check on Low Down and the bitch," Mac instructed. "I'm on my way up there now!"

Thinking fast, Mac called Prince while running up the stairs two by two. Prince had warned them that they probably haven't heard the last of Nella's friends. Mac thought back to the sophisticated earpiece and the bulletproof SUV. He had a feeling shit was about to pop off.

Just as he hurried up the staircase, Juice, Rio, and Maceo breached the main entrance. They cautiously fanned out like experts and covered as much ground as possible. Confident that the first floor was clear, they met back up in the lobby.

"No sign of Nella down here. We gotta hit the second floor," Maceo insisted. He was amped up and ready to get it crackin'.

"There's a freight elevator in the back, but it's too risky. I say we take the stairs," Rio suggested.

He was right, they did not know what to expect on the second floor. The freight elevator could potentially be their casket. They eased up the steps slowly. Rio took the lead, Maceo was in the middle, and Juice brought up the rear.

****

Once Nella realized that her crew was there to rescue her, she sprang into action. She knew the other hoods had heard the gunshot and was bound to check the room. She grabbed the dead man's wrist in a tight grip and pulled with all of her physical strength. Smeared blood painted the floor as she dragged the dead body out of sight. Then she crouched down by the doorway, prepared to attack anyone who entered.

While waiting, she folded her hands and whispered a prayer to God, thanking him for having her back so far. As she scooted into a more comfortable position, she felt something cold and hard. It was the gun. God was smiling down upon her.

The Streets Made Me

****

K-Roc pressed his ear harder to the door, hoping to get an indication of what was going on. The silence on the other side did not reveal any clues. He started to panic when he heard the bottom of Mac's shoes as Mac leaped up the stairs. K-Roc disliked the ridicule he often received concerning his intelligence. In his opinion, he was just as smart as anyone else, yet every time he was put in charge of something, he fucked it up. He hoped this was not another one of those situations.

He made up his mind, he was going in. He patted his pockets, but couldn't find the key. "Aww, man, not again." Moving too fast, he mistakenly kicked over his brown medicine bottle. The thick, purple fluid oozed onto the floor, spilling his liquid high. "Got damn it!" he cursed in an irritable tone.

He could hear Mac breathing hard as he rushed up the flight of stairs. K-Roc didn't want anyone to know he was sippin' on sizzurp, so he quickly bent down to pick up the medicine bottle. While doing so, he spotted the keys. Relief flowed through his body.

He fumbled with the lock then finally got the door open. The room was dark, but the moonlight shining through the window allowed him to see that Nella's chair was empty. An eerie feeling crept over him. Something wasn't right. He pulled out his heat, relieved that there was no need to cock it. He always kept a hot one in the chamber. He took a small step forward and aimed the pistol into the darkness.

"Low Down!" he called in a hushed voice. "Low Down, say somethin', Cuzzo!" He stepped further into the room to investigate, however, Mac made it to the top floor out of breath and stopped him.

"K-Roc!" Mac shouted. "Don't go in there, my nig, it might be a set-up!"

As soon as K-Roc heard Mac's warning, he knew he had stepped into a booby trap. His brain processed the words and transmitted a signal to his legs, but it was too late to retreat.

Larry D. Wright

The first shot is always the loudest and most painful. The fire hot shell collided with his rib cage and punctured a lung. Internal bleeding would soon drown his vital organs. The second shot is not as loud because your ears are usually ringing, but it's equally painful. Flashes from the muzzle allowed K-Roc to get a brief glimpse of Nella's profile before the tumbling slug ripped through his BBE T-shirt and pierced his chest. He stumbled backward on wobbly legs but refused to fall. His face twisted in agony as Nella smiled with pleasure.

If you are lucky enough to be alive when the third round penetrates your body, you typically don't feel a thing. The powerful adrenaline flowing through your veins numbs all other feelings. If you survive, expect to wake up with a shit bag attached to your stomach, or worse.

K-Rock wasn't as fortunate. The third bullet smacked him right under his left eye. The hot projectile ricocheted off his skull and bounced around inside his head like a pinball machine. His knees buckled, and he collapsed on the cold, filthy floor. His world went black.

Mac watched helplessly as three quick blasts of gunfire cut K-Roc down. Within seconds of hitting the ground, the lifeless body was lying in a river of dark red blood. Mac eased into the shadows for cover. His AR-15 with a clip taped to another clip was fully loaded and ready. From Mac's position, he could see the dead body. K-Roc's eyes were still open. If those eyes could see, they would've been the only eye witness to a gruesome and ruthless murder.

Rio silently slithered up behind Mac clutching the same Desert Eagle Juice used to shoot at the cargo van earlier that evening. He pressed the barrel against the back of Mac's dreadlocks. The cold steel felt like ice. Shivers shot down his spine. Mac dropped his weapon and raised his hands to surrender. He knew what time it was.

"Turn around, punk-ass nigga! I want you to see who murdered you," Rio demanded.

206

Mac turned around to face his killer. No fear registered on his face. His diamond-studded teeth glistened in the darkness as he smiled.

"You got any last words?" Rio asked.

Mac held his chin up and stuck his chest out. He had a lot of heart and a deep understanding that for niggas like him, there was no fairytale ending. When the curtain closed, it was life in jail or eternity in hell. The four cannons pointed at his dome did not faze him.

"Yeah, I got some last words," Mac declared and hawked a wad of phlegm in Rio's face. "Fuck all y'all!"

Before the words fully left his tongue, Rio, Nella, Juice, and Maceo squeezed off simultaneously. Mac was dead before his body hit the ground. His BBE shirt resembled Swiss cheese. Blood and mucus dripped from each of the smoldering bullet holes in his chest. The trigger has no heart.

Maceo stood over the dead body and let off one last shot. "That was for Yung Zay, fuck boy!"

The Body Snatchers wasted no time getting out of the building. They had to get ghost before the jakes had the area surrounded. Once outside, they piled into the stolen Escalade. Police sirens blared in the near distance. Maceo started the vehicle and smashed off. He had no idea where they were going but was relieved that they had rescued Nella.

"Yeah, that's what the fuck I'm talkin' about, my nigga! Do or die!" Rio screamed as him and Juice shook hands.

Maceo joined in the celebration. "See how I held the banger sideways and popped that fool? That's how you do it, dawg!"

The high fives and enthusiastic celebration ended abruptly when Nella inquired about the other teammates. "Where's Najee and Yung Zay? They missed out on all the action!" she said while rubbing her sore wrist.

The three men became unusually silent. No one wanted to be the bearer of bad news. They drove in awkward silence for two blocks before Rio reluctantly answered her question.

"We got some bad news to tell you."

Nella braced herself emotionally. "Well give it to me raw. This silence is killing me."

Rio took a deep breath before speaking. "Yung Zay didn't make it! The Knight XV flipped over during the chase. There was nothing we could do."

Nella lowered her head and squeezed her eyes shut. Tears rolled down her cheeks. She and Yung Zay had grown close. He was like a little brother to her. She couldn't believe what she was hearing. "And what about Najee?"

Rio was about to hate on Najee but decided to keep it one hundred. "Najee stayed back to look after, Yung Zay. That's when the one-time snatched him up."

A sense of relief swept over Nella. Knowing Najee was alive eased some of her discomfort, but the three dead bodies left in the warehouse were not enough retribution for Yung Zay's death or the agony she endured. One more person needed to be severely punished, his name was Prince!

Nella told them how Prince noticed her communication device and mistook her for a federal agent. She also explained his connection to Sosa and the Block Boy Empire organization.

"I think there's some type of rivalry brewing between, Prince and Sosa," she told her crew.

"What makes you think that?" Juice inquired.

"Just my woman's intuition. Plus, he flinched when I revealed the name of the snitch in their clique. I got a feeling he has something to hide."

"Well, he can't hide from us!" Maceo interjected. "His ass is toast, straight up!"

Maceo checked the rearview mirror periodically, he didn't observe anything suspicious. Had he received more training in countersurveillance, he would have noticed a black Bentley GT slowly trailing them at a distance. Prince stayed at least two blocks back.

CHAPTER 21

Power Moves

Prince took his foot off the gas and let the whip coast. He didn't want to get too close to the Escalade. When Mac called and told him about the gunshots, he did a U-turn, cut a couple of corners and doubled back to the warehouse, losing the unmarked car that had been tailing him for two-weeks. He could have shook them off at any time, but he was trying to determine whether it was them people or Sosa keeping tabs on him.

He was an expert at following vehicles. As a young pimp, that was a prerequisite of the job. When one of his whores got into a car with a trick, he would discretely follow them to make sure his girl and his money made it back safely. As he became more seasoned and his stable of women grew, he was unable to watch their backs. *Besides, it didn't take two people to sell one pussy*, an old pimp schooled him.

To make sure his money came back straight, he created rivalries amongst the women. He never gave them an exact quota per se. Most hoes are lazy and would stop hustling once they reached a certain amount. Prince was never satisfied, and no amount could appease him or pacify his appetite for the almighty dollar.

He was also a master manipulator and good at playing head games. If one of his new girls brought him a nice wad of cash, he would simply toss it on the dresser as if it meant nothing to him or nonchalantly stuff the bankroll in his pocket. *Never count hoe money in front of a hoe*, he was taught. If they saw a glimmer of satisfaction on your face, they knew in the future you'll accept the same or less. Always give them the impression that you're not impressed, and they will work twice as hard to please you. If a ho's money is starting to get funny, show her that her contribution is insufficient by ignoring her and praising the breadwinner. This will bring out the competitive nature in any woman.

As Prince cautiously followed the Escalade, the divine wisdom of an older pimp named St. Louis tumbled through his mind. Even after all these years, the lessons over games of high stakes 4-5-6 stuck with him. St. Louis was ultimately murdered in an after-hours gambling shack, leaving Prince and Mama Merl without a mentor.

His stable of women disbanded. Some became renegades while others defected to lesser-known pimps. Mama Merl, the queen bee of them all, chose Prince. She saw Prince's potential even before he did. Prince shook the images of the past out of his head. He hated being revisited by the ghost of his previous life. He made an effort to focus on the task at hand. The Body Snatchers were traveling South on the highway. He had a hunch that they were headed to the airport.

It would make good sense to get the hell out of town while they still had a chance, Prince reasoned.

The Escalade merged lanes and took Exit 72 Camp Creek Atlanta Airport. His assumption was correct. The luxury SUV pulled into the parking lot of the Baymont Inn. The four passengers jumped out and thoroughly wiped the vehicle down to remove any fingerprints. When this task was complete, they jaywalked across the street to a Radisson Hotel and entered the lobby.

Prince watched the scene unfold while sitting in Denny's parking lot with his engine idling. He waited patiently for twenty minutes. When the foursome did not return, he knew they had rented a room for the remainder of the night. That was fine by him. He needed to put his next chess move into play. He lit the tip of his Garcia Vega with the car cigarette lighter and blew smoke through the moon roof. He had been on edge all night. It was time to relax and strategize.

Prince checked his cell phone. No missed calls, no new text messages. He felt disrespected that Sosa did not have the courtesy to holla back. He was gonna have to teach him a lesson. First, however, he needed his own supply of cash. Success was the best revenge.

He had been depending on Sosa to fund all his business ventures, therefore making himself a subordinate. Sosa called all the shots and used the money to control him. Prince wanted to break that dependency, and the mil-ticket reward from Benzo Al was the blessing he needed. He took another long puff of the purple dro and coughed. The THC flowed through his system. His plan started to formulate.

The mastermind replayed the master scheme in his head. He would call Benzo Al and tell him that he located the stickup kids who have been hitting his spots. Benzo Al was offering a ticket for the group of bandits responsible for embarrassing him and causing ripples within the syndicate. Prince was almost double that amount in the rear with Sosa from failed business deals, but a million dollars was a good start.

Club iCandy was the go-to spot for Hot-Lanta's nightlife, but the establishment was plagued by lawsuits stemming from a number of violent incidents that occurred on the premises. On the surface, the club looked like it was thriving, but on paper, it was another bad investment. Considering the incident that happened tonight, he was sure the Alderman was going to suspend their liquor license. No alcohol, no partygoers. No partygoers, no return on the investment.

'*Damn*!' Just the thought made his palms sweat. He was depending on Benzo Al's reward money and Sosa's sloppiness to finance his new life. He would only ask for $500,000 in cash and the rest in dope. Fifty kilos was the number swimming in his head. He would stash the loot and step on the fifty yams and whip them into one-hundred, twenty-five recompressed bricks. He would then do a double back twist and sell the blow-up dope to Sosa's customers for seventeen-five a piece. By the time they complained about the poor quality, he would have over $2.5 million stashed away. On his way out of town, he would make one last shiesty move. But for now, he had an important call to make.

It was only 2:00 a.m. in Los Angeles, so he knew the boss would still be on the grind. Benzo Al picked up on the second ring. Music from a popular Mariachi band thumped in the background. Benzo was already in the ATL but didn't broadcast his arrival.

"Qué onda, ese? This better be good!" the fat Mexican growled into the phone.

Benzo didn't like snakes, which means he didn't like Prince. Something about the suave pimp made his spider-sense tingle. However, Prince was good for business, and he kept Sosa on point.

"I always come with that good shit. You know me, Poppy!" Prince replied, trying to be cordial. What he wanted to say was, *"Bean eating muthafucka', if it wasn't for me, those crazy cats from MS-13 would've shanked yo' fat ass when we were in the joint."* But he held his tongue.

There was no love lost between the two men. Their distaste for each other was evident, however, money was placed before bullshit. "Make it quick, I don't like cell phones!"

Prince ignored the comment and got right to the point, "I got a line on those stickup kids, four of them temporarily breathing, one dead on arrival."

The connect's mood brightened. He placed his Corona beer on the glass table and sat up straight. "Where are they?" His voice was barely a whisper.

"Right here in Atlanta. They tried to rob me at the club tonight," the lie easily slipped off his tongue. "But my boys dropped one of 'em."

A light clicked on inside of Benzo Al's head. The pieces were starting to fit into place. "So, that's what popped off at the club? Sosa claimed he didn't know anything about it."

"You hollered at, Sosa?" Prince asked.

"Yeah, we spoke 'bout an hour ago."

So he did see my number on the caller ID. Prince was furious. Sosa had deliberately ignored his call. To him, that was a declaration of war, but he was two steps ahead of the game. He decided to use the oldest trick in the book. Divide and conquer. "I don't know why he would lie to you, my man. He was directly involved."

Benzo Al twirled his rosary beads between his fingers. "Is that right? Sosa is pinche mentiroso." He called him a liar in Spanish.

"Don't tell him I told you this," Prince lowered his voice for effect. "He chose not to invite you. In fact, he didn't even want you

212

to know about the big party. I tried to talk him out of it, but what can I do? He's the boss," he knew his words would strike a nerve.

"No, I'm El Jefee. I'm the boss of all bosses!"

"I agree," Prince stroked his ego. "But you know these young guys, they start blowin' money fast, then forget how to slow down. I try my best, but hey, what can I do!"

"Don't worry about it, I'll take care of it. And if you found those pinche banditos, I'll take good care of you, too."

Prince licked his lips. "That's what I wanted to holla at chu' about. We don't want the whole mil-ticket."

Benzo Al leaned back on the leather sofa and sipped his Corona. Prince never turned down nothin' except his collar, so he knew something was up. "I'm listening, amigo," he said suspiciously.

"Me and Sosa were talking."

"Oh really." Benzo Al raised an eyebrow.

"Yeah, really. We thought it would be a good idea to take half the ticket in loose change and fifty Street Lit books." He talked in code.

There was a moment of silence. Prince could almost hear the gears turning inside of Benzo Al's head. If the kingpin did the mathematics, he would see that he was coming out cheaper than paying the whole million in cash. He was getting the cocoa from across the border at rock bottom prices, plus he wanted to personally send the banditos to hell after he tortured them. It was a win-win situation.

He took the bait. "You got a deal! Where are they?"

Prince let out a sigh of relief. His plan was coming together. "One of the cats got scooped up by the one-time. The remaining four just checked into the Radisson Hotel on International Boulevard by the airport."

"Don't take your eye off them. I'm sending some shooters your way. Call me ASAP if they get mobile."

"Gotcha! What about the package?" Prince wanted to know about the money. He could give a damn about anything else.

"I'm already in town, amigo. The drop is going down later. Tell Sosa he only has to leave seven rubber bands in the car. I'm sending one-hundred-fifty Wahida Clark books."

"But wait a minute!"

His words were cut off. Benzo Al had already hung up. Shit wasn't looking good. This was a new twist. What Benzo Al proposed meant that the next shipment would only cost $700,000 for one-hundred bricks instead of the normal $1.2 million. That's a $500,000 discount. He would also add an additional fifty bricks as part of the reward instead of the cash that Prince wanted all to himself. He had basically fucked himself by claiming that he and Sosa came to the conclusion about the reward money together.

He had to think of a new angle fast. The plug said they were gonna swap it out later that day. That was new news to him also. He wondered how long Sosa knew about the drop but wasn't telling him about it. Prince went from being calm and relaxed to straight pissed off. Sosa was fucking with his intelligence!

He took one more drag off the blunt, then crushed the tip in the ashtray. He had another ace up his sleeve. He scrolled down his contact list until he came across the number he desired, FBI Agent John Walker. There was no better ally than a crooked cop.

Prince glanced at his iced out timepiece. It was the wee hours of the morning. He decided to wait before he made the call. Today was going to be another long day. He laid back on the headrest and reclined his seat. The soft Italian leather cuddled his body. He didn't want to go to sleep, but his heavy eyelids betrayed him. He slowly drifted off. As always, he dreamed about Monica.

****

The sun was shining, and the palm trees swayed gracefully in the gentle California breeze. Prince was counted amongst the elite, the upper echelon of ghetto hustlers. Life was good, but along with the money came the issues, the haters, and the agitators. He had 99 problems, and yes, a bitch was one!

214

Prince looked over the top of his newspaper and shook his head. Monica was 8 months pregnant and big as a house. He had pulled her to the side on several occasions and asked her was she ready to get down for her crown. Each time, she used the baby as an excuse.

"Wait until I have my baby. I'm gonna be your star," she would swear, then kiss him on the lips, which was a no-no in the pimp ecosphere.

He tried to convince her that pregnant pussy was the best pussy. He would be the one to know. He constantly went against the rules of the game. He couldn't keep his dick out of her. She was playing him and he couldn't see it.

Others did see it. A pivotal moment in his career occurred at a well-known tavern on Sunset and Vine in the heart of Hollywood. Prince was in rare form. He was dressed to impress. His Fedora matched his shoes, and his shoes matched his cane. He had just beaten a local pimp by the name of Boulevard five times in a row on the pool table. Boulevard was reluctant to give up the pink slip to his Cadillac and caught a bad case of diarrhea of the mouth. Prince believed that pimpin' was a no-contact sport, however, he wasn't no punk. The two men squared off.

"What's the bizness, Boulevard? I beat you fair and square, so why you acting like a square?"

"Me, ah square?" Boulevard asked while pointing at himself. "Nigga, I'm ah pyramid. You the one in the way. Move over and let a real pimp get some paper!"

"Jive ass nigga, you wouldn't know what money looked like if you was trapped in a bank vault!" Prince shot back.

A bad vibe infiltrated the air. A crowd formed around the pool table. Boulevard knew he was out of order. He had gotten beaten fair and square, but he was waiting for a showdown with Prince. Now was his opportunity to prove that he was a contender.

"You ain't out here checkin' paper, chump. You out here rescuing prostitutes. You running a homeless shelter for pregnant women!"

The crowd roared with laughter. The things said behind his back were now being said in the open. Prince looked around with an uncomfortable look on his face. He needed a quick comeback.

"You got jokes, huh? You should've been a comedian because you damn sho' ain't no mack. While you was losing at pool, you was also losing yo' main hoe as well."

Boulevard looked around the tavern for his bottom bitch, Bunny. She wasn't hard to find, standing at 6 'feet with bleach blond hair, she stood out in any crowd. Candy and Sugar were escorting her out the front door. Boulevard was pissed. He ran after Bunny, but Prince grabbed his arm.

"You know the game, nigga. Now give up them keys!"

"I ain't giving you shit except a bullet in yo' ass if you don't let me go," he threatened and pulled out a snub-nose .38 Special. He jammed the gun against Prince's rib cage.

Mama Merl made her move as soon as he pulled the banger from his waist. She was an expert at concealing razor blades in her mouth. She slashed Boulevard across the cheek, leaving an ugly scar on his face.

Mama Merl made a dash for the front entrance. An old-timer named Godfather ushered Prince through the employee's only area and out the back door. They hopped into his old Buick and raced away from the scene. When the coast was clear, Prince reached into his pocket and pulled out a large bankroll. He peeled off two crisp C-notes and handed them to Godfather. The old-timer held up his hand to decline the offer. He had too much pride.

"Keep yo' money, young blood. You're like family," he said in a raspy voice.

Godfather pushed in an 8-track cassette tape, and the smooth voice of Curtis Mayfield singing Superfly oozed from the speakers. Prince unbuttoned his collar and relaxed a little. The music was the theme song to his life. He fired up a joint and passed it to the driver. They jammed to the soulful beat and smoked in silence until Prince realized what part of town they were in.

"Where you taking me, old man?"

"To Watts, there's somebody you need to meet."

Prince screwed up his face. "Who is this somebody?"

Godfather lowered the music and spoke in a serious tone. "I'm taking you to the projects to meet the voodoo lady."

"The who lady? Man, looka here, turn this space ship around and drop me off on the track! You done lost yo' damn mind!"

"Hear me out, young blood. I know what you going through. I been there, done that and can do it again if I wanted to. That chick Monica is gonna bring you down. She is dead weight player, trust me."

"Why should I trust you?"

The old-timer didn't answer. He made a turn off Imperial Highway and pulled into the Nickerson Garden Projects. They drove through a maze of buildings before they parked in front of one of the units. Before Godfather could knock, the door creaked open. The oldest, ugliest woman Prince had ever seen filled the door frame. She was blacker than a Goodyear tire and had roaming eyes that were yellow as egg yolk. When she spoke, she revealed a set of brown, rotten teeth.

"I was expecting you," she hissed in a Jamaican accent. "Quickly, follow me!" She turned on her heels and marched off. Prince wondered how she even knew they were coming?

The voodoo lady disappeared into the kitchen. When she returned, she had a single white pill in a clear baggie. She gave it to Prince.

"What is this for?"

"It will induce the pregnancy. You want baby to come?" she questioned in her thick Caribbean accent. "Crush the pill in orange juice, baby come faster."

Prince looked from the voodoo lady to the Godfather and smiled. 'This just might be the lick,' he thought. Once Monica had the damn baby, he would work her like a mule.

Prince looked over the top of his Wall Street Journal again. The voodoo lady had given him the pill a week ago, however, he still had reservations about slipping Monica the roofie. He was either growing a conscience or growing soft.

He watched her finish eating the pickle, then open a bag of Lays chips. When she licked the salt off her fingers and smacked her lips, he became irritated. Who was he fooling? His penthouse had become a shelter. A rest haven for hoes. Things had to change.

"Do you want something to drink, sweetheart?" he asked nicely. His scheme was in motion.

Monica was shocked. Prince never offered to do anything for anyone. He was a pampered man, the women catered to him. "Uh, sure, can you bring me a Pepsi?" she replied with a smile. "And while you're at it, bring me the hot sauce for these potato chips, honey."

"How about I just get you some orange juice. That would be better for the baby," he commented, concealing his anger.

Monica blushed. This was the first time Prince had shown any care or concern for her baby. Prince opened the well-stocked refrigerator. It was filled with every type of food and beverage except orange juice. He decided to improvise. Looking over his shoulder to make sure no one was watching he removed the pill from his pocket and crushed it inside a bottle of Pepsi.

'The voodoo lady said crush the pill in orange juice, but she didn't specifically say that juice was mandatory,' he reasoned. He hesitated for a moment, then said fuck it. By the time he brought the soda to Monica, the white powdery substance had already dissolved.

Monica died the same day while giving birth. Prince never fully recovered from that incident. The guilt ate away at his soul like battery acid. The doctors said she died from labor complications, but the autopsy report later revealed that she had high toxicity levels in her bloodstream. He felt like a murderer, not a player. He lost his lust to hustle and isolated himself inside a shell. He became what he despised the most.

His harem of women dwindled quickly. In the end, all he had is what he began with. Mama Merl, she stayed ten toes down through thick and thin, yet, in a murderous rage, he beat her into an unconsciousness she would never wake up from.

218

The Streets Made Me

While he was confronting his demons at San Quentin State Prison, he received news that he was a father. Mama Merl was pregnant at the time of her death. She concealed her pregnancy because she knew Prince would force her to get an abortion. She had been a whore all her life. She was turned out at the tender age of fifteen by her mother. Her own flesh and blood would exchange her young pussy for a shot Heroin and rent money.

Merl assumed she was damaged goods and unable to have children. After battling morning sickness for several days, she secretly bought a home pregnancy test. Joy filled her heart when the line turned blue. God had blessed her womb. She didn't reveal her secret to anyone, not even Prince.

When Prince heard the news from his prison social worker, his soul shriveled up inside of him. He couldn't cope with the blood that stained his hands. There was a time when he believed that a whore with kids was an anchor, dead weight, and an obstacle between him and his money. But, after holding Monica's newborn in his arms those feelings quickly evaporated.

Sitting across from his social worker and learning that his own son had been named and placed in foster care without his knowledge or input, drove him over the edge. In a fit of rage, he flipped over the social worker's desk and lunged at her. The goon squad quickly intervened. They maced him with pepper spray, and then viciously beat him with nightsticks like he was Rodney King. He kicked and screamed as they dragged him to the hole.

He was charged with assaulting a staff member and sentenced to do a three-sixty in solitary confinement. He was transferred to the secure housing unit. The SHU program is where California's most dangerous and infamous prisoners are housed. During his extended stay, he met Alonzo Guzman.

A deadly feud between the Mexican and El Salvadorian gang members was brewing. Prince alerted Benzo Al to a hit that was placed on his head and furnished the wealthy Mexican with a shank. Needless to say, Benzo was grateful for the favor and vowed to look out for Prince once they hit the bricks.

219

Years later, the Latino mobster kept his promise. In return, Prince introduced him to an up and coming hustler named Sosa. Within a year, Sosa was moving a hundred kilos per month. The money was loose change between couch cushions to Benzo Al, however, he admired Sosa's determination and enthusiasm. The two criminals forged an unbreakable bond.

****

Prince stumbled out of his dream in a cold sweat. He hated reliving the vivid images. Monica and Merl were names that haunted his past. Najee and Sosa were names that jeopardized his future.

He wiped the beads of sweat from his forehead and glanced at the digital clock on the dashboard. It seemed like he had been sleep for hours, but it was only six in the morning. The Denny's parking lot started to fill up as the morning crowd gathered for breakfast. The Escalade had not been moved, and the Radisson Hotel looked peaceful and calm. Prince was relieved to see that he did not miss any major action while he was sleep.

Right on cue, a blue '64 Chevy Impala swooped into the parking lot and pulled up beside the Bentley. Five menacing cholos huddled inside the low-rider. Prince shook his head in amazement.

"Why do Mexicans always pile up in one damn car?" he asked.

The driver got out and approached the driver's side door of the Bentley. He wore a crispy white wife beater and heavily creased tan Dickies. His muscular arms were littered with jailhouse tattoos. The large *13* tatted on his bald head added to his menacing look. The four other passengers shared the same deadly mannerisms. Prince rolled down the window, and the cholo got right to business.

"Where are they?" he asked bluntly. His English was surprisingly clear.

Prince nodded in the direction of the hotel. "They checked in a couple of hours ago, but I don't know the room number. I think they're waiting to catch a flight outta town."

"The only thing they catching today are some slugs. Here is how we 'bout to put it down, Ese!"

The Cinco Diablos street captain had everything figured out. Since Prince was dressed the most conservative, his task was to go into the hotel lobby and discreetly pull the fire alarm. When the hotel was evacuated, the Mexican assassins would pull up and push their caps back in broad daylight. They wanted to send the world a clear message, don't fuck with Benzo Al!

CHAPTER 22

Live Fast Die Faster

The king-size mattress had cool cotton sheets and fluffy goose feather pillows, but Nella was still uncomfortable. She tossed and turned while the men snored peacefully. Fully exhausted from the drama and mental fatigue, the men crashed out on the couch as soon as their eyes closed. Nella stared at the spinning blades of the ceiling fan. Multiple thoughts drifted through her mind, but her main thoughts were of Najee. She squeezed her sexy thighs tightly together. Just the thought of him made her nipples erect and her clitoris tingle.

"Why do I always fall for the bad boy?" she quizzed herself.

Najee was the epitome of thug passion. He was handsome, mysterious, and lived on the edge—attributes every woman secretly desires in a man. Nella was enticed by his lavish criminal lifestyle. She couldn't believe how quickly she went from being a professional woman receiving six-figure offers from corporate America to kickin' in doors wavin' the four-four! But she had no regrets. The money flowed, and his cause was noble. She would choose to be a ride or die chick over a slave bitch any day. She just hoped they lived long enough to express their true feelings for one another.

After tossing and turning for another hour, Nella was greeted with pleasant mental images as her mind drifted into a dream world. She was no longer in a low budget hotel. She was in the honeymoon suite at the Hedonism Resort in the Bahamas. Najee's soft lips sucked her toes, kissed her inner thighs, and finally found her brown nipples. She let out a low moan in her sleep when his fingertips slipped into the elastic of her panties. He stroked her forbidden fruit until sweet nectar dripped on his middle finger. The dream felt good, too good.

A presence in the room jolted her out of her peaceful sleep. Rio stood at the foot of her bed watching her with a lustful look in his glossy eyes. She felt naked and vulnerable laying there in her skimpy panties and bra.

"What the fuck are you doing in here, Rio?" she covered herself with the blanket.

"Stop trippin', I was just checking to see if you were straight."

"Yeah, I'm straight, so keep it moving."

Rio lingered in the doorway longer than necessary before he finally turned and left. Nella was pissed off. She got dressed and stormed out of the bedroom. Juice and Maceo were crashed out on the couch. A sisterly smile came to her face, but her head was still pounding. Her wrists and her jaw were also killing her. She had never been tied up, slapped, and called so many bitches in one night. Her makeshift ice pack was soggy, so she decided to take a trip to the ice machine.

The kidnappers had confiscated her iPhone, but Maceo's cell phone was on the table and so was his banger. She decided that it was better to be safe than sorry, so she grabbed both. She checked the Nina, a shell was lodged in the chamber. She checked the phone. The low battery indicator blinked rapidly, and there were two missed calls from a 404-area code. She figured it was probably some hoochie mama from the ATL that Maceo met on Instagram. She put the phone in her pocket, tucked the banger in her waist, and grabbed the plastic ice bucket.

Once in the hallway, she called Mufasa, her Somali connect. He had arranged the trip to the A and provided the guns and fly whips. Now she needed four tickets on the next thing smoking back to Los Angeles.

The line rang six times before a sleepy voice answered in an irritated tone. "Yeah, Mon', who the devil iz dis?" His Somali accent made him sound like Bob Marley.

"It's me, Yellow Gurl!" Her alias slipped off her tongue smoothly.

"Warya maxaad sheegtay?" he asked how are you in the Cushitic language of the Somali. "I wuz jus' dreamin' about you."

"Yeah right!" she replied dryly. Usually, she would playfully flirt back, or they would play the dozens. She loved cracking on him about his bad breath and terrible acne. Today she was in no mood for games. She wanted to get right down to business.

She had met Mufasa while at Club Rain in Miami. So far, he had proven to be a reliable source for exotic automobiles, automatic weapons, traveling arrangements and accurate information from the streets. Today was no exception.

"Seriously my sista, you got big problems. Your name iz ringin' on deez streets and your life iz in danja." Mufasa was known for keeping his ear to the block.

He continued talking, his heavy Somali accent was hard to decipher, but she understood what he was saying. "Taxadar warya, Yellow Gurl," he warned her to be careful. "Dem devils got major paper on your team. Dem no play games. Dem play for keeps!"

This information was nothing new to Nella. Every street nigga and crime family knew about the reward money for the jackers who were strippin' ballers from coast to coast. However, no one knew she was involved until now. Prince must have put the word on the street, she concluded.

"And there iz somethin' else, my sista." Mufasa cleared his throat and lowered his voice as if he was about to reveal a confidential government secret. "Ya boy Najee put big paper on Rio's head. When dem Shottas come, anybody standin' next to him iz gonna get wet up, including you. Ya know how sloppy dem get. Dem come through blazin' everything movin'!"

She almost dropped the ice bucket. She asked him to repeat his words, hoping she would hear something different. She had a million questions, all of which Mufasa answered, He had never been wrong in the past, so she took his word at face value. She hung up the phone and immediately called Najee. His voicemail picked up on the first ring. An automated voice informed her that the mailbox was full. Frustrated, she ran back towards the room.

On her way to their hotel suite, the fire alarm rang. The loud siren echoed throughout the hallway. Within seconds, curious heads peeked out of their doors. A hospitality worker yelled, "Fire!" All hell broke loose!

Half-naked hotel guests rushed out of their rooms. The hallway suddenly filled with screaming people. Nella pushed through the chaos. Their room was at the end of the hall by the emergency staircase. She could see people cramming their way through the narrow entrance. Finally, she made it to her hotel suite. She swiped her key card to gain entry. She busted through the door and discovered that Rio, Juice, and Maceo were gone. She turned back around and ran to the emergency staircase. The hospitality worker ushered the last guest through.

"Hurry, we don't have a lotta time!" He waved his hand frantically, leading Nella down the stairs.

As she rushed down the steps, a thought occurred to her. "I don't smell any smoke, do you?"

The hospitality worker paused and sniffed the air. "I don't smell anything either lady, but they don't pay me enough to sit around and get burnt up trying to find out. Let's keep it movin'."

Down in the lobby, she scanned the sea of people looking for her crew. While doing so, she caught a glimpse of a tall, light-skinned man in an expensive suit. He quickly walked out of the side exit. Red flags went up, and her heart pumped faster. She did not see the man's face, but her instincts told her that it was Prince.

'*This can't be*,' she thought. She pulled the nine-milli from her waist and held it down discreetly by her leg as she pushed her way through the crowd and out the side glass doors. When she got outside, the man was gone. She looked to the left, then the right, but he had vanished.

A Six-Foe Impala recklessly pulling into the parking lot caught her attention. The front passenger had a Tec-Nine. The rear passenger pointed a Mossberg 12 gauge pump out of the back window. It was a hit! Nella chased behind the car as the driver sped to the front entrance of the hotel. She turned the corner and watched paralyzed as a horrible scene took place.

Rio, Juice, and Maceo stood outside looking around, hoping to spot Nella. They did not see the blue Impala creep up next to them until it was too late. The Cinco Diablos assassin in the backseat gritted his teeth as he pumped the shotgun. The 12-gauge barked,

226

and fire spewed from the sawed-off barrel. Maceo didn't have time to react. The buck shots made twenty small holes in his chest. The force of the blast lifted him off his feet and slammed him into a large window. He crashed through the glass and landed on his side.

Rio and Juice upped their bangers but didn't get a chance to squeeze off. The vato in the passenger seat got out of the lowrider and let his Tech-Nine spit. Innocent bodies toppled over each other as the frightened crowd made their retreat. The shooter waved his deadly wand with reckless disregard for safety. The tattoo teardrops on his face cried out for murder.

Bullets cut down anyone in their deadly path. Rio and Juice scattered for shelter. Each of them posted behind one of the many large palm trees that lined the landscape. When the gunfire abruptly paused, they simultaneously made their move.

Every street nigga knows the problem with putting in work with a Tec. They have the propensity to jam. The shooter fumbled with the clip to no avail. The barrel was too hot. Juice squeezed off with the Desert Eagle, hitting the Diablo henchmen in the neck and shoulders. The Tec-Nine fell to the pavement followed by his lifeless body. The backseat passenger cocked the sawed-off shotgun again, but before he could bust, Rio let him have it.

The scorching hot lead whizzed by his head, missing the target by inches. It wasn't his time to go, but the backseat passenger sitting next to him wasn't so lucky. A slug drilled him in the temple. Blood, flesh, and bone fragments splattered brain matter on the custom leather interior. The smell of gunpowder and death lingered in the air.

The remaining survivors in the car urged the driver to take off, "Go, go, go!" they shouted. "Get the fuck outta here, Primo!"

"Un minuto, putos, if we fuck this up, we're dead, Ese!" If they didn't accomplish their mission, they were useless to Benzo Al.

The back window shattered. The driver ducked low and threw the Impala in gear. He smashed off, abandoning his desire to play the macho role. Glancing in the rearview mirror, he saw two men and a crazy senorita chasing the low-rider. Fire and lead burst from their weapons. He pressed hard on the gas pedal, desperately trying to outrun the shower of bullets.

Having only one last hollow point in his Desert Eagle, Juice stood over the lifeless body of the shooter who was left slumped at the curbside entrance of the hotel. He flipped the body over with his Nike and aimed his banger at the dead man's face. He yelled, "Rest in piss bitch!" Venom was in his voice as he squeezed the trigger. A large dark red puddle formed under the dead man's head and trickled into the gutter.

The fresh morning air was replaced by the stench of death. Police sirens blared in the near distance. It was time to go. Rio, Juice, and Nella sprinted toward the hotel parking lot where they left the Escalade. They were relieved to see that the SUV was still there. Rio hopped behind the wheel and turned the key in the ignition. The Flow-Master pipes rumbled. The On-Star Tracking device had not been activated. The arrogant owner was still crashed out from partying all night with his blonde mistress.

****

Mufasa ended that call and double-checked to make sure that the USB cord for his cell phone was plugged into his laptop, it was. He pulled up the Talk Tracker Software and double-clicked *Recent Activity*. He was on the phone with Nella for 13 minutes and 22 seconds, more than enough time to track her location. He logged off and dialed a number he knew by heart. His call was answered on the first ring.

"Yah mon', Yellow Gurl called me just like you said she would."

"Good, keep tracking her movements. We go where she goes."

"Insha'Allah." The line went dead. Mr. Meyers smiled and took a sip of latte.

****

Prince ducked low in the front seat as he watched the three remaining stick up artists run to the Escalade. The Mexicans had fucked up and let them get away. When the shiny SUV stormed out of the hotel parking lot, he sat up and banged his forehead angrily on the wood grain steering wheel. Shit wasn't going right.

"I can't believe them Spanish, rice-eating muthafuckas let them punk ass niggas get away!" He was a raging bull.

If he wanted anything done right, he was going to have to do it himself. He threw the Bentley in drive and followed the Escalade at a distance as the trio headed away from the airport. Keeping one hand on the steering wheel, he grabbed his cell phone and scrolled to the number of his unlikely ally.

The crooked cop didn't pick up until the fifth ring. "Special Agent Walker here," he sounded sleepy and grumpy.

"Man, iz you sleeping on the job? Wake yo' ass up. All kinds of shit been jumpin' off."

"Relax, I'm on it. I heard about the fight at the club and the shootout on Peachtree. In fact, one of the bad guys is in the morgue, and their leader is in custody." He intentionally left out the details concerning the side deal they had cut with Najee.

"That's just the tip of the iceberg. The three bodies found at the warehouse late last night were Block Boy Empire soldiers. And there was another deadly shootout at the Radisson Hotel a few minutes ago. Turn on your damn police scanner."

Agent Walker snapped to attention. He sat up straight in bed and shook his bisexual lover on the shoulders to wake him up. He placed the call on speakerphone so they could both hear the conversation.

His lover yawned and wiped the crust out of the corner of his eyes, then slowly inched his hands under the cover and massaged his partner's penis. Agent Walker swatted his hand away and placed a finger to his lips, signaling for Detective Donald Smith to remain silent.

"Now what were you saying? You got my full attention."

"I was sayin' that this shit is 'bout to pop off fo'real, fo'real! The Body Snatchers wasn't trying to rob, Sosa, they were trying to sell him information."

"What kind of information?"

"Last night we kidnapped a female member of the stickup crew. That's what the high-speed chase was about. Y'all got a major leak in the DEA's office. Someone gave them every single detail about the BBE indictment, including the identity of key confidential informants. To make matters worse, the bitch ended up escaping."

Agent Walker's eyes widened. "Whoa, whoa, hold up a second! Are you saying that the investigation has been compromised?"

Prince snapped, "Muthafucka', I'm sayin' they got my first and last name. Fuck the investigation!" he yelled into the phone.

They each knew the grave consequences attached to being labeled a rat. If the information got into the wrong hands, the snitch was a dead man. Prince was glad he acted on his instincts and abducted Nella from the club, but he was disappointed in himself for not putting a bullet in her forehead and burying his secret along with her body. Now he was counting on two crooked cops to straighten things out.

"I need you to run a license plate number for me. I'm following a black Escalade with three of the jackers inside. The Georgia plate number is One-One-Six-K-K-M."

Detective Smith sat on the edge of the bed and radioed in the request as Prince called out the digits. He received the results in a matter of seconds. He wrote down the information and handed the sheet of paper to Agent Walker.

Agent Walker examined the slip with a worried look in his face. "This vehicle is registered to the Mayor's office. What the hell is going on?"

"The whip is most likely stolen. They left a line of exotic automobiles in my VIP parking lot last night. What I need you to do is have your people activate the On-Star GPS locator, but don't hit the engine kill switch just yet. I wanna know where these muthafuckas' are going. And another thing, Alonzo Guzman is coming to town. The drop is going down today, so be ready!"

230

Agent Walker and Detective Smith scrambled from the bed and grabbed their wrinkled clothes off the floor. A pungent smell lingered in the air, a reminder of their night of sinful debauchery and unprotected anal sex. No words were passed between them until they were speeding towards the 1st precinct in a government-issued Chevy Malibu.

"That bastard Najee has been playing us all along," Detective Smith remarked and blazed a cigarette. "I wonder what else he didn't tell us?"

"Probably a whole lot. I think it's time we show his black ass who he's fucking with!"

Detective Smith agreed and pressed the pedal to the metal. His partner flipped the switch to activate the sirens. They desperately needed to get to the station before Najee was released. The detective maneuvered the unmarked police car in and out of lanes, but morning rush hour traffic had the roads congested. Thinking quick, Agent Walker radioed the precinct, hoping to stop Najee's release.

Larry D. Wright

CHAPTER 23

Chess Not Checkers

After a slow and grueling process, Najee finally made it to the glass property window. The grouchy jail clerk purposely ignored the annoying sounds of the phone ringing while he slowly filled out several forms. Once finished, he rudely shoved an envelope containing Najee's wallet, Hublot watch, canary diamond earrings, and cell phone towards him.

Once outside he inhaled deeply, allowing the fresh down South air to fill his lungs. The sun was inching over the horizon, promising another hot day. He looked toward the rays of light escaping the partly cloudy sky and gave silent thanks.

The low battery indicator on his phone flashed off and on, telling him that the device was about to lose power. He threw his Pelle jacket over his shoulder and strolled at a brisk pace while dialing Maceo's number. Confusion mixed with joy overtook him when Nella answered the phone. He was surprised to hear her voice.

"Nella, is that you?" His mood brightened.

"Oh my God, Najee! I'm glad you called, baby. So much has been going on!" Tears formed in her eyes, she couldn't hold it in any longer.

"I'm already knowin', sweetheart. I'm just happy you're alive. Them mark ass niggas didn't hurt you, did they?"

Nella's entire body ached from her scalp to the cuticles on her manicured feet, yet she didn't reveal the pain she endured. "I'm good," she lied. "But I got bad news, Maceo is gone, baby. He got dropped this morning. I feel like it's my fault, I had his gun," she managed to say through sniffles.

Najee looked towards the sun rays shining through the morning clouds and shook his head from side to side. All his life he had been surrounded by death. It was only a matter of time before the demons reached up through hell and snatched him into his grave.

"It's not your fault, Nella. Maceo was a straight-up rider and a loyal soldier. I see the same qualities in you as well. Hold ya head up because shit is about to get even more grimy. I need you now more than ever."

The seeds of confidence he planted in her heart blossomed immediately. She was his murda mami and would remain devoted until the wheels fell off and the muffler was dragging. She sniffled one last time and wiped the tears from her blurry eyes. Najee needed her help, and she wasn't going to let the man of her wet dreams down. She pulled herself together and held her chin high.

"Okay, baby, I hear you. Just tell me what you want me to do."

Najee lowered his voice to a whisper, "First of all, keep a close eye on, Rio. He can't be trusted. Where is he at anyhow?" he asked in a secretive tone.

Nella sat in the backseat while Rio drove and Juice rode shotgun. When she looked up, Rio was watching her through the rearview mirror with a suspicious look on his face, as if he knew his name had been mentioned. Their eyes locked for a brief second and she saw something in him that she never noticed before—jealousy!

"The guys are right here with me. Everything is Gucci," she said to throw Rio off. "I spoke to, Mufasa. He told me all about the Somalians."

Najee knew better than anyone how closely Mufasa kept his ear to the concrete. Mentioning the Somali assassins was her way of telling him that she knew about the paper put on Rio's head.

"Sorry, you couldn't hear it from me first. The decision hurts, but it is what it is. First, we gotta do what we came here to do, and that's get some bread from these Block Boy Empire niggas. Rio will get dealt with after that. We need him for now. Tell everybody to screw their wigs on tight. We finna run up in the Blood Bank!"

"How are we gonna do that? You saw the surveillance footage. The Feds got the whole block hot." She pointed out.

"Trust me on this, baby girl. I got this shit all figured out. Just meet me at the spot on Glenridge Lane, ASAP. I'll explain everything then."

Nella let out a long breath. The last time Najee said he had it all figured out, she woke up in an abandoned warehouse with her arms tied behind her back. She looked at the purplish bruises on her wrist and was reminded of the perverted goon rubbing his erect private parts against her thigh while shoving the barrel of his pistol under her chin. Thinking about the ordeal gave her chills. She squeezed her eyes shut and deleted the memory from her mind. Now was not the time to get scared.

"Okay, we're headed that way now. We're in a black Escalade. I'll call you when we hit the block. And one more thing, Najee."

"What's good, Shawty."

"No matter what happens, I just want you to know how much I luv—"

Before she could confess her love for him, the call signal was dropped, and they were disconnected. Najee looked at the face of his cell phone. Damn! The screen faded black. His battery was dead. He put his head down and walked faster, putting as much distance between him and the police station as possible. He needed to find a phone booth to call his people in Edgewood and arrange for a fast car and some high power, automatic weapons.

'Was she about to say she loved me?' Najee's lips parted into a Crest white smile.

He was so engrossed with pleasant thoughts of Nella that he didn't notice the Chevy Malibu slowly creeping up behind him. When he eventually looked over his shoulder, it was too late. He had been caught slippin'. Detective Smith and Agent Walker were experts at jumping out of moving squad cars and apprehending suspects. Before Najee could react, the vehicle bounced over the curb and rolled on the sidewalk. The car pinned him between the fiberglass bumper and the concrete wall of a tall building.

Agent Walker swung the passenger door open and approached him with the swiftness of a starving panther. His lips were screwed into an angry frown. Najee's body stiffened when he saw the menacing look in the officer's eyes, but he showed no fear. He played it cool and put his hands on the hood of the car. The hot engine scorched the bottom of his palms.

Agent Walker threw a lightning-fast right hook, punching Najee hard in the stomach. Najee folded over in pain. Agent Walker connected again with a ferocious punch to the ribs. Najee groaned while holding his midsection. Drool dripped from the corner of his mouth.

"That was for lying to my partner," he shouted while pointing his index finger in Najee's face. "And this is for lying to me, asshole!"

Agent Walker's powerful knuckles landed just below Najee's chest and dug into his solar plexus, knocking the breath out of him. His stomach muscles contracted as he bent over in agony.

His first instinct was to reach for the officer's throat and rip out his Adam's apple, but he remained calm. Fighting back was a losing battle and would only make matters worse. Police brutality was all too common in the concrete jungle. Law enforcement used it to break you down physically before they broke you down mentally. The only way to defeat them was having a strong mind, not strong fists.

Detective Smith remained behind the wheel with a wide grin on his face as Agent Walker led Najee toward the backseat and shoved him inside. He put the car in reverse and they were gone as quickly as they came. When Najee looked up, they were back at the 1st precinct. The sight of the brick and glass slave plantation gave him an instant migraine.

The crooked officers led him roughly by the elbows down a long, isolated hallway. They stopped in front of a nondescript wooden door and shoved him inside. The makeshift interrogation room was very small and bare, except for two worn-out office chairs and a metal table. There were no windows, the dim 60-watt bulb swinging from the ceiling was the only light source. This room was the infamous torture chamber which brought so much shame and scandal to the department. When Najee's pupils adjusted, he saw dried up blood splatter on the walls.

Agent Walker sat at the table, and Najee plopped down in the chair opposite him. The two men stared at each other without blinking. Najee's dark eyes burned a hole in the agent's soul. He detested those who abused their position of power to oppress the weak.

Detective Smith walked behind Najee and rolled up his sleeves. He cracked his large knuckles before he spoke. "We got a few questions for you, and you're gonna answer each one of them truthfully. If you get cute, I'm gonna make sure you're pissing blood for the next month, understand?" When Najee didn't answer, the burly black detective punched him viciously in the kidney. "Do we have an understanding?"

Najee clenched his teeth and absorbed the pain. He knew their tactics well. The years he spent in solitary confinement molded him into a master at mental chess. He would prove to the dirty cops that a pawn was the most powerful piece on the board. Move number one, cause a distraction.

"Would one of you pigs please tell me what the fuck this is all about? I thought we had a deal!" Najee stated with authority.

"We did have a deal until we found out you were withholding information from us." Detective Smith slipped on a pair of black leather gloves.

"What information?"

Swack!

Detective Smith punched Najee in the kidney again. The force of the blow knocked him out of the chair. The detective leaned over and whispered in his ear. "I got all day. Breaking down thugs like you makes my dick hard, so I hope you like pain as much as I do." His hot breath made the hairs on the back of Najee's neck stand up.

Agent Walker cleared his throat. His role in the interrogation was to be the level headed, friendly cop. "Listen, buddy, my partner gets off on dishing out pain, but I'm more civilized. We already know why you were at club iCandy last night. Just tell us what you know about the BBE indictment and who told you."

Najee sat up and calculated the math in his head. Something wasn't adding up. He wondered how the authorities found out about his failed scheme to give Sosa vital information about their investigation in exchange for cash. He decided to level with the crooked po-po. They had different motives, but fate had brought them together for one common purpose. Chess move number two, offer yourself as bait.

"I'll never give up my source, but that's not important. If I'm correct, what's important is the money? I thought you wanted me and my crew to stick, Sosa?"

Detective Smith's mouth salivated at the mention of money. "We do, but we don't need any cowboys. We need you to pull this off low key. You've barely been in town twenty-four hours, yet there has already been a high-speed chase, a rookie cop murdered, a politician's SUV was stolen, and at least seven senseless homicides. What do you have to say for yourself?"

Najee shrugged his shoulders, "If it makes any difference, I didn't have anything to with stealing the Mayor's Escalade."

"How did you know it was an Escalade?"

"How did you know what I was doing at the club?" Najee shot back.

Silence echoed off the eggshell white walls. Agent Walker and Detective Smith looked at Najee, then stared at each other awkwardly for a brief moment. In the years since local law enforcement and the DEA created a joint task force in Atlanta, the two officers made many enemies on the streets and within the prestigious circles of law enforcement. The crimes they had perpetrated concealed behind their gold shields could land them in prison for life if revealed.

Recently, they both had agreed that it was time to retire before the pieces crumbled. Sosa and his illegal fortune was their meal ticket, and they were convinced that Najee and his elite crew of stick up artists could deliver him on a silver platter. It was now or never.

Agent Walker let out a deep breath. "As you probably know from the DEA's dossier, the key confidential informant is a man named, Princeton Riedel. He is a slick-talking ex-pimp, also known as Prince. We flipped him a few years ago. What you and everybody else don't know is that Prince is Sosa's biological father. Even Sosa doesn't know the truth. Sounds crazy, but it's a cold world."

"Anyhow, he was sent to prison for viciously beating Sosa's mother to death. Sosa was shuffled from foster homes and juvenile detention centers until he found refuge in the streets. He was just another two-bit hustler until Prince popped back on the scene and introduced him to a major drug runner named Alonzo 'Benzo Al' Guzman. The sky was the limit from there. For years he has been literally untouchable."

The names Prince and Benzo Al burned Najee's eardrums. He closed his eyes and clenched his teeth. Agent Walker's lips continued to move, but Najee couldn't hear him talking. His mind drifted into a faraway time and place. A place where his faith was lost to the burning smell of gunpowder and the odor of innocent blood being shed.

He became nauseous reliving the brutal murders of his mother, his first love, and the only father he had ever known. The deep scars on his body and soul were constant reminders of what was taken away from him. Now it was time to make those who were responsible pay restitution. Chess move number three, make your opponent your ally.

Agent Walker was still speaking when Najee held up a hand to cut him off. "I've heard enough! I need you to call your people off, Sosa. Send them on a wild goose chase or something so me and my team can run up in the Blood Bank. And I need weapons, body armor, a burn out phone, and a fast vehicle. How quick can you arrange all of that?"

Detective Smith showed all of his yellow tobacco-stained teeth as he smiled. "Quicker than you think. You're sitting right above the evidence room." *CheckMate*!

Larry D. Wright

CHAPTER 24

The Blood Bank

Benzo Al stood in the middle of his humid warehouse issuing orders. "Rapido, move faster!" he demanded between sips of Tecate beer. He stalked back and forth, ruling his domain like a mighty lion.

The Mexican immigrant workers scattered like Santa's Elves. They were in one of several cocaine distribution centers in the ATL operated by Los Cinco Diablos. A yellow forklift swooped up and sat down a wooden pallet stacked with kilos of Mexico's finest agricultural export. Each of the neat rows of duct-taped bricks had a sticker depicting a goofy cartoon character of President Donald Trump. Several muscular Latinos wearing wife-beaters and holding choppers stood alert keeping a watchful eye on the product.

Workers loaded bricks of coke into the hidden compartments of three compact vehicles and a large custom tour bus. One of the Toyota's was for Sosa and his Block Boy Empire soldiers. Benzo Al didn't perform any physical work, yet the armpits of his silk Versace shirt were sweaty. Being a boss was a difficult task.

"Pinche, puto!" he shouted at one of the immigrant workers who fumbled and dropped an arm full of kilos. "Be careful with the merchandise, carbon!"

"Si, Señor," the worker nervously replied.

After overseeing the vehicles get loaded, Benzo Al slid into the backseat of his cocaine white Maybach. Against better judgment, he decided to accompany the mules and drop the shipment off to Sosa personally. He had grown bored with sitting idle on the throne. He missed the excitement and adrenaline rush that came with hustling in the trenches. His closest and most trusted lieutenants advised him about being hands-on with so much product, but he ignored their wise words, reminding them that he had more cocaine stuck under his fingernails than they had ever seen in their lives.

The Maybach followed the convoy of vehicles out of the warehouse. A heavily armed Diablo goon chauffeured the luxury whip while Benzo Al lounged in the back. His larger than life persona was shielded by dark tinted windows and privacy curtains. He ran a fat cigar under his nose, admiring the rich aroma. To him, only one thing smelled better than a Cuban Havana and that was the scent of money. He lit the tip with a gold butane lighter and imagined the bodies of his enemies burning in the blue flames.

****

Sosa woke up and stretched his long limbs. His mouth was cotton dry, and he had a severe hangover. He looked at the two beautiful women sleeping next to him and let out a chuckle thinking about the birthday bash he threw for himself. He had to admit that last night was lit despite some broke ass niggas starting a fight in the club. He reached for the nightstand and grabbed his cell phone and the ashtray. Some people needed a strong cup of coffee to wake up. He needed weed. He lit the other half of a leftover Blackwood and scrolled through his phone. He had several missed calls from a couple of greedy gold diggers that he wanted to fuck and six new text messages.

A text from one phone number in particular immediately caught his attention. It was from Benzo Al. He tapped the touch screen to retrieve the message. It read, *//: Change in plans, amigo. Me and the white girls R on our way 2 the Blood Bank. B ready!*

Sosa snapped to attention and crushed out the tip of his stale blunt. He needed to get moving fast. He jumped out of bed and snatched the warm blanket off the two women. Their lovely naked bodies were entwined between the silk sheets. He admired both of their clean, shaved pussies for a moment, then gently shook the female who resembled an Egyptian goddess. Even in the morning with no makeup on, she was still a dime.

"Wake up, shawty. Y'all gotta go," he whispered nicely into her ear.

The Egyptian goddess moaned in her sleep and rolled over. She didn't want to leave the fantasy world she had created in her dreams. Sosa glanced at the face on his Audemars and grew impatient. He

242

walked over to the curtains and snatched the drapes open. Bright sun rays beamed directly on the bed like a spotlight.

The chocolate skinned club hostess was exhausted from a long night of partying and wild rough sex, but she woke up with a devilish grin stuck on her face. She blew him a kiss, slid out of bed and walked to the bathroom, making her plump booty bounce with every step just in case Sosa was watching. The Egyptian goddess, however, was angry as a vampire. She put a pillow over her head trying to block out the shining light. The pills, weed, and alcohol had worn off.

Sosa became irritated. "Bitch! Get cho' black ass up. Not now, but right now!" his thunderous voice sounded like a lion's roar.

The Egyptian goddess threw a pillow at him, then stomped to the bathroom and slammed the door. Sosa ignored her childish tantrum and looked out the balcony window. Something else had caught his attention. He looked down at the brown UPS delivery truck parked in the driveway and wondered how long it had been sitting there.

He glanced up and down the block. All of the exotic cars and tricked out SUV's from the night before were gone. The only vehicle left was a black Escalade sitting on 26-inch Forgis, a champagne-colored Range Rover, and his candy painted Rolls-Royce Wraith. He knew that the Range Rover belonged to his bodyguard, Bones. The Cadillac truck was unfamiliar.

It probably belonged to one of the workers, he surmised. The sound of Bones talking and laughing with someone downstairs eased his paranoia. He closed the drapes, then foolishly left his Heckler & Koch on the nightstand and joined the two women who were soaping each other up in the shower.

The soothing hot water hit his back as he contemplated the possible reasoning behind the plug making the drop himself. It was a risky move. The only conclusion he could come up with was that Benzo wanted to check on his operation to make sure everything was running smooth. Sosa humbly admitted that he had been trickin' off lately and burning through a lot of cash. He vowed to tone down his flamboyant lifestyle and get back on his square.

****

On the first level of the opulent mansion, Bones parted the bamboo blinds and squinted at the UPS delivery truck. Over the past two weeks, he had noticed several questionable vehicles and a suspicious lady walking her dog. His radar was up, but the sexy delivery lady disarmed him. "Damn, Cuz! Come check out this UPS chick, she thicker than a Snickers!" When he smiled, his platinum and diamond grill sparkled.

His companion, 2Face clicked buttons on a game controller and cussed at the high definition graphic flashing on the 85-inch flat-screen. His mind was engaged in a game of NBA Live.

"Ohhh wee, you missing the show, dawg. This bitch got a phat ass!" Bones informed him.

The delivery lady bent over seductively and sat two Dell computer boxes on the ground. Her brown UPS shorts inched up into her crack and exposed the bottom of her smooth ass cheeks. She retrieved her clipboard from the truck, then sashayed up the cobblestone pathway leading to the front entrance.

Bones swung open one of the large oak doors before she rang the bell. He greeted her with a grin, displaying his diamond-studded smile. His lustful eyes traveled up and down her luscious body, stopping at her juicy breasts. The top three buttons on her uniform were open, giving him an unobstructed view of her sexy cleavage. Blood drained from his brain and went straight to his dick. She had that effect on most men and a lot of women, too.

"Good morning, I have a delivery for this address. Would you mind signing for it and helping me with those big packages?" she asked politely and pointed toward the two boxes sitting on the ground.

'*I got a big package of my own I can help you with,*' Bones joked to himself.

He looked over his shoulder and saw 2Face sitting on the leather couch clutching the Xbox controller and cussing at Kobe Bryant on the TV. He turned back toward the UPS delivery lady and

244

determined that she was harmless. He followed her to the back of the truck, admiring her mesmerizing hips as they swayed from side to side. She was just his type.

"I hope my bluntness doesn't offend you, baby gurl, but you killin' them shorts! What's yo' name?" he inquired while giving her the Denzel look. Not many women turned down a baller on his level.

"Some people call me, Huny. Some people call me, Yellow Gurl, but you can call me the bitch that set you up!"

"Huh, what did you say?" he asked with confusion on his face. His question was quickly answered. Rio and Juice were hiding in the back of the UPS truck with their weapons locked and loaded. Bones had two automatic weapons pointed at his dome. He knew what time it was and put his hands high in the air. His Denzel look transformed into a treacherous mask

Chic! Chic!

The sound of metal scraping against metal drew all of their attention to the front entrance. 2Face stood boldly in the doorway with a Givenchy hoody over his head and pointing an AKM automatic rifle in their direction. An AKM is a shorter version of an AK-47 and was the weapon of choice for Saddam Hussein's deadly soldiers. 2Face gritted his teeth and squeezed the trigger, launching scorching hot bullets in their direction. The slugs turned the side of the UPS truck into Swiss cheese.

Rio, Juice, and Nella ducked behind the truck for shelter. Thinking fast, Bones broke free and ran toward the house. Rio tried to shoot him in the back but didn't have a clear shot. In an astonishing display of calmness amid chaos and mayhem, 2Face kept blasting like he was a member of the Taliban. The gunfights he survived in the hood, and the many hours he spent playing Call of Duty, prepared him for this day. He was a young rider.

"Hurry up nigga, get in here!" he yelled.

Bones dove through the door and landed hard on his baller belly. 2Face let off another rapid burst of shots before slamming the front door. He lay on his back on the floor and inserted another clip into the bottom of his stick.

The team didn't hesitate to follow pursuit. Juice jacked a round into the chamber of an RPK light machine gun and tossed it to Nella. After peaking around the corner, he yelled, "Go, go, go!" They stormed the house and placed their backs against two large pillars that decorated the archway entrance.

Bones crawled to the couch and lifted one of the leather seat cushions. He pulled out a big black AR-15 with two clips joined together by electrical tape and then stuck a Glock with an extended clip into his waistband.

"These muthafuckas want war? I'ma take 'em to war! I'ma show these cockroaches how BBE get down!" He was gassed up and in full Tony Montana mode.

Upstairs in the steaming hot shower, Sosa heard the thunderous clap of gunfire. His heart thumped in his chest. He turned off the water and listened intensely. The two frightened women hugged each other tightly. Their annoying whimpers broke his concentration.

"Shhh, shut the fuck up! I'm tryna' hear what's goin' on out there!"

To his dismay, the Egyptian goddess started to cry louder. "Don't tell me what to do, I don't wanna die like this. They after you, not us." Tears ran down her cheeks.

Sosa wanted to smack her ditzy ass but somehow knew that his mother, wherever she may be, wouldn't approve of him hitting a woman. He grabbed her roughly by the shoulders but spoke softly, "Listen shawty, you need to be quiet and let me focus. Whoever is doing all that shooting probably is after me, but do you really think they gon' let the witnesses survive?" He regretted the comment as soon as the words left his lips. She became hysterical and sobbed even louder.

As quickly as the gunfight started, the shooting suddenly stopped. The two petrified women took that as their opportunity to leave and ran to the bathroom door.

"No, don't go out there!" Sosa protested.

They ignored his warning. Sosa stepped out of the shower with urgency and wrapped a white cotton towel around his waist. He

246

grabbed the .22 that he kept taped under the toilet and checked the clip. It was fully loaded. He cautiously crept out of the bathroom. The house was quiet, a little too quiet. From his angle, he had a view of his bed and the nightstand. His gun was gone, but someone had left the bullets behind!

His heart rate increased. He gripped the banger tighter and slowly inched into the bedroom. A cool breeze caused the balcony curtains to flap in the wind. Sosa froze, someone had opened the sliding glass window. The shooting outside started again. He could hear the sound of empty shells clinking off the ground.

"Drop the gun!" Najee demanded.

He clutched two chrome .40 caliber handguns. One was pointed at Sosa, the other was aimed at the two women with their backs against the wall trembling with fear. Sosa swung his pistol in the direction of the deep voice. His nervous trigger finger shook like he had Parkinson's disease, but he held his ground. The two men faced off, sizing each other up.

"You got until the count of three to stop pointing that small ass strap at me, or I'ma shoot one of these bitches!" Najee's threat sounded like a promise, but Sosa remained defiant. If it was his time to go, then he was gonna go out with a bang. The intruder started counting slowly. "One—two—"

Bluka!

Najee didn't have the patience to count all the way to three. He aimed at the prettiest girl and squeezed the trigger. The slugs slammed the beautiful Egyptian goddess into the wall. She looked at Najee with disbelief in her tearful eyes as she clutched her stomach, trying to keep her insides from spilling out. Sosa watched her body slide down the wall in slow motion. Her body jerked before it expired.

"Okay, let's start over," Najee said with the calmness of a serial killer. "Drop your gun before I shoot this other hoe!"

No one doubted his words. The chocolate skinned club hostess begged Sosa to put down his weapon. Her desperate pleas drowned out the sounds of the violent shootout.

"*Fuck that!*" Sosa mumbled to himself. There was no way he was going to disarm. Not without a fight first. "Who sent you?" Sosa asked. "Was it that punk ass nigga, Prince? I knew he was a fuckin' snake from the jump!"

Najee aimed both of the twin barrels directly at Sosa. "I thought Prince was your right-hand man?" he quoted the information given to him by Jezz and Dee in the 1st Precinct holding tank.

"He is, I was taught to keep my enemies close. So, if it ain't Prince, then it's gotta be my money hungry bodyguard, Bones. I guess he's tired of skimming off the top and making side deals behind my back."

Najee eased up and lowered one of the pistols. "Damn, bruh! You don't trust nobody, do you?"

Sosa thought about the tattoos on his face. "With all the shit I been through, I can't afford to. I give 'em enough rope to hang themselves in the air, then I kick away the chair."

The front door crashed open and more gunshots crackled. Najee backed up slowly and checked the hallway while keeping a cautious eye on Sosa and the naked girl. The coast was clear, but a fierce gun battle could be heard downstairs.

"Listen, homie, we don't have a lot of time, so I'll break this down quick. Prince is a snitch! The Feds about to hit you and twenty other BBE associates with a conspiracy charge and some more shit that I can't even pronounce. But I know everything about the sealed indictments. The names of the informants, who being followed, which spots are being watched, everything you need to fuck up their case. I was at the club last night to see how much money that information was worth to you, but Prince ran interference."

Sosa jaws dropped open as his brain sautéed the stranger's words. "I knew Prince was a shiesty nigga, but I never would've guessed that he was working with them, people. He ain't even built like that."

"There's more," Najee paused before dropping the most devastating bombshell, "Prince is your father! He went to jail for beating your mother to death when she was pregnant with you!"

248

The Streets Made Me

Sosa was speechless, he stumbled backward on weak knees and sat on the edge of the bed holding his head in his hands. A buffet of emotions ran through his heart. Hurt, anger, disbelief, and revenge.

"How do I know what you're saying is valid? You come stormin' up in this bitch like you Clint Eastwood. Wavin' guns in my face. You done kilt one of my bitches. Nigga's is shootin' outside. What the fuck is going on?"

Najee lowered the other gun to his side. He empathized with the powerful drug dealer, in many ways they were just alike. Their mothers had been killed by the same man, they were raised by the streets, and they both had been betrayed by someone close to them.

Najee contemplated telling Sosa about his own biological mother Monica and the toxic pill that Prince slipped in her drink, but the subject was too painful to talk about. Instead, Najee told Sosa about the crooked cops and their elaborate plot to rob and assassinate him. In return, Sosa offered Najee a deal he couldn't refuse, half of the money he had stashed in a secret underground bunker in exchange for helping him escape. They shook hands, cementing their alliance. Najee glanced at his watch and then ran to the balcony window to check the scene. Time was running out.

249

Larry D. Wright

CHAPTER 25

Rat Trap

Across the street, Prince carefully climbed up the wooden scaffold attached to a house that was under construction. He found the perfect spot to post up, and then laid on his stomach. He cussed under his breath at all the dust and filth staining his expensive suit. He quickly set up his SK sniper rifle equipped with a 10 power Unertl scope and looked through the viewfinder. Nella was locked in his sight as she stormed the front entrance, exchanging gunfire with Bones and 2Face.

Seconds before his index finger squeezed the trigger, he was distracted by three loud gunshots coming from Sosa's bedroom. He aimed the highly accurate rifle at the open balcony window and watched as Sosa and Najee faced off. He recognized Najee as one of the Body Snatchers from the club, but something else about his features looked familiar. He just couldn't put his finger on it. He watched the men through the scope and became enraged when Sosa shook hands with the enemy.

Prince tracked their movements and smiled when Najee looked out of the balcony window and gave him a clear shot. The powerful scope made the Polo logo on Najee's shirt look like it was next to his eyeball. He squeezed the trigger.

Bluka!

Birds scattered from the treetops as the lava hot ammunition sliced through the air and slammed into Najee's chest, knocking him off his feet. Najee was unconscious before his body hit the floor. One shot, one kill! Satisfied with his work, Prince recalibrated the scope and aimed the SK at Nella. The yellow and brown UPS emblem on her uniform appeared in 3D.

Frightened birds flying from the safety of their nests gave away Prince's position. Juice pumped the action grip on his sawed-off Street Sweeper and blasted buckshots in his direction.

"Sniper at six o'clock!" Juice yelled and took cover.

Nella dropped to one knee just in time. A bullet from the sniper's rifle whizzed over her head and knocked a large chunk of plaster out of the pillar she was standing next to. She applied pressure to her trigger and retaliated with a rapid succession of shots, spraying the rooftop from left to right. Prince zigzagged while running for shelter with the SK rifle strapped over his shoulder. She recognized him immediately.

"Prince is on the roof! Get that nigga!" Nella screamed while pointing in his direction.

Nella and Juice simultaneously lit up the vacant property like it was the fourth of July. Rio kept his weapon trained on the mansion. He loved using the M-240 Gulf machine gun that Najee borrowed from the police evidence room. It had been confiscated from the Outlaw's biker gang during a raid on a meth lab. The belt fed rounds ate through the solid oak door, leaving it smoldering and slightly ajar.

Bones and 2Face took positions flat on their stomachs as bullets shattered glass all around them. "On the count of three, I want you to swing the door open with your foot. I'm finna air these fuck niggas out. You with me?" Bones whispered.

"Let's get buck in the bitch!" 2Face replied with courage. He rolled onto his back and nudged the door open with the toe of his Air Jordan's.

Bones rushed through the door letting his AR-15 spit. The fully-auto jerked in his hands. Fire spit from the muzzle. Expended shells discharged from the shaft.

Flack! Flack! Flack!

Following Bones' lead, 2Face rose to his feet with the chopper extended towards the enemy and squeezed off. The powerful slugs knocked chips out of the cement pillars. Rio dove for cover. Nella and Juice pivoted towards the mansion and returned fire. The faint sound of approaching police sirens inched closer.

Bones and 2Face stood side by side holding it down for the BBE name and reputation. They were two soldiers who lived and were obviously ready to die by the gun. Fire flashed from the muzzle of their killing machines as they held the thieves at bay.

Despite their valiant efforts, their zeal and bravery was no match for trained warriors with superior artillery. Teflon coated slugs and double-o-buck shots tore through their torsos. They collapsed in a twisted tangle of bloody flesh. The plush white carpet soaked up their life. The team bum-rushed the door, stepping over the dead bodies as they entered the house with caution.

Upstairs in the master bedroom, Najee was stretched out on his back staring at the spinning blades of the ceiling fan. The last time he was shot, he woke up with a clear tube in his nose, an IV in his arm, and a catheter in his penis. This time he was thankful for the Rhino body armor. Thanks to the bulletproof vest, he was only knocked unconscious and suffered bruises to his rib cage.

As Sosa analyzed Najee's wounds, Juice kicked the bedroom door off the hinges. Rio and Nella barged in. For the second time that morning, Sosa had multiple guns pointed at his face.

"Drop the gun!" Nella demanded.

'*Here we go again,*' Sosa thought as he dropped his iron and raised his hands.

The petrified club hostess used her hands to cover her big breasts and shaved private parts. The team turned their weapons on her next.

"Bitch, you ain't special! Put your hands in the air, too!" Nella ordered.

Noticing Najee on his back, she rushed to his side and dropped to her knees. She observed a quarter-sized burn mark in his shirt where the Polo logo used to be, and tears swelled behind her eyelids. Despite not seeing any blood, she thought the worse. She was relieved to learn that the Kevlar had absorbed the slug.

Najee grunted in pain and reached up to pull her into his warm embrace. She tried to speak, but his full lips pressed against hers and stopped the words. Nothing needed to be said. Their tongues slow danced to the melody of love. At that moment, nothing else mattered. They were suspended in time. He pulled her closer, never wanting to let go.

Sosa cleared his throat. "Ughh, ummm, I don't mean to break up this happy reunion, but we gotta get ghost," he insisted while tapping the face of his sixty-three thousand-dollar Audemars Piguet.

Nella cupped the back of Najee's head and helped him sit up. He shook the dizziness off and slowly climbed to his feet. He was sore but ready for action. The wailing sound of police sirens was getting louder. Najee snapped into combat mode, issuing instructions with the confidence of a boss.

"Sosa is right, we gotta bounce, but first we're gonna load up the UPS truck with some bags. Nella, I want you to tie up the female. If she gives you any static, shoot her. Juice, I need you to stay up here and stay on point. You can see whose coming and who's going from the balcony."

"I'm down for whatever, B, but I need some heat if I'm gonna be on security. I only have one shell left."

"I feel you. Rio, give him the M-240 and you take this." He passed Rio the Heckler & Koch Sosa left on the nightstand. "Then I need you to go downstairs and pull the UPS truck inside the garage. That's our ticket out of here. I'll meet y'all in a minute, there's something I gotta do."

Everyone fell into position. Rio slowly backed the truck into the garage. Sosa assisted him with the expertise of an airport worker guiding an airplane on the runway. Once the delivery truck rolled over a large slab on concrete, Sosa held up his palms, directing Rio to stop. He ran to the utility box on the far wall and pushed a green button that engaged the hydraulic floor. The truck and slab of concrete slowly sank into the ground. This was big boy criminal enterprising. The Block Boys were on a whole 'nother level.

"Well, I'll be damned!" Nella remarked. She admired the sophistication of Sosa's organization. Being plugged with Los Cinco Diablos had its perks.

Everyone paused when they heard a single gunshot explode from the Street Sweeper followed by Najee rushing into the garage. No one noticed that he had changed clothes. The Givenchy hoodie and retro Jordan's that 2Face had on fit him perfectly. All of them climbed down the ladder that led into a climate-controlled bunker.

They were greeted by several brown boxes stuffed with cold hard cash. A golf cart was plugged into an electric charger.

"Don't waste your time with the duffel bags," Sosa instructed. "They're filled with low denominations. We don't have a lot of time, so concentrated on the boxes filled with blue faces. Oh, yeah, watch out for the rat traps." Sosa made eye contact with Najee as he spoke.

They formed a soul train line and quickly tossed the packages into the back of the truck. As they were loading the boxes, Sosa's last phrase tumbled through Najee's head. *"Watch out for the rat traps—watch out for the rat traps!"* The warning held a deep symbolic meaning, but he couldn't decipher the cryptic words.

Once complete, Rio jumped back into the driver's seat, everyone else rushed up the ladder. Sosa pressed the green button again, and the pressurized hydraulic pumps lifted the truck with ease. The concrete slab slipped back into place, concealing any evidence of an underground chamber.

Right on cue, Juice stepped from the shadows brandishing the deadly machine gun. Najee was happy to see him. "Good timing, bruh, let's get the fuck outta here while we still got a chance."

Juice didn't budge. He kept the barrel of the M-240 aimed at his target. Najee looked into his eyes searching for an answer, but Juice lowered his head in shame. The full weight of Sosa's words fell squarely upon Najee's shoulders. Juice had betrayed him. Disgust and disappointment left a bitter after taste on his tongue.

Rio climbed out of the truck brandishing the Heckler and Koch. "Thanks for leading us to the paper. It's been fun but we gotta run," he remarked sarcastically and removed the two chrome .40 calibers from Najee's waistline. He kicked them under the truck, a smug look of victory and satisfaction was smeared on his face.

Najee ignored the comment and focused on Juice. "I know why Rio snaked me. He's been a player hater all his life. But why you, my nigga? This is how you treat me, huh? After all the shit I've done for you?"

"After all you've done for me? Nigga, please! You using us as toy soldiers in your own personal war, B. Fuck that! Double-crossing you was my idea."

As the last words left his lips, Najee attacked with a swift left jab and right hook. The mighty blows slammed into Juice's face and crushed the cartilage in his nose. He dropped to his knees, blood dripped from his nostrils like a leaky faucet.

After watching Juice fall, Najee dashed towards the RPK machine gun that Nella left propped against the wall. He grabbed the weapon and spun around but came face to face with the dark barrel of a 9mm.

"That bulletproof vest ain't gon' save you this time!" Rio clenched his teeth and pulled the trigger.

Click! Click! The gun didn't fire. *Click! Click! Click!* Rio kept squeezing the trigger unwilling to believe the obvious. He had been tricked, the clip was empty.

Najee laughed. "The art of war is mental. Did you really think I would give yo' fool ass a loaded gun?"

He didn't wait for a reply. He emptied the whole clip into Rio's chest. Rio's agonizing screams drowned out the tink-tink sound of empty shells hitting the concrete. The force of the blast knocked him flat on his back. White smoke and thick blood poured from the gaping bullet wounds. His insides burned. His eyelashes grew heavy. He fought to keep his eyes open but was losing the battle. His mouth moved, but no words came out. Najee moved closer to read his lips.

Rio managed to whisper, "I'm sorry." His body went limp, and his condemned soul descended into purgatory.

Najee didn't have long to mourn the twisted, fatal death of his childhood friend. Juice was on his feet waving the lethal M-240. "Y'all know what it is. Everybody get the fuck up against the wall."

No one was close enough to attack. They had no choice but to comply with Juice's demands. They lined up against the wall like sitting ducks, the movie of their lives flashing before their eyes in high definition. Death was certain, but surprisingly, Juice cautiously backed up and climbed behind the wheel of the UPS truck. A collective sigh of relief could be heard as the truck rolled in reverse out of the garage.

Pac! Pac! Pac! Pac!

Juice didn't get far, the echo of an assault rifle penetrated the silence. "Get down, get down!" Najee cried out and used his body as a protective shield as he pulled Nella to the ground.

Two muscular Latinos with bronze skin and angry war faces stood in front of a Toyota Camry spraying bullets from an AR-15 and AK-47. The lethal slugs chewed through the loading door of the UPS truck. Juice mashed on the accelerator and rammed the rear metal bumper into the fiberglass front of the Camry. The two Los Cinco Diablos goons jumped out of the way and continued to spray the truck with slugs. They had him trapped.

Juice put the stick shift in drive and drove forward. He then slammed the stick shift into reverse gear and smashed into the Camry again. He kept his heavy foot on the gas. The tires spun out, polluting the air with smoke and burnt rubber as he pushed the smaller vehicle out of his path.

Benzo Al watched the scene unfold from the security of his Maybach. The smoky aroma of his expensive cigar was replaced by the stench of death. Had he arrived minutes earlier, he would've gotten caught up in the mix. His chubby fingers calmly rubbed his wooden rosary beads. He thanked the Virgin Mary for her mercy and protection.

Benzo Al's driver pulled off slowly. As they cruised down the winding suburban thoroughfare, a convoy of police cars and unmarked law enforcement vehicles raced past them in the opposite direction. Benzo Al had dodged another bullet and would live to trap another day.

As he rolled the beads between his fingers, a wicked grin formed on his lips. You could almost see the mental gears churning inside his head. He had finally discovered who was behind the notorious stickup crew known as the Body Snatchers and why he was their main target. He ran another Havana under his nose and clipped off the end. Before he fired up the cigar, he slapped his thigh and roared with laughter. Najee was a grown man now, but he remembered the curious little boy sitting in Boulevard's Cadillac like it was yesterday.

Benzo Al's grin swiftly transformed into an evil frown. He put away his rosary beads and pulled out his trusty, pearl-handled gun. His finger massaged the trigger as he remembered the stern warning he gave Boulevard about fucking with his money. He vowed to teach Najee the same lesson.

The sound of police sirens was no longer a noise blaring in the distance. The long arm of the law had arrived. Black and white squad cars with red and blue flashing lights descended upon the scene like army ants. A navy blue SWAT van blocked off the driveway. The sliding door swung open and six trained members of the Special Weapons and Tactics team deployed with their automatics drawn.

The cartel gangsters ignored the commands to drop their weapons. They didn't speak English. Furthermore, surrender was not in their vocabulary. They stood shoulder to shoulder and opened fire on the police. The jakes responded with their own deadly arrows and chopped the two men down on the front lawn. Their blood watered the grass.

Juice was less brazen. He ran back into the house and tripped over the two dead Block Boy Empire soldiers as he rushed through the doorway. He grabbed Bones' AR-15 assault rifle and tried to scramble to his feet but slipped in blood.

Najee, Nella, and Sosa were still in the garage. They remained prone on their stomachs as gunshots rained around them. Najee saw Juice make a run for the house and couldn't resist the temptation to grab his twin .40 calibers and chase after him.

"Where you goin', mane? We gotta bounce up outta here. The Alphabet Boys got the spot surrounded!" Sosa stated. He made a dash to the far wall and pressed the green button that controlled the levitating cement floor. "Two years ago, I had a tunnel built below that leads to a house I bought on the next block. That's how we smuggle the money in undetected."

The modest single-family home he spoke about sat one street over and directly behind the infamous Blood Bank. Once again,

Nella was impressed with the cleverness and vast amount of resources Sosa's criminal enterprise had access to. The hope of escaping reenergized her soul, but Najee had other plans. Prince and Benzo Al had gotten away, which increased his burning desire to exterminate Juice.

He walked over and gave the drug lord a firm handshake. "Get her out of here safely, Sosa. I got some loose ends that need to be tied."

Nella blocked his path when he turned to leave. She didn't want him to go. "Baby, are you crazy? We have a chance to escape. We finally have a chance to be together," she pleaded.

"Move out of my way!"

"No!"

"I said move!"

"Give me one of your guns. If you ride, then I'm riding with you," she declared.

Najee studied the features of her angelic face. She was beautiful. She was extraordinary, but most importantly, she was loyal. He felt as though he didn't deserve her. Everything he touched somehow crumbled. His lips gently touched her forehead before he spoke. "Go with Sosa, Lil' mama. I'll meet you on the other side. I promise."

Nella reluctantly followed Sosa down the ladder. It took them deep into the secret bunker. Najee blew her a kiss, and then pressed the switch that lifted the concrete slab back into place. He hoped this wouldn't be the last time they saw each other.

It was a risky move, but Najee made a mad dash for the mansion just as the two cartel members were chopped down by the SWAT team. He zig-zagged through a hailstorm of police bullets and burst through the front door, tripping over the lifeless bodies of Bones and 2Face. He fell on the blood-soaked carpet in time to see Juice sliding open the glass patio door. Juice turned around and let the AR-15 spit. Deadly .223 ammunition whisked by Najee's dome and tore chunks out of the drywall.

Najee rose up and tried to clap back, but he lost his footing and slipped. He landed on the soggy carpet and watched Juice

259

effortlessly tumble over the backyard fence. Najee clenched his jaws and let both .40 calibers loose, missing Juice by inches. He rose to one knee and continued squeezing the trigger, but his efforts were useless.

Juice dashed through the normally peaceful neighborhood until he spotted a middle-aged white lady unloading groceries. He jammed the stick into her rib cage and demanded the keys to her Tesla.

Inside the hidden bunker, Sosa moved quickly and unplugged the golf cart from the battery charger. A ramp lowered revealing a long tunnel. It was rumored that the contractors who dug the underground passage were executed once the project was complete, ensuring that only a select few knew of its existence.

"Give me a hand with these duffel bags, Shawty. We can't take 'em all, but we're not leaving here empty-handed either."

Out of curiosity, Nella leaned over and unzipped one of the oversized, Gucci bags. She was greeted by three long slabs of illegally obtained U.S. currency shrink wrapped in clear plastic. Benjamin Franklin's big face was the centerpiece of each $100 dollar bill. She zipped the heavy bag and tossed it on the golf cart.

Sosa read the question on her lips before she asked, "There's one million compressed dollars in each duffel bag. I haven't survived the game this long by being a fool. Feel me? Niggas like Rio and Juice are fueled by greed. That's why the boxes are decoys filled with dummy money!" He loaded four more duffel bags onto the golf cart before getting behind the wheel.

The bumpy dirt road in the tunnel was only 145 feet long, but the trip felt like a mile. The air quality was stale, and Nella felt claustrophobic, but Sosa operated the buggy like a vet. He had taken this route many times before, eluding federal agents, nosey neighbors, and the stickup kids.

Halogen headlights illuminated the dark, chilly path making Nella feel like she was traveling through an MRI machine. Just when she thought she would suffocate to death, they came to the end of the tunnel.

Sosa climbed up a rusty metal ladder built into the concrete and twisted open a steel security latch. He carefully pushed open a hidden panel that led up to a fake fireplace. He stuck his head through and scanned the humble-looking living room. The house was just as he left it.

Nella handed Sosa each duffel bag, and he shoved all five through a narrow opening. He climbed up first and then reached down with one of his long, strong arms to assist Nella. Once she made it inside the house, she took a large gulp of fresh air. They were dirty and visibly shaken but happy to be alive. That joy was short-lived.

Nella smelled his expensive cologne before she felt him pointing his gun. She spun around and saw Prince leaning coolly against the dining room wall. Their eyes locked, but this time she did not turn away. She met his intimidating glare with an intense stare of her own. Sosa stood defiantly by her side with the money bags at his feet.

Prince licked his lips, openly giving Nella's body a once over. The tight UPS uniform showed off her curvy figure. "We gotta stop meeting like this," his words dripped with sarcasm.

She charged at him swinging her small but solid fist. "You bastard!" Sosa grabbed her arms to restrain her before she got a chance to scratch his eyes out.

Prince chuckled as she kicked, thrashed, and struggled to break free. "You better keep that bitch in heat on a leash before I stick this pistol up her pussy and squeeze the trigger," he snapped.

"Fuck off you, rat!" she screamed with venom. "You're a snitch! Your name is Princeton Riedel. I saw how you flinched when I said your name back at the warehouse. You're an informant and a washed-up, fake ass pimp!" Her words broke bones like stones.

Prince raised his pistol and cocked back the hammer, but Sosa bravely stepped in front of Nella. "You wouldn't shoot your own son would you?" He enjoyed the look of surprise on his father's face as he revealed the truth.

Larry D. Wright

Prince's facial expression went blank. "How long have you known?"

Before Sosa could respond, Detective Smith burst out of the kitchen with Agent Walker following closely on his heels. Their presence shocked Sosa and Nella.

"He won't shoot you, but I will! So, step away from my money, asshole!"

Sosa and Nella stepped away from the money. Walker and Smith scooped up two duffel bags apiece leaving one for Prince. It was his Judas reward for selling out his own flesh and blood.

The ex-pimp stopped at the front door with the Gucci bag strapped over his shoulder. He turned and offered a few consoling words, more to soothe his own lost soul than anything else. "I wish thangs could've turned out different, son, but this is real life. This ain't the Cosby Show or one of those fake ass street literature books. Know what I'm sayin'? You got a good heart. I hate I even introduced you to this scandalous game. I advise you to get out before you end up dead, or even worse, become like me!"

"I'll never be like you!" Sosa yelled with anger.

Prince pretended like the comment didn't sting, but once outside, he leaned against the door and let out a deep breath. His guilty conscience felt heavier than the duffel bag containing the million dollars. He looked up towards the sky. Something didn't feel right. The bright sun felt hotter as if Lucifer himself had deliberately turned up the temperature.

Neither Prince nor the crooked cops paid attention to the three Kawasaki motorcycles revving their souped-up engines as they zoomed down the narrow residential street. They were deep within their own selfish thoughts.

When Prince finally noticed the motorcycles, it was too late. The first thing he saw was three armed men dressed in black. The last feeling he felt was pain.

Flacka! Flacka! Flacka!

Gunshots from the three fullies disturbed the peace. The Somalis on steel horses sprayed everything in sight. No person, animal, or structure was exempt from their reckless gunfire. They

262

had a reputation for being careless and sloppy, however, their ruthless method of execution was highly effective. Shoot everything moving, and you'll never miss your target was the assassin's creed they lived by.

Detective Smith and Agent Walker were viciously gunned down in the streets as they loaded the duffel bags into the trunk. Agent Walker took two shots to the back and a lethal shot to the dome. Unmerciful hollow-point bullets turned his internal organs into mush. As his body dropped, Detective Smith reached for his holster and drew his weapon.

Experience and a stronger will to survive allowed him to live a few seconds longer, but death was inevitable! The department issued bulletproof vest offered protection for his chest and midsection, but the gunslingers were aiming for the neck up. Detective Smith popped off two wild shots before he was sprayed in the face with a fully. His lifeless corpse fell hard on the curb. His fluids seeped into the concrete cracks.

Prince was struck several times in the spine as he banged on the door, desperately trying to get back inside the house. Hot lead brought him to his knees. His sweaty hands slipped off the doorknob, and he landed face down on the porch. He coughed and hacked up thick blood clots and slimy saliva as a cloud of blackness hovered above him.

The gunners did a U-turn at the intersection and came back to admire their destruction. Nella looked out of the window. One of the bikers lifted the dark, tinted shield on his helmet to make sure the vic's were dead. Nella's mouth dropped open. It was Mufasa! Their eyes met briefly. He winked at her before his back tire burned rubber.

Sosa and Nella eased out of the house and watched Prince squirm in agony. He tried to crawl down the steps but collapsed into a puddle of his own blood. Even while gasping for his last breath of air, he was still arrogant and greedy. He clutched the duffel bag tightly in his fist as if he could take the money to hell with him. Nella reached down and pulled his .44 Bulldog from his waistline. Anger, bitterness, and hatred flowed through the bone marrow in her trigger finger. She wanted to blast him but watching him suffer was equally rewarding.

Prince looked up at Sosa, pleading for help. His red eyes silently begged for mercy. The slugs in his back released poisonous toxins, which attacked his central nervous system and caused his legs to go numb. He was dying a slow, painful death. If he was lucky, paralysis would kick in before his body went into shock. He coughed up more brownish-red blood.

"My son, please don't let me go out like this. I know shit ain't been right between us, but I'll make it up to you. On my word."

"Oh, now I'm your son, huh? Fuck that, mane! All the shit I've been through. Now you wanna make it up to me?" He turned to Nella. "Clap this nigga and put him out of his misery."

Nella stepped closer and aimed the barrel at his melon. "Wait! Wait!" Prince pleaded. "Don't let that bitch shoot me, son. Take my gun away from her triflin' ass and help me get out of here. I promise I'll make thangs right between us. You gotta believe me, Marcus. At least give ya pops a chance."

Hearing his real name caused a voltage of electricity to shoot through his body. He thought about all the foster homes, project buildings, and correctional facilities that raised him. He thought about all the holidays, birthdays and lonely nights he spent wondering who he was, where he was from, and where he was going. Shady characters became his siblings and the cold streets became his caretaker. Thinking about the unnecessary pain he endured made him despise his dead beat father even more.

"Let me smoke his punk ass, Sosa!" Nella begged.

Hearing his hood name snapped him back into reality. He looked at Prince one last time, searching for a trace of sincerity or physical resemblance between the two of them. He didn't see any of either. He was still standing tall through it all, and Prince was shrinking right before his eyes. Killing him would be easy, he deserved to suffer in Hades.

"Let him die slow. He's not even worth the bullet," Sosa said as he pried the duffel bag out of Prince's stiff fingers and walked away.

264

"Sosa! Sosa!" Prince screamed in agony. "I'll see you in hell, muthafucka!"

Nella pried the keys to the Malibu from Detective Smith's cold fingers and tossed them to Sosa. They drove off just as a hooded figure stood on the porch watching the ex-pimp crawl on his stomach like a snake. Prince felt a commanding presence towering over him. He thought it was Sosa.

"My man, I knew you wouldn't leave me hanging like this. I'm gonna keep my promise and change my ways, that's on everythang." He hacked up dark clumps of blood as he spoke.

The hooded figure grabbed a fist full of his bullet-riddled shirt and flipped him over. Prince looked up startled and confused. The man snatched the hoody off his head to give Prince a better view. Their eyes locked. Prince instantly recognized the facial features of his executioner.

"Before you do anything crazy. I just want you to know that I truly loved your mother."

Najee didn't give Prince a chance to repent. He pressed the cold barrel of the burner between his bushy eyebrows and squeezed the trigger.

Prince went into severe shock and started to convulse. His organs stopped working, causing his bowels and bladder to let loose. His last act on earth was pissing and defecating in his pants. Exhaling one last painful breath, the infamous pimp was dead. Flies buzzed around his crotch area enjoying the aroma of postmortem flesh.

****

Later that night at the Hilton Hotel, Nella soaked her aching limbs in a soothing bubble bath, neither the hot water nor the chilled bottle of Moscato could wash away her sorrow. Her life would never be the same.

She took a long swallow straight from the bottle and let her arms dangle over the edge of the tub as she poured out a drop of liquor for each of her fallen comrades. She was fucked up in the head over their greed and treacherous betrayal, but she still loved them like brothers.

News channels headlined the day of deadly events with special interest. Had it simply been a shootout in the ghetto, the story would have only received a limited amount of coverage, but a tantalizing story about money, murder, and mayhem erupting in an upscale suburban neighborhood was too irresistible for the national media outlets to ignore. CNN and TMZ camera crews swooped in like vultures.

Nella turned up the volume to the flat screen monitor that was mounted in the bathroom and listened to the local news for the fifth time that evening. She watched as several reporters shoved microphones in the police spokesman's face, overwhelming him with questions. *"Do you have any leads? Is the Mayor somehow involved? Are the reports about an underground tunnel true, and if so, is there any connection to similar tunnels that were discovered in Arizona and Mexico?"* The spokesman declined to comment, pushed his way through the thick crowd of journalist, and ducked under the yellow tape. The cameras then switched to a shot of the bullet riddles mansion.

Nella hit the power button and closed her eyes. She tried to concentrate on the two duffel bags sitting in the next room and how she would use the two million dollars to complete the Alive365 project, but she couldn't focus. The news anchor's booming voice and the graphic images of bodies covered with white sheets replayed in her head. A cocktail waitress who worked at Club iCandy was the sole survivor. She politely declined medical treatment and refused to cooperate with law enforcement officials.

Najee reportedly took multiple gunshot wounds to the upper torso and a fatal gunshot blast to the face. Because of the condition of the corpse, authorities could not positively identify the body. They were relying on a California driver's license that was found on his person. Nella heard the news and her heart shattered into tiny jagged pieces. She poured out a drop of liquor and a bucket of tears for Najee. The sound of her sobbing was the balled of a dead soldier.

CHAPTER 26

The End of the Beginning: Los Angeles, CA

The cloth bandages wrapped tightly around my head made me feel like a mummy. I was relieved when Renee gently removed them. She had graduated from UCLA and turned out to be an excellent plastic surgeon. Her clientele included rich housewives, Hollywood actors, and several mob figures. I had looked her up when I got out of the joint, and we've been in close contact ever since.

She handed me a mirror, and I took a deep breath before coming face to face with my new face. I didn't know what to expect and was kinda nervous. Getting cosmetic surgery was very necessary, mandatory in fact. This wasn't a gimmick or a scene from a low budget, straight to DVD movie. This shit was trill!

My name was ringin' from coast to coast. I had instantly become an urban legend, the topic of conversation in every barbershop, nail salon, and corner bodega. I had street niggas gunning for me, Los Cinco Diablos, and the most dangerous organization of them all on my ass—the police! I chose to be the hunter instead of the hunted by faking my own death, a skill I learned by studying the cunning tactics of Machiavelli.

What I saw in the mirror pleased me. "Not bad for a dead man!" I complimented her work and smiled back at my reflection.

"I like the old Najee better. Mmm, mmmm, you sho' was one fine black man," Renee teased. "The only time I think about sinning is when I think about you."

Ever since she had gotten a divorce, she had been dropping little hints and throwing the pussy at me like crazy. She said her ex wasn't puttin' it down right, and that I was her dark chocolate temptation. Sometimes I would flirt back, but for the most part, I would just keep it gangsta and give her a devilish grin. I already had too many complications in my life.

After the bandages were removed, I sat in Renee's Beverly Hills clinic sipping Ciroc while we talked about the past and the future. On the reals, I was seriously contemplating murkin' her. She was the only person who knew about my new identity. That was a potential problem.

I quickly pushed the thought out of my mind. She always kept it one hondo with me, and her father, Detective Mark Brooks, was my inside source for information. He was now working as a liaison for the DEA and was the person who put me up on the Block Boy Empire indictment.

Renee suddenly switched gears and started to preach to me about the Bible, "Najee, you are a hot mess, my brotha. You need Jesus!" Her lips were smiling, but her tone was serious.

There was a lot of truth and wisdom in her words, but I wasn't trying to hear it. My heart wasn't ready. I gave her fifty bands then bounced. I didn't want to be late for my own funeral.

****

God's Temple: Torrance, CA

When I arrived at Love, Faith, and Charity Church in Torrance, California, the pastor was comforting the weeping congregation with tales of the dead man's fruitful and productive life. The eulogy was so positive, I thought I had stepped into the wrong chapel. My life was far from perfect. Only holy water could wash the bloodstains from my hands, but I appreciated the man of God for omitting my sinful characteristics and highlighting some of my positive attributes.

I didn't have any next of kin, so the body was happily released to Nella. She did a great job of putting my funeral together. My casket was beautiful. If a casket was a vehicle that transported you to the next life, I was being chauffeured in a Maybach.

It had been a long time since I had stepped foot in a church. I sat all the way in the back, hoping the pews didn't catch on fire. From my seat, I could see a gold frame picture that accompanied the closed casket and a beautiful woman sobbing uncontrollably. Black mascara and tears slowly ran down her cheeks. Even from behind the large Dolce & Gabbana sunglasses, I could tell that the mourning lady was Nella.

My heart skipped a beat! I wanted to reach out and touch her. I wanted to let her know I was still alive and only did this shit to deceive my enemies, but it wasn't time yet. I didn't want to put her life in further danger.

It hurts to see someone you care for cry. I didn't deserve her salty tears, however, I didn't deserve what happened next either. As the deacon pried Nella away from my casket, the church's large wooden doors crashed open. I turned to see four masked men. Their Remington AR-15's added to their menacing presence. They were professional soldiers sent by Benzo Al.

I reached for my heat ready to get it crackin', but I didn't want to blow my cover. I'm a beast in these streets, but I was in no shape to take on four contract killers with assault weapons.

One of the intruders shot a burst of gunfire into the air. The congregation screamed and rushed towards the nearest exit. I watched in horror as the tallest and most muscular goon snatched open the coffin. They dragged the lifeless body out of the church and dropped the corpse on the filthy concrete steps.

I slipped outside and blended in with the shocked crowd just in time to witness one of the goons splash the body with gasoline. The leader struck a match and enjoyed watching it burn before he dropped it. The body instantly burst into flames.

Loud sirens quickly approached, but the threat of police did not deter them from committing one last unspeakable act. Each of them unzipped their pants and pulled out their dicks. The crowd expelled audible gasps as yellow streams of urine doused out the flames.

I pulled out my .44 Magnum and held it down by my leg. Even though it wasn't my grave that was being desecrated, I was still furious. Their appalling acts were symbolic, Benzo Al was sending a message.

I stood there watching, plotting and calculating my next move. A light tap on my shoulder broke my concentration. I spun around and found myself face to face with Nella! I tucked the heat in the small of my back just as a Mercedes Benz slid up to the curb. The

24-inch black Giovanna rims matched the paint and dark tinted windows.

She took off her D&G shades to get a better look at me. We stood there staring at each other until I broke the silence. "How did you know it was me?"

Her lips curled into a smile. "Your eyes, baby. You can change the face, but I'll never forget those incredible eyes!"

She stood on her tippy toes and kissed me. In return, I pulled her into my strong arms, hoping that our souls would merge into one. I felt complete, I had what all thugs are looking for, true love.

"Are you still willing to go where I go?" I asked. She answered by lifting the hem of her skirt to reveal a chrome .380 strapped to her laced garter belt.

"Does this answer your question?"

I didn't get a chance to reply. A gloved hand gripping a Russian Luger was extended from the passenger side window of the Benz. The shooter squeezed off six rounds. Three of them struck Nella in the back. Her limp body collapsed into my arms. Even in stormy weather, the shooter's diamond Block Boy Empire medallion glistened. I fell to my knees on the church steps. Blood was on my shirt, vengeance blazed in my heart.

****

Rose Hill Memorial Park: Whittier, CA

Sosa walked through the pristine cemetery. He passed several well-kept graves sites until he found the burial plot he was searching for. He kneeled down on his knees and placed a dozen fresh roses at the foot of a tall, marble cross. This was the sixth visit he had paid to his mother's gravesite since finding out where she was buried yet tears still tumbled from his eyes. He removed the gold-rimmed Prada shades and ran his fingers across the precious words carved into the expensive slab of stone. The message read: *In Loving Memory of Merilyn 'Mama Merl' Fischer.*

Sosa had accomplished what every street nigga dreamed of. He left the game caked up with no mud on his name. He happily left behind a life filled with violence, deceit, and ultimate betrayal in order to become a successful restaurant owner. According to Forbes magazine, his chain of drive-thru soul food restaurants called Mama Merl's was well on their way to becoming the fastest-growing franchise in America. He was also featured on the cover of Black Enterprise. The publication praised him for exchanging the street corner for a corner office.

Retirement was treating Sosa well, but he failed to realize that there's no leaving the life without paying the ultimate price. Once you're married to the game, it's blood in blood out. He would soon learn that the game is a jealous bitch.

****

Rancho Hacienda: Acapulco, Mexico

Juice used a warm wet nap to dab the excess salsa from the corners of his mouth. He had easily demolished the plate of carne asada enchiladas, Spanish rice, and refried beans. He rubbed his full belly while admiring the Latina hostess. The naked senorita tucked a loose strand of brunette hair behind her ear and flirted with him while removing the dirty dishes and plastic tablecloth. She made sure he had an unobstructed view of her soft, round ass. Juice reached out and smacked the colorful butterfly wings that were tatted on each cheek. When her booty jiggled, it looked as though the butterfly was flapping its wings.

Six months had slipped by since Juice betrayed Najee. After his brazen escape from Sosa's mansion, he had nowhere to go. Fueled by greed and envy, he contacted Benzo Al with a tempting proposition. Juice knew Nella wouldn't miss Najee's funeral for the world. He convinced Benzo Al to pay him a handsome fee in exchange for killing the person closest to Najee's heart. Benzo Al eagerly agreed. He even supplied a diamond sprinkled BBE medallion so that witnesses would pin the murder on Sosa.

271

Benzo Al felt that Sosa had betrayed him by becoming allies with Najee and his clan of urban pirates. The loyalty and love he once had for his young protégé had evaporated. Nothing could make him feel better than seeing Nella swimming in a pool of her own blood and Sosa rotting in a prison cell, but things didn't go as planned.

Benzo Al stepped outside onto the patio and took a seat across from Juice. He didn't speak, he merely stared at his guest with contempt. The orange flame on the tip of his Cohiba glowed brighter with each puff. He looked like a Mexican version of Suge Knight. Even when he smiled, a permanent scowl disfigured his face. His gold crucifix was lost in a thick patch of chest hair.

Juice squirmed uncomfortably in his seat. "Is everything okay, bawse?"

Benzo leaned back in his chair and crossed his legs. "I'm afraid not. You fucked up, homes! That chica is still alive, she survived!"

Juice's throat became extremely dry. His shirt collar tightened like a noose. He knew the severe consequences for failing a Cinco Diablos mission. "On my word, I can fix this. Just tell me where she's at, B. I'll creep across the border tonight, *bam, bam, bam.* Take her out and be back by sunrise."

Benzo Al dropped his cigar in Juice's drink. The flame sizzled. "Your word means nothing to me. In this organization, we don't tolerate fuck ups. Entiendes?"

Through his peripheral, Juice caught a glimpse of the naked Latina quickly approaching him. Her cordial smile had evaporated. She wrapped a sharp wire around his neck and twisted it into a firm knot. She was a sicario, an assassin, and her method of killing was called the Spanish guillotine. She loved the thrill of the kill. After her first murder as a child, she never looked back.

Two Mexican soldiers in black army fatigues with the word policía stamped across their chest appeared and held his arms. Juice kicked and thrashed for his life, but his efforts were futile. The heartless Latina frowned and tightened her death grip until his lungs were deprived of oxygen. He threw up his last meal and suffocated in his own vomit. Finally, his feet stopped twitching. Juice was dead. The policía dragged his limp body away.

Benzo Al's savagery was not complete. He wanted to send a clear message to those who opposed Los Cinco Diablos. "I feel like having grilled swordfish tonight. Chop his dick off, put a hook through it, and use it as bait." Even his assassins cringed at his cruelty.

Benzo Al stood on the patio watching the blue waves crash into the white sandbanks. After each savage murder, his peers gave him more power and respect, nevertheless, peace eluded him. He didn't know how many more of Najee's followers were out there. They could strike at any moment. A gust of ocean breeze brought a foul odor to Benzo Al's nose. He raised his hand and sniffed his armpit, he smelled fear!

****

Sofitel Hotel: Red Light District—Amsterdam

Nella snuggled against Najee's muscular chest as he ran his fingers through her silky hair. Each time they made love the sex was deeper, harder, and better. After the shooting in front of the church, Nella was rushed to Cedar-Sinai Medical Center. Three of the six slugs ripped through her back, leaving her in critical condition. Najee never left her bedside. For six months he held her hand and begged God to spare her life. Now they were tangled together at the exquisite Sofitel Hotel in Amsterdam, dining on French cuisine and exploring each other's body.

"What are you thinking about, Najee?" Her fingernails gently raked his chest hairs. "I can tell when you're in deep thought."

Najee looked towards Nella's empty wheelchair, then he kissed her softly on the forehead. "My mind is on the past, the present, and the future." In reality, his mind was on revenge, vengeance, and retribution.

"Don't lie to me, and don't worry about me either. You got all the physical therapy my body needs. Last night you even made my

273

toes curl. Plus, Attorney Meyers took care of all the arrangements for Yung Zay, Maceo, Rio, and their families. Blue and his sons are holding it down at the Alive365 headquarters, and we're gonna get Benzo Al. So, stop thinking too hard."

It was easier said than done, but Najee managed to push all the negative thoughts out of his mind in order to concentrate on his woman's delicious treats. Nella shivered when Najee's mouth touched her nipples. Her vagina muscles quivered when his middle finger caressed her clit. He slowly worked his way down to her stomach, planting affectionate kisses here, there, and everywhere. Finally, he came face to face with her juicy fruit. He used his thumbs to spread open the outer lips of her wet peach. Nella moaned when Najee blew warm air on her pussy. She screamed when he used the tip of his tongue to spell his government name on her clit. He licked her sticky spot like a postage stamp until she came. Then they made love!

A Los Cinco Diablos, henchmen stood under the canopy of a nearby café. From his position, he had an unobstructed view of the hotel's front entrance. He used his trigger finger to punch in Benzo Al's phone number.

"Buenas noches, El Jeffe! We located the chica."

Benzo Al ginned; murder was on the menu.

To Be Continued...
The Streets Made Me 2
Coming Soon

Submission Guideline

Submit the first three chapters of your completed manuscript to ldpsubmissions@gmail.com, subject line: Your book's title. The manuscript must be in a .doc file and sent as an attachment. Document should be in Times New Roman, double spaced and in size 12 font. Also, provide your synopsis and full contact information. If sending multiple submissions, they must each be in a separate email.

Have a story but no way to send it electronically? You can still submit to LDP/Ca$h Presents. Send in the first three chapters, written or typed, of your completed manuscript to:

LDP: Submissions Dept
Po Box 870494
Mesquite, Tx 75187

DO NOT send original manuscript. Must be a duplicate.

Provide your synopsis and a cover letter containing your full contact information.

Thanks for considering LDP and Ca$h Presents.

Larry D. Wright

The Streets Made Me

Larry D. Wright

By Blakk Diamond

THE DOPEMAN'S BODYGAURD II

By Tranay Adams

TRAP GOD II

By Troublesome

YAYO III

A SHOOTER'S AMBITION II

By S. Allen

GHOST MOB

Stilloan Robinson

KINGPIN DREAMS II

By Paper Boi Rari

CREAM

By Yolanda Moore

SON OF A DOPE FIEND II

By Renta

FOREVER GANGSTA II

GLOCKS ON SATIN SHEETS II

By Adrian Dulan

LOYALTY AIN'T PROMISED II

By Keith Williams

THE PRICE YOU PAY FOR LOVE II

DOPE GIRL MAGIC II

By Destiny Skai

THE LIFE OF A HOOD STAR

By Rashia Wilson

TOE TAGZ III

By Ah'Million

CONFESSIONS OF A GANGSTA II

By Nicholas Lock

278

The Streets Made Me

PAID IN KARMA III

By **Meesha**

I'M NOTHING WITHOUT HIS LOVE II

By Monet Dragun

CAUGHT UP IN THE LIFE II

By Robert Baptiste

NEW TO THE GAME II

By **Malik D. Rice**

Life of a Savage II

By **Romell Tukes**

Quiet Money II

By **Trai'Quan**

THE STREETS MADE ME II

By **Larry D. Wright**

Available Now

RESTRAINING ORDER **I & II**

By **CA$H & Coffee**

LOVE KNOWS NO BOUNDARIES **I II & III**

By **Coffee**

RAISED AS A GOON I, II, III & IV

BRED BY THE SLUMS I, II, III

BLAST FOR ME I & II

ROTTEN TO THE CORE I II III

A BRONX TALE I, II, III

DUFFEL BAG CARTEL I II III IV

HEARTLESS GOON I II III IV

279

Larry D. Wright

A SAVAGE DOPEBOY I II

HEARTLESS GOON I II III

DRUG LORDS I II III

CUTTHROAT MAFIA

By **Ghost**

LAY IT DOWN **I & II**

LAST OF A DYING BREED

BLOOD STAINS OF A SHOTTA I & II III

By **Jamaica**

LOYAL TO THE GAME I II III

LIFE OF SIN I, II III

By **TJ & Jelissa**

BLOODY COMMAS I & II

SKI MASK CARTEL I II & III

KING OF NEW YORK I II,III IV

RISE TO POWER I II III

COKE KINGS I II III

BORN HEARTLESS I II III

By **T.J. Edwards**

IF LOVING HIM IS WRONG…I & II

LOVE ME EVEN WHEN IT HURTS I II III

By **Jelissa**

WHEN THE STREETS CLAP BACK I & II III

THE HEART OF A SAVAGE I II

By **Jibril Williams**

A DISTINGUISHED THUG STOLE MY HEART I II & III

LOVE SHOULDN'T HURT I II III IV

RENEGADE BOYS I II III IV

PAID IN KARMA I II

By **Meesha**

280

The Streets Made Me

A GANGSTER'S CODE I &, II III

A GANGSTER'S SYN I II III

THE SAVAGE LIFE I II III

CHAINED TO THE STREETS I II

By J-Blunt

PUSH IT TO THE LIMIT

By **Bre' Hayes**

BLOOD OF A BOSS **I, II, III, IV, V**

SHADOWS OF THE GAME

By **Askari**

THE STREETS BLEED MURDER **I, II & III**

THE HEART OF A GANGSTA I II& III

By **Jerry Jackson**

CUM FOR ME I II III IV V

An **LDP Erotica Collaboration**

BRIDE OF A HUSTLA **I II & II**

THE FETTI GIRLS **I, II& III**

CORRUPTED BY A GANGSTA I, II III, IV

BLINDED BY HIS LOVE

THE PRICE YOU PAY FOR LOVE

DOPE GIRL MAGIC

By **Destiny Skai**

WHEN A GOOD GIRL GOES BAD

By **Adrienne**

THE COST OF LOYALTY I II

By Kweli

A GANGSTER'S REVENGE **I II III & IV**

THE BOSS MAN'S DAUGHTERS I II III IV V

A SAVAGE LOVE **I & II**

BAE BELONGS TO ME I II

Larry D. Wright

A HUSTLER'S DECEIT I, II, III

WHAT BAD BITCHES DO I, II, III

SOUL OF A MONSTER I II III

KILL ZONE

By **Aryanna**

A KINGPIN'S AMBITON

A KINGPIN'S AMBITION **II**

I MURDER FOR THE DOUGH

By **Ambitious**

TRUE SAVAGE I II III IV V VI

DOPE BOY MAGIC I, II

MIDNIGHT CARTEL I II

By **Chris Green**

A DOPEBOY'S PRAYER

By **Eddie "Wolf" Lee**

THE KING CARTEL **I, II & III**

By **Frank Gresham**

THESE NIGGAS AIN'T LOYAL **I, II & III**

By **Nikki Tee**

GANGSTA SHYT **I II &III**

By **CATO**

THE ULTIMATE BETRAYAL

By **Phoenix**

BOSS'N UP **I , II & III**

By **Royal Nicole**

I LOVE YOU TO DEATH

By Destiny J

I RIDE FOR MY HITTA

I STILL RIDE FOR MY HITTA

By **Misty Holt**

282

The Streets Made Me

LOVE & CHASIN' PAPER

By **Qay Crockett**

TO DIE IN VAIN

SINS OF A HUSTLA

By **ASAD**

BROOKLYN HUSTLAZ

By **Boogsy Morina**

BROOKLYN ON LOCK I & II

By **Sonovia**

GANGSTA CITY

By **Teddy Duke**

A DRUG KING AND HIS DIAMOND I & II III

A DOPEMAN'S RICHES

HER MAN, MINE'S TOO I, II

CASH MONEY HO'S

By Nicole Goosby

TRAPHOUSE KING **I II & III**

KINGPIN KILLAZ I II III

STREET KINGS I II

PAID IN BLOOD **I II**

CARTEL KILLAZ I II III

DOPE GODS

By **Hood Rich**

LIPSTICK KILLAH **I, II, III**

CRIME OF PASSION I II & III

By **Mimi**

STEADY MOBBN' **I, II, III**

THE STREETS STAINED MY SOUL

By **Marcellus Allen**

WHO SHOT YA **I, II, III**

283

Larry D. Wright

SON OF A DOPE FIEND
Renta
GORILLAZ IN THE BAY **I II III IV**
TEARS OF A GANGSTA
DE'KARI
TRIGGADALE I II
Elijah R. Freeman
GOD BLESS THE TRAPPERS I, II, III
THESE SCANDALOUS STREETS I, II, III
FEAR MY GANGSTA I, II, III
THESE STREETS DON'T LOVE NOBODY I, II
BURY ME A G I, II, III, IV, V
A GANGSTA'S EMPIRE I, II, III, IV
THE DOPEMAN'S BODYGAURD
Tranay Adams
THE STREETS ARE CALLING
Duquie Wilson
MARRIED TO A BOSS... I II III
By Destiny Skai & Chris Green
KINGZ OF THE GAME I II III IV
Playa Ray
SLAUGHTER GANG I II III
RUTHLESS HEART I II
By Willie Slaughter
FUK SHYT
By Blakk Diamond
DON'T F#CK WITH MY HEART I II
By Linnea
ADDICTED TO THE DRAMA I II III
By Jamila

284

The Streets Made Me

YAYO I II

A SHOOTER'S AMBITION

By S. Allen

TRAP GOD

By Troublesome

FOREVER GANGSTA

GLOCKS ON SATIN SHEETS

By Adrian Dulan

TOE TAGZ I II

By Ah'Million

KINGPIN DREAMS

By Paper Boi Rari

CONFESSIONS OF A GANGSTA

By Nicholas Lock

I'M NOTHING WITHOUT HIS LOVE

By Monet Dragun

CAUGHT UP IN THE LIFE

By Robert Baptiste

NEW TO THE GAME

By **Malik D. Rice**

Life of a Savage

By **Romell Tukes**

LOYALTY AIN'T PROMISED

By Keith Williams

Quiet Money

By **Trai'Quan**

THE STREETS MADE ME

By **Larry D. Wright**

Larry D. Wright

BOOKS BY LDP'S CEO, CA$H

TRUST IN NO MAN

TRUST IN NO MAN 2

TRUST IN NO MAN 3

BONDED BY BLOOD

SHORTY GOT A THUG

THUGS CRY

THUGS CRY 2

THUGS CRY 3

TRUST NO BITCH

TRUST NO BITCH 2

TRUST NO BITCH 3

TIL MY CASKET DROPS

RESTRAINING ORDER

RESTRAINING ORDER 2

IN LOVE WITH A CONVICT

Coming Soon
BONDED BY BLOOD 2

BOW DOWN TO MY GANGSTA

The Streets Made Me

www.ingramcontent.com/pod-product-compliance
Lightning Source LLC
Chambersburg PA
CBHW070557260626
47161CB00002B/631

* 9 7 8 1 9 5 1 0 8 1 9 3 5 *